Ring of Truth

by

Susan Vaughan

Devlin Security Force, Protecting Priceless Treasures, Vol 2

Ring of Truth

Cover Art by *Kim Mendoza*

The Wild Rose Press, Inc.
PO Box 708
Adams Basin, NY 14410-0708
Visit us at www.thewildrosepress.com

Publishing History
First Edition, 2023
Trade Paperback ISBN
Digital ISBN

Devlin Security Force, Protecting Priceless Treasures, Vol 2
Published in the United States of America
Previously Published 2015 by Gullwood Press

Dedication

Ring of Truth is dedicated to my dear aunt Rhoda Hofstetter, who contributed the cameo idea in a key scene. Even when she could read only by a special magnifying device, she read and commented on my books. I miss her sense of humor, her caring and compassion, and her zest for life. Rhoda, you left us way too early at the age of 102.

Chapter One

Infamous jewel thief dies in prison
By Rona Laughton
WASHINGTON DAILY NEWS
An international jewel thief who eluded law enforcement for five decades and stole a small nation's crown jewels from a national U.S. museum has died. Leon Jones, known as the Jeweler, died on April 16 at the age of 68 of complications from cancer, in the Devens, Massachusetts, Federal Medical Center.

Jones pulled off his last and biggest theft twelve years ago at the Smithsonian Museum of Natural History in Washington, D.C. He made off with the crown jewels of the principality of Gramornia, including a scepter, the royal crown, swords, and rings.

Mistakes during the break-in led to the Jeweler's arrest and conviction. His son, Cortez Jones, was also convicted of the theft and served a short sentence. The Gramornian crown jewels have never been recovered, according to the FBI and Global Insurance.

For five decades, the Jeweler's heists from museums and mansions confounded law enforcement agencies from the Riviera to San Francisco and...

****

Two weeks later
CORTEZ JONES WAITED behind a pillar where he had a clear view of the parking garage's level-two

1

elevator.

The Marton woman wouldn't answer his phone calls, so here he was. His father's attorney had given him her license plate number and work address in Crystal City, Virginia. Less intrusive and a whole lot less threatening than approaching her at her apartment.

Cort had made an effort to look respectable. Even wore a long-sleeved polo to cover the prison tats. No luck. The guard at the security desk took one look and showed him the damn door. On impulse, he ducked into the garage as somebody drove out. Once inside, spotting her car was a cinch. No missing that bright red coupe.

He needed to be careful. Diplomatic, low-key, so she didn't freak and call security. Scaring her was the last thing he wanted.

He needed her help.

If she would listen to the ex-con son of the Jeweler. But if Leon's deathbed story panned out, he had a way to get the FBI off his back. Once and for all.

If Leon had conned him—wouldn't be the first time—he'd go on with his backwoods life. Shit. A half-life. No life. Now that an ember of hope ignited, the possibility flamed into a need that burned in his soul. He wanted more. He wanted out from under FBI and Gramornia pressure. He wanted to hold up his head.

He wanted a life.

News dating from the Gramornia crown jewels theft investigation said that Quincy Marton's widow was Korean. Cort had figured spotting the daughter would be easy.

But he didn't count on the building's employees being the United Nations. Several women about the right age with dark hair and vaguely Asian features exited the elevator while he waited. None of them went to the red coupe.

The elevator bell dinged and the doors opened. Another young woman stepped out into a halo of light. About his age. Black hair to her shoulders, high cheekbones, eyes with an exotic slant, but that could be makeup. If she was Mara Marton, she'd inherited her father's height—five-eight or so. Dark pants. Bright blue sweater with glittery stuff swirling across breasts that begged for male attention.

Cort shook his head, banished the inconvenient sexual awareness. Had to keep focused on business and not on a hot female. For luck, he fingered the ring in his pocket. Leon hadn't lied about that much. As for the rest, he would see.

Mouth tight, the woman scanned the open lanes and the parked vehicles. She clutched her bulky orange purse beneath her arm. And headed directly for the little red car.

Another female, a redhead in a blue jacket and khaki pants, stepped from behind a panel van and intercepted the brunette.

Uncertain, he stayed put to observe.

"Ms. Marton. Mara," said the redhead, holding up an ID and a small digital recorder. "Rona Laughton, *Washington Daily News*. Please give me a few minutes of your time."

Marton wheeled. Anger flashed in her dark eyes. "I told you on the phone I have nothing to say to the media. No comment means no comment. Leave me alone."

Cort hunched his shoulders, backed deeper into the

shadows.

"Your father, an investigator for Global Insurance," the reporter went on, undaunted, "was implicated in the Gramornia crown jewels theft from the Smithsonian. My paper would like to review that case, a sort of where-are-they-now story. What's your reaction now that Jones is dead? How do you feel?"

When crimson highlighted Mara Marton's cheeks, Cort clenched his hands into fists. How the hell did this cold bitch think she felt? The attacks in the news media and accusations by the FBI had broken Quincy Marton. He died of a heart attack in the middle of the investigation. Not unlike Leon Jones. Fitting. Ironic.

Tears glistening, Marton headed for her car. Laughton stopped her with a hand on her forearm. Marton was taller but the reporter had twenty pounds on her. And more nerve than a high-wire walker.

Cort should stay light years away from the media but he couldn't stand by. He slipped from behind his pillar and hustled over. Held his arms loose at his sides, hands open so both women could see he meant no physical threat. His height and build made him intimidating enough. "The lady said she doesn't want to talk."

The reporter stepped back, her mouth set in lines of frustration, showing her age, on the hard side of forty. Her gaze skewered him. "Who the hell are you?"

"Just making sure everything's all right." He turned to Marton. "This chick bothering you?"

She stared, eyes wide and round as hubcaps, then blinked as she took in his question. After a breath, she said, "She was just leaving."

Cort gave Laughton his patented hard-case look,

the one prison dawgs called the Murder-One stare.

She fired a death stare of her own. Then, face scrunched and red at seeing a story slip from her grasp, she stalked away. Her heels clicked on the cement leading to the stairway exit.

Softening his expression for the woman standing nervously before him, he scratched his nape. "Where's security when you need them?"

Her shoulders relaxed but she eyed him with suspicion. Why wouldn't she? They were alone in that section of the cavernous garage. She held her keys like a weapon between her knuckles. "Thank you for your help."

"Ms. Marton, I'd like to talk to you too. It's important. I'm Cortez Jones. Leon Jo—"

"I know. You're the Jeweler's son." A frown formed a line between her dark brows. "I'm surprised that reporter didn't recognize you."

"After she thinks about it, she will. The media haven't tracked me down yet. Only a couple people know where I am." His boss and the attorney. "The name Jones makes staying incognito easier. Thanks for not outing me to the *Daily News*."

She flushed, apparently just realizing she could've escaped by siccing the press babe on Cort. "How did you find me?"

"Leon's attorney said you might be able to help. I got rid of the reporter babe for you. I figure you owe me a little time."

Lips pursed, she seemed to consider. Her mouth looked clean of lipstick, soft, natural. He dragged his attention up to her eyes.

Curiosity warred with fear in those tilted cat-eyes.

She kept the keys in defensive mode. "He did phone me, but forget it. I owe you *nothing*." Her chin trembled. "Your father could have cleared my father. All he had to do was speak up. But for eleven years he told nothing but lies. Dad *died* trying to recover the crown jewels. He had nothing to do with the theft or hiding the stolen property."

She edged toward her car.

His pulse raced. He had to grab her interest now. "I can help you clear your father."

She stopped, a foot from her car, eyes narrowed. "For all I know you're as much a liar as your father."

"I'm sorry Leon didn't confess. Hear me out. *Please.*"

She stared at him, speculation in that exotic gaze. More people exited the building into the garage. In the next aisle, a car door slammed. An engine coughed to life.

"Okay," she said, her gaze as wary as a frightened fawn. "I'm listening. You have five minutes."

"Deal." He had to talk fast before she bolted. "Leon's death leaves issues about the Gramornia crown jewels case."

"I'd offer my sympathies on your loss, but I can't say I'm sorry he's dead."

"No sympathy needed or wanted." No tears from him. That man he'd seen two weeks ago in the prison hospital was a stranger. His only reason for regretting Leon's death was that it came a few days too soon. "The FBI and Global Insurance won't talk to me, let alone help. Your father's working files could have key answers."

"I hold *your* father partly responsible for the death

of *mine*. Why should I help you?"

"The Feds have never been able to prove the identities of Leon's accomplices, including yea or nay on your father. I have information that could ID the accomplices." Showing too much of his hand was a bad idea. Maybe this much would satisfy her.

Her eyes narrowed. "You were one of the thieves. You don't know the others?"

"Leon dragged me into the job at the last minute because his other guy broke a leg in a car accident. He kept me in the dark. I knew only my part of the job, nothing about other accomplices. I stayed on the roof. Never saw anybody but Leon."

"Yeah, yeah, that's what you said eleven years ago. This is about finding the jewels, isn't it?" She flung the last words like a dagger and, for extra measure, speared him with an accusing look.

He stiffened, his hands curling into fists before he forced them to relax. Dammit, he didn't want to scare her. "Partly. I did my time. Paid for my mistake. The FBI came to the furniture school in Maine where I work to grill me. They threatened to keep harassing me. I could lose my job. But the Feds won't let me off the hook."

She bumped up against her car. "They think you know where he hid the jewels?"

Shit, he *was* scaring her. He held out his hands, palms up like the damn beggar he was. "If I can help return the loot, I can live my life without that sword hanging over me. I need your help."

She looked down her slim nose at him. "*Return the jewels?* Ha! I suppose you have a bridge to sell me too."

7

"I'm not surprised you don't believe me. But what I say is true." *As far as I know.*

She clicked her key fob and opened the door. "I don't believe you. Not for a nanosecond. And I won't help you." Mashing her bag against her chest, she dove inside and punched down the door lock.

Cort grasped the door handle as she started the engine. "Don't you want to clear your father?" he yelled over the car engine's noise.

The car accelerated backward so fast he had to scramble out of the way. He watched, fists clenched, as the car sped off. Its tires squealed as Mara Marton accelerated up the out ramp.

****

Cort swore. He returned his cell to its belt holster. He leaned against his workbench.

Damn. Just like the FBI to make things as tough on him as possible. At least his boss let him know an agent showed up again at the woodworking school. Last thing Cort needed. The Birch Lake Woodcraft Center had a solid rep in the state and in the New England woodworking community. It didn't need a sideshow. And neither did he.

He held a great deal of respect and gratitude for his boss, who'd hired an ex-con on a buddy's recommendation. Cort would hate like hell to lose his assistant instructor job.

Whatever the ring brought down on his head, he didn't want it to ruin this work that brought him a measure of peace. Would the Feds ever give it up?

No was the answer. No more than the incessant spring rain would cease drumming on the metal roof of this barn. Hell, he should've known his father wasn't done with him. If he could turn Leon's puzzle over to the Feds, he'd be out of it. If only.

The odors of glue and wood shavings permeating the shop soothed his rattled senses. Caressing the grain of the cherrywood plies he would laminate to create the curved front of a hall table, he felt the life in the wood. He lined up the plies in preparation for gluing. Picturing how the grain pattern would play out smoothed the tension in his shoulders.

He snatched an armful of clamps from the wall rack and dumped them on the workbench.

"You can never have too many clamps."

The familiar voice snapped Cort to attention. He gave himself a mental dope-slap for not hearing the visitor—correction, intruder—arrive above the rain's patter. Seven years out of prison he was growing soft. Having the FBI agent greet him with the mantra of all woodworkers only ratcheted up the irritation factor.

Leaning against Cort's drafting table, the stocky agent drummed the fingernails of his left hand on the table's cluttered surface, as was his irritating habit.

"It's been awhile, Kaplan," Cort said, noting the requisite Feeb dark suit as usual looked like the agent had slept in it. "I figured since Leon's gone, you'd leave me alone." He marched to the mini-fridge and grabbed a bottle of green tea.

Someone who didn't know Kaplan might not notice anything, but the blank look in his drooping eyes shifted a fraction at Cort's lack of hospitality. Too damn bad.

"You figured wrong, Jones. And that's *Special Agent* Kaplan."

Kaplan had caught the case eleven years ago as a

9

new agent. Because of the man's sagging features, Cort thought of him as a human basset hound, and like a hound on a scent, Kaplan never let go.

Cort downed a long gulp of tea before returning his attention to his nemesis. "If you're here to offer your condolences, get on with it so I can get back to work."

"Condolences? Yeah, I'm sorry as shit about the old Jeweler. I was at his funeral Saturday. Didn't see you."

"I said my good-byes two days before he died." A phony service in the medical-center chapel? Not for him. They'd be sending him Leon's ashes. What the hell was he supposed to do with them? Trash them with the ashes from the wood stove maybe. He finished the tea while he waited for the agent to get down to business.

"Tell me about that conversation." Kaplan hitched a hip onto the table and leaned back against the wall, making himself comfortable. "He must've bragged about how he put one over on the government."

Cort tossed the empty bottle into the recycle bin. "No deathbed confession, if that's what you mean."

"If you insist on not sharing," Kaplan said, "you could be charged with withholding information. Or your boss might find official visitors at the school again. Soon. Augusta's close enough the local special agent can pop in nearly every day."

Kaplan was full of crap about the withholding thing. But he'd make good on his threat to have the local agent show up on a regular basis. Sue for harassment? Before Cort could even dial Leon's attorney's number, the school would boot him out on his ass. He wrapped his hands around a clamp to keep them steady. Here was his opportunity to turn everything over to the FBI. His chance to dig out from under.

He reached in his jeans pocket as he crossed the room. He placed the ring piece on the draft table and pushed it toward Kaplan. "Leon directed me to this."

Chapter Two

"Gramornia royal family in turmoil."

MARA SHOULD'VE KNOWN the Jeweler's death would revive media interest in the case and in her father, the insurance investigator. And now this online article.

Today's gossipy piece covered the principality's distress over not having the royal paraphernalia on the first of June to crown the new prince. The legendary crown and scepter symbolized the royal family's legitimacy. Rumor had it that the ambitious prime minister would use the issue to eliminate the royals altogether and consolidate his growing power, seen by many as a danger to the tiny democracy.

Head pounding from the incessant barrage about the old robbery, Mara exited and reached in the desk drawer for ibuprofen. A few moments later, her headache subsiding, she returned to her research report and clicked the printer icon. While the pages slid onto the printer tray, she leaned back in her desk chair and read an earlier printout—her research on Cortez Jones—one more time.

After their encounter she'd had to stop the car a block down Crystal Drive until her tears dried. Tears of fear at being face to face with the Jeweler's son. Tears of anguish at believing her father would never be cleared. Tears of frustration at wanting to trust what

Jones said and knowing she shouldn't.

Her sister Cassie accused her of always trusting everyone. She'd rather trust people than live behind a wall of distance and distrust like her father. But trust Cortez Jones? No. There lay too much danger.

"Mara, you're here late."

Straightening at the familiar voice, she stood to greet Thomas Devlin. "I wanted to finish this report on the Chinese horse. The authenticator's analysis took longer than usual. No excuse. Sir." She'd been a bit off lately but he didn't need to know that. She tamped down the swell of emotion.

The head of Devlin Security Force stood in the doorway of her cubicle. A formidable man, Devlin had started the high-end art-and-artifact security and investigation firm with a few former Special Forces buddies. Today DSF had museum and gallery clients all over the world. Trim and fit in a gray hand-tailored suit, he leaned one muscled shoulder against the cubicle support in a pose that appeared casual, even lazy. Mara had seen him go from languid to deadly in a nanosecond in defense of one of his people.

She gathered the report, fastened the pages with a banker's clip, and handed it across. "I'm afraid this bronze horse is a copy. A very good copy. The composition and the measurements are only slightly off, like the one from the British collector."

Devlin's dark brow lowered. "Another. That's three. Damn! At this rate, we'll be years tracking down the original."

Two years ago thieves had stolen the second-century sculpture from the Tate Museum in London. Since then, copies kept turning up, sold to private collectors as the real thing. The Tate director and Lloyd's wanted results, not more mystery.

"I could ask Ivan to go over the data again, in case there's a mistake," she said.

"No need. You're always thorough and methodical. If you think he's accurate, I'm satisfied. No data left unturned." He grinned.

"Thank you, Mr. Devlin." She relaxed, warmed. And relieved at the high compliment rather than a reprimand.

"The death of Leon Jones must be upsetting. Must bring it all back." His eyes crinkled with sympathy before his gaze settled on the unofficial report beside her keyboard. "I see you're researching his son."

Her stomach tightened and she crossed her arms as she followed his gaze. If he reprimanded her for using company resources for private reasons, so be it. She'd suppressed her anxiety so she could complete her official report. She suddenly felt too tired to stand.

Nodding, she sank into her chair. "He contacted me. He says he can help clear my father. Claims he has new information but needs to see Dad's working files." Telling Devlin seemed to lift the burden weighing on the nape of her neck, where the muscles kinked into walnut-sized knots.

He bent toward the printout. "May I?"

"I have no secrets from you." Devlin knew her past. Her father's past. He'd hired her anyway. He'd even put a man on the case then, but found no proof of her dad's innocence or guilt. When the investigation served only to upset her mom and sister, she'd asked him to drop the matter.

She handed him her report on Cortez Jones.

Devlin read the half page before his laser stare settled again on her. "Released from prison eight years ago. Steady job in Maine. Keeps his nose clean. Is this all?"

"Everything I could find." On a sigh, she added, "Maybe I should just put it all behind me and move on."

"The truth will come out someday. But if you want to pursue this lead, go ahead, but be careful you don't get in over your head." He set the paper on her desk and turned to leave.

Mara thanked him and swiveled her chair away, too moved to say more. Whoa. Not only didn't he rap her knuckles, his warning included the implication she could continue to use DSF resources.

If there was a chance to prove once and for all that her father didn't conspire with Leon Jones, she ought to take it. The authorities, including Global Insurance, looked only at the surface, at how his seemingly friendly relationship with Leon Jones implicated him in a cover-up after the actual robbery.

They hadn't grown up in a household with her dad instilling integrity into the very corn kernels he used to pop for family movie night. This was the man who never cheated at solitaire even when Mara secretly watched. The man who pored through every receipt to make sure he was absolutely honest with his taxes. The man whose disappointment at her youthful lapses had cut her to the bone. And the man who doted on his wife and daughters even when his wife didn't love him. That little fact, Mara had gradually realized, was the source of unhappiness and increasing distance in their marriage.

She shook away her mother's calculating view. Not the sort of marriage she intended to have. True love between her and her future mate, that was for her.

She owed her dad. Her love for him demanded she prove his innocence. She'd let it go too long. To hell with her sister's sensibilities. And Mom? Well, she'd deal. Clearing her dad could force Global Insurance to reinstate the pension her mom needed. Finding the truth was worth risking more hurt.

She picked up her cell from the desk, hesitated, her finger hovering over the keypad. To hell with caution. She tapped in the number Jones had left on her voice mail.

****

On Friday night, Cort left his truck in a garage on New Hampshire Avenue and walked from Dupont Circle to the bar where he was meeting Mara. Neutral territory.

She wanted to talk to him. Wherever she wanted to meet worked for him. He rolled one shoulder, then the other to dislodge the tension. And exhaustion. He'd driven straight through—twelve hours.

Inside Sean and Tony's Pub, the sounds and scents of a neighborhood establishment washed over him— conversation punctuated with laughter and argument, aromas of ale and wine and fried food. Over the bar the TV showed a silent pre-season baseball game while stereo speakers played "Glory Days." The walls were lined with souvenirs from Ireland along with autographed sports posters and team banners hanging beside Blarney Castle and the Ring of Kerry.

In spite of his tension, Cort smiled as he surveyed the packed room. A slender woman sat in a back booth.

Her dark hair draped her face as her thumbs skated across her cell phone, but he knew her instantly. Mara Marton.

When she saw him, she scooped back her hair. It fell around her shoulders like a curtain. Would it feel like silk? She dropped the phone in her sweater pocket and lifted one hand in a tentative wave.

"Thanks for meeting with me," he said, caught by her unexpected soft smile and the keen intelligence in her eyes. He seated himself opposite her. Felt calmer already. "Why the change of heart?"

"Mr. Fox called to vouch for you." Color matching her hot pink blouse bloomed in her cheeks. "And I checked up on you. Where you live, your job. Research is what I do."

No big surprise. He'd expected as much. Hoped for it. "So you decided I'm clean?"

"Clean enough for more questions."

He liked her voice, low and husky, now that she wasn't yelling at him. The oil lanterns on the tables and the low lighting set a romantic stage. *Don't even think it.*

When a white-aproned waiter hustled over, Cort ordered a lager. Mara already had an untouched goblet of red wine. Either she hadn't waited long or she was so nervous the glass was her second. The alert look in her gaze made him opt for the former.

He shrugged off his windbreaker and stuffed it into the corner. He glanced at the sandwich menu in the stand by the lantern. When he looked up, she was staring over her wine at his forearms.

The sleeves on his knit shirt had gotten pushed up some. Pulling them down to his wrists, he shrugged.

"Prison tattoos."

She shook her head. "Lots of people have tattoos. I didn't mean to stare."

But his black scrolling lines and spider webs weren't civilian tats. His were thick and chunky, intimidating. "Some prison tats are artistic, but most are for protection."

"What do you mean?"

"Medium security at Allenwood isn't as tight as max. More freedom inside means more chances for other guys to hurt you." If a guy let himself get beat up, stabbed, or raped, he lost all respect. Cort had protected himself and bloodied a few guys with his fists in the process. He wasn't about to give details. "To be safe I needed respect. Show I was tough, sit still for tattoos."

"My God, you were only nineteen." Her eyes grew huge as the implications sank in.

"I survived. I'd get rid of the ink but laser surgery costs money I don't have."

She made no response but he was ready to change the subject anyway. "If you haven't eaten, we can order dinner. My treat."

"We'll see."

Ah, she was still skittish. Wanted to be able to walk away at any moment. The robbery had devastated her family as well as his. He wanted to reassure her that she wouldn't be hurt again. But he couldn't promise that. He couldn't promise a damn thing.

She lowered her gaze to the menu.

Good. She was considering his offer.

He already knew from seeing her in the harshly lit garage she was gorgeous. The restaurant's soft light gave him a chance to view the details—fine-boned features, dark-chocolate cat-eyes, warm-honey skin. And hints of both strength and vulnerability that tugged at him.

Curb it, Jones. He hadn't been that long without a woman. He shifted on the bench seat and studied the menu.

When the waiter brought his brew, Cort suggested they order. He awarded himself a virtual high-five when Mara relented. They chose—the corned beef for him and a chicken-salad wrap for her.

After another sip of wine, she said, "You said before the FBI won't help you. But if you have some sort of lead, shouldn't you try?"

He lifted one shoulder noncommittally as he took a drink of beer. "I did try. Every year since he went inside, Leon concocted elaborate scenarios for where he hid the jewels. As far as the FBI's concerned, my story was another of his hoaxes. They might take notice if I walk in wearing the Gramornia crown and carrying the scepter."

"A joke. You surprise me." She chuckled, an infectious sound that resonated deep inside him. "I'm trying to imagine you wearing a jeweled crown."

He couldn't help a grin. "Not a pretty picture."

"Their resistance makes no sense. You say the FBI harasses you often, yet they won't listen to you now."

He shrugged. "My lead comes from an untrustworthy source, the Jeweler."

When he'd laid out Leon's strategy for protecting the loot's hiding place, Special Fucking Agent Kaplan had laughed at him. Laughed at the puzzle ring piece and walked out. His skepticism matched Cort's, but the rejection and derision rankled.

A small bowl of snack mix and their silverware arrived.

Mara picked out a sesame stick. The corners of her mouth ticked downward, and the warm humor in her eyes cooled. "I didn't meet you here because I wanted to chat. I might consider helping you, but I need some answers first."

"Shoot." He sipped his beer as he helped himself to pretzels and peanuts.

"I gather you're searching for the jewels because of something your father told you. Why do you need to find the other accomplices, if they exist?" She popped the sesame stick into her mouth and watched him with wary curiosity.

Cort chewed over how much to tell her. Fox had said her father's reputation was for thoroughness. Looked like she inherited that trait. Good. He might have to spill everything. But he couldn't afford to trust her any more than she trusted him.

A quick survey of the room reassured him of their privacy. "Leon didn't give me much but I'll tell you what I know."

The waiter whisked over with their meals. Cole slaw and curly fries smelling of salt and spices surrounded the thick sandwiches. When Cort asked if Mara wanted more to drink, she shook her head, indicating her half-full goblet. He ordered another draft.

They ate in silence until the beer arrived. "Leon was a complex man. His cryptic brain suited his professional distrust. He made a puzzle ring."

"The kind of ring you wear?"

"Bigger. It's a sort of jigsaw puzzle. When I was a kid, he made me one. When you fitted the three pieces together correctly, they formed a whole. Inside mine was a picture. This new one contains words, clues to where he hid the jewels."

"And he gave the separate pieces to his accomplices and kept one. Is that it?"

"Right. No one of them could retrieve the loot without the others."

"What happened to honor among thieves?"

"I asked him that. He said honor went only so far when big money was involved."

"The FBI didn't believe you, but *you* believe *him*? Why now, after all these years?"

"I have doubts, I admit. He was dying, so why lie to me? I have to take the chance. No pain, no gain, as they say. But I want more proof, like another ring piece." The old man's story had holes, too many dots unconnected after too many years of lies. Still, Leon had seemed sincere, as sincere as he could ever be.

"They had to trust *him*," she said. "I mean, he knew where the jewels were."

That aspect bothered him too. "If they wanted in, they had no choice. Cops in more than one country picked him up but they never had enough evidence to charge him. So he expected even if the FBI questioned him, he'd be free in a matter of days. The bunch would retrieve the loot together once the furor died down."

"He didn't count on going to prison." Mara dabbed at mayonnaise on her lower lip.

He dragged his gaze upward before his jeans became too tight. "I think he still figured on following through once he was released. When he knew he was dying of cancer, he sent for me."

"But he wouldn't just tell you where he hid the

stolen crown jewels?"

Cort dipped a fry in catsup as he considered the old man's motives. "True to form, he doled out his secrets one at a time. He told me where he hid his ring piece. He wanted me to take it to him before he told me the rest, but his heart conked out."

Cort had found the first ring piece no problem, the same day he saw Leon at the prison hospital. But couldn't leave work until the next weekend and missed his chance to learn more. He refused to feel guilt about any of that. From the get-go, Leon should have told him everything.

She set down her fork and leaned forward, her gaze soft, sympathetic. "He wanted an excuse for his son come visit him again."

Cort huffed his disdain. Manipulation suited the old man more than family feeling. "More likely he wanted to make sure the ring section was still there. If it was gone, he'd figure one of his partners got the loot."

"You did find the ring section?"

"I found it. That much was true." He ate some of his sandwich as he waited for her next question. The corned beef was tender and juicy, with a tangy sauce.

"Do you have the ring piece with you? May I see it?"

He dug in his jeans pocket, then dropped the shiny circle into her upturned palm.

"This is big enough to be a napkin ring," she said. "Definitely not jewelry."

"The toothed, curved edges are where this piece would fit the others on each side."

"Gold?"

"Looks like ten carat. Probably from some other

22

heist. He liked to work with gold. Malleable and doesn't tarnish. This piece seems to have the middle of the clue."

She turned the gold circle to catch the light from the oil lamp.

He'd memorized the words inside, for all the damn good it did. Reading the precisely engraved script down the circle's inner arc, you got part of each of four lines.

THE
AND
FOUNT
OUR

After reading it, she looked up, frowning. "Not much help."

"No sh— No kidding. Now you know why I have to identify the other accomplices."

"What about this raised arc on the outside?"

"Haven't figured that out. Knowing Leon, it's not just decoration but another key to the puzzle." He held out his hand.

She returned the gold circle with obvious reluctance. The corner of her mouth ticked down again as she took her lip between her teeth. Instead of asking more questions, she devoted silent attention to her sandwich.

Cort stuffed the ring piece in his pocket and finished his meal as he gave her time to think. "That's all I have. Will you let me examine your father's files?"

She touched her napkin to her mouth. Her exotic eyes looked almost black, impenetrable, and her expression interested but wary.

"You want me to help you so I can clear my father's reputation. Obtaining the rings will identify the accomplices. Is that it?" Her expression said she found the flaw in his plan. Or flaws.

"That's part of it. The Feds questioned dozens of suspects and so did your father. If I can narrow down the field from his notes, maybe I can track the other ring pieces. I need proof the ring leads to the jewels. Proof I can take to the FBI." How he'd obtain the ring pieces from Leon's partners in crime was another problem. One thing at a time.

"I see." She folded her napkin and laid it beside her plate. "Dad didn't get the case until after the robbery. He was suspected because he knew the Jeweler from other cases and because they appeared too friendly. He wouldn't have had a ring piece. I don't see how identifying the accomplices by who has the ring pieces will do anything to clear his name."

His pulse kicked up. "Just so we're clear, no guarantee. But wasn't your father suspected first because he requested the case?"

"Yes, but not because he was in on the robbery, like the FBI suspected." If her eyes could shoot daggers, he'd be a dead man.

"Hey, I didn't say he was. Here's another angle the police could've thought of. You'd be surprised how porous jail security is. Leon could've arranged from inside for somebody on the outside to involve Marton. Once I find the accomplices, they might know something that'll clear him. Either way, I have to ID Leon's accomplices."

She chewed her bottom lip as she thought about it. "I need some time to decide. Unless you want coffee, I think we're done here."

Did she really need time? Or was this a brush-off?

The fries sat in Cort's belly like a clump of wet sawdust. He tossed down money to pay the bill.

"I'll pay for my own," she said, eyebrows lifted in objection.

"This was my idea. My treat."

"Then thank you." Pulling her sweater around her, she wove her way through the tables.

Damn if he was going to let her walk away without giving him another chance.

Chapter Three

OUTSIDE, MARA SHIVERED as she tied the
sash of her wrap-around sweater. A light mist fell and
she wished she'd worn a raincoat. She stuffed her hands
in her pockets. Anxiety tightened her shoulders. This
was her only chance to clear her father's name. How
much could she trust this man?

"I'll walk you to your car," Cort said.

She started, only then realizing he was standing
beside her. His jaw worked back and forth as storm
clouds darkened his eyes. Guarded and still, he seemed
to have a volcano seething beneath the controlled
surface.

Her stomach swooped and not with fear. She'd be
safer if it were fear. Her research on him along with the
past hour she'd spent with him had dissipated any
lingering fears for her safety. "I walked. But there's no
need for you to escort me."

No smile but his eyes softened. "I already know
where you live. And I won't let you walk alone this
time of night."

Her stomach fluttered again at his offer of
protection. Being a gentleman? Or making time for one
last plea?

"I wasn't worried." Just surprised. She headed
across the street. "It's this way." But of course he knew
that.

As they proceeded side by side down the narrow sidewalk, she didn't mind his escort. He was rugged and rough-edged, with brown hair curling onto his collar and the hint of dark beard on his jaw line. He radiated vitality and dominance, not just physically, but with the force of his personality.

Light from building entrances glistened on the wet pavement. A few cars passed. A skinny man hunched beneath a hooded sweatshirt ambled toward them. A vomit-green recliner, its padding erupting through the flowered seat, blocked the sidewalk.

Cort's big hand touched the small of her back, indicating she should precede him. Frissons of awareness eddied down her spine from the momentary warmth.

"Quiet here," he said. "The D.C. I remember from college days was a lot noisier."

"Quieter in Maine, I imagine," she observed when he caught up to her. "How did you end up so far north?"

"One thing led to another. In high school I took wood shop, built some furniture. When I got out of prison I still had thirteen months supervised release."

"Probation?"

"The federal prison system doesn't call it probation, but yeah. I worked as apprentice to a cabinetmaker near Pittsburgh. From him I heard about the furniture school in Maine. He recommended me, so when my time was up, I went. Spent some time there as a kid."

Ah, yes, his arrest had interrupted his freshman college year. He'd put that behind him and lived a solitary life in the woods. She started to squash her sudden spurt of compassion but remembered something. "My research said your mother is gone."

His step hitched and he jammed his hands in his jacket pockets. "She died while I was in prison."

The grim line of his mouth told her he didn't want sympathy but she couldn't let the comment pass. "I'm sorry. I still have my mother, but you've lost both parents."

"I lost my father a long time ago."

His statement was uttered flatly, without emotion. That, together with his earlier comments about his father, told her theirs had not been an easy relationship. His demeanor with her was low key, but she sensed the passion and determination in his soul.

The mist turned into a light rain as they walked in silence to her front stoop. She climbed the first step and plucked her keys from her sweater's deep pocket.

"Thanks for walking with me." She extended her right hand.

The streetlight sparkled on the moisture beading his hair and cast a shadow on his face. He stepped closer and clasped her hand. His was tanned and tough in contrast to her smaller, paler fingers. Callused palms from hard labor, as well as scarred on the backs. His grip was gentle but unbreakable.

Holding on as if to keep her from running inside, he pinned her with his gray gaze. "You haven't told me what you decided. Will you let me see the files?"

Savoring the feel of his palm, she didn't pull away. Maybe he'd go along with her compromise. "I'm not comfortable letting you look through my father's papers. I'll go through everything this weekend. Then I'll phone you with a list of names."

His jaw firmed. "It's not good enough. Look, I—"

"Research is what I do. Take it or leave it." She glared at him eye to eye, the step raising her to his level.

He nodded, releasing her hand. "I'll take it."

The sad desperation in his eyes nearly undid her.

"Good night." She darted up the three steps, inserted her key, and ducked inside before she could relent. Through the side window she saw him striding back the way they'd come. Her hand tingled from his grip and she swiped it against the sweater's rough knit. His imprint remained.

Cort Jones was a study in contrasts. She shouldn't be drawn to him, but she couldn't help being intrigued.

A big man, hard and lean, with bulges of muscle testing the seams of his knit shirt, he was all edgy intensity and coiled energy. Yet he gave her space and reassured her. His square jaw tightened with agitation. Yet his voice was gentle and resonant—raw, as if he rarely used it, deep and dark and very male. He had eyes of steel. Yet shadows lurked in their depths. Of loneliness? Pain? Prison would do that to a man. So would a lonely life. She shivered at the thought.

He was an ex-convict. A criminal. Hadn't Dad always said, *"Once a crook always a crook"*? His investigative work had taught him healthy skepticism, and he'd tried to pass it on to his daughters. In more ways than one. She sensed there was a lot more Cort wasn't sharing. What he said seemed straightforward. She'd have to proceed methodically. And carefully.

Leaving the foyer, she opened the inner glass door. The hallway was dark, lit only by the dim light filtering through from the foyer. She felt along the wall toward the light panel and flicked the switch. Nothing.

Drat. The overhead light was working when she left.

A shadow of apprehension nibbled at her mind. Her pulse jittered. Maybe she should've had Cort walk her inside. No, she was being foolish. It was just a burned-out bulb. She'd report it in the morning.

Good thing she lived on the first floor. The brownstone had three stories with two apartments on each floor. She edged her way along the wall toward her door, first on the right. When she reached the frame, she sighed in relief and felt for the keyhole.

She heard a board creak and tensed, started to turn.

Hard arms grabbed her from behind.

She dropped her keys. Heart racing, she struggled, but a vicious grip twisted her left arm behind her. She opened her mouth to scream. All she managed was a whimper of pain.

A sharp point jabbed her throat. "Quiet, bitch. Or I'll cut you."

Mara's attacker thrust his upper body against her, ramming her against her door.

Her pulse pounded in her ears. Where were the other tenants? Why didn't someone come down the stairs or open their door?

Her next-door neighbor took out her hearing aids at night. She wouldn't hear her scream, but upstairs they might. And Cort! Was he still close enough?

The mugger wrenched her arm tighter behind her back. Pain rocketed through her shoulder. Her heartbeat clattered and her throat closed tight with terror. She could barely breathe, much less call for help.

He jabbed the knife harder beneath her chin. "What

did Jones want?" The voice was half whisper, half growl.

The reek of checkout-counter cologne and sour breath gagged her. Dizziness swam in her head. She couldn't fathom his question. She was too trapped. Her stomach lurched and her knees buckled. She'd have fallen if he wasn't propping her against the door.

Apparently concluding he'd squeezed the breath from her, the man eased up his body pressure against her. But not the knife. "What did he want?" he repeated.

She dragged air into her starving lungs. In the darkness, her other senses came into sharp focus. She was aware of the blood rushing through her veins, aware of her heart pounding hard enough to rock her body—and aware of her right arm.

It was free. She pressed her palm pressed flat against the door.

Swallowing down nausea, she forced herself to think, to make sense of what the man demanded. No common mugger, he knew who Cort was. Instinct told her not to mention the rings. "He... he just wanted to talk."

She couldn't escape, but she could stall. She had to get help. She inched her right hand toward her sweater pocket.

"Talk. Not good enough. What did Jones want?"

She coughed, slumping against the door as she slipped her hand into her pocket. "Nothing! Only to apologize for my father's death."

The man growled an obscenity in her ear. "You bitch. You're lying." The knife point bit harder.

Mara winced at the sharp sting. "That's all. I

swear! Don't hurt me. Please let me go."

She squeezed her eyes shut and concentrated on what she had to do. Concentrated on closing her fingers around the cell phone. She eased it around and felt the screen for the right place.

****

Head bent against the now driving rain, Cort jammed his hands in his jacket pockets. Telling Mara about the puzzle ring had made him relive his visit to the prison hospital.

The reunion replayed in his mind.

He'd searched for deception in the watery eyes. "You conning me?" he'd asked the shrunken old man in the wheelchair.

"Why would I? Especially now?" Leon said. "Your mother, bless her departed soul, was the one who lied to you."

Cort's chest tightened. "She was trying to protect me."

"Yeah, from your old man. I never lied to you. I'm not conning you now." Again his gaze didn't waver.

"But why tell *me*? Why not the FBI?"

"The Feds would arrest everyone who had a ring. I'm no rat." Leon's tone implied that should be obvious. He had his own code of honor, logical and reasonable to him.

Cort stared at the man he used to believe was larger than life. Scalp pale through his thin hair, and in pain and weakness, he hunched his bony shoulders. Hands once infamous for their skill and steadiness trembled. Eyes that used to glow with charisma and dreams of big capers were watery and yellow. Disease had aged him beyond his sixty-eight years.

The dimmed eyes studied Cort with fervor. "You're a hell of a lot bigger than me but your face is mine at that age. Same gray eyes and stubborn square chin. Uncanny."

Only one of many reasons to hate the son of a bitch. He wouldn't give in again to the bad seed within him. Staying in the woods kept him out of the light and out of further temptation. Cort clenched his fists. He schooled his emotions against the anger roiling in his belly. "A burden I have to live with."

After some dancing around the subject, Leon got down to business.

"Those days are over," he said. "The Jeweler's days are over. I want to make things right. For you." He gestured at the nearby chair.

Cort lowered himself onto the cool metal. He wasn't convinced but curiosity gripped him. "Deathbed conversion?"

"More like yielding to reality. I'm never getting out of here. Not alive. I'm never going to reset those jewels like I planned." He straightened, the gleam in his eyes reminiscent of the old days when he'd been a notorious man of mystery. "A perfect caper. The Smithsonian, no less. And you should've seen the crown. The diamonds and rubies in the scepter. Glorious. I—"

Cort had interrupted him to ask about the accomplices. They were to get a cut. Except for Cort. He'd refused any part of the take. But about the others, he'd hit a wall, a slippery wall named Leon Jones.

And tonight with Mara had he slammed into another wall? Global Insurance wouldn't trust him. The FBI wouldn't listen to him. And Mara...

He pictured her face, her expressive exotic eyes

and lush mouth. She was an enigma, skeptical and distrustful yet compassionate and warm. She looked delicate and soft, but he sensed a steely strength inside. And he'd felt the impact of her smile. It had seeped into him, infusing a ray of light into the dark place he barely acknowledged as his soul.

He shouldn't be attracted to her. Their fathers had been on opposite sides. Hell, if there was an afterlife, they still were. She didn't trust him and she shouldn't. His mother had trusted him, and he'd abandoned her to die alone.

Trust is for fools.

Nobody should trust him and he trusted nobody. He'd trusted his old man and look where it got him.

So he shouldn't... couldn't trust Mara. But she was all he had. Maybe her search of the files would yield names. He'd feel a hell of a lot better if he could see the notes.

He reached the corner and saw Sean and Tony's Pub two blocks away. He could go there and drown his sorrows. But that'd accomplish nothing except a headache in the morning and a higher parking fee. He probably already owed the parking garage the cost of a winter's firewood.

Cort turned left toward Dupont Circle.

His cell phone chirped. When he looked at the screen, he recognized Mara's number. His pulse skipped. Did she change her mind? He pushed the button to answer. Before he could speak, the voice he heard kicked him in the gut. Not Mara but a man's rough voice.

"You bitch. You're lying."

Then a whimper, and Mara's voice. "That's all. I

swear! Don't hurt me. Let me go."

His adrenaline spiked like a jet streaking for the sound barrier. He swung around and raced toward Mara's building.

The voice growled out of the cell again. "The Jeweler's rings, you got one of 'em?"

Cort dropped the phone in his pocket and stretched his legs, pushed harder. Ignored the rain soaking through his jacket and dripping into his eyes.

Reaching the building, he took the steps two at a time. Where was she? Did the rat bastard hurt her? He yanked at the door handle. Locked. Mara'd used a key. He cursed the building security that let in her mugger but not her rescuer. His hand shaking, he jabbed a call button beside the door.

Nothing.

He jabbed another.

Still nothing.

He pressed more buttons. Leaned on them.

Finally some trusting fool buzzed the door lock.

Cort barreled through the two doors into darkness. Flattened against the wall and fished in his pocket. Flicked on the mini-flashlight attached to his keys. Swept the thin beam over the stairs, then the hallway.

"Who's there? Look out!" Mara called out.

A heavy weight slammed onto the side of his head. He toppled like a load of mahogany.

Chapter Four

"CORT?" PANIC SHARPENED her voice.

"Stay put. Call the cops." Cort's head spun. Pain fractured out from where the creep hit him. He heard footfalls down the hallway toward the back of the building.

Shaking off the blow, he pushed to his feet and started toward the sound. Was it running feet or did he hear only the pounding in his skull? He blinked at the gloom ahead, stumbled on the uneven floor. His tiny flashlight scarcely penetrated the darkness, and he groped the rest of the way along the wall.

A door banged shut. He surged ahead but smacked into cold metal.

He tore open the heavy door. Rain drenched his face. He sucked in the cool, damp air. Still dizzy, a gong ringing inside his head, he stumbled down metal steps into an alley, dimly lit by windows in surrounding buildings.

Three cars, one of them Mara's, sat in lined spaces beside a couple of trash containers. Cascading water from a downspout churned a stack of newspapers into a sodden mess.

Nobody.

Dammit, he'd been too late to nab the mugger. Gingerly he touched his aching head and felt a lump beginning to bloom above his left temple. In the bad light, he couldn't tell blood from rainwater. He searched the alley further, then tromped back inside.

Light spilled from Mara's apartment onto the tiled floor. She stood in the doorway, hair damp and disheveled, hands knotted in front of her.

"He got away. Broke the lock on the alley door. Got in that way," he said. "Did you see him?"

"It was too dark." Her forehead crimped as she closed the door behind him. "Thank God you came. I couldn't cry out. You were the last person I called, so I pushed Redial."

"Smart move."

She clutched his arm and tugged him inside, into the light. "You're bleeding."

He felt like he'd stuck his head in a drill press, but his vision was clear. "It's not bad. A glancing blow. No concussion."

She slid the dead bolt into place. Her warm-honey skin was ashen. Her shoulders trembled. Crimson smeared her throat and stained her shirt and sweater.

His stomach clenched at the thought of what might've happened if he hadn't gotten here in time. He shouldn't have involved her. His pressure on her led the scumsucker right to her. "Damn, he cut you. You're bleeding too."

"He had a knife. He—" She touched a finger to her throat. Losing more color in her face, she crumpled.

Cort curved his arm around her waist to support her. She was slim, with soft curves, and her hair smelled like a summer rain. Awareness surged into him.

Bad timing.

His gaze took in the apartment—living room with lights blazing, bar to a kitchen, hallway that must lead

37

to the bathroom and bedroom. "It doesn't look deep but we have to stop the bleeding. Bathroom back this way?"

She nodded. "Past the kitchen. I don't mean to go all woozy on you. I don't know what's the matter with me."

"You're in shock. No surprise." He guided her into a bathroom the size of a cupboard. He made her sit on the commode lid.

"And *you're* all right? With a head blow?"

He smiled at her spunky retort. "I've had worse."

"Hard head."

"Runs in the family." He handed her a washcloth from the towel rack. She pressed it against the cut while he rummaged in the medicine chest for bandages and antiseptic.

She looked so fragile sitting there, trembling, leaning against the sink in her bloody blouse. He wanted to carry her away and keep her safe from muggers.

Even if he could, this intruder was no garden-variety city mugger. That was for damn sure. "Did you recognize the guy? Has he bothered you before about the ring?"

"The first I heard about the ring was from you tonight and I never got a look at the mugger. All I can tell you was he was big." She eyed him up and down. "Bigger than you. And so strong I could barely move. I couldn't breathe when he mashed me against the door."

If he'd walked her to her apartment door, he could've prevented her injury. He shouldn't have involved her but what other choice did he have? And now it was too late. "He was smart, cutting the light, keeping you from seeing him. Don't think about him now. Try to relax while I clean your wound."

He tore off his sopping windbreaker and tossed it into the bathtub. Most women would yell at him for dripping all over her carpet, but her first concern was for *his* noggin. For a man she didn't trust and didn't like. Yet she'd called on him for help.

After running warm water in the sink, he wet a clean washcloth. He wrung it out and turned carefully, too aware of the intimacy in the tiny bathroom. Scents of feminine soap and shampoo surrounded him, the source of her summer-wildflower scent. Mara sat inches away, beautiful and pale and shivering. He swallowed.

She looked shaky and her eyes were unfocused. He had no choice. He bent toward her with the wet washcloth.

"I can stand." She shrugged out of her sweater. Holding onto the sink for support, she levered to her feet. Tugging down the shirt collar to give him access to her cut, she lifted her chin. "I'm afraid to look. How bad is it?"

He stood close enough to her to dance cheek to cheek, close enough to inhale her fragrance. Close enough to see the tiny mole beside her nose.

Too close for comfort. His comfort.

His pulse raced and his body thrummed with heat. *She* seemed perfectly at ease baring her soft skin for him.

He patted her throat where the blood was drying. Good, his hand was steady. "Bleeding's stopped. A small puncture wound. You won't need stitches."

"Great. I hate doctors. Hospitals are where people go to die."

Like her father. Guilt twisted through him and tightened his mouth. He would help her prove her father innocent if he could. If any of what he wanted to do was possible.

He cleaned her wound and dabbed on antiseptic ointment. Beneath the shampoo scent was another, more subtle, the female sweetness of her skin. He finished the doctoring with a gauze pad and tape. Done. He couldn't take much more.

"That'll do it," he said, stepping back the inch the linen cabinet would allow.

She tilted her head this way and that, inspecting his handiwork in the mirror. When she turned to him, her wide smile lit him inside.

"Thank you. Now it's your turn. Have a seat." She indicated the throne she'd recently vacated and offered him a hand towel. "Dry your hair and I'll have a look at that bump."

He didn't need nursing, but he couldn't bring himself to refuse her touch.

Switching positions meant doing a little close dancing, his hands on her shoulders. Her breasts brushed against his ribs. Sweat trickled between his shoulder blades.

He dropped his hands from her shoulders. Some chicks got a kinky thrill from hooking up with an ex-con, but not a classy female like her. She wasn't even looking him in the eye. He sat down heavily and rubbed the towel over his hair. He determined to ignore the feel of her gentle fingers on his scalp. Maybe now his head would clear.

Mara watched him towel his hair and saw the pain in his eyes. He'd taken care of her while his head was pounding. She handed him a paper cup and a bottle of ibuprofen. "You should take a couple of these. No, three."

A protest appeared to form on his lips but then he caved and accepted the pills in his palm. He was so big, so potent, so very male, smelling of dampness and fresh-cut wood. She took care not to touch him. But of course she'd have to so she could clean his wound. She busied herself with rinsing the bloody washcloths and running clean water. Her pulse drummed in her ears.

She considered her bathroom cramped, not intimate. Until now. He wasn't hovering over her, but he filled the room anyway. She felt his gaze as she tried to calm her breathing.

Yes, he'd rescued her, maybe saved her life, but she couldn't forget who he was. He'd served his time, and his record seemed clean, but she couldn't ignore what her dad had always said. On the surface, what they wanted seemed the same, but it wasn't. As long as he found the rings, he wouldn't care who had them. Why should Cort care what she wanted, clearing her father's name and helping her mother?

She turned to him with a clean, damp cloth. After the towel drying, his hair spiked up in all directions. Resisting the urge to finger-comb the thick, wavy strands, she dabbed at the growing lump above his left temple. "It's only a small cut, more of a scrape, but you should put an ice pack on the swelling when I'm finished."

"What the hell did that guy hit me with?" Cort muttered. "A brick?"

"Close." Smiling, she pulled a curved red shard from his hair and handed it to him. "A clay plant pot.

The leaves and dirt are all over the hall floor."

"Guess I should be glad I didn't get a haircut." He looked up at her sharply. "Cops're taking a hell of a long time. I thought they'd be here by now."

She stepped back and wrung out the washcloth. She motioned to him to hold still while she smeared antiseptic on his cut. "I didn't call them."

A long swallow as he processed what she said. Then finally: "Why not?"

She draped his dripping jacket over the shower curtain and hustled from the bathroom. She had no choice but to explain—some—but she'd rather talk in the kitchen. "Didn't you hear him on the phone?"

"About the Jeweler's rings. I heard. So?"

Temporizing, she searched the freezer compartment. "I have a gel ice pack in here. I use it sometimes after a hard tennis game."

She pulled the pack from behind the coffee beans, then grabbed that container too. When she turned around to hand the pack to Cort, she found him close behind her, his gray gaze intense and penetrating.

She edged away and began measuring coffee beans into the grinder section of her coffeemaker, but her hands still shook. Did she really want caffeine after all? Too bad she had no brandy. Folding her arms, she turned to face him. Might as well jump in before she wimped out and changed her mind.

He leaned a hip against the bar and held the frozen gel gingerly against his head.

When he winced, she caught a glimpse of the little boy he'd been. Tousled hair, skinned knees, freckles—

She squashed the image. That boy grew up with a criminal for a father and became a criminal himself.

Tough and hard. Never mind he was studly and sexy and he made her pulse race and all that crap.

"Why not the cops?" he prodded.

"Don't you see? The mugger must be one of the two other accomplices. That means the rings exist. Your father didn't make it up."

"So it seems. Too bad it took you getting cut and me whacked on the head to convince us. But this attack gives me enough to grab the FBI's interest."

Her pulse skipped, and she almost reached for his arm before she hugged herself. "No, no, please. No FBI. Not until you have real proof. I don't trust them. It was the FBI and the insurance company that persecuted Dad until his heart couldn't take the pressure."

His brows jammed together in a skeptical expression. "The FBI might catch on. They think I kept quiet because I want the loot. Secrecy will convince them of that for sure. I *won't* go back to prison."

The ferocity in his last statement startled her. But *did* he want the jewels? Even if he did, she couldn't let that stop her. "You and I heard what the intruder said. No one else. Unless your cell phone recorded his voice, no proof exists about anything except that one ring section. The police would say the attacker could be a regular mugger after money or drugs."

"I hate to admit it. You're right. Hell, I'm no detective." He drove the fingers of his free hand through his hair, then winced.

"But *I am.*" When his brows shot up at her admittedly absurd statement, she said, "Well, I do research, but I have access to most of the company's databases. Once we have the names, I can find them. My boss might even offer his cooperation."

"You said *we*. Does that mean you intend to help?"

She touched a trembling finger to her bandage. Her stomach flip-flopped. She couldn't believe what she was about to say. "I do want to clear my father's name. And I can't thank you enough for tonight. You may have saved my life. I owe you."

"I've rescued you twice. Hope it doesn't become a habit." A grin flashed, sexy and brilliant, then faded just as fast, humor replaced by suspicion. "So I can see the files?"

"I'll work with you. I'll let you see Dad's files. On one condition."

"No FBI."

"See, your head's better already." She smiled, mental fingers crossed that he'd not change his mind.

"Yeah, better. Thanks." He laid the ice pack on the counter. "So when do I get a gander at the files?"

"They're in the basement of my sister's house. I'll get them tomorrow."

"No. *We* can get them tomorrow." His tone of voice and the set of his jaw brooked no argument. "I'll come back in the morning." He headed for the living room.

With a start, Mara realized he was leaving. With Cort here, she felt safe. Strange, but there it was. Now she'd be alone.

She followed him. If the intruder came back, her double locks might not be enough to keep him out. A spasm tightened her throat.

"Wait. Your jacket." How needy did she sound? Her friend Sandi would tell her to grow a spine.

He shrugged. "It's too wet to do me any good. I'll get it tomorrow." Finger on the door handle, he turned.

"The alley door is useless as security."

"I'll call the landlord. He's usually quick with repairs. He has certain companies he uses." Now she was babbling. *Shut up, Mara.*

"That won't help you tonight. Be sure to lock up."

She twisted her hands in front of her. "Yes, fine."

He stared at her for a long moment, his gaze every bit as penetrating and mind-reading as her boss's. Maybe more. "You don't look fine. You're still shaky. Will you be all right?"

Mara hesitated. Before she could fold and ask him to stay, she forced herself to shrug. "Absolutely. Double locks. I have that dead bolt." Mr. Devlin would fire her if he knew she didn't have a security system in place. With all the computer gear and electronic gadgets she had? Geesh. She'd take care of it ASAP.

His brow furrowed. Eyeing the sofa, he said, "I could crash there."

"Wait. You? Stay here? No, out of the question. I'll be okay." She stepped forward to herd him closer to the door but he stood his ground.

"I'm too tired to be a threat. Left Maine at two this morning. Drove straight through. I can probably find a hotel. But I don't feel right leaving you. That guy might return."

Which was riskier, having this ex-con sleeping on her sofa or lying awake all night listening for the mugger trying to break in? Either way, she wouldn't sleep.

Her breath hitched. "My sofa folds out into a bed. You might as well stay."

He reached up to rub the lump on the side of his head. "I must've been hit harder than I thought. Did the woman who doesn't trust me just *invite* me to stay here?"

"Yield to the inevitable is more like it." She marched to the hall closet and returned with a pillow and blanket. Sounding resentful was a tough order when relief was her primary reaction. That and a hefty dollop of anxiety. She couldn't let his protective attitude get to her. He was a dangerous man and she couldn't forget that. "And don't think for a minute I trust you."

But who was she trying to convince?

Chapter Five

LATE SATURDAY MORNING, Cort steered his pickup into Mara's sister's neighborhood in Dundalk, a suburb of Baltimore.

He'd spent the night on the sofa-bed trying to adjust his knees and hips so he wouldn't sink into the mattress fold's permanent dent. In the morning, he hoofed it to the parking garage to retrieve his truck and his overnight bag. On the way back, he picked up pastries and coffee for them both at a coffee place he passed. Popular place. Two taxis were parked outside while the cabbies ordered their morning joe. Joe for him, too. Colombian, black, and something for her called a venti non-fat, no-whip, no-foam mocha. Fancy name for caffeinated hot chocolate, if you asked him. But it suited her somehow.

By the time the two of them came out to head to Dundalk, a locksmith was hard at work installing a new lock on the alley door. Impressive results, Cort said, especially on a weekend. A good omen, Mara had said. The woman was way too optimistic. He didn't believe in omens. He didn't believe in much.

Mature maples and oaks lined Dundalk's street and yards. The rain had moved on. Moisture on the trees' new leaves glistened in bright sunshine. Late April in Maine, trees were barely budding. 1950's-era frame and brick houses in the lower middle-class neighborhood, not upscale. Plumbers, shop owners, teachers. Factory workers, if any factories remained. Not unlike the Springfield, Massachusetts, neighborhood he'd lived in with his mom. Leon offered dough but she wouldn't let him pay for anything upscale.

"That house on the left," Mara said, pointing to a brick ranch-style. "I grew up there. Mom grew flowers and vegetables in raised beds in the backyard. She loved working in the dirt. She lives with her sister in San Francisco now. My aunt's row house has only a paved patio."

He said nothing as he pulled into the blacktopped drive and stopped behind the Subaru sedan in the carport. "You going to be okay with this? You said your sister didn't sound happy."

Mara hoisted a shoulder in a gesture of nonchalance that didn't fit the tight set of her mouth. "These days Cassie never sounds happy." On that enigmatic note, she opened the passenger door and slid out of the truck.

He hoped to hell he didn't end up in the middle of some family squabble. All he wanted was the files so they could get back to D.C. "Don't tell her about the rings."

"I already told her on the phone." She gaped at him. "You don't trust my sister?"

"The fewer people who know about the rings, the safer we all are." And no, he didn't trust her sister. He couldn't.

"Come in the side door," a raspy feminine voice called. He hadn't noticed anybody seated in the breezeway.

Mara replied with a casual wave. "This way," she

said to Cort. They headed through the carport past gardening tools and a watering can.

The aromas of coffee and cigarette smoke enveloped him as he entered the screened-in space. Her sister lounged in an Adirondack chair, a ceramic mug in one hand and a freshly lit cig in the other. The ashtray beside her held three butts.

With similar features and hair color, the two women were clearly sisters. Cassie was a few years older and a few pounds heavier, same glossy hair but hers was cut chin length. The style gave her a harder look. Her dark eyes held more bitterness than distrust as she openly appraised him.

Mara made the introductions, and he muttered a greeting.

Cassie merely nodded. "I made coffee. Help yourselves. It's in the kitchen."

"Where's Livvie?" Mara asked, looking toward the open kitchen door.

"At her dad's for the weekend." She took a deep drag on her cigarette.

"Mom would have ten fits if she knew you were puffing away again." Mara fanned blue fumes away from her face.

"I don't smoke in the house." She inhaled and blew smoke. "Or around Livvie."

"You know that's not what I meant. What is this, a thirty-something version of teenage rebellion?"

Cort hadn't grown up with siblings but he recognized when family pushed each other's emotional buttons. Marton had been a heavy smoker. The case probably wasn't the only factor in his death, but Cort would keep that opinion to himself.

Cassie blew a lung full directly at her sister. "She'd have *twenty* fits if she knew you wanted to dig around in the case."

"I'm not going to argue with you. I said it all on the phone." Mara turned to him. "Come on. I'll pour you some coffee before we head downstairs."

In the kitchen she poured aromatic brew from a drip coffeemaker into two bright red ceramic mugs and added cream and sugar to hers. "Basement door's over here." The handle rattled when she tried it but it didn't turn.

Arms firmly planted on her hips, she stalked to the breezeway. "Door's locked."

Cassie laid her smoke in the ashtray and swung out of the deck chair. "I've changed my mind. I don't want you to take those files."

Cort retreated to a dark corner of the unlit kitchen to watch the battle.

Mara chewed on the inside of her cheek for a moment. "They're Dad's files. I have as much right to them as you do."

"But it's my house now, not Mom's. What you're doing can lead to nothing good. Dredging it all up again."

Mara looked like she'd been slapped. "You think he's guilty." Apparently she'd just realized the source of her sister's resistance.

Cassie lifted one shoulder in dismissal. But the red flush on her face said the accusation hit the bull's-eye. She was named right. Cassandra, the predictor of doom.

Time to step in. This was his fight. "Mara isn't doing this only for herself," he said. "It's partly because I asked her."

"You just want the *loot*." Cassie's mouth was tight with emotion.

"I want my life back. I paid my debt to society, but the FBI won't let me move on. If I can lead them to the crown jewels, I'll be free once and for all." He could hold up his head instead of holding out a damn tin cup for crumbs.

"Not my problem, is it?"

"Cassie!" Mara knitted her hands together in supplication. "This is for us, for Mom. She could have Dad's pension if he's cleared."

"And if he isn't?"

"At least I tried." Mara's mouth was tight, her shoulders hunched. "Don't forget you still owe me thousands for my half of this house. If I took you to court, that line you've drawn in the sand would be blown away. Is keeping me from Dad's files that damned important to you?"

Red faced, Cassie shook her head as if to clear her thoughts. "I didn't think of the pension. This search, investigation, whatever—it better not hurt Mom. The key's in the junk drawer."

A short while later, Cort followed Mara outside with one of the two file boxes. He enjoyed how her jeans fit her curvy butt. He wanted her but couldn't afford to alienate her. He needed her. But no stopping the fizz of chemistry in his veins. And he liked her. She was feisty and smart.

"You know I hate this, Mara," Cassie said, her smoker's rasp adding another layer of doom. "Opening up Dad's last case. Cozying up to this, this—"

Sparks flared in his veins. "Thief? Ex-Con? Those the words you want?"

He shoved the two boxes into the truck bed and slammed shut the cap gate. When he saw her tears, the fear and pain, he reminded himself she was justified in her fear.

On a deep breath, he calmed his expression, his voice, kept it even. "I promise to do all I can to keep Mara safe. She believes in your dad. If we can figure out who my father's accomplices were, your dad is in the clear and so am I. So chill."

He climbed into the driver's seat and breathed deeply in a rhythmic pattern—an exercise he'd learned in prison anger management classes—while he waited for Mara.

****

Cassie reached for her sister's hand. She had to try to talk her out of this misadventure. "If he has to keep you safe, what didn't you tell me?"

"He's just the protective sort. I'll be all right," Mara said. "Mr. Devlin's going to help us with the investigation."

How could Mara bear to go through this again? Her throat tight, Cassie shook her head. "Let Jones take the boxes. You stay out of it."

Mara's eyes widened. "Now you trust him more than I do. I don't plan to let Dad's files out of my sight. If Cort took off on his own, clearing Dad would be a dead issue."

"He's a good-looking guy. I saw the way he looked at you. You sure this isn't—"

"Whoa!" Mara held up her hands. "No way. You can back off on that one. He may be a hunk but I'm not going to be like Mom."

"Whatever. But what if you go on this wild goose

chase and still don't clear Dad? You don't know what dangers you might be facing." Cassie sniffed back her tears.

Mara looked about to say something but only handed her a tissue and hugged her.

Cassie mopped at her eyes and kissed her sister on the cheek. "You always were stubborn. Just make sure your methodical ways keep you safe."

Mara grinned. "I never even asked you about Livvie. How's my fave niece?"

"Your only niece, kiddo," Cassie replied. The tension in her throat relaxed now they were on safer ground. "What can I say? She's eight going on twenty. Wants a tattoo on her ankle. I'm hanging tough but I only hope Walt doesn't cave under the wheedling."

Mara opened the truck passenger door. "Look it up on the Internet. Tattooing anyone that young is probably illegal."

Cassie heaved a sigh. The ash on her cigarette had grown nearly an inch and she tapped it onto the pavement. "You've just saved me a headache."

"Until she's sixteen or so." Mara held the door partway open. "And promise me you won't tell Mom about this. I don't want to worry her."

Cassie pressed her lips together in thought. "I don't know."

"Look, I'll tell her myself if we get anywhere. If nothing pans out, she doesn't need to know. Okay?"

"I guess. Deal."

Cassie watched as the big black truck pulled around the corner and disappeared. Too-trusting Mara didn't know what she was getting into. After all these years, no way were they going to get anywhere finding proof of Dad's innocence. Or those jewels. All they'd find was more trouble. And more pain.

****

The truck rolled away and Mara waved goodbye. She noted Cort's thin slash of a mouth and set jaw as they reversed their route. He kept his emotions under tight control, but she was beginning to read him. He kept a lot of hurt buried.

Cassie'd gone on the attack, but even she yielded to his potent maleness and the internal scars he couldn't conceal. "Sorry about my sister. She's five years older and defensive."

He hit her with his stone-gray gaze. Hypnotic when he really looked at her. As if she were the only person in the world. She could barely drag her eyes away.

"Not a problem," he said. "I just want to get these boxes opened up."

"Exactly what I want." Why she'd never examined them before, she wasn't sure. Maybe too heavy a burden to go through what the FBI had already searched. If they came up empty, what could she find? And, like Cassie, she dreaded the pain of opening old wounds. But now with a ray of hope, she had to take the chance. "Plus, the divorce has her all on edge."

"I gathered that. The daughter was with the ex." He frowned at the side mirrors.

"Tough situation. Cassie came home from work early to find Walt in bed with her best friend. To her credit, she kicked both of them out of her life that very day. Walt and the best friend aren't together now but Cassie doesn't forgive."

"Don't blame her. I know what it's like to be screwed over."

So did she. Her dad was innocent. He had to be. *Once a crook, always a crook.* His favorite saying. Too painfully ironic if it applied to him. And her as a transgressor.

"You tell her about being attacked last night?" Cort asked.

"No way. She'd have called Mom, gotten her on my case. One of her Korean lectures is all I need."

"Your mom teach you girls her language?"

"We learned some when we were kids but both of us lost interest by high school. Even in Korean I'd know I was on the receiving end of a scolding."

He grinned then straightened in his seat as he checked the mirrors again. "Get a hold on that safety handle above you."

She blinked. "What?"

He reached across her, blocking her view. "This."

She slid her gaze along his sinewy forearm to the handle above the door. "You don't trust the seatbelts or something?"

"You're gonna need it. Humor me."

As soon as she had a firm grip, he shifted to Neutral. He yanked the steering wheel a hard left and stood on the brakes. In the middle of traffic, the truck swerved into the opposite lane in a tight U-turn.

Tires shrieked. Horns blared.

The move flung Mara right shoulder first into the passenger door. Her breath blew out in a whoosh. Her fingers froze around the safety handle.

When the truck threatened to fishtail, Cort corrected the steering. His jaw set in stone, he shifted to Drive. The truck shot forward, laying more rubber with an ear-splitting squeal. The G-force thrust Mara back in her seat. They zoomed the opposite direction down the street, zigzagging around traffic so fast she barely registered the other vehicles.

"What the hell is this, NASCAR?" she croaked.

"Losing our tail."

"What?" She peered back between the bucket seats. "Someone's following us?"

"Watch for a black SUV."

At the next intersection, he made a hairpin turn right onto a one-way street the wrong way. He squealed around a green van headed their way. After that she didn't want to look.

"Anybody back there?"

Turning around, she dared a peek. "A few shocked motorists giving you the one-finger salute out the windows." She closed her eyes, picturing what she'd seen. "Maybe a black SUV. But it didn't turn into this street."

"Good. I'm not done yet. Hang tight."

Chapter Six

ANOTHER SHARP TURN followed that one, and
another, careening the truck nearly off its tires. Now
she knew what the expression *heart in your throat* felt
like. The pickup bounced across railroad tracks, and
they entered the industrial area near the marine
terminal. Finally Cort reduced the break-neck speed and
zipped through an open chain-link gate into an
abandoned shipping business. The pickup rolled to a
stop behind a warehouse.

"We'll wait here a while," he said. "Allow time for
them to give up looking."

Mara released her grip on the handle, one cramped
finger at a time. "What the hell was that about?" she
said when she could trust her voice again.

He rolled down the driver's window and adjusted
the side mirror. "The SUV picked us up the block after
Cassie's house. Hung back a car length or two but
stayed with us."

She twisted her fingers together. "You think it's the
thug who attacked me last night?"

He covered her shaking hands with one of his
rough workingman's hands. "Maybe. Could be FBI.
They're driving dark SUVs now instead of sedans."

Any minute she expected to hear sirens. When after
a few minutes, all she heard were the normal, distant
traffic noises, she breathed easier. "Where did you learn

to drive like that?"

His mouth curved in a teasing smile that dented the small new-moon scar on his left cheek into a dimple. She'd have to shore up her resistance to this boyish side of him.

"Misspent youth doing some street racing. Used to sneak out of the house after midnight. Mom went ballistic when she found out. Even Leon disapproved."

"What father wouldn't?"

He lifted a shoulder as if to dismiss Leon's attempt at discipline. "He was afraid it'd draw police attention onto him."

"It's possible he genuinely feared for your safety."

He grunted his doubt of that and started the engine.

He brushed off his hurt, kept it unspoken but the aura of anguish around him was palpable. How sad to be betrayed by his own father. Her dad, no, never.

They drove home the longer way, across the Francis Scott Key Bridge and via the Baltimore-Washington Expressway, a route no one would expect them to take. She hoped.

****

At the end of Cassie Marton's street, Rolf Rousso stabbed the End Call button on his phone and muttered a string of profanity. He should've known that con would lose them. But the greedy pair were his only connection to the puzzle rings.

The Jeweler had led Centaur on a merry chase for years. He would not let the son do the same to him. Retrieving the Gramornia crown jewels would be his ticket to move up in the smuggling syndicate, to be management. He would no longer have to sit in a rental subcompact and rely on local idiots for assistance.

He had grown up sleeping on the floor beside his snoring older brothers. Their father drank most of the money their mother earned on her back. Rousso had grubbed for every coin he could beg, con, or steal. He was never sinking again to such misery.

Never. The Gramornia jewels were as good as his. As Centaur's, he amended.

He turned the ignition key. No purr or roar of a finely tuned engine, only a basic vehicle, nothing to attract unwanted attention.

Jones and the Marton girl had led him to what he suspected was their weak link. A little research and he would know exactly how to use her.

****

Later that night Cort dug into Mara's cooking at her cocktail table as they finished with the first box of files. So far the only indication of her father's possible guilt or innocence was the lack of any. No proof of anything.

"Ate in a Korean restaurant in Boston once. This dish isn't exactly rice with tofu and kimchi," he teased as he forked up a bite of chicken and pasta primavera. She'd accompanied the dish with a fresh green salad.

"The only Korean dish I know how to prepare is *gam-ja-tang*, a pork stew with potato and vegetables. Dad was a meat and potatoes eater. And kimchi?" She affected a shudder. "Way too eye-watering for this girl. I prefer Italian."

"I'll eat this anytime." He scarfed down more.

After thanking him, she nibbled from her plate as she organized the mess of files they'd examined in the first box. Somebody had stuffed copies of police reports in folders with Marton's notes and insurance reports.

Elegant and exotic even in a simple lime-green jersey, faded jeans, and flip flops, she seemed to have settled down after their dodge-'em maneuvers in Dundalk. She'd pulled her glossy hair back in one of those scrunchie things. He took in how the thick chunk of it slid onto one shoulder as she bent forward. When she reached for the piles nearest him, her knee pressed against his and her scent underlined with savory sauce swirled in his head.

To distract himself he looked around the room. Comfortable furniture in primary colors—reds in the sofa and pillows, strong blues, greens—elegant and feminine but not frilly, like the woman. Family photographs and bold abstract paintings scattered the walls around shelves. A yoga mat lay rolled up in one corner beside a tennis racquet and bag.

She'd set aside in a stack her magazines—*Wired, PC World, Smithsonian Magazine*—before they sat down. She was meticulous about the filing, to the point of adding new folders and labels. With a felt-tip pen, she labeled the next folder "Police Reports," with the dates involved. Her lips were pursed in concentration.

Soft and kissable, he bet. He needed to ditch those thoughts. Hell, he wasn't here for fun and games and neither was she.

He set his empty plate on the table and noted she'd barely touched her food except for the salad. Methodical and exacting, good qualities. But was she overcompensating for the cloud around her father by trying to be perfect?

"I'm surprised your father was so disorganized." He enjoyed a swallow of cabernet.

"The files were probably in folders or neat piles on

Dad's desk when the FBI took them away. When they returned the boxes, Mom stored them away without looking at the files." Her voice caught on the last word but she firmed her mouth. "I don't know who to blame for the mess—the FBI or the DSF operative who dug into the case later."

"Does organizing matter now? We've examined them."

She glanced up from the label she was affixing to a folder. The stress and exhaustion showed in fine lines around her eyes. "Not enough. We may want to go through those papers again in case we missed something."

Thorough, he'd give her that. "What about computer disks?"

"Maybe in the other box. Back then he backed up his files on floppies. I'd have to take those to the office to see if they're corrupted." She edged back and picked up her plate.

Cort looked at the short list he'd made in his spiral notebook. Marton had eliminated most of the people the FBI questioned. "Looks like he narrowed the suspects to the security guards and Leon's usual partner. Must've figured Falco knew something even if he didn't take part in the burglary. Falco might tell *me* what he wouldn't reveal back then."

She cocked her head. "*You* took his part in the break-in. Why don't you have another one of the ring pieces?"

"I refused a cut." He should've refused the whole dodgy enterprise, but he'd been a dumb-ass kid and Leon a smooth talker. "Maybe he gave that piece of the ring to Falco before the job and didn't have time to get it back from him."

"A possibility." Appearing to take his hint not to grill him further, Mara peered at her laptop screen. She scrolled down the names and the scant information. "This guard, George Hauptman, stayed in the central security headquarters, monitoring the closed-circuit system." She worried a corner of her lower lip between her teeth.

"The cameras as well as the alarms and motion sensors were disabled temporarily—probably Leon's doing—but they'd gone on the fritz off and on for a week and the FBI couldn't prove Hauptman had anything to do with it that night. The technicians said the interruptions could've been due to the frequent thunderstorms that June."

"What if he caused it all to divert suspicion?"

The FBI and Marton had covered all this but what the hell. "Either of the two other guards could've arranged the disruptions. But maybe guilt has weighed on the guy all this time and he's ready to spill his guts."

"Or another one is. A hopeful thought. Too bad you have to go back to Maine tomorrow." She stabbed a bite of chicken with her fork. "If Hauptman still lives in Kensington, I can go talk to him."

His hand jerked, nearly knocking his plate on the floor. "Whoa, whoa. No way." For someone so logical and careful, how could she be so naïve? "Go interview possible criminals by yourself? Unless you're more than a research tech at Devlin Security?"

She shut her eyes briefly and sighed. "Nope, strictly an office grind. I have no self-defense expertise at all. You're right, of course. I'm just antsy. I want to *do* something."

"And you can. You told me research is what you do. So research. Get on the 'Net and find out where all these guys are, where they live, what they're doing now. Everything you can get on them since the Gramornia crown jewels were taken. And don't—"

"I know. Don't tell anyone at work about the rings. Hush-hush. But I have to keep my boss in the loop."

"Better if nobody knows what we're doing." How could he trust a man he'd never met?

"Thomas Devlin offered to help, remember, offered the resources of DSF. I think he'll give me clearance for access to more secure databases. And time to do this research. He'll be discreet." She laid a hand on his knee. "You want me to trust you, so you have to trust me."

If secrecy and security were the man's business, maybe it would work. But if others started looking for the rings, he could lose all control of the search. And the jewels. Trust her? Maybe this far. "Only Devlin, okay."

"Then what? You'll be in Maine."

"I have some things to finish, a two-week course, some other business." He'd finish the latest commission. Take leave from his job if necessary. "Then I'll come back. We might find more names in the second box and notes about Leon."

"Or something about the puzzle ring." The tightness of her mouth said she hoped not. "Tell me about finding your ring piece. Where'd he have it hidden?"

He considered. Couldn't see why not. "Behind the house where I used to live with my mom. I was lucky the present owners weren't home. The back side of the stone wall abutted a drainage ditch. He'd tucked the ring piece into the stone wall. That niche used to be a drop for him and me."

"A drop?"

"A secret stash, for notes mostly."

Her eyebrows winged upward. "You had to pass notes in secret to your dad?"

"When I was a kid, Mom thought she was protecting me by keeping Leon's profession a secret. We moved from Marseille to Milan and different places in the States, supposedly because of his jewelry-designing business. He did design jewelry, but I knew where some of the *supplies* came from."

"Do you look like him?"

"Some. Less now. I'm built like Mom's family, not wiry like... like a second-story man." Leon had asked if he worked out. Yeah, he worked out. Exhaustion from running and lifting helped him make it through the night. Maybe making this right would let him sleep.

She'd finished—about half of what was on her plate, as much as she ever seemed to eat—and he followed her into the kitchen with his plate.

"You lived with your mom. They were separated?" She scraped the plates into the garbage and placed them in the sink.

When she moved to cover the casserole and put it away, he took her place at the sink. Might as well earn his keep. And standing closer to her allowed him to breathe her scent. "When I was twelve, she discovered he'd been teaching me certain skills."

He wouldn't go into how Leon used to tell him stories about the glamorous world of jewel theft. He attributed the twinge in his chest to too much pasta.

Memories of the arguments and his mother's increased drinking hammered at him. Especially after that day. "She packed me up then and there. We left."

She took coffee beans from the freezer and shook her head. "What sort of skills was he teaching you?"

"Off and on he had me practice climbing walls and walking across the roof. To strengthen me and build agility for sports, he said, but I knew better. I heard enough to know why they argued about it. Mom caught him showing me how to pick locks." He'd kept the set of tools Leon gave him. A point of pride they remained unused. And would.

"No surprise you did what your dad wanted. A guy thing." She dumped coffee beans into the high-tech contraption she called a coffeemaker. When the thing finished whirring like a power drill, she set up the brewing. "Was he a good dad except for… you know?"

He shrugged that off and reached for a bowl. Finished rinsing the plates. His wet fingers brushed hers as he handed her a dish, and her cheeks flushed a nice pink. As she arranged the dirty dishes and silverware in the dishwasher, she kept her face averted. He grinned, pleased he affected her. Not that anything between them should go further than a simple touch.

"Did they divorce?" Her expression held curiosity and interest, not pity or disdain.

He poured wine and leaned back against the counter where she'd set her cell phone in a dock with an iPod. She had games too. All the toys, this pretty geek. He swirled the dark red liquid in his goblet. "She moved us to Massachusetts, where she grew up, and divorced him. Their agreement was that he'd see me only under her supervision."

Susan Vaughan

"But Leon didn't stick to their deal. Again, no surprise." She shook her head and sipped wine.

"You're catching on."

"Your dad made his life seem exciting and adventurous. Heady stuff for a boy," she said. "And your mom disapproved, so you were caught in the middle."

"Most of the time it was okay. Going into the relationship, she knew what he was. Then she couldn't take the secrecy, the unsavory hangers-on, the constant moving."

"Did they love each other?"

"Love? Is there such a thing? Can't prove it by me." He barked a harsh laugh. "She said she loved him. Just couldn't live with him. Didn't want me to end up like him."

And first chance he got, he followed in good old Dad's footsteps.

He set down the glass with careful control. "Never again. And I'll prove it if I have to drag Leon's partners into the FBI office and make them hand over their ring pieces."

Mara crossed the tiny kitchen and placed her small hand on his chest in comfort, as if she'd read his mind. As if she'd said, *"You're not your father."* Or was he?

In reply to that gesture, he said, "I should've known not to trust him."

The press of her soft palm and the tips of her fingers revved his pulse to a higher gear. He inhaled—the fruity shampoo that permeated the bathroom and the fresh rain scent that seemed to be hers alone—and his blood simmered again.

When she lifted those dark liquid eyes to his, he

had to taste her. Her generous words and tender touch seeped into his chest and something shifted. Before whatever it was could take hold, he held her away from him. He was spending another night in her apartment. Best not to start something he couldn't finish.

"You were only a boy." She backed up, effectively snapping any connection, probably all in his mind. And lower.

"Does that mean you trust me now?"

Her eyes flashed with irritation. "We'll see. I know you haven't been involved in any criminal activity since you got out of prison."

That much was all he deserved. "I have to head to Maine tomorrow, and we have another box to go through. We might find more suspects. Or the proof you need." If the FBI didn't find anything to exonerate Marton, it was unlikely they would. But he didn't say so.

"My thoughts exactly." She poured two mugs of the brewed coffee. She handed him one before doctoring hers.

He waited for her to precede him, watching the sway of her ass as she walked into the living room.

Chapter Seven

BY THE NEXT Friday, Mara's eyes were blurry from research. All week she'd had a full load of regular assignments—gathering info on known collectors of Chinese artifacts, artifact forgers, and thieves. A fourth fake Han period horse, copies of the stolen one, showed up, this time part of a California collector's estate. Someone was cheating the cheats. Hard not to smile at the irony, except for the loss of the original horse.

Her lunch breaks and scarce spare time went to researching suspects in the Smithsonian theft—the three security guards and Leon Jones's usual partner.

She picked up a short stack of file folders and stuffed them and her flash drive into her tote, ready to head home. Online research had given her addresses for two of the three possible owners of ring pieces. She'd find the third eventually. The second file box yielded no more information than the first.

Nothing incriminated her father. Nothing cleared him either.

"Devlin give you time off for this project, Mara?"

She looked up to see her friend Sandi at the cubicle entrance. Also a researcher, Sandi sympathized with Mara's situation.

"Didn't ask. Not yet anyway," she said. "I'll wait and see if it's necessary." She aimed to turn in her reports early so if they had to travel, she could take personal days.

"I saw Cortez Jones's photo. Even holding a number in front of him, he looks hot." Sandi winked, waggled her water bottle and the fountain of brown curls on top her head. "I'd sure want to spend some days with the guy. And nights."

Mara rolled her eyes. "We're just working together. That's all."

"Sure, sure." She didn't sound convinced. "What'd you find on your list of suspects?"

"Background checks, current addresses, jobs, finances, families. Nothing suspicious. One person has died."

"Guess they won't be much help."

Sandi's lighthearted attitude was contagious, and Mara joined in her laughter. "Gotta count on the families."

"Well, good luck. Let me know if you need any help. You could introduce me to the hottie." She strolled off, tossing this last over her shoulder.

Like that would ever happen. Cort's reasons for not trusting were valid. And she'd sworn both Sandi and her boss to secrecy. If Cort knew she'd included her friend, he'd have a cow, to quote her sister, but she needed Sandi's expertise in using the unfamiliar databases. And she might need her help again.

She picked up the tote and her hand-painted designer purse. The chirp of her cell phone had her huffing. When she saw it was her sister, she almost let it go to voice mail. But no. She set down her bags.

"Hey, Cassie." They hadn't seen each other since collecting their father's file boxes. She'd returned them to the basement but Cassie hadn't been there. "What's up?"

"You met with that ex-con again yet?"

She felt her shoulder muscles stiffen. Cassie refused to refer to Cort as anything but *that ex-con* or *him.* "Cort's coming in another week. I told you that."

She heard Cassie blow out a breath. "You haven't gone off on your own to see the others, have you?"

Mara scowled at her sister's implication, mostly at herself because Cassie was right. But Cort had talked her off that ledge. Then memories of the behemoth who'd attacked her had kept her double-locked in her apartment with the new security system coded in and set. "No way. He and I will do that together."

"Good. You never think anything bad will happen. Amazing for someone who researches criminal stuff. I'm afraid. You can't trust him. I don't like it either way."

She was used to her sister's criticism but it rankled. "I'm okay. I'll let you know what I find out."

"Good. That's good. Well…"

The hesitation meant something was up. Cassie hadn't phoned only to check on her. "What's going on, sis? Is it Livvie?"

"Livvie's fine." Ah, the catch of breath, her sister's pause for effect. "I've met a guy."

Of course. Ever since her divorce, Cassie'd swung from down in the dumps to a peak of on the hunt so she could flaunt some guy in front of her ex. Mara sought patience.

"Hold on a sec," Cassie said.

Mara heard a male voice in the background. *Here we go again.*

But she mustered up some enthusiasm. Maybe

Cassie would focus on romance instead of ragging on Livvie and her. "Hon, that's great. Is that his voice I heard?"

Cassie laughed. "That's just the cable guy. Some problem with connections. They're checking every box on the street."

"I don't have much time but tell me the important stuff. Where'd you meet him? What's he like? And I don't mean the cable guy."

Her sister's raspy chuckle hummed through the line. "Good thing. Met André at work. He came to my desk to open a checking account. We're going to play tennis and have dinner tonight. He's sophisticated and *sooo* charming. Looks like that hot French guy who's on *Devine Secrets*, Gilles something, but a little older, forty maybe."

"Gilles Coreau? Whew, I'm heating up just hearing about André." True, but that condition had nothing to do with Cassie's new guy.

She'd remained hot ever since Cort nearly kissed her. Fantasies of his hard mouth and harder body warming her inside and out filled her thoughts whenever she wasn't focused on work. Knowing he was so the wrong man didn't make any difference to her body. Whenever he phoned to check on her research, his low rumbling voice caused the same heartbeat rev, the same tingle she'd felt when she pressed her palm to his solid chest and his eyes went to smoke. Was this how her mom had ended up married to a man she didn't love? Did the heat of passion mask their basic incompatibility?

She chatted a moment longer before begging off. She promised herself to be all business when Cort arrived. Clearing her father and finding evidence for the FBI had to be her priority. Not drooling over a guy, like Cassie. Or going soft in sympathy.

She exited the building and drove across town, taking side streets to avoid rush-hour traffic. And to shake anyone following her. Mr. Devlin had explained how to watch for a tail. A DSF tech guy searched her car for a GPS tracker and found nothing, thank goodness.

Cassie's warnings were unnecessary. She knew to be careful. If they didn't trust each other, following up on any attraction was out of the picture. Trust or no trust, she needed to know more about what made Cortez Jones tick. And how involved he was in his father's nefarious business before they robbed the Smithsonian Museum of Natural History. The bare facts she'd researched and her short acquaintance with him didn't begin to address his motives then. Or now.

****

Cort tested the finish. Solid and dry. Good. On his own time, he'd busted ass finishing this commission. Six chairs to match the cherry dining room table built for a regular customer in Connecticut last year. Now he could pack them up to deliver on his way to D.C. He flicked off the workshop lights and headed across the dooryard.

His time back in Maine had dragged like a load of logs behind a skidder. Assisting a guest instructor from Vermont in a course on boxes with inlays kept him hopping from nine to four through the work week.

His mind kept wandering to Mara Marton. They'd spoken on the phone while he was away. Usually about what she was uncovering on their suspects and once about her new security system, but whenever he heard her sexy voice, the world went away.

He rammed a hand over his hair as he passed through the shade of a spruce tree. Shit, he wasn't the kind of guy a classy woman like her should get involved with. She deserved better than hooking up with an ex-con, a loner who lived a hermit's existence. Special Agent Kaplan had accused him of hiding in the woods. Yeah, so? But starting on the road to changing things made him hunger for sunlight and a new beginning.

When he opened the cabin door into the darkened living room, he walked into a battering ram. The blow dropped him to all fours and knocked all the air from his lungs.

He gasped for breath. His stomach rolled. Three sets of legs in dark trousers and polished shoes surrounded him. Brutality wasn't the usual FBI tactic. Who then?

Meaty hands dragged him upright and held his elbows in a vise.

"Merely a tap, Mr. Jones. I hope I now have your full attention." The deep voice held the merest trace of a foreign accent.

A click and the table lamp beside the sofa came on, better illuminating the intruders. The fiftyish man watching him with deep-set black eyes pointed a black automatic pistol at his belly. Close-cut hair either white or pale blond. A military demeanor that implied who'd sent him. His two playmates could've been his clones, except for the eyes. No intelligence and cunning, only the empty eyes of professional muscle. Years since he'd faced the type but he hadn't forgotten the soulless look.

Cort straightened his shoulders and affected an air of confidence. "I told the duke's man I was searching for the crown jewels. He didn't have to send his enforcers."

The man withdrew a pack of cigarettes from an inside pocket of his black leather jacket. He smiled thinly, revealing bad teeth. "I am aware of the duke's efforts. The prince's younger brother is competent but conventional and irrelevant. Allow me to introduce myself."

The words threw Cort into Mick Jagger's song. It would be a mistake to underestimate this man whether he was the devil or merely imitating him. Cort's nerves crawled like a nest of spiders.

"I am Colonel Yerik of the Gramornia Security Police, under the command of His Excellency Prime Minister Turkof." He made a small bow and clicked his heels together. "The prime minister has a different priority."

"Yeah? And I should care because?"

One of Cort's bookends cracked a fist against the back of his head. He jerked forward, head swimming, but didn't make a sound. He knew not to show weakness, let alone pain. Been there, done that, learned the fucking lesson.

"Pay heed, Mr. Jones. Or my men will reinforce my words with their fists." Yerik blew smoke in his face, then tapped the ash onto the floor. He pocketed the pistol, apparently believing it no longer necessary to ensure Cort's submission.

"I'm all ears."

Yerik ignored his insolent tone. "You will cease your search. You will continue to tell the FBI and the royal family you have no way of locating the jewels. Do you understand me?"

If the clones hadn't been holding him fast, he'd have stumbled backward in shock. The FBI and the Gramornia royal family had pressured him for years to return the crown jewels, and now this KGB-type creep wanted him to leave them hidden? Had he fallen down the damn rabbit hole or was there something funny in the colonel's cigarette smoke?

Another second and it hit him. Not silly smoke, but political smoke and mirrors. Dirty smoke. Without the crown and scepter and the other trappings of royalty, would there even be a coronation? A ruthless prime minister could foment general unrest and eliminate the royals altogether. Maybe the entire democracy while he was at it.

All Cort had to do was… nothing. Yerik's mistake was in thinking the threat of a beating would accomplish that. A fist in the gut or a broken nose and the promise of pain weren't enough to stop him from turning his life around. "So what's in it for me if I go along with this plot?"

Yerik clucked his tongue, a disgustingly wet sound. "*Plot* is such an ugly word. I prefer to think of the plan as an alternative. And you? I will allow you to live, Mr. Jones."

"For sure I can trust you on that. Why bother? You could kill me today and your worries would be over."

"A tempting suggestion. However, your sudden death or disappearance would lead to more investigation than the prime minister would appreciate. So you will be allowed to live. Unless you resume your search. Then I must re-examine our bargain." He dropped the butt and ground it into the throw rug with his heel.

Cort couldn't figure out what the catch was. Except that once the coronation date passed, probably so would he. "Say I agree. Then you walk away and leave me alone?"

"In principle. You will be watched. Closely. Trust but verify, I believe one of your presidents was fond of saying." He held up a fist.

A signal? Cort braced himself.

In a practiced move, the two clones grasped both arms. Clone One slugged him in the chin. Pain ripped through his head as it snapped sideways. His brain did a sickening spin. Black spots danced around the room. The other clone kicked his legs and he toppled to the floor.

"Fuck you, Colonel!" Cort spat through bloodied lips.

"One final word of advice and a warning, Mr. Jones," Yerik said. He once again held the automatic. "I understand you and Ms. Marton are working together. From reports, it appears you've moved in with her. You will recover from the little reminder my assistants will administer, but would she? You will say nothing of this conversation to her or to anyone else. If you do, not you, but the lovely Ms. Marton will suffer. I assume I need not be explicit."

A poisonous storm broke loose in Cort's head. He exploded upward. *"You fucking cowardly bastard!"*

The two no-necks tackled him before he could reach Yerik. Their powerful fists rammed into his ribs, his chest, his jaw. One kicked him in the back. He welcomed the blows, each one splintering knives into a new part of his body. Oblivion would come. The suffering was temporary.

Pain cleared the mind. Pain clarified. Pain focused.

Chapter Eight

AS THE SUN was setting, Mara pulled into a space behind her building. Cort was waiting for her. The surrounding buildings reached up to the sky, painting his rugged features in shadows. His raw masculinity frightened her a little. At the same time, his protective aura, as if he'd never allow harm to come to her, eased warmth into her stomach. Maintaining detachment around him took effort. She slid out and grabbed her tennis bag and tote from the back.

"Hey." He stepped forward and took her tote. At the brush of his fingers against hers, her pulse did a little dance. "Everything all right?"

When she looked up at him, she gasped. A greenish bruise surrounded one eye. Scrapes and scabbed-over cuts marred his jaw. "What in the world happened to you?"

He hoisted a shoulder in a show of nonchalance but winced at the movement. "Nothing serious. Got in the way of a load of falling lumber."

"And I'm the tooth fairy, but if that's your story, I won't pry."

"Thanks." That was all. He didn't elaborate but his expression was as grim as death. Even so, an appreciative gaze perused her legs.

A little fizz jazzed her pulse higher. She should've changed from her shorts and sneaks after her sets.

"You can have an ice pack once we're inside." Fighting? An explosion of temper? Maybe she'd been mistaken about his tight control on emotions. Another reason not to trust him. She'd have to control her own better where he was concerned. "Your boss okay with you taking off?"

"I have the next workshop session off. Boss said he'll need me after that. I'll work out something if I need to."

The strained optimism in his voice plucked at her chest. As an assistant instructor, Cort couldn't make much money, yet he was putting his livelihood in jeopardy to prove he was no longer a thief.

"You can stay here again. I mean, if you want. Hotels in D.C. and the suburbs are pricey." Dammit, she didn't want to make him think she was coming on to him or offering charity. But if he'd been fighting, maybe her offer was a stupid move.

To her surprise he grinned, actually looking relieved. "Thanks. I'll take you up on that offer. I've been paid for a couple commissions so I'm okay, but who knows what expenses we'll have from here on out."

"Commissions?"

"Working at the school's not my only job. I build furniture on commission. Desks, chairs, tables. I delivered a set of chairs on my way here." He pushed open the building's back door and stood aside for her. Pride in his work shoved aside the shuttered pain she usually saw in his eyes.

Custom-made furniture could cost the earth. He wasn't living hand-to-mouth. *Never assume.* Suddenly she felt small. Without intending to, she'd belittled him.

"If you'd rather stay elsewhere, I'd understand. My sofa's not exactly orthopedic." She'd noticed him stretching his back after the last night he'd slept on it.

"No, I'm good. My back kinda got used to the um, unusual contours of that mattress."

She laughed, reassured, as they entered the building.

She mentally rehearsed her new security code before inserting her key in the apartment door lock. "You're carrying my research results in that tote—in my tablet and printouts for you. What I think we need to do is begin with the suspects who live in the D.C. area."

"I'm guessing if you found anything to exonerate your dad, you'd have said so."

The gentle support in his voice buoyed her. "You got that right. I did find his notes about meetings with Leon in jail." She didn't feel right saying *your dad* when Cort didn't call him *Dad*. Calling him the Jeweler seemed confrontational, so she'd settled on Leon.

"The same notes the FBI thought incriminated him?"

She nodded, fumbling with the key ring. "Dad apparently liked Leon. He mentioned his gregarious nature and his use of entertaining stories to detour an interrogation. From his choice of words, I believe Dad was leading him on, befriending him in hopes he'd be persuaded to reveal his big secret—the crown jewels' hiding place."

"Sounds reasonable, but it doesn't help your cause." He jerked a nod at the briefcase in his hand. "Your notes tell you if Leon's old partner is still around here?"

"Dante Falco lives in College Park." Maybe this was her opening to broach her other issue. Her pulse jittered at the thought of quizzing Cort about his criminal past but she wanted—*needed* to know everything. Maybe he would also tell her about his busted face—and ribs, judging from the stiff way he moved.

"You doubt Leon's usual partner has a ring piece."

She turned the key in the deadbolt. "That and—" The motion met no resistance. Ice scraped her spine. Her heart rate stumbled. "Oh my God! The door's unlocked."

Cort nudged her to one side. He turned the knob and pushed the door inward. When he emitted a low whistle, she had to see.

Furniture, books and DVDs on shelves, and plants were turned over and tossed around. "Like a tornado went through."

A grim look on his face, Cort gripped her shoulders, stopping her from entering. "I once saw a cabin where a black bear got trapped inside. Tore the place apart looking for food and an exit. That was destruction. *This* was a search."

No need to hold her back. She was frozen in place and a fist squeezed her chest. But the protection of his arms kept her from shattering into pieces. "F-for the ring p-piece they think I have?" Damn, did she have to sound so shaky?

"Or for what we know." He opened his phone. "This time we call the cops." His tone brooked no discussion.

****

Uniform cops responded to the 911 call within

fifteen minutes. The two officers quickly cleared the apartment. One took pictures and dusted for fingerprints around the alarm keypad, the locks, and the computer desk. The other asked questions and took notes. Because violence wasn't involved, they, not a detective, would handle the case. Just as well, as far as Cort was concerned. The fewer cops the better. Even these two made him nervous, as if he'd committed the crime. He doubted they'd find much.

Mara's hands and shoulders shook as she surveyed the mess. The ring piece was safe because he carried it. And her hard-copy notes and tablet were safe, in her tote, which she'd kept with her. The only items missing turned out to be her laptop and the desktop computer CPU. The only loss that threw her was the disabling of her new security system.

About that, the note-taking cop clicked his tongue. "Burglars are savvy these days. Illegal code-breaking devices are available on the Web. These guys came prepared. Odd they took the computers and not the rest of the components. Or the game consoles."

Sniffing back tears, Mara indicated the mess in her living room. "Maybe they didn't see them. Or they wanted money or jewelry instead. Who knows?"

Yes. Cort mentally pumped a fist at how smoothly she'd handled the cops' questions so they thought they were dealing with ordinary burglars. But he figured these creeps were after the ring and any info about the treasure they could find, paper or in computers. *Who* was the question. The rat bastard colonel who'd had him thumped? Or one of Leon's accomplices, greedy for the jewels?

As soon as the uniforms left, Mara slapped a hand

over her mouth. *"Frak!"* She raced to the bathroom and he heard the sounds of her losing lunch.

Seeing her so affected tied a knot in Cort's gut. This was worse than the thug's attack. He raised his hand to knock on the bathroom door. His fist hovered an inch from the wood. Hell, he had no idea what to do if she opened up. What did you do with a sick person? He backed away.

A memory brushed his mind—his mom pressing a damp cloth to his forehead. He'd been eleven, sick with the flu. She rubbed his back and eased his fever with the cloth as he hugged the porcelain god and heaved his guts.

Banishing the throat-tightening memory, he strode to the kitchen and dug around in drawers until he found dishcloths. He ran cold water on one, wrung it out to an inch of its life, and returned to his post. A gentle tap on the door should be enough. "Mara, you all right?"

"Better." The door opened slowly. "Just, it got to me. I don't throw up when a mugger holds a knife to my throat, but I do because one touches my private things. A violation. Stupid."

"Not stupid. Seems like it's piling up on you."

She was mopping her face with, yes, dammit, a washcloth.

Shit. Now what should he do?

Before he could hide his offering behind him, she said, "Thanks. This one's dried out."

He let out the breath he'd been holding and handed over his cloth. When she gave him a tremulous smile, he felt like a hero. Idiot. She looked whiter than her computer printouts. He knew what he'd do for himself under the circumstances. A shot of something alcoholic.

But she'd already started on the mess, scooping dirt back into the plant pots. He helped her right the living-room furniture, and then they started on the shelves.

He reached for the game consoles on their backs like overturned turtles. "I don't think these are broken. Wii, iPod, *Wired*, computer with two monitors—you're a geek all the way."

She folded her arms and glared, dark eyes flashing with life finally. "Be grateful I am or we wouldn't have all the data on our suspects."

"Whoa, don't freak on me. I think it's sexy as hell." When she looked uncertain whether he was hitting on her—he was—he decided to lighten up. "But *Frak*?"

She wagged her head, a pretty blush returning some color to her honey-toned cheeks. "Swear word from *Battlestar Galactica*. I like it better than the f-bomb."

His laughter deepened her blush and she jabbed him in the biceps with a small fist.

"Mara, the f-bomb's the mildest curse I heard in prison. You won't damage my ears with it. Or with frak."

The bedroom was worse, drawers of clothing dumped, the computer desk a total loss. It would keep, she told him. He sent her to rest on the sofa. Downed a shot of brandy and poured two for her.

"I don't need this," she said, even as she accepted the glass. She stared at the amber liquid with no life in her eyes. She didn't argue. Not like her. Her lack of resistance wound his gut tighter. "You should eat something. Sit there and I'll see what I can do."

Her fridge held an array of food but the only

ingredients he could make a meal with quickly were bagels and an omelet. Eggs should be okay on a queasy stomach. Probably.

He glanced at her as he cooked. Eyes closed. In the lotus position on the sofa, her breasts rising and falling with deep breathing. Maybe yoga would calm her. Seeing her stretching that lithe body and arching her back sure wasn't calming him. She was tough and vulnerable, smart and beautiful, and he wanted her bad. More than that he wanted to be with her. He liked just talking to her. But they were so wrong for each other it was laughable. The cynical loner and the trusting geek. All that brought them under the same roof was their mutual goal. That's what he needed to concentrate on. Not getting Mara naked.

He flipped the omelet, catching it with the pan. Hadn't forgotten how. After release, part-time work as a short-order cook had paid off in some skills even if the job had paid squat.

After dumping in grated asiago and chopped vegetables, he folded over the eggs. "Omelet's ready." He headed to the table armed with silverware and a tub of cream cheese.

"I'm okay now." She pushed off the sofa and came toward him. "The eggs look wonderful. But I don't think I can eat."

Okay? No way. He wanted to bundle her off to Maine. "You look shell-shocked. You need to eat."

She shook her head. Lifted his hand and pressed his knuckles to her cheek.

He wanted her to keep his hand there forever against that warm soft skin. Heat flared briefly in her eyes before she banked it. Just as well.

"Thank you for being so thoughtful," she said, regret in her voice. Or in his mind. "But I'm going to bed now."

So he consumed the entire omelet and two bagels and shoved the sofa-bed against the door. He stretched out there—alone.

****

On Thursday, Cort headed to Crystal City for a powwow with Mara's boss. He could come and go as needed from the apartment now that she'd given him a key and installed his fingerprint access to the new security system installed by Devlin Security Force. Poring over her reports had taken up most of his time since the break-in. He had to give her credit for thoroughness. She uncovered details of their suspects' histories and current lives.

He exited the crowded Metro car at the Crystal City Station with a throng of late-afternoon commuters. Another mob waited on the platform to enter the cars, headed south on the Blue Line and home for the evening.

A lanky teenager with enough piercings to sink a boat slunk by him, plugged into a cell phone. Body spray of the kind supposed to attract females trailed in his wake. Cort stifled a gag reflex as the car door whooshed closed behind him. The train rumbled to a start and whisked away.

The public transport ride threw him back to his year of college at GW. He'd grown up in major cities in Europe and the States so subways were nothing new to him. As a student living on his own for the first time, he'd been enthralled with exploring and with the night life, but he'd known even then urban life wasn't for him long term.

No matter what happened with the Gramornia loot, not the life he wanted. No crowded commute for him. Give him trees and quiet and work with his hands.

He stood facing the Metro System map so he could study stragglers in the scratched Plexiglas reflection. Prison had taught him how to watch his back. The warm temperature meant no coats to cover pistols tucked in waistbands. He froze to attention when a middle-aged man in a Nationals cap stepped aside to unfold a map. When the guy moved toward the exit, he exhaled. A trio of women stopped for one of the group to dig something out of her bag. Gradually the crowd dispersed. Nobody paid him any mind.

No tail.

He'd lost the tails earlier. Maybe the guys who followed him from Dupont Circle realized they were made and gave it up.

Pocketing his Farecard, he headed for the escalator to the surface. The open space of the station kept the air from being stale and overpowered by humanity but once through the gate and the exit, he welcomed the sunshine's warmth on his face and the fresh air, laced with the scent of potted flowers at building entrances on either side.

The man with the map had disappeared. After another survey found nobody turning away abruptly, nobody dawdling in front of a reflecting surface like he had, nobody otherwise suspicious, he headed toward his destination.

Officially part of Arlington, the commercial and residential center sat south of D.C., surrounded by the Potomac River, Reagan National Airport, and the

Pentagon. Nearly every building, including the speckled-granite tower he was passing, bore *crystal* in its name. Something to do with a crystal chandelier in the first office building, Mara'd told him.

Last night's burglary had ratcheted up Devlin's interest in their "caper," enough reason for a meet with the big honcho. Was it the case or his pretty employee that interested Devlin? Cort hunched a shoulder. Why should he care? He just wanted the information Devlin said he uncovered.

He checked the street sign and turned the corner.

Mara's determination to prove her dad innocent earned his admiration. Cort had dragged her into this search, into danger, had given her hope. His need for exoneration made her vulnerable. No time to waste— less than two months to the coronation. He had to set some sort of plan in motion. If Yerik caught wind they were continuing the search— The constant knot in his gut wrenched tighter.

If he could get her out of this mess, get them both out, he should try.

One more time.

He'd spent the better part of the last two days trying to talk to Al Kaplan again. The special agent was in conference or on the phone or on fucking Mars for lunch, but he sure as hell wasn't available to Cortez Jones. He'd called Global Insurance, but got only a bullshit answer—*"Leave your number and an agent will get back to you."*

Heaving a sigh, he took out his cell phone and stepped away from the traffic hum across the street from Crystal Arches, where the Devlin Security Force logo, a stylized Greek delta bearing the firm's initials, ranged above the entry. DSF occupied the top floors of Crystal Arches and ran the security for the whole shebang.

Odors of hair chemicals and perfumes puffed out of a hairdresser's shop when a customer opened and closed the glass door. He punched in the memorized number without much hope.

"Special Agent Kaplan speaking."

Cort nearly dropped the phone. "Cortez Jones here."

After a pause, the agent cleared his throat. Cort figured he was ordering a trace on the caller's location. "Don't tell me you've decided to come clean on the jewels."

"You already know everything I do," he said. "You probably also know Mara Marton is helping me track down the other pieces to Leon's puzzle ring."

"What do you want from me?"

Interesting Kaplan didn't deny the assumption. The fucker. Cort's shoulder muscles tightened. He inhaled deeply to calm the tension. "I want you to do the investigation, not me. I've involved Mara in this mess. We've gone through her father's papers and come up with a list of possible accomplices who might have the other ring pieces. But the search is getting dangerous."

"Yeah? How so?" Cort's phone picked up the habitual rhythmic drumming of his fingernails on his desk. In the background, a phone rang, a printer whirred.

"Last night somebody broke into Mara's apartment and stole her laptop and desktop computers. She called the D.C. cops. You can check."

The squeal of Kaplan's desk chair told Cort he'd

gotten the agent's attention. Finally. "I'll do that."

Cort told him about the thug who'd grabbed Mara in her foyer and the SUV that followed them in Dundalk. Not that he could prove either one. "She didn't want to report the first attack because she doesn't trust you guys, and I figured the SUV might *be* you guys."

"Wasn't FBI." Kaplan's tapping resumed. "The mugger wanted the ring, or so you say."

Cort gritted his teeth. The hell with deep breathing. "Kaplan, I don't give a flying fuck if you believe me but Mara Marton doesn't deserve to be harassed or hounded by the FBI or some assholes who want the jewels. Maybe her old man conspired with mine. Maybe he didn't. But she's an innocent who believes in Marton's innocence. I read Gramornia's putting pressure on the U.S. to find their crown jewels. Can't you take over here?"

"Granted, the Gramornia ambassador and the junior senator from Maryland—she's got a Gramornian grandmother, I hear—are leaning on the Bureau." His voice came across muffled, as if he didn't want others in his office to hear his words. "But you're my best lead, Jones. One ring piece and your puzzle story aren't enough for my SAC to authorize more than I'm already doing on this case."

What Kaplan meant was his hands were tied. Pressure on his boss meant pressure on him but no support and no resources. Typical bureaucracy. "So you want *me* to handle the FBI's case for *you*. That it?"

Again the chair squealed in protest at the agent's fidgeting. Fingers drummed louder. "The suspects on your list haven't talked to the Bureau in eleven years.

Doubtful they'd tell me squat now. They'd more likely talk to the Jeweler's son."

The statement rocked him back against the wall. The agent believed Cort's story. But why? When Cort had laid out Leon's ring story, Kaplan stalked out of his workshop with threats to hassle him until he yielded the treasure. And now the FBI wanted an ex-con to do their investigation? Great. Not only was he searching for himself and Mara, but for the damn FBI. All while pretending *not* to search, for Yerik's benefit. He shook his head, as if the motion would tumble his dilemma into a coherent answer.

"This is bullshit. Suddenly you believe my story? Are you on some new meds? What the hell changed, Kaplan?"

Chapter Nine

THE POWERPOINT GAVE Mara something
positive to do even though Cort had said the slide show
was overkill. Not unexpected from a non-techie. She
needed to act, to move ahead so they were ready to
interview the next suspect.

Slipping the flash drive containing her little show
into her jacket pocket, she headed for the elevator.
She'd expected support from Mr. Devlin but he'd gone
above and beyond. He even set up this meeting with her
and Cort this afternoon. Maybe a ploy to check out the
ex-con.

Not that she minded the buffer. She needed to
cultivate a purely professional attitude toward Cort.
Having him spend nights at her place put him too close
for her peace of mind. She kept picturing him in bed.
With her. A man who was the antithesis of all her father
stood for.

If my dad's innocent, a little voice said.

She pushed away the traitorous notion. If Cassie
had doubts, Mara did not. Quincy Marton didn't
conspire to hide Leon Jones's loot. Then why did her
inner voice of doubt make her feel tainted and dirty?

She found the administrative assistant's desk
unoccupied, her boss's door open, and the aroma of
fresh iced tea in the air. Francine had been busy
preparing for the meeting. Mara was touched by

Devlin's consideration.

She didn't know much about his family background. No one in the company did, no one who'd talk about it, even his admin. God knew Mara had pumped her enough. But his taste for sweet tea hinted at a southern heritage, maybe South Carolina or Georgia.

"Come on in, Mara." He'd apparently seen her on his office screen. Closed circuit cameras were ubiquitous throughout the company's corridors and offices.

When she entered the inner sanctum, Thomas Devlin replaced the phone handset in its cradle. He tugged off a royal-blue silk tie as he rose from his executive chair. His charcoal linen suit jacket hung on a rack behind the desk, a gleaming metal-and-glass construction, a contrast to the antique wall clocks he collected. The desk was more art than furniture.

"Just finished a meeting with a new client. Then the phone call. Couldn't wait to get that noose off." He grinned, his eyes crinkling at the corners.

Her employer's informality would probably make Cort feel more comfortable, and she said a silent thank you. He'd placed a yellow legal pad and pen at the head of the conference table. At the other end, a tablet would connect wirelessly to the overhead projection module.

He waved her to the table. "Go set up your slide show. I have a little matter to take care of before we can begin."

She noted the time on the 1800's banjo clock beside the security screen. Her stomach tightened. Cort was late. Not a good sign. A moment later she saw him on screen and awareness sped up her pulse. When she took in the whole picture, her heart took a nose dive.

No. Oh no.

Pivoting, she rushed to the door.

Devlin already had already gone to the anteroom.

Cort marched in and stopped six feet from Devlin. Two security guards followed close behind and flanked the visitor in a military stance she'd heard called parade rest.

Guards, a grinding reminder of prison. Cort might as well be made of stone, he stood so still, so silent, so stoic in his pressed khakis and teal dress shirt. His arms hung loose at his sides, his broad hands open.

His facial wounds had healed but he looked like a battle-hardened warrior. His mouth was drawn into an edge as straight and sharp as a guillotine, and his eyes, blank granite, stared straight ahead. Only the twitch of a jaw muscle betrayed his emotion. Embarrassment, fury, hurt—Mara could only guess.

Her eyes burned along with her cheeks. She could only look on and hope Cort observed and appreciated her empathy. And her inability to act. This was the boss's call.

Devlin said, "Mr. Jones, give me a moment, please."

When Cort inclined his head, Devlin linked his fingers behind his back, the superior officer reviewing troops. He turned his attention to the guards. "What's the meaning of this?"

One man cleared his throat. The name on the company ID pinned to his green uniform shirt was Mannion. "Eddy said this guy has an appointment but—"

"But you didn't like his looks so you took it on yourself to escort him. That it, Mannion?" Her boss's words were soft, but his rigid posture said they were only smoke preceding the flame.

Prepare to be scorched and barbecued. She knitted her fingers at her waist.

Behind the three men facing Devlin, another man entered the office.

Max Rivera, one of DSF's field operatives and as imposing a figure as Devlin and Cort in his size and dynamic aura. He and Devlin had served in Iraq and Afghanistan together. Max had told Mara that but not much more.

But why was the Latin hunk here for her meeting?

As if sensing her gaze, Max sketched a salute. His teeth gleamed a white, cocky grin against his bronze skin. Folding his arms, he hiked a jean-clad hip onto the desk and settled to watch their boss dismantle the two guards.

Mannion hitched his shoulders and nodded with emphasis as he answered his boss's question. "Yes, sir, Mr. Devlin. Thought he needed an escort. Can't be too careful."

"Generally speaking, I value independent thinking and initiative. I encourage it among my employees." Devlin took a second to observe the sage nods of the two guards. "But I also expect my employees to check their facts."

Mannion looked blank.

Cort didn't move but his expression shifted to sharp interest. He apparently caught on that the guards had stepped in it up to their hips.

"Did Eddy also tell you I'd personally cleared Mr. Jones?" Devlin asked.

The two guards exchanged glances. The other

man's gaze skittered away. He looked as if he'd like to sink into the floor. Ah, Devlin's phone call had been from Eddy at the lobby security desk. The little matter he needed to take care of.

"Well, no, sir," the guard began, "he didn't. I—"

"—never asked," Devlin finished for him.

The guard shuffled his feet. His silence spoke for him.

"So not only did you proceed without the facts, both of you left your assigned posts without justifiable cause. And you've insulted my visitor. Does that about sum it up?"

The two guards swallowed, then nodded.

"You will apologize immediately to Mr. Jones. Then return to your duties. I'll talk to your supervisor later."

Mara bit back a smile as the two red-faced guards muttered apologies in the form of insincere drivel. They'd be lucky to keep their jobs.

When they'd left, tension released from Mara like a balloon hissing away its helium. She nearly ran to Cort, to wrap her arms around his lean waist, to soothe. But no sooner did relief chase across his features than his stoic face returned. Reality slapped her with good sense.

All business, Mara Lin, all business. She locked her feet in place and her fingers behind her back. Instead of unwanted sympathy, she sent him a smile.

When Devlin stepped toward Cort, Mara stayed put. No need for introductions. The two men shook hands with assessing gazes and firm grips, but without the contest of strength she'd anticipated.

"My deepest apologies, Mr. Jones," Devlin said.

"I'll let those two stew awhile before I deal with them. Rest assured their insult will not happen again."

"No problem," Cort said. "Goes with the territory."

If he meant insult was what he had to deal with on a daily basis because he had that hardened look about him, no wonder so many ex-cons returned to crime. Her throat tightened.

Devlin introduced Max. "One of my best agents. He'll be joining our meeting. Rivera has some information I think you'll be interested in."

"Jones." Max extended his hand and Cort grasped it.

They took the high-backed chairs around the conference table, a gleaming match to Devlin's desk. She steeled herself to hold her own amid all the testosterone in the room.

Her boss sat at the head facing the wall screen, with Max to his left. Mara beckoned Cort to join her on the other side. She'd feared he might walk out when he realized their circle of secrecy was widening in spite of his precautions and caveats. But he hadn't batted an eyelash.

In the table's center sat a tray with a pitcher of tea, glasses, cloth napkins, and small glass plates. "I can offer you iced tea," Devlin said to Cort. "Or I have a full bar if you'd prefer something hard. It is after five."

Cort took the seat beside Mara. "Tea's fine. Thanks."

Devlin was pouring the tea as his admin whirled in with a bakery box.

"Hope everyone enjoys this." Slim and rigid as the sharpened pencil she kept tucked into her steel-gray French twist, Francine's voice wavered. Flustered because of the ex-con elephant in the room? "My lemon bread. The bakery was out of cookies."

She fumbled as she opened the box. A delicious lemony fragrance rose from the plate she removed.

"You didn't have to go to all this trouble." Cort said accepted a pale yellow slice. He winked at her. "But I'm glad you did."

Her cheeks flushed the hue of her candy-pink lipstick. A first.

So, Cort had an effect on all females. Didn't he put her at ease after her initial jitters when she met him? The same tough look that made men wary seemed to convey to the female sex a sense of protection and sensuality. Or she was reading more into this than she should.

"No calls, please, Francine," Devlin said. "It's late. You go on home."

"Good call on the lemon stuff, darlin'," Max said in his Texas drawl, helping himself to a second slab of the treat.

Francine smiled her thanks.

When the door had closed behind her, Devlin nodded to Mara. She clicked the remote to launch her presentation. The slides covered the facts as they knew them and the background information she'd gathered on the suspects. She finished with a slide of questions to be answered.

"In my view, these are the most pressing." She inclined her head to Devlin. "Who is our competition? Who mugged me and searched my apartment? Who followed us in Dundalk? Who else is after the ring pieces?"

"And the Gramornia crown jewels?" Cort finished

for her.

She found herself too aware of him to pay the attention she should to the enigmatic look exchanged between Devlin and Max. She watched Cort's wide hand holding his drink, his scarred forefinger tracing the condensation on the fragile glass, the five-o'clock shadow darkening his stern jaw. When had she ever been so conscious of a man? Not since she was a teenager. Forcing herself to look away, she noted her boss had been making notes on his legal pad.

Devlin downed his tea and slid another slice of lemon bread onto his plate. "You've hit on the main reason I wanted this meeting. Max and I have *some* answers."

"You know who else is after the crown jewels?" Cort asked, leaning forward.

Mara poured more tea into his glass. His eyebrows had twitched at the first taste of the pre-sweetened tea, but then he drank up without comment.

"Some information has come our way," her boss said, doodling in the margins of his pad. "Max, please."

The operative set down his glass. "Y'all probably are aware Gramornia is pushing the U.S. to find the crown jewels in time for their big shindig later this summer." He folded his hands on the table. At ease and confident, he seemed to be the only relaxed member of the group. Even Devlin's tension showed in the set of his jaw.

"June second." Mara clicked to a new slide showing the online news story. "Crowning of the new prince."

Cort swiped a hand across his mouth. Covering his amusement at the technology? Tough. "We have less than two months."

"Exactly," Max said. "Seems the Gramornians don't feel like relying on Uncle Sam. You can hardly blame them. The FBI has produced nada in the years since the robbery. Gramornia is on the hunt for the jewels. The Royal Guard sent an agent here undercover."

She choked on her tea. "A Gramornian *spy*? That little country. You're joking."

"You'd be surprised," Max said. "I have a buddy in the country. Knew him in the Stan." At her blank look, he added, "Military slang for Afghanistan. Gramornia sent troops as part of the NATO forces. When he went home, he moved up to the Royal Guard. Happened to mention in an email the palace scuttlebutt about the UC agent. There's other political dirt but it probably doesn't connect to this."

She doubted the buddy just *"happened to mention"* the agents. More likely Max led him to the revelation.

"I was followed on the way here," Cort said. "About five-ten, big nose, receding hairline. Lost him at Metro Center."

Mara pictured the huge transfer station, an octopus of connecting lines. Definitely a place to lose a tail. Cort continued to impress her with his resourcefulness. He covered her hand with his, maybe to reassure her. It didn't.

Max shrugged. "My buddy didn't mention descriptions or names or the number of agents. If I ask, he might balk. Catch on I was pumping him."

"First the over-muscled gorilla who grabbed me. Now this guy," she said. "Are they working together or are there separate factions?" Her head reeled. Were she and Cort in danger from all sides? Feeling surrounded by enemies, she wiped her palms on her pants.

"I have no intelligence on the connection between those two or their stake in the jewels. But clearly we have more than one faction." Devlin's chair rolled a little as he leaned back. To Cort, he said, "Your father ever mention a group called Centaur?"

The question threw Cort. Brow tight with perplexity, he slid his hand from Mara's. Time to focus and not on the sympathy in her eyes or the fear emanating from her. "You mean like the mythological part horse-part man?"

"This Centaur is an international criminal syndicate involved in stealing and selling art and artifacts on the black market. Centaur's relatively new, formed in the last several years." Devlin waited, his penetrating blue eyes watchful and wary.

Cort shook his head slowly, meeting Devlin's gaze. "The only time I talked to Leon since my trial was two days before he died. He never mentioned any criminal gang."

"He told you only about the puzzle ring?"

"Yes. He said he'd leave up to me what I did with the jewels once I found them. Wouldn't surprise me if he'd heard about this Centaur in prison."

"Or if they'd contacted him."

The air snagged in Cort's lungs as the import of Devlin's suggestion sank in. If Leon knew Centaur wanted the Gramornia crown jewels, would he have put them on the trail of the puzzle ring? If true, another betrayal. Then why send Cort for the first ring piece? Mara placed her hand on his knee. The contact anchored him, brought him back. No, Leon making a deal from a prison he'd never leave made no sense.

"What about Centaur?" she asked, breaking the suffocating tension.

Apparently satisfied Cort knew nothing about the criminal gang, Devlin nodded. "I started picking up mention of Centaur a few years ago. Then Max had a run-in with their activities last fall. Word is they began in Europe. Started small but various groups of art thieves around the world have joined them. Besides black-market dealings with unscrupulous collectors, they're involved in art forgery."

"And now they want the crown jewels?" Cort asked.

"While I doubt Gramornian agents would attack anyone or break into an apartment, at least with such appalling lack of finesse—" he tilted his head toward Mara "—I know for a fact Centaur agents employ violence without compunction."

Cort blew out a breath. "Mr. Devlin, if your offer still stands, I'll have that stiff drink now. Bourbon on the rocks if that works." The break would give him time to consider bringing Devlin in on his other problem. The man might have the connections he needed.

"No problem, and make it Thomas. I'll join you. Anyone else?" The others shook their heads. He crossed to the wall cabinets. An opened panel displayed crystal decanters and an ice bucket. A moment later he handed Cort a glass and sat down with his.

Cort thanked him and downed a healthy gulp. The amber liquid spread its warmth down his throat. He recognized the rich flavor and smoky aroma. Had tasted it once or twice before. Too pricey for his wallet.

"Big Nose could've been either Centaur's man or a

Gramornian agent," Max put in.

"Or FBI," Mara said.

"Not FBI," Cort said, shifting in his chair. "FBI tail was a different guy. Crew cut, shades, windbreaker to cover his sidearm. They have a look, these Feds. I lost him too."

Max sputtered a laugh into his iced tea.

"And there's something else," Cort continued. "I talked to Kaplan—that's FBI Special Agent Al Kaplan—before I came here today. They want *me* to lead *them* to the jewels."

Devlin leaned forward, planted his elbows on the table. "Why would they subcontract to the Jeweler's son? What's going on?"

"I asked Kaplan that. It took me a while to get through his doublespeak but here's the crux. He'd hoped Leon's old partner Dante Falco would spill on the hiding place. Until last night. Falco was found dead."

Stunned silence, the same reaction he'd had when Kaplan laid it on him.

"Go on." Devlin picked up his whiskey. "How'd he die?"

"Preliminary police report said it was an accident. He'd just robbed a condo in Alexandria. Owners were out to a party. He fell from their ninth-floor balcony."

Devlin's pen flew across his paper. "How did he gain access?"

Falco might've used the same technique Cort remembered from the Smithsonian job—a grappling hook and rope. Or maybe he'd climbed the bricks and then jimmied the slider. Speculating aloud might implicate him. He shrugged. "Kaplan didn't say."

Max emitted a cynical huff. "People think balconies on the high floors are secure. So they don't lock the sliders. An old hand like Falco would know how to take advantage."

Cort nodded. Leon had taught Falco all his tricks, probably that one. "He apparently fell on the way back down with his loot. His backpack was loaded with jewelry and cash. One of the tenants found him on the ground. Broken neck."

A nine-floor drop. He guessed a fall like that would break more than a neck but didn't say so when he caught Mara's ashen face.

For a few moments the only sound in the room was the ticking of the antique clock and the scratch of Devlin's pen.

He flattened a palm on his pad. "You think it was really an accident?"

Chapter Ten

CORT LIFTED THE box containing Mara's new desktop computer. She'd crammed the car's hatchback with state-of-the-art electronics. They'd stopped at an office supply store for the PC and a laptop.

He'd restrained himself from whistling when he glimpsed the bills over her shoulder. Her money. Her tools. He would've spent that much on power tools if he had it. And insurance would cover most of her cost.

Mara carried out a bag of Chinese take-out. The aromas had tortured him for the past half hour. The meeting had run until seven and his stomach needed more than lemon bread.

She locked the car and headed into the building. "You never answered Mr. Devlin's question."

No, he'd needed time to process. Analyze the possibilities. Consider the odds.

"Believe Falco's death an accident?" he said finally. "As much as I believe in the Easter Bunny. Leon called him the Human Fly, like he had suction cups on his feet and hands. His taking a header at this particular time is too big a coincidence."

And too big an opportunity to pass up. Kaplan had insisted the cops didn't find a ring piece in Falco's house. Didn't mean one didn't exist.

"And what did my boss want when he pulled you aside after the meeting ended?" She angled her head, suspicion crimping her brow.

No reason not to tell her the first part of their conversation. He grinned at her over the big box. "Not much. He delivered a warning."

"About me?"

"Wanted to make sure I wasn't playing you."

Devlin had put his warning in no uncertain terms. His tone low but lethally clear. *"My file on you says you're on the level but who knows. Mara's savvy and sharp, but I wouldn't want some asshole taking advantage of her soft heart. If you're conning her or if she gets hurt, you'll have no place to hide. You'll wish you were back in a nice safe, fucking prison. You hear what I'm saying?"*

Cort heard him all right. Loud and clear. *You hear what I'm saying?* The question he'd heard in stir from the COs. Except the correction officers delivered their warnings at bullhorn decibels.

She huffed in exasperation. "I can take care of myself."

"Mara, he was only doing what he does best— protection, security. Chill."

Because of that, Cort had made a leap of faith and asked for the man's help.

"There's another player in this game," he'd said, "on the opposite side."

"The guys who gave you those?" Devlin indicated the fading wounds on his face.

Gratified Mara's boss respected him enough to assume it was more than one, Cort nodded and explained. "Mara can't know about any of this, but I'm asking for your help."

Devlin studied him for a long moment before he

spoke. "What do you need?"

"Know anybody in the Gramornian embassy?"

"Matter of fact I do." Devlin smiled and handed over his card. "Call my private number and we'll talk more."

Feeling more hopeful than he had since Colonel Yerik and his clones showed up, Cort had shaken the man's hand with enthusiasm.

Inside, he watched as Mara punched in her new code and pressed her thumb to the biometric pad. Her bunched-up shoulders relaxed as the device flashed a green light. The living room looked the same as when they'd left it. No breach, no burglary, no threat. For now. Her face had that wide-eyed, scared expression, probably the result of the meeting's revelations. The main reason he'd called Kaplan and spoken to Devlin about Yerik still stood—her safety.

"Put that here for now." She deposited their dinner on the small dining table opposite the kitchen bar. "I have to do something about the desk before I can set up in the bedroom."

The aromas of sesame chicken and Hunan beef made him salivate like a retriever. Ignoring her directions, he kept walking. Maybe his surprise would cheer her up. Or not.

For the first time since he'd surveyed his handiwork, second thoughts crowded his brain. Had he crossed some invisible line? Maybe she'd hate what he did. Shit, did he screw up? His gut clenched tighter than a vise grip.

"Cort, where are you taking that?" She trotted along behind him down the hall. "Not the bedroom, it's—" Her almond-shaped eyes widened when she spotted the new desk.

He set the box on the floor. "I wanted to build you a desk, but I don't have the tools or work space. This was the next best thing."

She wandered to the new installation and ran her small hand across its polished surface. "Cort, you did this for me." Wonder floated in her words.

"I wanted to repay you for putting me up. And putting up with me." He tried a smile but his mouth was too stiff. "The salesman said this L-shape was better for the corner space than one long desk like the original. More room for the two monitors and the new laptop. It's wood, sturdier than that orange-crate the burglars crushed. If you don't like it, I can take it back."

"Never." She'd thrown her arms around him and pressed her warm little body against him before he realized she'd crossed the room. "Thank you."

She bestowed a tremulous smile on him. Tears like iridescent jewels shimmered.

"You're crying. I wanted to make you happy."

"You did. I love it. This is the nicest thing anyone's ever done for me." She tipped her head back, offered her lush mouth.

He needed no further invitation. He lowered his mouth to hers and feasted on her sweet taste, her heat and hunger that matched his. In only a few short weeks, this woman had tangled up his mind and jump-started something in his chest he thought was dead. Her arms slid up to tighten around his neck like she too felt the heat detonate between them. He slid his hand to her mass of hair, wrapping his fingers in it, reveling in its warm slide.

The power of his kiss had every muscle in Mara's

body going lax. His rich, dark taste exploded on her tongue. She'd tried to protect herself against the sensual onslaught but his generosity and his hard-soft mouth crushed all her defenses and aroused a hunger more intense than any she could remember. Deep, burning kisses, drugging and devastating.

His hands trailed fire everywhere he touched. Her head, her throat, her breast. She gloried in his scent—fresh-cut wood and male—in the scrape of his chin, in the press of his arousal. No man had ever kissed her with such urgent hunger. Desire flooded through her. Before she lost control, she had to stop him. She didn't do impulse sex.

When he rained kisses down her neck to the open collar of her blouse, she whispered, "This is happening too fast. We're all wrong for each other. It's insane."

"Not insane," he said. "I want you. You want me. We're free adults. What's wrong with that?" He nibbled her ear and her lower lip before molding his mouth to hers again.

She absorbed the sharp thrill. No denying that she wanted him, wanted this.

Her passion was only natural. She hadn't been with a man in months. But this wasn't just any man. This was Cort Jones, a man she couldn't afford to trust. *Once a crook, always a crook.* Somehow her dad's motto rang false. Or did she just not want to listen to the little voice?

The question brought her back from the brink. She flattened her palms against his chest—his very hard chest, where his heart pounded a heavy beat—and pushed. "Cort, stop."

He went rock still, then released her and stepped

back.

She swallowed and straightened her blouse.

"I'm looking for happily ever after, and you're not it. I can't allow sex to confuse my emotions," she said, her voice unwillingly rough. "I wanted to thank you for my beautiful desk. I didn't mean to do it with more than a simple kiss."

His gray eyes gleamed dark as charcoal and his breath rasped, as if he'd run miles. "Nothing simple about that kiss. The chemistry between us is explosive. So are the complications. Life has taught me control and patience, but you make both damned hard."

Heady words. Her body pulsed. He was right about the chemistry. And the complications. After that kiss, he knew how much she wanted him. No time to be reckless when danger surrounded them like cobras ready to strike.

He turned toward the door. "I'll get the other box."

Control, yes, essential where Cort was concerned. Patience? He wasn't giving up. Her racing pulse hitched a beat.

****

Mara observed Cort across the table trying to manage rice with chopsticks. Sinewy muscles rippled beneath the tattoos of his free arm as the hand fisted.

The two of them sat at her small table, the food containers between their plates. From the speakers, Marcia Ball sang "Red Beans" and boogied on her piano. Not the right ethnic group, but food for the soul.

When most of the clump of rice dribbled from his awkward grip, she decided he'd had enough. "Yeoman effort. Give it up and use the fork."

A sigh of frustration escaped him. "You don't have

to say it twice. I'm starving. No wonder so many Asians are skinny." He dropped the chopsticks as if they were live wires and snatched up his fork.

She enjoyed watching him put away the heap on his plate. He must need a lot of fuel to power that strong body. Shoving away the sensual memory of their hot kiss, she scissored up a bite of chicken but her real enjoyment came from watching Cort enjoy his meal. Her nerves were still strung tight as her tennis racquet. She could barely swallow.

"Me being followed, the break-in, the added players we heard about today—all that has you tied in knots," he said.

Damn, she'd hoped to keep her fears to herself. "The danger seems to be growing exponentially."

As she thought about the threats all around them, her heart thumped hard and her stomach twisted. In spite of her resolve, she wished she could throw herself into his arms and forget everything except the heat they generated.

Her appetite gone, she set down her chopsticks. "The situation reminds me of that old movie *It's a Mad, Mad, Mad, Mad World*, where all these different people race to find a buried treasure. Don't they try to kill each other?"

Outside, a horn blasted, slamming Mara's heart into high gear. Her hand flat on her uneasy stomach, she crossed to the speaker dock. She stabbed the button to turn it off, shuddering involuntarily at Coldplay's "Death and All His Friends."

"Don't make it worse than it is," he said, studying her when she returned to her seat. "These guys want what we have or might find."

She drank some more wine to calm her nerves. "Don't be too sure. Maybe whoever took my computers used the files to find Falco."

And kill him. He swore, as if wishing that conclusion were fantasy. "Like I said in the meeting, the FBI will keep tabs on us but not interfere. If we get into trouble, they'll step in. So the players we have to worry about are Centaur and maybe the accomplices."

"Unless there's only one now that Falco's dead."

"We'll figure that out soon enough." He slugged down the rest of his IPA.

The local beer's weird label gave her the creeps but her nerves had nothing to do with the graphic. "I don't like the FBI being involved. I don't trust them."

"Me neither." Cort said. "But I trust them more than the devil I *don't* know."

Although she wasn't convinced, his concern made her smile. "After we eat, I intend to set up both computers and transfer my files."

"Even though copies of our stuff are on your tablet, those bastards got all your other files. Tough break." He raised his bottle of beer toward her in a sad toast, then added more Hunan beef and another egg roll to his plate.

She shook her head. "*Not* all my files. The tough break is they know what we know. They have our research."

"*Your* research. Take the credit, Mara." He lifted one thick, slashing eyebrow as he dipped his egg roll in hot mustard. "What do you mean they didn't get all your files?"

"I double save everything, including email, on an external drive." She saved everything to a cloud site as well, but he'd only tease her about her geekiness if she told him. "It's not very big. They must not have seen it partially hidden under some printouts. Or they didn't care. Just unplugged everything and took off."

"I'm glad. One less thing to worry about."

Too true. She had plenty else to handle. Not the least of which was probing Cort. The break-in had shattered her plan the other night to quiz him. Knowing more about his part in his father's crimes should solidify her resolve, which at the moment was as firm as warm pudding, not to follow through on their mutual attraction.

"Was the Smithsonian burglary your first?" Chagrinned by her blurted question, she felt heat climb up her cheeks. She wove her fingers together in her lap. "I mean, did you work with him before? The newspapers didn't talk about you much, just the Jeweler. I'm sorry, but—" Damn, she should just shut up.

He shoved his chair back and went to the kitchen. Not another beer but one of the bottled green teas in hand, he leaned against the bar like a western-movie gunslinger, dangerous and sexy. His jaw worked.

"It's okay. You deserve to know the details," he said finally. "The Smithsonian burglary was the first time I crossed the line. Leon tried to lure me in before, but I always made it clear I didn't want that life. And I didn't want to let Mom down. That excuse was the only one he accepted." A shadow passed over his expression before he banished it. Another mystery to probe.

"How did he convince you that one time?"

Cort's gaze lifted to the ceiling. "He met me after my final exam that Wednesday. Told me his partner went to the hospital with a broken leg from a bad car accident on the Beltway."

"That was Falco." She knew that already but Cort seemed to need her urging to continue.

He nodded. "Leon said he had this big job lined up on the Washington Mall, all on a timetable. He had to go with the plan. Couldn't abort because it was coordinated with others. We'd go in and out fast. No risk of getting caught. He made it sound like an adventure. I'd use the climbing skills he'd taught me."

His father had rooked him into the crime. She never met the man, hated him for years because of her father, and now detested him all the more because of what he did to his son. She stifled the urge to hug Cort. "Leon conned you."

He tossed his napkin on the table. "I was young and stupid. He could charm January snow into flowers with his smile and slick words. Convinced me he never robbed anybody who couldn't afford the loss. Conned me? No shit." He chuffed a bitter laugh. "He reminded me he was paying the full boat for me to attend one of the finest colleges in the country. And he was—"

"Your dad. You looked up to him."

"That was the last time." His jaw seemed set in solid steel. "So I climbed up the rope onto the roof. Helped him up. He wasn't as agile as he used to be. Didn't want to fall. I waited while he did the deed. Sweated bullets the whole time, expected spotlights to blind me and the cops to arrive any minute. We got away clean. I figured I was clear, except for my conscience. I didn't sleep for two days." He fretted his napkin into shreds.

"Until the cops showed up?"

"Yeah. Falco's accident meant Leon had to work alone once he got inside. Time was tight and the cameras came back on. One caught his profile clear as a mug shot."

"And you? How did they know you were involved?"

His jaw worked again as if it ached from tension. "I told them."

"What? You confessed?"

"The FBI knew Falco was out of the picture and I was in D.C. When they came to talk to me, yeah, I confessed. I was that disgusted with myself. I'd have gone to the cops if they hadn't showed up. But for the confession, the judge would've given me more prison time."

Her vision blurred. This true confessions session didn't work as she'd planned. The FBI must've searched his mother's house and questioned her. Mara wanted to ask but the lines bracketing his mouth made her hold off. "I'm sorry you had to go through that."

"I deserved what I got. I made the most of it."

"Your woodworking."

He nodded. "What I make of my life now is my doing, not Leon's." He reached for one of the fortune cookies. "Maybe this will help." His crooked, boyish smile nearly undid her.

She snapped open a cookie. "*Mountains can move, but not your character.*" Her throat felt too tight to eat the almond-flavored treat. Did the saying confirm her dad's? Or did Cort's situation prove that one mistake didn't make a crook? He'd confessed and paid his debt to society but society was still exacting a price—the return of the Gramornia crown jewels. She forced herself to swallow. "True. As far as it goes. Your turn."

He opened his cookie and popped half into his mouth. She heard it crunch while he read his slip of paper. A slow, sexy smile widened his mouth. A Washington summer had nothing on the steam heat in his eyes. *"The best lovers make love on a full stomach."*

Suddenly she felt hot all over. She wanted the passion he offered but she couldn't. She still couldn't trust him, and worse, she couldn't trust herself.

Chapter Eleven

CORT TOOK A circuitous route to shake off Colonel Yerik's clones in their black sedan. They'd been watching the apartment from the other side of the street. No sign of a tail now. Mara looked sufficiently occupied on her phone not to notice. Maybe he ought to tell her but he hated scaring her. He left the main drag and steered the pickup along the quiet suburban Maryland street.

"That was my sister," Mara said, stowing her cell in her humongous purse. "She wants us to meet André and her for dinner tomorrow night."

"*Us?* As in you and me?" Like a date? Like normal people?

She waggled her shoulders and huffed a sigh. "Yes, you and me. I guess I can go alone if you want to do your hermit thing."

He slanted a glance her way, saw her sassy grin. Teasing him. When was the last time anybody teased him? He couldn't remember. "I'm just wondering why me. A hot chick like you, don't you have a boyfriend?"

"Eeuw, *boyfriend*? You have been out in the sticks for a long time. This isn't high school. And for your information, I'm in no serious relationship right now but there are a couple guys I hang out with sometimes."

Something more was going on than her just wanting company. He pulled over to the curb and turned off the engine but left his hands on the steering wheel. Otherwise, forces beyond his control might tug them over to touch her smooth skin. "But you're not asking those guys. You want *me* to go with you. Your sister doesn't like me, doesn't trust me. What's the angle?"

"Exactly that. Because you read people and you're always looking for their angle."

First the hermit thing. Now this. She'd figured him out. A tossup if that was good or bad. "You want me to scope out Cassie's new guy. That it?"

"Bull's-eye!" She scooted around in her seat to face him. "Cassie met André at the bank where she's in charge of new accounts. He asked her out that day. They played tennis and went out to dinner. I don't think they've been apart since."

"So? Lust at first sight. It happens." No shit. With Mara, it hit him like a two-by-four. Now he knew what the term *pole-axed* meant.

She rolled her eyes. "Yes, and it happens to Cassie all the time. At least since her divorce. Usually I let her crash and burn by herself. But this time is different."

"Because of our search for the jewels."

She air-chalked up a point. "You're on a roll, big guy. So will you come with me?"

"Why do you need me? Didn't you do your Internet voodoo search thing on the jerk?"

Her brow crimped with what looked like frustration. "He comes up clean. Exactly who he says he is. A wine importer with a family vineyard in France. But... it's Cassie." Her embarrassment hung in the air between them.

Ah, why would a rich international businessman be

interested in a small-time single Korean-American mother desperate for love?

The pleading and worry replacing the playful look in Mara's brown eyes reached into his chest and squeezed. "On the off chance this André is one of our bad guys, I'll do it. But for real your sister included me in the invitation?"

She turned to look across the street from where he'd stopped. Avoiding the question? "Maybe she wants André to scope you out. Should be interesting, the two of you eyeing each other like rival lions." She pointed. "Is that Falco's house?"

No yellow police tape fenced in the white-painted brick Colonial. Just as Cort had hoped. Cops must've searched it. But Falco died in Virginia, so his College Park, Maryland, house wasn't a crime scene. Shades and drapes were closed.

"Modest home for a high-level jewel thief. Well, modest for around here," Mara said, peering around him from the passenger seat. She tucked a strand of midnight hair behind her ear.

"I don't know how high-end he is—*was*, but he tried to stay low-profile. After the Smithsonian job, the cops kept a close eye on him. Quiet, older neighborhood. I guess it suited his cover as an insurance salesman."

She blinked in surprise. "Did he really have a day job?"

He snorted. "His day job was probably casing his next burglary job. According to Leon, Falco always worked a day job as cover. Lexus salesman, real estate appraiser, and personal trainer once because it gave him entry to wealthy people's houses."

No comment was necessary. Her downturned mouth made her disapproval clear.

"For him and for Leon, it was as much about the adrenaline rush and the challenge, the nonconformity, as it was the money. For the Jeweler, it was also about the gems themselves." He rolled down his shirtsleeves, switched off the engine, and climbed from the truck.

"Wait. What are you doing?" Mara's shock raised the pitch of her voice.

All he'd told her was they were going to look at Falco's house because the truth would've had her digging in her heels. "I need to know if he had one of the ring pieces. Kaplan would've told me if the cops found it. He didn't, so it could still be in the house."

Brow furrowed in obvious confusion, she walked around to join him as he extracted two clipboards and a canvas bag from behind the seats. She peered from the official-looking forms to the magnetic sign he'd slapped onto the pickup's door earlier without her noticing. *Westchester Appraisals, Inc.*

"The trick is to look and act official, like you know what you're doing and you're supposed to be here." Giving her a clipboard and pen, he hustled her up the driveway before she could protest.

She took it but her wide eyes said, any second she was ready to rebel. Distrust tightened her mouth. "That fake sign. These official-looking papers. You *have* done this before."

"No. Leon just bragged a lot about casing jobs."

She didn't protest again but she'd squawk loud and long soon.

He handed her the tape end of a fifty-foot rule. Made a show of measuring the carport and side entrance before extracting his key ring from his jeans pocket. On his way to the backyard, he flipped through his keys as if he had one to the house. The small lawn led to a flagstone patio shaded by maples and one newly leafed cherry tree like the ones by the Jefferson Memorial. Falco'd probably enjoyed its blossoms last month. Damn shame.

Worse, if his death was murder.

Mara clutched her clipboard against her chest. Cort pried it from her death grip and set both on a patio table. Wrought iron. Too cold and dark. Teak would be warmer, lighter.

"Now nosy neighbors believe we're official." And if they didn't, tall shrubbery hid the backyard from view. The lawnmower next door, with its coughing whine of a giant dying insect, would cover their voices.

"You intend to go inside? But Falco lived alone," she said. "We can't go in unless—"

Her brows lifted and her eyes widened in comprehension, a comic-book parody. He'd laugh except he didn't like this either. "Unless we break in. So I finally get to use Leon's lock-pick set."

After studying the façade, he smiled. No slider. Falco had known not to make his house vulnerable. Cort headed for the atrium door beside the picture window. Wired for an alarm. Another given. Vertical shades over the windows hid the interior from view. He pocketed his key ring and slid out Leon's leather case.

"No, we can't do this... this breaking and entering." she said, fear and doubt clearly scraping her voice raw. "*I* can't break the law, I mean."

Her stricken appeal pinched something in his chest. He'd brought her along for two reasons. Having a woman along was good cover, and he needed to know how much he could count on her in a pinch. And hell, he just plain wanted her with him.

But here they were and he had to get the door open, had to search *now*. He might not have much time. Or another opportunity. "I don't like it either, Mara. Yeah, technically it's breaking the law. But the risk outweighs the need for more ring pieces. For me."

She shook her head. Stared at the ground. Visibly torn between what she needed to prove and what she had to do to achieve it. Searching Falco's house meant only touching a toe across the line. Who knows what else they—*he*—might need to do? Could he trust her?

No time to deal with that now. "Falco is dead. He won't care. We're not stealing anything. He'd probably want me to find the ring piece."

"*If* he had one."

He winked as encouragement. "Only one way to find out."

"The house could have electronic protection. Alarms."

"Definitely. Falco would have the best." He grinned, grasping Leon's adrenaline rush, and immediately regretted the lapse. "I'm prepared for that too."

She narrowed her gaze as if trying to see inside him. "The sign. The clipboards. Did my boss help you with this scheme?"

No surprise she figured it out. And dammit, Devlin would've advised him not to bring her along. Stupid of him to put her at this much risk. "At Devlin's invitation, I dropped by this a.m. Max introduced me to all sorts of cool gadgets." He held up the canvas bag. "Including a handy-dandy electronic decoder to disarm the security. Gave me scrambler chips and GPS blockers for our phones. Also something called an RFD to check for listening devices."

"RFD, a radio frequency detection unit." A sigh expressed her exasperation. "A bug sweeper in lay terms."

"He checked my truck for a GPS tracker. Took off one he said might be Centaur's." Could be the colonel's, but why have his men watch them if he had a bug? He held up the lock pick and raised an eyebrow in silent question.

"It's a conspiracy." She gave a fluttery wave of her hands. Nodded. "Okay. I guess. Go ahead and pick the damn lock."

He inserted the small tool. No resistance. Bony fingers of cold dread slid down his spine. "Looks like I don't get to use the pick kit after all. Someone else was here first."

"Not the police. They'd have Falco's keys." Mara stared at the lock. "Left unlocked, just like my apartment."

"Yep. Could be the same burglars. They're long gone." *Shit, how can I be certain? If they're inside, I'm five kinds a damn fool bringing her along.*

He pocketed the lock-picks. Grabbing the clipboards with one hand and her arm with the other, he marched back to the street.

"Hey, hey, hey what's the rush? I thought you, you wanted to get inside?" she sputtered, jog-walking to keep up.

He didn't speak until they were back in the truck. "I was an idiot for bringing you. The burglars could still be inside. I'll come back later. You don't need to be involved anymore. I can go on alone. Whoever the bad guys are, they have your computer files. They know what we know. They'll leave you alone." Not exactly the case but all he had for now.

"I'm not quitting." She huffed. "Yes, I'm scared. So are you. We have different agendas. You need to find the jewels. I need to find the truth."

Kee-rist on a cracker. First she won't help me. Now she won't back out. "You don't trust me."

"Should I? Can I? Do you trust me? You don't trust anyone."

"Ouch." He rubbed his chest, miming a direct hit, but where he really hurt was his head. A dull throb from temple to temple. "But I have good reason. We can't be sure who our adversaries are. Or how many, like Devlin said. I haven't seen a tail but they could still be following us. Watching us."

She cast a furtive glance at the quiet street before returning her gaze, filled with fear, to him. "You must be anxious too. Even frightened."

"A guy'd be crazy not to be. But I know how to protect myself. You don't. I'll talk to suspects, search Falco's house, keep you informed. You stay out of it. Stay safe."

"No deal. I'm in the middle of this mess." She hugged her bag as if armoring herself. "The same thugs or different thugs might come back. What do I do? Announce on Twitter or Instagram saying I'm no longer involved in finding Leon Jones's puzzle pieces or the Gramornia crown jewels?"

He waited to reply until a tan Suburban passed with a mother yelling at a bunch of kids in the back. He took her hand and linked fingers with her, as if that would make what he was about to say easier on her. "If I'm away from you, they'll track *my* movements, not yours. Me being with you is part of the problem. Your problem."

She started to yank her hand away, but he held tight. "I know that stubborn look," she said. "I can do stubborn too. And no. Different agendas, remember? My problem is Global Insurance believes Quincy Marton conspired with Leon Jones. I need to prove he didn't. Without me, that goal will get lost in the race to find the jewels."

Pain ricocheted across his forehead. He deliberately relaxed his jammed eyebrows. The curse that erupted from between his clenched teeth came out as an unintelligible growl. He concentrated on his calming-breath technique until the pain eased.

He turned toward her, his left arm across the steering wheel. "I get that you'd like to clear your dad, even that you'd like your mom to have his pension. Makes you a good daughter and all that. But it doesn't explain why you're risking your life after all this time. You have a good job. Nobody looks at you crosswise. Your life'll go on pretty much lah-di-dah if we walk away now. Why are you nearly as desperate as me? What's your stake, really? Worried Quincy Marton was dirty after all?"

From staring out the windshield at the expanse of green suburban lawns, she spun on him. Her brows shot up and her mouth turned down. Pain filled her eyes as twin flags of crimson blotched her cheeks. "*Never.* Dad's innocent. I know it."

He thought about her anguish at breaking the law

about entering Falco's house. About her drive for perfection, her eagerness to please, her almost forced optimism. "Because if you find out he's guilty, that makes you dirty too?"

"*No*. How could you say that?" She sniffed away the welling tears.

"You keep trying to be perfect. Why, unless you have some big transgression to hide? You can't be blamed for what your father might've done."

"What are you, a shrink?"

"I just want to understand why you need so bad to clear him? Will it clear you?"

"Frak it, I don't know! Maybe. Yes. I'm not perfect. Growing up, the times I messed up... the disappointment in his eyes, in his voice... If Dad's character wasn't as strong as I think, maybe there's something tainted in me too." She blew her nose on the tissue he handed her. Once she'd calmed, she raised somber reddened eyes. "He was scrupulously honest in everything, but he didn't believe a criminal could change. He always said, 'Once a crook, always a crook.'"

Cort's whole life, he'd had to struggle with his conscience. When Leon wanted to teach him burglary skills. When Leon portrayed his capers as glamorous escapades like in the movies. When Leon and he exchanged secret notes in the stone wall. No wonder Marton's slip from grace, if he *did* conspire with Leon, came as such a shock to her.

"So that must mean if he screwed up once—taking a bribe from the Jeweler—he must've been a crook all along," he said. "Then what chance does that give you?" *Or me.*

"Something like that. I don't know anymore." She dabbed at her eyes with a tissue and looked in her bag for more.

He handed her the box of tissues from behind the seat. "Think about it. I grew up with a thief for a father. Not just any thief, but world-class. Leon ate, drank, and slept larceny."

Her eyes widened. "I didn't mean— But you paid for your crime. I'm sorry."

"Shh, we're cool. I gave in to Leon that one time, and no matter I've done my time, it made me a crook in the eyes of the world. The world can shove it. Prison counselor told me my scars will remind me where I've been but I don't have to let them dictate where I'm going." He told himself that every day.

Eyes soft with affection, she touched an index finger to the dimpled scar on his cheek. "That's pretty profound."

"I hope so. People face choices every day, choices where they can do the right thing or the selfish thing or the impulsive thing. Everybody's flawed. Sometimes we give in to the wrong impulse. It's human to be flawed. *You're* human." *He* was human. God help him, he'd fight the family legacy running through his veins.

His time in stir had shown him true evil existed. He hoped the people they were up against now were merely flawed, greedy humans and not evil, but after two murders and the assault on Mara, doubts outweighed the hope.

A smile lifted the corners of her mouth. "I'm not sure you're right. But okay for now. Like in AA, I'm Mara and I'm flawed. Today I will not commit a crime."

He whooped a laugh. Before he could do a U-turn to their original conversation, she grabbed his shirt collar and pulled down his head for a hard kiss that was like swallowing sunshine. A hot wave of longing swept through him. Dizzy and drunk on her taste, he nearly yanked her across the console again, but she pulled back.

"You're not getting rid of me." A cream-lapping-cat smile curved her lips. "Some people won't open up to that tough mug of yours. You need my sweet, innocent face to help open doors. Without my full participation, you won't have my tech support. Who knows what new barriers you'll run into? Without me, you could crash."

"Mara, I promised to help you prove your dad's innocence, and my word is good. It would kill me if you got hurt."

"I appreciate that but I'm in all the way."

"You know we may find nothing about your dad. Nothing either way. If we do find evidence against him, can you face that truth?"

She lowered her gaze and chewed her lower lip. When she looked up, her eyes were clear with determination. "I want the truth."

He knew when he was beat. He held up his hands in surrender. "All right. We're good to go. But with two provisions."

"What now?" She huffed a sigh of exasperation.

"The bad guys, whichever bunch they are, know what we know. Have what we have."

"Except for your ring piece."

"Except for that, and my knowledge of how Leon's mind worked. I want to keep it that way. Somebody's on the same trail we are. We need no leaks about our plans. From here on out, we tell nobody what we're doing. No emails, no phone calls, zip."

"Cassie," Mara said, twisting in her seat. "I hate keeping her in the dark. She worries so. She won't tell anyone."

"Maybe not. But whoever followed us knows where she lives. The less she knows, the safer she is. We don't tell the FBI *or* your sister."

"Trust no one."

"The motto I live by. You took the words right out of my mouth." How the hell was he going to keep her safe?

"And I'm going in that house with you." She jumped out of the truck and jogged across the street.

Back where they started, he stopped her from entering ahead of him. "I got a second provision. If you insist on seeing this through, you have to put up with me being protective."

She grinned and blew him a kiss. "Oooh, that just makes me hot, Mr. Caveman."

Shaking his head, he turned the doorknob and pushed the door open. "Bet I won't need the security decoder."

Casting an anxious glance over her shoulder, she hurried in behind him.

No red or green light on the security panel beside the door. Dark. Disabled.

No sounds in the house other than the hum of the refrigerator. When his eyes adjusted to the dim interior, he saw they'd entered the dining area of a great room. To their right was the kitchen, before them, toward the front of the house, the living room area.

Everything, everywhere a junk heap.

Chapter Twelve

THE UPHEAVAL IN Mara's apartment couldn't compare with the destruction wrought in Falco's house. Furniture overturned, smashed, and shredded. Holes gouged in the walls and flooring. In the kitchen nook, the refrigerator stood open. Its light spilled onto the tile floor, littered with broken food containers and dishes. The stench of rotting food choked him.

Mara's hands flew to her throat. "Why did they do this?"

"Something pissed them off big time. I'm hoping it's because they found squat."

His cross trainers crunched pottery shards and dried flowers into the carpet as he wandered through the mess. His heart dropped to the soles of his feet. Why hadn't he visited Falco early on? Maybe he could've prevented his death. And this. He dropped onto a straight-backed chair, the only piece of furniture untouched.

Mara picked up a bent silver picture frame. The cracked glass distorted the portrait of Falco's grown daughter. He'd have to call Isabella. If he could figure out what to say.

"Centaur? The gang Devlin described?"

Not the colonel or his men. They'd have no reason to search this house. "Centaur. An accomplice. The Gramornian agent. Take your pick. But my bet's on

Centaur."

"Then they could have Falco's ring piece."

If Centaur or anyone they didn't know about had one of the ring pieces, they were dead in the water. "Or they ran amok because they *didn't* find it." He stood and crossed to where she stood at the edge of the slashed and stained carpet. "Falco was smart. He wouldn't choose an obvious place to hide something so important."

"But where could we begin in all this mess?" She spread her arms in demonstration.

"Looks like the house has a basement. First place to check."

"Where should I look? Upstairs?" She glanced at the stairs with trepidation.

"We should stay together."

"I understand the safety issue, but I'm here. Now let me help." She folded her arms.

"Okay, but let me clear the upstairs first." Before she could argue, he bounded up the stairs and checked each room. "Nobody in the closets or under the beds. Go for it."

"Maybe he has a computer that'll tell us something."

Once she waved him away, he located the basement door in the kitchen. At the bottom of the wooden plank steps he found a large, unfinished space. In one corner, Falco had installed weight-lifting equipment and a treadmill. Everywhere else more evidence of the search littered the floor.

He remembered Falco as an orderly man, methodical. He would've hated this mess. That made the thief not unlike Mara. He smiled.

He picked his way through a litter of paint cans and overturned storage boxes to a workbench where tools hung against their outlines on bead-board paneling. The searcher had moved along, emptying every container and drawer as he went. He'd dumped out a toolbox onto the bench. Mixed in with innocuous items like wrenches, odd bits of copper piping, and vise grip pliers were the tools of Falco's trade—a bump key, padlock shims, a keybit.

A crash from upstairs brought up his head so fast he nearly cracked his skull on a low beam. *Mara?* "What the hell!"

****

Mara found the bed neatly made in the master suite, shirts draped on doorknobs, but no socks on the floor or toothpaste tube open on the sink. No evidence of a search. Only the normality of a male living alone. A neat male.

In the other bedroom a laptop sat on a small desk beside an all-in-one printer. A man like Falco would have the computer password protected. Maybe they could take time for her to tease out the password.

Downstairs, glass shattered with a deafening crash.

A startled shriek tore from her throat. *Cort!* She turned and raced to the stairs.

From farther below came, "What the hell!"

His exclamation reassured her but curiosity propelled her downstairs. She stopped at the edge of the living room carpet. She barely heard him pounding up the basement steps as she stared at new destruction.

The picture window's vertical shades shook from the blow, clattering against the wood frame. Glistening slivers added to the carpet debris. A softball-size rock rolled to a stop on the littered carpet.

Cort arrived from the basement at the same time.

"Why would someone do that? What for?" Mara started to step away from him.

He pulled her back. "*Don't*. Let's get out of here."

Another object whizzed through the broken window. More glass splintered, followed by the acrid odor of gasoline. He tucked her behind him, sheltering her with his body.

A fireball erupted in a cloud of black smoke.

****

Her heart still pounded like a Thoroughbred's hooves down the stretch at Pimlico when Cort's truck sped down Queen's Chapel Road. Neither of them saw the vehicle or the thrower. A Molotov cocktail, he'd told her as they fled the burning house. Whatever the blasted thing was called, it exploded into fire like a bomb.

Sirens screaming in the distance reverberated inside her and spread outward from her chest. Her stomach rolled as the tremors radiated into her arms and legs. When she felt her legs, then her feet and each toe quiver, she pulled her knees up to her chest and wrapped her trembling arms tight around them. If she let go, she would fly into a million pieces like the window. Her teeth chattered, and she lowered her forehead to her knees. She would not throw up.

The truck pulled over and stopped on the roadside. She felt herself hauled over the console and onto Cort's lap. He cuddled her under his chin and held her as if he knew her state.

"It's okay. I've got you. You're safe," he murmured into her hair. "Hey, I'm shaking too. Nobody ever threw one of those things at me before either."

She started to push at his arms. But she wanted him to hold her. Resistance was useless and childish. She gripped the knit of his Henley and buried her face against his solid chest. Her tremors eased and she savored the feel of his strong arms around her, the new-wood smell he always carried on his skin, and the rumble of his voice as he murmured unintelligible words of consolation.

When she felt more rational, almost normal, enough to let go of him and sit up, she leaned back and looked into his shadowed face. He'd put himself in front of her when that thing exploded. "You were in front. Were you burned?"

"Sweetheart, holding you like this would make any man all right. I'm fine. You okay?"

She tried and failed to keep the flush from her cheeks. "I'm okay now. Thanks."

"Long as you're sure," he said, his expression neutral as he helped her back to her seat.

She was sure of nothing. He hadn't caressed her. He hadn't kissed her. He'd only held her while she recovered, despite the hard ridge pressing against her bottom. She wasn't feeling bold enough to thank him for his restraint. Besides, being on his lap like that made her want to throw her restraint out the window and do the wild thing with him. Whoa.

He turned the key in the ignition. "What now?"

"You'll think I'm crazy. I want to see the gem collection at the National Museum of Natural History. If people are going to throw bombs at me, I want to see for myself the scene of the crime. You'd probably prefer not to go back there."

Staring at his hands on the wheel, Cort mulled her idea over, then lifted one shoulder. "I'd prefer if the museum was never the scene of a crime. But it's past time I see the gem gallery."

His shoulders knotted, but he'd suck it up. Yeah, no problem passing through security, having suspicious guards stare at him, through him. He nosed the truck back into traffic.

"I think whoever trashed the house was covering their tracks. They weren't trying to kill us. We were parked across the street. They probably didn't know we were there," he said. "If it's any comfort."

"Minimal." Her tremors seemed to have dissipated but her gaze was still stark with fear. "And we've lost our chance to search for Falco's ring piece."

"But if our competition didn't find it, they lost out too." He couldn't hide the bitter disappointment in his tone. "*If* Falco had one."

"He did have a laptop. But I didn't have time to check it out. And it's too late now. But no ransacking upstairs. All neat and organized."

"Systematic search in the basement." Something about that scene bugged him.

"The police and FBI could've overlooked Falco's ring piece, but our competition knows what they're after," she said, drawing in a quick breath. "What if Centaur or another one of Leon's accomplices has it?"

"If it's an accomplice, he could have two now." His voice sank like his spirits.

Mara slumped in her seat.

If some son of a bitch got away with the crown jewels, Kaplan would think he'd lied about the puzzle ring. He'd have no way to find the stash, no way to prove his cooperation. The FBI would have no grounds to arrest him, but they could make his life a living hell.

With her guidance, he drove to a parking garage near the Federal Trade Commission, where he took the last parking spot in the far corner. They walked without talking to the museum's Constitution Avenue entrance.

As they approached the tall glass doors, Cort felt his shoulder muscles bunch. Again. Mara looked up, studying him. Hell, his tight face probably announced he expected to be pulled aside by guards and frisked. Or worse, arrested. He could get through this. This was a museum, not a fucking prison.

At the security stop, a table and metal-detector portal, the uniformed guard's bored gaze passed over them. "You folks enjoy the exhibits. We close in thirty-five minutes."

No frisk after all. He willed the muscles to unkink, the iceberg in his gut to thaw. Mara reached for his hand and squeezed as they sauntered through the Ocean Hall, scattered with tourists and school groups. Everywhere around them, voices reverberated against the hard surfaces of the structure.

He led Mara past a poker-faced guard to the wide marble staircase. A glance at her beautiful face, still pinched and pale, clamped his chest. They were facing more danger than he'd imagined when he began. He hated dragging her into it.

He checked behind them before he spoke. "The Gramornia crown jewels were taken from the Janet Annenberg Hooker Hall of Geology, Gems, and Minerals." They climbed away from the milling crowd.

"You know all about it. No surprise. Tell me more."

"What I know about the place I learned from research while I was in prison."

"Because you never got inside that night."

He nodded. "I came here that spring with a bunch of guys from college, but we mostly goofed around in the dinosaur section."

"I toured the museum with my eighth grade class." Her heels clicked on the hard floor. "All I remember seeing in this gallery is the Hope Diamond. I read it's been reset. An updated design meant to show it off better."

"Most of the gem and mineral exhibits were already here but not as secure and not displayed as well until a mega donation. They'd built this hall a couple years before the robbery. The security wasn't all in place for exhibits on loan."

"Ah, the reason for the robbery's timing."

He thought about it. "That and Leon knew he didn't have many good years left for second-story jobs. He wanted one last big, high-profile heist."

When she didn't reply, he knew what she was thinking—*Yeah, high profile, he accomplished that all right.*

In the second-floor gems hall, people clustered around the four-sided glass case in which the famous blue diamond rested on a rotating pedestal. Above the display arched a small dome with a skylight in its center. Mara indicated a man in turquoise-and-pink plaid pants and a purple-striped shirt as he hunkered down to snap a flash shot. Her humor meant she'd nearly recovered from her fright. Cort gave the tourist and the Hope only a cursory glance. They went on through the gallery of celebrity jewels.

They found the small Special Exhibit Gallery beneath another skylight. A sign proclaimed the current exhibit a loan from the Egyptian government, jewelry and other items unearthed during the discovery of Cleopatra's tomb a few years ago.

"I read about this show." She bent to examine the Queen of the Nile's necklace, a chin-high, shoulder-draping choker of gem-encrusted gold. "The tour goes to several major cities. I think Paris next. DSF might even have a contract for part of the security."

Gaudy stuff. Leon would've loved it. One reason he liked to reset hot rocks. Plain gold was okay, but Cort preferred the simple grain and elegance of wood.

He clasped her elbow and pulled her aside, out of view of the ceiling cameras. "This gallery probably has all the bells and whistles the other rooms have, like infrared beams. That case with Cleopatra's choker must have motion and weight sensors. Back then all Leon had to worry about in here was cameras and motion sensors." No visible sign of any security devices other than the cameras, but unobtrusiveness was the point.

"So did your father come in through that skylight?"

He shook his head. "Doesn't open, but it was wired. Cracking the glass would've broken all hell loose in the form of alarms." He gestured toward a wall vent. "An air circulation duct that vents on the roof. I lowered Leon down on a rope."

"I've seen the air ducts in the DSF building. Narrow. *You*'d never fit inside. That why Leon went in alone?"

"Probably. He never asked me. Maybe because he knew I wouldn't do it. Maybe because he knew I wouldn't fit. Maybe because I'd have no clue what to do once inside." He shrugged away the issue. "Doesn't matter. I helped him open the shaft and waited for him to climb up with the bag of *loot*." He pantomimed air quotes with the last word. "Then we ran to where we'd left the grappling hook and hit the ground running."

When she looked up at him from the exhibit's sparkling gems, her dark eyes glistened. "You were scared."

Scared didn't begin to describe it. He'd heard descriptions of soldiers facing battle. Shaking limbs, clammy hands, pounding pulse, loose bowels. He'd experienced all but the last. Like now, his gut had frozen. "Hell yeah, I wasn't sure my legs could carry me to the car. Satisfied now you've visited the scene of the crime?"

She frowned. "I'm not sure satisfied is the right word. But I'm glad we came."

When a guard announced the museum was closing and they'd have to leave, they followed the stream of tourists back to the blue whale and their exit.

"I guess seeing the scene of the crime got you through the aftermath of that fiery cocktail. But you have to know it may not be the last danger we face."

"I'm aware of that." Her chin lifted. "I won't be such a wuss the next time, I promise."

The resolute look in her eyes convinced him she meant it. Next time. Shit, for sure there'd be a next time. June was coming up too damn fast.

****

Rousso paced the hotel room's plush green carpet.

Two hours since he had given the order. Where *was* the man? Muscle with the brain of a turnip but he did follow orders. But little better than a turnip.

He stomped to the mini-bar and poured a glass of Perrier. When his cell jangled, he jumped. "What?"

"Mission accomplished, Mr.—"

"No names, remember?" He had checked the phone for listening devices but one never knew. If the fool wanted to incriminate himself, that was one thing, but Rousso would not allow himself to be dragged along with him to prison.

"Yeah. Sorry. Um, house burnt to the ground. Fire department couldn't save 'er," the voice on the other end said, glee apparent in his tone.

"What about the two you are trailing?"

The other man hesitated, uttered unintelligible grunts, as if searching for words.

Rousso sipped the sparkling mineral water. "The second transponder, does it work still?"

"No problem. It works good. Just it, um, led me to the, um, thief's house."

Rousso closed his eyes for strength against his frustration. Of course Jones went to search his father's old partner's house. He should have sent this man sooner to eradicate his sloppy search, a big mistake. "Do not tell me they were inside when you threw in the device."

"They didn't see me or nothing. I floored it outta there. Then I hung back outta sight when they split."

"Vhere—*where* they are now?"

"Went into the District. They parked the pickup in a building downtown. Near the Federal Triangle stop."

"And they went?"

"Dunno. You said not to follow them on foot. I shouldn't be seen."

Dolt. Yes, he obeyed orders. But too literally.

Rousso gritted his teeth and gripped the phone nearly tight enough to crack the case. He called on willpower not to beat his head against the wall.

Federal Triangle. He glanced at the Metro map open on the bed. Did they go to the museum? Why? What was there so many years later?

"What do I do now... sir?" He was an overgrown puppy ready for the next trick.

"Hang up. Go home. Await my call."

Chapter Thirteen

THEY CLEANED UP at Mara's apartment before driving north for dinner. As she pulled into the jammed parking lot of the Severn River Marina, the rearview mirror revealed the same big black sedan she'd noticed behind them as they left the District. It had followed them all the way to the restaurant. Centaur's man? Or was Cort keeping another threat from her? Now wasn't the time but she'd grill him later.

"You sure this is where Cassie said to meet them?"

Cort's dubious tone triggered her chuckle as she shut off the car engine. The marina, with weathered boards and a sagging wrap-around porch, looked like a place to avoid, not where a respectable fishing boat would dock.

"The place isn't much to look at," she said, "except for that new blue metal roof. Dad used to bring the family. They receive fresh catches daily. Best crab cakes in Maryland. Spiced shrimp and hush puppies too. Dad liked the cheap prices and it didn't matter if we made a mess."

"My mouth is watering already," he said as they climbed from her car.

Her mouth watered too, and not from the aromas of spiced shrimp and boiled crabs wafting by. Cort looked way too hot in the same khakis and blue dress shirt he'd worn to DSF the other day. The light touch of his big hand sent tingles up her arm and across her scalp. She shouldn't think of this outing as a date.

When they entered the dining room, she spotted her sister immediately, at a prime booth for the water view. Cassie started to wave but her hand froze and her eyes narrowed.

"She didn't know I was coming," he whispered. "Why did you bring me?"

"You know why." Although having him scrutinize the new guy wasn't her only motive. She wanted his company, his solid presence and frankness. "And she did know. I told her. She's just not happy about it."

"Hostility's great for the appetite."

"The digestion too. Suck it up, big guy."

"I'll just order a stiff one. Or two. André looks like he'd rather be on the tennis court."

"Or in a magazine ad." The pale yellow cable-knit draping his shoulders typed him. That and his dark hair and soulful eyes. She pictured him with a racquet in his hand instead of the wine goblet.

They threaded through the plain wooden picnic tables to where her sister and André sat by a window overlooking the docks.

Cassie made hasty introductions and the two men shook hands. Mara couldn't help a smile when she saw the other man wince at Cort's grip. Not that Cort meant a warning. No way.

A waiter whisked over to take their drink order and left the four of them to stare at each other. Mara chalked it up to nerves when she and Cassie gushed family stories about meals at the restaurant and about the gorgeous view of the river. Finally they ran down like wind-up music boxes.

"Did you drive, André?" Mara said, searching for a new topic, a neutral one, a safe one. "I didn't see my sister's car outside."

André and Cassie exchanged amused glances. He slung an arm around her shoulders and kissed her forehead. "We came by boat. The romantic way to travel."

No wonder Cassie was falling for this man. His voice was velvet smooth, his accent French with a trace of British.

"André's boat." Cassie snuggled closer.

Blushing, hanging on him like a teenager. Whoa. Mara had never seen her sister so blown away. She'd been hot for several guys since the divorce but not like this. No cigarettes either.

"The sailboat?" Cort nodded toward the craft at the end of the marina dock.

"Not the skipjack," Mara said. "That's—"

"Sis, please don't," Cassie said, holding up a hand in a stop signal.

Mara stifled herself. "Okay." She managed an apologetic shrug.

"What?" Cort said. "What's the deal about the skipjack?"

Mara's glance darted among the three of them, settling on Cort and pleading with her eyes for him to drop the matter. "Nothing. Just local trivia."

"Hell, now I'm curious," he said. "Go for it."

"Please," André said, his gaze encouraging. "I would like to know."

After a reluctant nod from Cassie, Mara said, "To conserve the oyster fishery, Maryland law allows only sail-powered boats, and skipjacks are the original

Chesapeake oystering boats. The V-shaped hull and the square stern are distinctive. Most skipjacks, at least the few remaining that still fish, are forty to fifty feet long. Like this one. It's a working boat. See the winch above the hold and the dredging rig?"

"Why you said André's boat wasn't the skipjack," Cort said.

"You got it." Better to stop at that. They didn't want the rest of what her magnet of a brain had acquired about dragging for oysters.

"Mara's head is chock full of all sorts of odd factoids," Cassie put in. "If I don't stop her, she bores people with useless facts."

"Unless, like now," Cort said, with a pointed glare, "the factoid wasn't useless but pertinent."

Cassie looked away but didn't squirm or make excuses.

"And fascinating." André nearly blinded Mara with his smile.

Cassie might be melted into a puddle of mush and lust, but André's charm and looks had little effect on her.

"My boat is the cruiser on your right, with the inboard motor," André said, indicating a low-slung burgundy speedboat. A scrolling font on the hull identified it as *Vendange*. "Traveling from Baltimore under sail would require many hours."

"Sweet. Cigarette boat. Those babies go like hell," Cort said. "You must do all right. What business did you say you were in?"

And so the match begins, Mara thought. Serve over the net to opponent.

"*Vendange* means *vintage*," Cassie chirped,

watching the two males as intently as Mara. "André's in wine imports."

The Frenchman's grin became sharklike. Response ready for the ball swooshing through the air. "From France, Italy, Spain. My family has a vineyard in the south of France. *Mon père* has retired. My brother runs it now, but travel appeals to me more than pruning vines."

"He's here to arrange a deal with several of the big hotels," Cassie said.

"That is enough about me, *chérie*. Now I am the one who does not want to bore."

Oops, ball out of bounds. But before Cort could serve another, the waiter arrived with Mara's white wine and Cort's vodka tonic and a crab cake appetizer served with a creamy herb sauce. With their meal order, André insisted on a bottle of chardonnay, one imported by his family company.

As they ate, the match progressed but with Cort observing André quietly. Assessing, analyzing, figuring the man's angle, Mara suspected. André quizzed Cort about his furniture building, asking intelligent questions about wood and dovetail joints. When Cassie looked puzzled, Mara smiled but remained quiet as Cort explained that dovetails were interlocking wooden pins and tails. No reason to rile her sister again. Let her enjoy time with her new guy for as long as it lasted.

Later, after seeing the new lovers off in *Vendange*, Mara asked Cort's opinion.

"Hard to say. The man's slick but he seems to be what he says he is. Your research found nothing to the contrary?"

She shook her head. "I found the family vineyard,

the company, even André, online. Some education in England, which explains the mingled accent, a business degree in Lyon. No children, not married. I'll show you on my tablet later. Could he be with Centaur anyway?"

Cort's jaw worked over the question as he pulled out of the restaurant parking lot. "He seems to care for your sister, but there's a hard layer to him. You noticed the way he deflected questions about himself. Slippery. Makes me think he has something to hide."

****

Cassie poured a brandy for André. She ought to have a proper snifter. At least she had wine glasses and not just her Target tumblers. André was way more sophisticated than any man she'd been with, and she felt like a bumpkin.

The hour was late, after eleven. She normally wouldn't stay out so late on a weeknight. School and work meant early bedtimes. But she didn't have to be at the bank until nine and Livvie wasn't here. Cassie had gotten on her daughter's good side by agreeing to let her stay overnight with a friend. To work on a science project, Livvie'd said in her most annoying wheedle. Cassie huffed at that but trusted the parents to keep the girls corralled in the house. So she was free to enjoy the evening—maybe the entire night—with André.

"I am not certain of your sister, *chérie*," André said, "but her friend did not like me."

"You're imagining things," she said, astonished he lacked any confidence about himself or care what others thought, much less express it. She didn't enjoy the taste of brandy but she poured one for herself and joined him on the sofa. "It's me Cort doesn't like. Because I disapprove of this adventure he's talked my

148

sister into."

"Adventure?" André's gaze turned upward as if remembering. "You mean he is the son of the jewel thief, the one you told me about? We had dinner with a criminal?"

Cassie set down her glass and reached for his hand. What if he left? What if he refused to see her again because of Cortez Jones? "I apologize. But I didn't know. I warned her not to bring that man. Like I warned her not to go along with his scheme. But she doesn't listen to me anymore. I—" Her voice cracked and she stifled tears.

When he lifted her hand to his lips, she melted at the romantic Gallic gesture.

"It's not your fault, Cassandra." He raised one shoulder. "I am merely concerned for Mara, as you are. But perhaps what they do is not so dangerous if they are simply examining your father's files."

Maybe she shouldn't have told him anything about the Gramornia jewel theft. Maybe she should've kept it all inside. But André'd entered the room when Mara was telling her on the phone about being followed. She freaked out, cried like a fool, and he was so comforting, so sympathetic, the whole story came pouring out. Including her father's role. If he had a role other than insurance investigator.

She pressed a hand to her stomach. "I'm afraid it's gone beyond that now. The whole thing—Jones, my sister, the jewel hunt—just makes me crazy. I can't talk about it."

He tipped up her chin and kissed her lightly. "Then do not. When you feel better, you can tell me anything you like."

She gave him a tremulous smile. "Maybe later."

After a deeper kiss, one that sizzled her senses and drove all thought and worry from her brain, he clasped her hands and pulled her to her feet. With his arm around her shoulders, he nudged her down the hallway to the bedroom. "For now let us not talk at all."

****

"Two men in a black car are watching this building from across the street," Mara said, every word stiletto sharp. "They followed us to the restaurant and back."

Shit. Oh shit. Cort hurried to finish brushing his teeth. She'd spotted the Clone Brothers. Had to happen sometime, but why now?

Barefoot and shirttail loose, he crossed the darkened living room to where she stood looking out the front window and pulled her back into the shadows. "Probably FBI. Nothing to worry about."

She stiffened. "In a luxury sedan? Two ugly-mean dudes in black? They look more like enforcers for the mob."

When he said nothing, she eyed him with suspicion narrowing her eyes. "Cort, what's going on? You're hiding something from me."

He rubbed his nape and looked away.

"If you don't tell me everything," she continued, "I'm going out there and confront them."

"Dammit, Mara." She was too smart and too naïve. She might actually do it. When she made a start for the door, he snagged her hand. "Okay. But check the apartment again with Devlin's fancy bug detector. Leave the lights off."

She glared at him for a moment before fetching the RFD unit, the size of a TV remote, from her purse.

After she declared the apartment clear, they went to sit on her bed where, as she informed him, she could see his face as he 'fessed up. He finished his narrative about Colonel Yerik with an apology for his secrecy but without mention of the beating.

She sat staring at him. Fear joined the ire in her eyes, along with an emotion he couldn't read. Her silence made sweat break out along his hairline.

"I didn't tell you because I didn't want to scare you more than you already are. I've enlisted... assistance in stopping their plot but I need time. I'm doing everything I can to keep you safe and make the son of a bitch think I'm doing nothing to find the jewels. That's all I can tell you for now." His backstage tinkering had to remain just that. A slip could blow it all to hell.

Her expression gentler, she pressed a soft palm to his jaw. "The wounds on your face, the bruises. You didn't get in a fight at all. They beat you." When he merely shrugged, she tsked. "You've been holding all this inside. No wonder I hear you tossing and turning every night."

She wasn't cursing him for endangering her or lying by omission. He'd feel less guilty if she did. He kissed her palm and released her. Lowered his head in his hands. "Should've walked away from the whole thing. Then you'd be safe."

"And we'd both be sorry the rest of our lives."

That brought up his head. Did he hear her right? "What?"

"You told me you have to return the jewels so you can hold up your head. You've given me hope of clearing my father. Giving this bum and his gorillas what they want isn't an option. They're betraying their country. In the end, they would kill you anyway. And me."

"You're not pissed I didn't tell you?"

"You better believe I'm pissed." She smiled, a gentle curve of lips that loosened the knot in his chest. "But I understand. And the whole thing will end soon."

Her unfailing optimism was one of the things about her he appreciateed. And agonized over. "Soon, yeah. Time is tight. Eleven days. But who's counting?"

"Gives *deadline* a whole new meaning, doesn't it?"

Her words conveyed cockiness but he wasn't buying it. The quiver in her voice said different. He deserved to die a slow, agonizing death if anything happened to her. But only after he delivered the same to Yerik and company.

Her eyes met his and the look in them blanked his mind. Not fear but heat. Arousal flared between them, molten, stunning.

When she leaned closer and brushed back a lock of his hair from his forehead, he bent his head to hers. "Mara?"

Her dark eyes flashed. "I fought this, but no more. I want you, Cort. Now."

He grasped the back of her neck and rocked his mouth over hers. Her scent made his nostrils flare in demand to absorb the rest of her. The kiss devoured, igniting to fiery heat and pent-up longing, drugging kisses and dueling tongues. Her sweet taste drove out his anger, his pride, filling him with unabashed need and an inchoate connection he couldn't name.

Her hands made short work of his shirt buttons and glided over his chest, the soft sensation making his body tighten like the bass drum thudding in his chest.

She was flame licking over his flesh. Barely suppressing a groan, he captured her close against him, found her breast, the nipple hard against his palm through the thin blouse and bra. With the pad of his thumb, he rubbed slowly back and forth, feeling her hunger matching his as she moved against him and uttered little sexy, breathy sighs.

"Too many clothes," she murmured, tugging at his sleeves. Color suffused her cheeks beneath her lowered lashes.

He peeled off the shirt, then lay back on the big bed and let her divest him of his pants and boxers. "Now who has on too many clothes?"

When her short skirt hit the floor, he let his gaze crawl up her tennis-honed legs to the flare of her hips in red bikini panties. He ran his hand along her thigh, satin and firm muscle.

"Beautiful. Perfect," he murmured as he tugged off her tank top and bra. "And this you've been hiding from me." His index finger outlined the tiny tattoo on her left breast and her nipples hardened in reaction. "Now I need you against me. Full body contact sport."

Her response, a deep chuckle, stoked the flames higher. The rest of her clothes melted away.

He scooped her up and on top of him, her delicate curves soft against the rough angles of his body. He caressed and suckled and tasted as she writhed against him with fluid grace and greedy heat. When she cupped him and sketched her nails over him, she damn near burned him alive. Gritting his teeth to hang on, he stroked her liquid heat until she moaned. Without warning, her arms left him and she squirmed away.

Not again. "What the hell?" He heard a drawer

open and a shuffling sound.

"Protection." She tossed a foil packet on his chest. "Hurry."

She didn't have to say it twice. He sank into her, slowly at first, struggling not to hurt her, but the warmth of her, the joy of her shuddered through him and his heart took off like a dragster and the room lost all oxygen. Heat exploded between them and she responded, moving beneath him, clutching at him, kissing him, racing with him as his climax tickled at his spine, until she arched and her body clutched him with her spasms, and he joined her in a convulsive rush.

Chapter Fourteen

"IN THIRTY FEET, turn right... onto Crosslyn Avenue," the female voice directed in a crisp British accent.

The Washington area street map on Cort's lap rattled as he consulted it for verification of the Kensington, Maryland, street. Their first interview, now that Falco was dead, was the widow of retired security guard George Hauptman, who had died five years ago of cancer. Mara, ever hopeful, suggested the widow might still have his effects and had made an appointment with Twyla Hauptman. Not mentioning Cort being involved seemed an easier door opener.

This morning, they'd slipped out the back alley and taken one of the cabs parked outside the nearby coffee takeout to the closest car rental place. As far as Yerik's clones knew—he hoped—he and Mara were hanging out in the apartment after the morning grocery shopping. Or maybe the jerkoffs imagined they were doing the horizontal bump and grind. If they only knew.

In keeping with her bent for Crayola colors, she wore a slim denim skirt and layered tops in bright orange and yellow. Riding beside her gave him occasional whiffs of her sweet scent. An added bonus.

"Not impressed with Rosie?" Mara asked, with humor in her tone. Rays of the late afternoon sun gleamed on her dark hair.

Cort kept his hands on the map. "Impressed is the wrong word. Hell, even with Internet directions I want real map back-up. A voice from a plastic box is too far from reality to suit me. I use a computer and cell phone only out of necessity."

"You work with power tools."

"All the technology I need. Plug 'em in and push a button."

She sniffed. "I don't believe it's quite that simple, big guy."

He shot a sideways glance at her in the driver's seat. They had sure pushed each other's buttons last night. One button in particular. After they'd come down, he'd circled his index finger around her tattoo. "What's with the green apple?"

She tugged the sheet higher over her breasts. "Not an apple. That's the computer power button."

He bent nearer for a better view. "Green for *On*? Oh, baby. Just press here?" She hadn't responded, only eyed him warily until he'd quipped, "You still gonna make me go out there and sleep on Old Lumpy?" Then she'd laughed and relaxed against him for the night.

Still, he could tell she'd held back, kept a barrier up even though she came. Hell, no surprise she didn't trust him in bed any more than she trusted him otherwise, so he meant to keep things casual. He'd refrained from pressing her for another round, although it had pained him.

"You sure no one followed us?" She glanced in the side mirror as they made the turn into Mrs. Hauptman's development.

"I'm no expert but I haven't seen the same vehicle twice. Checked license plates too." What worried him more than another Molotov cocktail was not being able to keep one step ahead of the bastards. Losing Mara's files was too much of a setback.

They continued past bungalow-style and ranch houses. Bicycles and pop-up campers vied for space in driveways and carports.

"Not too different from Dundalk," he said over the Brit's next instructions. "No conspicuous consumption here. Vinyl siding. Bastardization of American building."

"Spoken like a wood man."

"Brick and stone are fine. Natural materials." He checked to see if she was teasing him but her expression was serious as she searched for their target address. Maybe she didn't trust technology all the way. "Neighborhood in transition. Trending up or down?"

"Kensington's always in transition. You're thinking the widow's not spending ill-gotten gains."

"If old George was a crook, he was either a bad one or the Gramornia heist was his only job. One that paid zip."

"Arriving at destination, on right." The tiny screen displayed a checkered flag.

Mara pulled into the paved driveway of a vinyl-sided ranch and parked behind a two-year-old station wagon. "Lawn's mowed. Trimmed bushes and geraniums in pots. Door painted. No sign of neglect here."

"What conclusion do you draw from that, Detective Marton?"

She wrinkled her nose and grinned. "No conclusion yet. It's early. Only data to input."

"Spoken like a techie." When she popped her iPod

157

into her bag with smart phone, he tested the weight. "You know, I read somewhere they have devices now that do all the work of these two toys you lug around."

"I know. Luddite that I am, I hang on to old technology." When he raised an eyebrow, she added, "More secure having the functions separated."

"A wary geek." Good plan, especially given their situation.

They exited, and he waited for her to lock the car. A faint aroma of barbecue hung on the breeze. In the next yard a dog barked and another neighbor started up a lawnmower.

Yesterday's shared scare and last night's lovemaking had made them easier with each other. In spite of her meltdown afterward, she was tough and determined. "Doesn't seem the bad guys have gotten to Mrs. Hauptman ahead of us."

"Now who's drawing a conclusion?"

"You got me there." He touched a hand to the small of her back, intending support for her, but the connection eased his own tension. "I know we agreed you'd take the lead. I want you to know I—" He didn't know how to express his thanks for her understanding.

Lame, but she smiled anyway, one of her golden smiles that warmed him inside and out. "I know."

As they approached the entrance, the door opened. Twyla Hauptman greeted them with a spare, prim smile. "Ms. Marton?"

"Hello, Mrs. Hauptman," Mara said. "Thank you for agreeing to see us."

The widow Hauptman was short and compact, somewhere between forty and fifty-five. Hard to see the real woman through the hard mask of makeup. Or past the frozen smile and wary eyes. With her curly blonde do, she reminded Cort of a poodle past its prime trying to hang onto cute and cuddly. On the other hand, she looked exactly like what she was, bartender at a rockabilly and blues bar on Georgia Avenue. She wore her work uniform of tight black skirt, white blouse, and a plastic name badge.

He knew the moment she recognized him. Her mascara-caked eyelashes blinked and her eyes widened before they narrowed.

"The Jeweler's son." Her glare shifted to Mara. "I didn't know you were bringing *him*."

"We're working on this together," Mara replied evenly. "As I said on the phone, I have some questions related to the Gramornia crown jewels robbery. May we come in?"

Hauptman glared at him a long minute, then stepped aside and gestured for them to enter.

In the living room, Mara sat on a loveseat opposite the widow's armchair. Not ready to sit on the clear plastic covers shielding every piece of upholstery, Cort leaned an elbow on the white-painted mantel above a gas fireplace. The room reeked of air freshener. Cheap reproduction antiques in a mash-up of styles, family photos, and a mirror in a gilded frame crammed the small space, and revealed zip about the dear departed George.

"You have a lovely home, Mrs. Hauptman," Mara said. A casual dip into a pocket on the outside of her purse started a tiny digital recorder.

"Thanks. I do try. Hard on a limited budget." The widow simpered. "Make it Twyla."

The two women discussed upkeep on the house for

what seemed to Cort endless minutes. Mara had gotten interrogation hints from her boss. The best way to elicit information was by leading them to like you, to *want* to help you. So far a bang-up job for someone without interrogation experience. Great. Okay. But he itched to move this along.

Suppressing his impatience, he turned to the family photos on the mantel. George and Twyla in a formal department-store-special portrait. He looked hunched and haggard. Maybe a last portrait before he died.

Various photos showed a younger Twyla with her parents and three siblings, two slim girls, and a teenage blimp in a football uniform. Other frames held more family snapshots and portraits.

"We're a large family," the widow said, apparently taking his curiosity for interest. "George and I had no children, but my sisters made up for it with four kids each." Her mouth tightened.

Mara tsked in sympathy and asked about the brother.

"That's Hugo. My baby brother's still single. I couldn't manage without him. He's such a big help."

Come on, let's get to the real reason for the visit. If he sat beside Mara, maybe he could hurry her process along. When he planted his butt on the loveseat, he suppressed a shudder at the creaking plastic. The ring piece in his pants pocket burned against his leg. He worked his jaw. Flexed his fingers on his knees. Cleared his throat.

Mara exchanged a glance with him before turning back to their hostess. "Twyla, we don't want to take up too much of your time. I apologize if asking about your dear husband brings up sad memories. Did he ever describe any of the talks he had with the insurance investigator?"

She huffed her disdain. "Talks? Interrogations was more like it. Just like the police questions." She picked at a piece of lint on her skirt. "That was your father, right?"

When Mara nodded, she relented. "George didn't say much. Mostly they asked what he knew about the robbery. He told them he didn't know anything. He had nothing to do with the electrical glitches that shut down the security cameras and other stuff."

"Nothing else?"

"That's all I remember."

"Did George leave anything in his effects that seemed… well, odd or unusual?"

The older woman straightened, cocked her head to one side. "What sort of odd thing?"

They'd agreed to reveal as little as possible, but Cort figured it was time to ask the hot question. "A ring. Gold. But too large for a finger. Yay big." He formed an *O* with his right thumb and forefinger.

A tiny frown crimped the flesh between Twyla's thin eyebrows. Her lips pruned. A flush stole up her neck. "This is about the robbery. You think my George was involved."

Cort held up his hands. "I don't know. Ma'am, this kind of ring might give me a clue to finding the jewels. The FBI—"

"FBI, my ass." Her face a red mask of indignation, Twyla shot to her feet. Gone was the gracious hostess. "You want everything for yourself. I got no ring. George had no ring. He wasn't part of no robbery. He lost his job on account of those accusations. Your old man caused that. My George never got over it."

"We don't know who was or wasn't involved, Mrs. Hauptman." Forget the first-name basis now. "And we're not the only ones searching. You need to be careful—"

"Who I let in my house. For damn sure. Get out. Now." She stood rigid, arms folded.

Mara took his hand. "We're going," she said, urging him toward the door. She deposited her business card on a table by the coat rack. "But if you should find that ring in your husband's things, we'd appreciate a phone call."

****

"Any luck on Inglish?" Cort growled, barely raising his head.

Mara's internal sigh of frustration must've leaked out. She looked up from the screen. "No joy yet. Give me a few minutes."

Her gaze blurred as she stared at yet another database, this one for drivers' licenses in the state of Illinois. No Danita Inglish. The museum guard had moved to Chicago eight years ago, but pinpointing an address sent Mara chasing shadows. Inglish was a prime suspect because she, along with George Hauptman, had access to the security diagrams.

They needed to move ahead, and fast, after hitting dead ends with Falco and now the widow Hauptman. As the weekend wore on, Cort had sunk further and further into the cushions of her sofa, seeming to close in on himself. He was fretting about how long he could put off the scary colonel. The man phoned several times to pressure him about what was going on.

A hot affair, Cort said. Hot was right. The hot

charge of chemistry kept them both steaming in and out of bed. Yielding to her desire for him had filed the jagged edge off their relationship but tangled up her mind. Her previous sexual relationships stayed casual, even recreational, without strong emotions. Not like the wild possession in Cort's arms. They didn't wring from her such intense reactions, such frenzied carnality that might lure her to mistake lust for love. And she liked him. His protectiveness, his inner strength, and in spite of his intensity, the comfortable silences they shared gave her a sense of safety.

But his present mood, as cloudy as this Sunday, was bringing her down. She wanted to see the dimple a smile carved into his cheek. While she worked on her laptop, he sucked down green tea and pored over printouts in hopes of finding something everyone else had missed.

Missed. What had she missed in her search for Danita Inglish? Struck by the obvious, she tapped more keys. A few moments later, she smiled. "Got her."

"Yeah, where? Timbuktu?"

"Almost. You won't like it. San Francisco." She didn't like it either. The golden city on the bay was also the current home of her mother. "Oakland, actually."

His muttered curse reverberated inside her. "I should've known finding these people wouldn't be a cinch, but the other coast? Shit. And the widow's a bust."

"Give her time to get over her mad. We've raised questions. In the meantime, let's get out of here." She shut the laptop lid and stretched. "If I look at any more lists on-screen today, I'll need eye surgery."

Chapter Fifteen

HALF AN HOUR later Cort stood at the Great Falls National Park overlook. Only feet below them, the waters of the Potomac foamed over and around jagged rocks in a series of cascades. The river's angry churning had nothing on the violence inside him.

"Now don't you feel better?" Mara, beside him, leaned against the wood-and-stone barrier. She turned as if to read his expression as he stared into the gray waters.

He felt the corners of his mouth lift. Her gentle question did make him feel better. No point in taking out his frustration on her. "Nothing like watching water to soothe the beast. According to the plaque back there, the Potomac's too rough for navigation from Cumberland to Georgetown. George Washington started a company to create the canal."

"He had to give up the project when he was elected president. There's a museum on the Maryland side of the river. Um, we can go there later. If you're interested, that is."

Her sister had tried to keep the lid on Mara's vast store of factoids, out of jealousy or self-centered embarrassment, whatever. Not him. He admired her memory for detail and attention.

"I'm *very* interested. If there's time before I have to leave."

He took her hand as they started walking, and she curved her fingers to fit his grip. The softness and warmth of her skin gave him thoughts that must've heated his gaze, judging from her flushed cheeks.

A movement in his peripheral vision prompted him to glance at the others around them. Clones One and Two had tailed them only as far as the parking lot. On foot they'd have been too obvious in this sparse mix of families, young lovers, and senior citizens. "Looks like most people are heading upstream. Let's follow the water."

"Figures you'd prefer the way less traveled."

He slung an arm around her shoulders and kissed her temple. "That way I get you all to myself."

Her murmur told him she wasn't immune to even that brief caress. "Or that was a ploy to see if anyone is following us."

"Busted. Doesn't mean I didn't enjoy the diversion." His lips again found the pulse in her temple. "Seems you didn't mind it either."

They set off down the paved path toward Mather Gorge. Maples and sycamores arched toward them on the land side, mingling their scent with that of the rushing river.

"Cassie always put down your store of knowledge like she did the other night?" he asked, trying not to sound too critical.

"Sibling rivalry." She sighed. "She resented, maybe still does, the fascination for all kinds of information I shared with Dad. She and Mom hated going to museums with us. Dad and I would pore over every exhibit, read every placard, while they couldn't wait for the gift shop."

"Not too different from the push-pull in my family." Cassie had more problems than he knew if she still resented Mara. How far would she go to stop their search?

A group of chattering teenagers came up behind them, so they walked in silence. Farther on, where the trail split, the teens took the right fork toward the canal, and they continued along the river. A jogger passed in the other direction. No one else nearby.

He pulled her from the path and toward the river. They climbed across great slabs of rock for a better view of the gorge, where the waterway widened and leveled off. Mara hopped boulders ahead of him, allowing him the opportunity to enjoy her perfect butt in skinny jeans.

When she started to teeter on an uneven surface, he wrapped his arms around her. "A little early in the season for a swim."

She eyed the rough waves. A nervous laugh escaped her. "Thanks."

When she turned in his arms to face him, he said, "While I've got you, I want to know when you were planning to tell me how you found the other museum guard."

She tilted her head, circling a manicured nail on his sternum. "I thought you'd never ask." She grinned. "Facebook."

The word struck him dumb for a long moment. He bent to touch his forehead to hers. Soft. Warm. Smooth. "Get out. She posted her personal info on Facebook?"

"For everyone, not just friends. She moved near her daughter and grandchild. Even posted pictures of the baby. Danita works for the city of San Francisco.

Then I found her address in the online city directory. If she's gone public, maybe that means she wasn't involved and has nothing to hide." Her face fell. "And no ring piece."

From optimist to skeptic in a heartbeat. "More likely she feels safe after eleven years. The FBI didn't hound the others as much as me. And she wouldn't know about Centaur."

"Wish *I* didn't know about them. And the dirty politics in Gramornia. Sort of." She didn't move out of his arms, letting him steady them both on top the boulder.

The breeze wrapped him in her scent, and his body went on alert. He couldn't wait until tonight to taste her again. Her mouth was hungry under his. Sleek and fluid, she tried to hide her sensuality but slowly, she softened, her breasts pressing against him, her tongue seeking his, and need scorched through him like the river's rush before reality pulled him back from the brink.

Breathing hard, he nuzzled her forehead, letting her spring scent soothe him. "You don't have to stop me. I'm not into getting it on with an audience."

"All I'd have to do is give a push, and you'd cool off fast enough."

He looked over his shoulder to see he'd backed up to the boulder's edge. Regrouping, he picked his way toward the path. She danced, laughing, over the rocks beside him with easy balance. Made him wonder if she'd wobbled earlier so he'd save her. So he'd kiss her. Maybe she trusted him more than she let on.

She shouldn't.

The looming clouds spattered fat raindrops on their

heads. The leading edge of a squall turned fast into a steady rain, driven by the wind.

Now the damn weather conspired against them. He muttered a few choice words.

"Couldn't have said it better myself," Mara said, turning back the way they'd come. "Mother Nature's herding us to the truck. I need a good run. Haven't played tennis lately."

He ran behind her as she took off at a sprint, her toned legs eating up the trail. He'd been running every day to burn off the tension and frustration. And to give Clones One and Two some diversion. Today was no different, just rainy. He hung back so he could keep the rhythmic movement of her legs and swinging hair in his sights.

Saplings swayed in the wind, their leaves darker green and shiny wet. Rain wrinkled the river's surface like curly maple. The teens who'd passed them earlier challenged each other for speed as they ran in their drooping jeans and long tees.

When they reached the truck, both were drenched. He handed her a towel from behind the seat and watched as she mopped her hair, then peeled off her sweatshirt. Trying not to stare at the twin nubs against her thin tee, he gripped the steering wheel.

When his cell jangled, a glance at the caller's number made him clench his jaw. Couldn't be good news.

"I better get that," Cort said.

"Hauptman?"

"No."

****

Cassie waved from the bleachers as Livvie's team

took the field in the bottom of the third inning. Her daughter waved back, beaming a huge smile brighter than this cloudy day.

Unlike sometimes, today Livvie was her little girl, not a rebellious preteen. The middle-school years could be tumultuous. She sure as hell remembered having friends one day who the next were clawing her in the back. Add to that the boy-girl thing, and you had hormone overload. Livvie's dad sure never made any of the games, was spending less and less time with her. So she needed her mom. Recently she'd taken more time for herself. André was her major focus. Cassie vowed she'd make more time for her daughter. Soon.

She sighed, her mind drifting to the man who'd sailed into her life and into her heart. His soulful eyes. His sensuous caresses. His gentle understanding. He made her feel beautiful again, and loved. Not that either one said a word about love. But soon, maybe...

"What a catch!" Another mother seated behind Cassie whacked her on the shoulder. "Livvie just made a great play." She stuck her bag of popcorn in front of Cassie.

The smack and the salty aroma woke her. She blinked and focused soon enough to see Livvie trotting off the field. She'd apparently caught a fly ball to end the inning. Rallying, Cassie shot to her feet and cheered. From the chatter around her, she realized the bases had been loaded. If Livvie hadn't dived for the fly, the other team might've scored more than one run.

"Thanks." She took a handful of popcorn. Now she'd pay attention to the game.

Once the crowd settled, she saw André making his way past admiring young mothers. In Euro-cut jeans and a black polo, he looked tastier than the popcorn. As he joined her, he smiled and kissed her cheek.

"Exciting game, *chérie*?"

Her neighbor fanned herself and grinned. Cassie linked her fingers with Andre's "Livvie just stopped the other team from scoring."

"A daughter to be proud of." He waved at Livvie, but the girl didn't see. "I cannot understand your American football, but baseball is beginning to make sense. It has nuances and strategy I can understand."

"Except this is softball. Bigger ball, different pitching style."

"Basically the same, is it not?"

Laughing, she conceded the point.

André joined her in watching the game and cheering for the home team. By the seventh-inning stretch, they led by three runs. He looked around at the cheering fans. "Does your sister ever attend these games?"

"Once in a while," Cassie said. "Her schedule doesn't allow the time. Plus she gets to travel, which I don't. She jets off to see our mother twice a year. I can't afford to go more than once every other year. In fact, she and Cort are taking off for San Francisco soon." She wasn't supposed to talk about their crazy quest for the mysterious puzzle ring pieces, but making it sound like Mara went to see their mom wasn't giving away any secrets. Besides, who would André tell?

"Then I hesitate to divulge my news."

She studied his regretful expression. "Bad news?"

"Possibly. My father has a heart condition. Last night he had an 'episode,' the doctor called it. At eighty, one never knows. I must return to France see him in hospital."

"I'm so sorry." She pressed his arm. "I'll miss you." Oops, that sounded selfish when she should be concerned about his father. "Will he be all right?"

"I pray he will. I shall return in a few days, as soon as he is stabilized." He lifted her hand and kissed the palm. "The next time I fly to France, I shall take you with me. You will love the wine country."

"That's so sweet. I'd love to go, but don't feel you have to—"

The crowd erupted in cheers.

The woman beside her pounded her shoulders with both hands. Popcorn sprayed over them like snow. "Whoo hoo, way to go, Livvie!"

Too late, Cassie leaped to her feet to discover not only had the teams played half an inning, but her daughter had just hit a home run. She yelled and waved as Livvie touched home plate. Her screaming teammates surrounded her, and she didn't look up.

****

Mara watched Cort listening to his phone, but he said nothing more. Probably wanted privacy. She grabbed the umbrella behind the seat. "I'll try Twyla Hauptman now."

She hopped out and ran for the visitor center. Under the entrance roof, she punched in the widow's number. After three rings, a tentative hello.

"Mrs. Hauptman, this is Mara Marton. I talked to you the other day about the Gramornia crown jewel robbery."

The widow's sharp inhalation could've been a suppressed sob. "You have some nerve calling me again! You should see the mess here."

What was going on? "Don't hang up, please. What happened?"

"I got home from work last night and found my back door wide open. Somebody went through drawers and cabinets and tossed everything around."

Cort had tried to warn the woman but now was not the time for *I told you so*. Mara chewed her lower lip. "How terrible. Did they steal much? Did they get the ring?"

The woman actually growled. "Ring, ring, that's all you people care about. I got no ring."

"Did you search for it?"

"Had to, didn't I? I went through George's things. No ring. Maybe them burglars were you. Or you led them here. Then the cops made another mess. Don't call me again. I told the detectives about you, so stay away from me." She slammed down the receiver.

Exhaling slowly, Mara disconnected. "That went well."

She dashed back to the truck through the downpour. Thunder boomed in the distance. She fumbled the umbrella as she clambered into her seat. Cort barely looked at her, just stared straight ahead. No wonder. She was a mess. Stringy, wet hair. Frak.

"You get Hauptman?" he said.

"For all the good it did." She described the call.

"Sounds like the same scenario, a search masked by vandalism. And no ring?"

"She yelled those words." She pulled her hair back and fastened it with a butterfly clip. "Say Centaur's man or someone else killed Falco and burned his house and also trashed my place. They must figure the Jeweler's son has one of the ring pieces. Why haven't they gone after you?"

"I've asked myself that. Maybe they're letting me do their legwork. Maybe they're waiting to find another ring piece. Saving me for last. Who the hell knows? But if you found Danita Inglish, they can probably track her down too."

Mara's pulse jolted. "So she could be in danger. Even in California?"

"Devlin said Centaur has long arms. We need to fly out there. Can you get away tomorrow?"

"I'm sure I can. But your job, you have to be back for another class."

"Not anymore. That call was from my boss. He fired me."

"Oh no! Why?" Seeing the grim line of his mouth tightened her throat.

"Said the local FBI agent visited the school twice last week. Bad luck for me the second occurred during a board meeting. A dozen big-money types watched as the Fed flashed his badge. He might as well have waved a cape at a herd of bulls."

"Didn't your boss stand up for you?"

"He did before when only a few board members heard about the FBI badgering me. But this time with all of them looking on, he had no choice."

"That's so unfair." She ached to offer the comfort of her arms but he'd surrounded himself with an invisible wall.

His shoulders raised and lowered stiffly in a show of nonchalance. "Not totally. He suggested I could return to the job once I resolved my problems. I still have my consignment business."

All he needed was another instance of being

rejected, being shunned because of his record. He needed to be accepted before he could brush that boulder-sized chip off his shoulder. And he needed to *know* he could trust someone before he could trust himself.

Apparently that someone wasn't her. She *was* keeping secrets from him. Necessary secrets. And how much could she trust him? She swallowed over a hot lump in her throat.

Chapter Sixteen

CORT AND MARA landed in San Francisco just before noon. The city was always cool and usually foggy, she'd said. He zipped up his windbreaker. Cool, yeah, but the sun shone in a clear bowl of sky.

She was chewing on her lower lip. Anxious about seeing Danita Inglish? Or worried about what she'd tell her mother? She'd worked late and then slept most of the way on the plane, her head against his shoulder. He'd gotten a cramp in his thigh from sitting still for so long, but she'd smelled so fresh and felt so good against him he'd kept still. Even after the long flight, she looked smooth and hot in black pants and a neon-orange jacket.

They'd used her frequent-flier miles for the plane tickets, and her boss gave her authorization to use a condo DSF kept in the city. Cort could manage on his own, but he wasn't stupid even if Devlin's high-handedness ticked him off.

Mara must've gauged his mood because she didn't object when he insisted on paying for the rental car. He followed signs out of the airport then turned north toward the Bay Bridge. The high-speed traffic and all the rapid-fire signage allowed little opportunity to watch for a tail. He mentally crossed his fingers that their last-minute arrangements caught the bad guys with bare asses in the wind. They'd left the Clone Brothers in a traffic snarl near Dulles.

Research didn't yield much about Inglish. She'd struggled in menial jobs after losing her Smithsonian security-guard position. She and her daughter had lived in a one-room D.C. apartment on welfare until she parlayed her technical skills into a traffic-control monitoring job in Chicago. When her grown daughter moved west and had a baby, Inglish followed. She moved several times since, each time to a better situation. She'd turned her life around. Cort half hoped the woman was innocent and didn't have a ring piece.

Where would that leave him? Dead in the water.

"She never answered my phone messages," Mara said. "I ought to try her now to see if she's home. She might be at work. I couldn't get her schedule."

"You're worried about her." He placed a hand over hers, felt a slight tremble. Wished again he hadn't involved her in this mess. But only for a second. Caved because weak bastard that he was, it'd mean he wouldn't have her soft hand to hold. And her soft body beside him at night.

"Why wouldn't I be after what happened to Falco?" On a sigh, she added, "No answer."

They'd find out soon enough, but he didn't like the odds.

Mara's phone GPS guided him through an Oakland middle-class residential neighborhood of colorful stucco homes with well-tended yards. They turned from a wide boulevard into a neat development of garden-style apartment buildings. He pulled into a guest parking space near the entrance to Inglish's building. Another car drove into the complex behind them but veered off toward distant buildings. Nobody else around.

He exited and walked around to Mara's side of the rented car. "Car in slot 213 says Inglish is home. Either she slams the door in our faces, or we grill her about the ring."

"Grill?" Mara said, grinning.

"Nicely."

They took the elevator to the second floor. Their strategy was the same as when they'd approached Hauptman's widow. Mara would lead and Cort would try to look nonthreatening. A tough order, with his nerves ready to burst like nuked popcorn kernels. Everything had gone against them. He had no reason to hope this would be any different.

When the elevator door swished open, they stepped into the opening.

A large, dark blur surged toward them from the left. Cort threw up his elbow, blocked the fist aimed at his temple.

He countered with a right cross to the attacker's jaw. Big brute recoiled at the blow but swung again. Cort ducked the massive fist. He swung up one knee to smash the guy's nuts. The bastard sidestepped and heaved a mighty shove that knocked him against Mara. She cried out as she fell to the floor. He recovered his balance, fists ready, but found only air to punch.

A door slammed and footsteps echoed in the stairwell. Two pairs of feet, not one.

Mara rose to her feet, her face a mask of shock but not pain. He hadn't hurt her, thank God.

Grabbing her hand, he scrambled to the window overlooking the entry. "Got to get a look at them."

Through the dusty pane, he saw the two men run

from the building. Big bastard who'd nearly cold-cocked him, six-five or more, in dark pants and windbreaker. The other, dark hair, average height, business suit. Their black SUV peeled out with a screech of tires.

He slammed a palm on the window frame. *Another fucking ambush.* "Shit! I saw only their backs. Didn't get the license number either."

"I never saw the smaller man," Mara said. "The guy who attacked you was huge. But I guess he could be the man who mugged me."

"You see his face? This guy, I mean."

She shook her head. "But I got the beginning of the license plate. *3AAL.*"

"Better eyes than I have. Way to go."

"Should I call the police?" She took out her cell.

"No. I'll get the FBI on it later." His gaze caught on the long hallway ahead of them. The attackers had come from the direction of apartment 213. He pushed away from the wall. "But damn, they got here ahead of us."

"Danita," she whispered, dread hanging on every syllable.

He prayed with every step down the hall the creeps hadn't gotten in, that the door was still locked, that they didn't have time to break in or trick Inglish into opening up. His adrenaline spiked, and he fisted his hands. The throb in the knuckles of his right was a souvenir he could ignore for now.

No answer to the doorbell.

"Try the door," she said. "Her car's there but maybe she went out with someone."

The handle turned easily. *Shit.* He pushed the door

inward. "Ms. Inglish? You home?"

When no response came, he stepped inside, trying to keep Mara behind him. She ducked under his arm and around him.

A rusty, coppery smell greeted them. Blood. But where?

Living room directly ahead. Pictures smashed, drawers emptied, cushions slashed. He muttered a curse. A door leading from the room might be a bedroom. "Ms. Inglish?"

"*No, no.*" Horror etched on her features, Mara clutched at his arm. She stared to her left, into a galley kitchen.

Danita Inglish sprawled supine on the tile floor. Blood soaked her clothing and fanned a crimson puddle on the floor. Beside her lay the remains of a chocolate cake and a blood-stained carving knife.

The dread knotting his gut was confirmed by the bloody scene, he blew out a breath and his shoulders slumped. They were too late. Again.

Mara started toward the woman but he held her hand. "We shouldn't touch anything."

"But she might still be alive," she protested.

"Be careful then." No choice now but to call the local cops. He pulled out his cell and punched 911.

She hurried to kneel beside the woman and felt her neck. "There's a pulse. Faint but she's alive. *There's so much blood!*" She grabbed a dish towel and pressed it against the wound.

****

Rousso observed through binoculars the police and ambulance frenzy outside Inglish's building. He and his local hire sat in a nondescript sedan parked across the street from the apartment complex. In case Jones had seen the big SUV, they'd obtained new transportation outside a supermarket. Willy wrapped his wounded arm with bandages purchased in the market.

He spewed curses and pounded the dashboard with the fist of his uninjured arm. He should have ensured Inglish's demise before they left. If he had not sent Willy to watch from the hall window, they might have missed Jones and the woman arriving until too late to avoid damage control. As it was they didn't reach the stairs before the elevator door opened.

"She has to be dead. Why would she not be dead?" he asked the abused upholstery.

Willy wisely said nothing, only gripped the steering wheel, ready to flee if necessary.

Rousso closed his eyes, searching for composure and resolve against the stinging pain in his arm. He should not have lost his temper and slapped her. He should have had Willy tie her up. She could not have attacked him. Then he lost it, as the Americans say, when she sliced him.

She would hand over nothing to him now. His search had yielded nothing. He was certain Inglish had a ring piece. Obtaining it himself was a lost cause now, with blue uniforms swarming everywhere. He would have to depend on Jones.

No matter, Rousso would possess that ring piece soon enough.

He would possess *all* the ring pieces.

Alive, Inglish could identify him and Willy. Jones had seen him before, so simply passing in the hallway was not an option. Willy's ambush made certain they did not see either of their faces. "You know this city.

Where they will take her?"

Willy worked his jaw and rubbed at the blooming bruise from Jones's fist. Thought rumpled his broad face like a Shar-Pei's. "County morgue. Dunno where that is."

"And if by some quirk of fate she lives still, what hospital?"

"Probably Highland General. Big trauma center. North of here. Not far."

Rousso thought about it. If the morgue, he was all right. The hospital, no. Obtaining access to a critical care unit was impossible without adequate time to plot a course of action. Staying in the San Francisco area for long could endanger everything.

"There they go," Willy said. He started the engine.

Lights twirling, the ambulance pulled slowly out of the apartment complex and onto the boulevard. No sirens.

"Do not lose them." Rousso concentrated on planning an attack if necessary.

The ambulance weaved in and out of neighborhood streets toward the highway. When it entered I-580 headed north, the vehicle sped up. The siren screamed.

The bitch is alive.

He checked his pistol, the silenced pistol Willy used to take care of Inglish. Clicked off the safety. "They must not reach the hospital."

Willy gaped at him in astonishment. "You gonna shoot at an ambulance? In traffic?"

"Theatrical, yes, but I—*we*—have no choice. I am a good shot. At the hospital, guards and many people could identify us. In traffic, I have the element of surprise. I assume your handsome face appears in local police records?"

Reality slapped the thug's mouth shut. He accelerated, staying one car behind as the siren cleared the left lanes for the ambulance's passage. After a few exits, the ambulance moved toward the right lane and signaled to exit. The sign read Beaumont Avenue.

"That's the exit for Highland General," Willy said.

Rousso lowered the passenger window. "Go! You must be closer. Be ready to brake."

The highway angled higher, above the wide avenue below. *Perfect.*

The ambulance zipped down the curving exit ramp, their stolen sedan on its rear bumper. Rousso released his safety belt and leaned out the window. He fired three shots in succession at the ambulance's rear right tire.

The third shot connected but the ambulance kept going.

He cursed and fired more shots. He would shred the damned tire if required. He did not care who witnessed this. He would be gone in moments.

The tire went flat. Black strips flew away as the rim chewed through rubber. Sparks fired like shooting stars as metal hit pavement.

Rousso ducked inside the car. "Brake, Willy. Now!"

Willy stomped on the brakes. Gripped the wheel against the fishtailing sway.

Rousso jerked against his shoulder harness. The force exploded agony in his arm.

Brakes screeched. Behind them a box truck jerked to a halt. Horns blared.

Ahead, the ambulance snaked along as the driver

tried to gain control. It careened sideways and toppled over the ramp's edge onto the surface below. The top-heavy ambulance rolled over. Once. Twice.

With the crunching of metal and plastic came screams of terror and pain. Finally the vehicle settled on its side, crumpled and silent between the off ramp and the traffic-filled street.

Willy swallowed hard and looked to Rousso for orders.

"Drive closer. Keep down. I must make certain my work is finished."

****

Mara sat on Danita Inglish's pretty blue-flowered sofa with her handbag clutched in her lap. She tried not to look toward the kitchen where the crime-scene techs were still working. A gunshot, not a knife wound, she'd heard a policeman say. Maybe Danita used the knife to defend herself.

EMTs had long since taken the poor woman to the hospital but the cloying smell of her wound hung in the air. Mara needed no reminder. Blood smeared her pants legs. She'd tossed her orange jacket, stained with rusty crimson, into the crime scene techs' evidence bag. She couldn't bear to wear it again anyway.

While the detective questioned Cort in Danita's bedroom, she might have time to get answers from DSF. She had to do more than just sit and wait. She and Cort would have to talk to the woman's daughter sometime, to find out if she knew of a ring piece. Mara ached at the image of them accusing the injured—if she made it—mother of being involved in the crime. The daughter would probably throw them out with nothing. But they had to try.

Fingers trembling, she keyed Sandi a message asking for the daughter's address and the SUV's owner. *DI shot. Nd dtr Ellen Plante addy. Nd owner lic nmbr bgng 3AAL. ASAP.*

Finished, she looked up, expecting to see Cort leave the bedroom. *Hoping* to see him was more like it. He was her rock in the middle of all the chaos Leon Jones's demise had unleashed. He was becoming more important to her than she wanted to admit. A hard man, he was gentle with her, treating her more like a partner than she'd expected.

She wanted true love with the right man, not just passion. Passion fooled a woman into thinking she'd found true love only to discover he was the wrong man. And yet she couldn't deny her passion for him. Or his for her. Yet when this was over, he would return to the wilds of Maine and solve that problem.

Sandi's reply jarred her from her thoughts. *OMG. UOK?*

OK, Mara typed. *TY.* Thank you. She slipped the phone into her bag. Okay? Sort of. Every nerve in her body vibrated but she was holding it together. Tears, but no nausea. No panic attack.

She and Cort had taken turns trying to staunch the blood until the EMTs arrived. She couldn't do CPR because of the wound's placement. Before anyone arrived, she and Cort agreed to reveal only why they were there—to investigate whether her father was involved with the Jeweler after the robbery—but nothing about the puzzle ring.

First uniforms, then a detective questioned them. The Asian detective with a shaved head possessed a laconic manner. Deadpan, he scribbled in a small notebook as she related what had happened.

She tried to describe the man who assaulted Cort but all she could really be sure of was his mammoth size. It all happened so fast, she told him. The detective showed more animation, a lift of his sparse eyebrows, when she recited the beginning sequence of the SUV's license plate.

That had been more than half an hour ago. He sent the vehicle information somewhere to be checked and told her to wait here while he questioned Cort.

The bedroom door opened. The detective emerged talking on his cell phone.

Cort walked out behind him. His gaze searched for her, the set of his shoulders and his mouth easing when he found her. The softening of his gray eyes wound heat through her in spite of her resolve and these circumstances. He joined her on the sofa.

"You look like you're making it," he said, perusing her face.

She nodded. "Guess I'm toughening up."

"That, and the attack wasn't personal this time. You jumped into action to help that woman. Impressive as hell." His eyes flickered over her, the admiration in their depths a virtual caress that tickled awareness across the surface of her skin.

A flush heated her cheeks. "Mr. Devlin makes sure all his employees can perform basic emergency techniques. This is the first time I've ever had to use the training for anything but a drill. Do you think she'll live?"

As reply, he curved an arm around her shoulders and kissed her forehead. She wanted his warmth, needed it. And the strength of his arm around her. His familiar scent comforted her, but the tension in his body said he was seething with frustration and fury. He might need her support just as much.

"Maybe we can talk to her in the hospital," she said.

The detective strode into the room, a grim look on his face.

"Any luck finding the green SUV?" Cort let his arm drop away from her as he stood. But he reached for her hand, and she grasped the lifeline as she rose to her feet.

"That's the least of my worries at the moment." The detective rubbed his nape. "Might as well tell you. All the local news channels will broadcast it soon. The ambulance crashed at the interstate exit to the hospital."

She shot to her feet. "Danita! Is she—"

His head shake cut off her question. "Looks like they were forced off the road. Inglish, the driver, and the two EMTs, all dead. Bullet to the head."

No. She slumped against Cort's side. That poor woman had fought for her life against those monsters. She took a shuddering breath, dug for control.

"Was it that SUV? Any witnesses?" Barely seeming to breathe, Cort waited, rigid.

"There were pile-ups. The crash happened too fast." The detective's jaw was tight. "The killer fled the scene in a light-colored Ford sedan, only thing we know for sure. No descriptions of the shooter yet. He must've figured Inglish could ID them."

"They switched cars. They must have," Mara said. "Stolen?"

"Good guess. Officer answered a car-jacking call at a Safeway not far from here. Two men dragged a shopper at gunpoint from her car." Tight-lipped, he shook his head at the casual violence. "Officer spotted the green SUV in the lot. Stolen plates."

He turned to Cort. "This professional-style hit goes a long way toward clearing you two of any suspicion. But don't leave town. And I'll need the number of that FBI agent."

"You have the address where we're staying across the bay," Cort said, pulling out his wallet. "Here's Special Agent Al Kaplan's card."

While the two men finished talking, Mara reached for her phone for something to do with her shaking hands. A message from Sandi gave Ellen Plante's address but indicated the license number would take longer.

Mara keyed, *TY addy. Lic NM.* License, never mind.

Chapter Seventeen

CORT LEFT A voice-mail message for Kaplan. Toss-up who'd get to the agent first—him or the detective. He needed Kaplan to clear them with the Oakland PD so they could leave town.

The two-story penthouse owned by Devlin Security Force was in an exclusive area south of Market Street and only blocks from the bay. Mara had supposed that if not for the fog creeping in, they could see the Bay Bridge from the bank of living room windows.

Devlin had good taste, for damn sure. Or his people did. Leather-upholstered furniture and paintings with objects or scenes a man could recognize, not just smears of color. Although the dining room boasted computer connections and desks along the wall, the table and chairs were of real cherry. Table had a classy touch—lengthwise strips of walnut and American holly down the center.

On the way from Oakland, Mara had phoned her mother to postpone their dinner until tomorrow. After they looked around the condo, she disappeared with her overnight bag into the en suite bedroom. Said she needed some time alone. He couldn't blame her.

What he needed was some hot, sweaty sex with her to get the frustration out of his system. Physically he craved her with a need that steamed his blood. Mentally, he liked her, admired her grit, her chisel-sharp mind. She didn't deserve... no, not going there. He couldn't afford to feel more than heat.

For now he'd opt for a different kind of exercise. He had plenty of time for a good work-out in the mini-gym that took up the third bedroom. On his way to change, he heard feet pounding on the treadmill. He was pulling on shorts when his cell rang. *Kaplan.*

"You've been a busy boy," the FBI agent said.

Damn, the detective got to him first. And double damn, Cort hadn't informed Kaplan he was headed west. "I suppose the cop told you all about it."

"I got the official version. I'd like yours." The rapid clicking of his nails on his desk announced the level of his irritation.

Cort gave him the condensed version before adding, "We're going to try to talk to Danita Inglish's daughter. Maybe she knows about the ring piece. A long shot but all we have."

"Now you see what the FBI has faced."

At least nobody'd died while the Feds investigated. But Danita Inglish would've been targeted regardless of what *he* did. "Now it's worse. Leon's death has invited a free-for-all."

"I do have something for you. Three days after the Jeweler's death, a man named Rolf Rousso took a Lufthansa flight from Munich to Boston. My contact at Interpol said they believe he's an agent of Centaur. Rousso's only one of several aliases. Traveled on a Polish passport. They're sending me a description and photo."

"He could be the big-nosed guy who followed me in the Metro." Maybe Cort would recognize the man. "You have any news about the break-in at Hauptman's house?"

"Hauptman? First I've heard of it."

Cort sat on the king bed and jammed his feet into sneakers. "Mara phoned Twyla Hauptman on Sunday. The woman complained about a break-in Saturday night. Didn't say what they took, only that they trashed the place. Said she told the cops about us, that we hassled her. Accused us of the burglary. But the local cops there haven't contacted either one of us."

"I'll check with Montgomery County PD," Kaplan said. "Anything from her on a ring piece?"

"Claims she went through her husband's stuff and came up empty."

"Do you believe her?"

"I don't believe anybody. Not until this plays out. Will you clear it with the detective here so we can head back east?"

"Not up to me. I verified your story. That's all. How do I know you're not involved?"

Kaplan had another call and disconnected. What the hell? Now *he* was pulling back? Afraid he'd get burned if Cort and Mara had something to do with killing Inglish? Cort was right in the first place not to trust the FBI. Bunch of suspicious paranoids.

Shit, how long would he be stuck in a holding pattern? Picturing Inglish shot and bleeding out in the wreckage of the ambulance, he grimaced.

They needed to return to D.C. Mara had to get back to work, and he had other possible accomplices to chase while they continued to play house for the benefit of the Clone Brothers. The week remaining wasn't much time to interview two more security guards and the museum director. He grabbed a gray T-shirt as he headed for the "gym."

He froze in the doorway, mesmerized. In lime green nylon shorts and a tank top, Mara jogged on the treadmill. The flexing of her toned body and strong legs made his mouth water. But she wasn't in the mood for sex, he reminded himself. Biting back expletives, he sketched a wave as he headed for the free weights. She dipped her head in greeting. Maybe she was so in the zone she wouldn't notice his body's condition, all too obvious in thin cotton shorts.

Warm-up had a whole new meaning. Eyeing the banana seat on the stationary bike, he scowled. Symbolism and more torture. And a ride meant staring either at the floor or at Mara on the treadmill. He swallowed and eased onto the torture seat before pumping his legs. The exertion would distract him.

Yeah, right.

Then his gaze zeroed in on the damp spot on the cotton between her breasts.

His leg rhythm faltered and the bike's sprocket protested loudly. Shit. Enough. He'd grab the treadmill when she was done. He mopped his face with a towel from a stack, then tossed off his already soaked T-shirt. He selected a weight. His biceps routine would be something he could get into. He'd forget all about the delectable female across the room.

Right arm and then left, he strained with each set of curls until his arms screamed and sweat poured from his chin and ears. Satisfied he'd given his muscles enough stress, he deposited the weights in the rack. He mopped his head and chest with the towel, and then glanced at her.

His gaze tangled with hers. The naked hunger on

her face made him gasp for breath. She was walking her cool-down but there was nothing cool in her gaze.

"Like what you see?" He spread his arms and grinned.

"Not anything I haven't seen before." The cheeky toss of her head flipped her ponytail.

"But something you want. Your eyes don't lie, sweetheart." His speeding pulse had nothing to do with his workout. He crossed to the treadmill. "Enough of a workout."

"Time for stress reliever sex?" Another flip of hair and she kept walking. But she was chewing one corner of her mouth.

For the first time he noticed her eyes were red. "You've been crying. I damn near broke down myself. Inglish didn't deserve that, no matter what she did."

"I started changing clothes and it all came crashing down on me. Guess I needed a good cry. I'm okay now." Her chin quivered but she shook off the emotion. "I heard your phone ring. Kaplan?" Her gaze flicked from his face to skim his body.

She hadn't cooled off. Neither had he. "Yeah. I don't want to talk about that."

And then he did the damnedest thing. He hauled her off the treadmill and into his arms. Before she could resist, he lowered his head and captured her mouth. Damn, he loved her taste. Her mouth felt soft as silk under his, and she smelled of spring beneath the sweat. Gradually she swayed into him with a little sigh, becoming soft and pliable, fitting just right against his body.

"You don't want *me*," she murmured against his lips even as she pressed her breast into his palm. "It's just the stress. We don't—"

"Have anything in common but our mutual goal. I know. But this chemistry between us says that doesn't matter. We're combustible in bed. And we need a break from reality."

She clutched at him, her cheek against his shoulder, her short nails scraping his skin.

Heat burned through his skin, and his body clenched so hard he ached. Heat poured through him. She had to feel his straining arousal pressing against her belly.

She lowered her lashes and swayed in his arms. And then she kissed him back.

Their tongues met and danced together as she gave herself up to the moment. He pulled her tank top loose and found the soft skin of her belly. As if on auto-pilot, his hand glided upward to push her sports bra aside and cup the fullness of her breast.

After a moment, she leaned back, gasping. "We're both all sweaty."

"There's a remedy for that." Grinning like a fool, he scooped her up in his arms.

Mara would've protested but he kept her mouth too busy as he carried her down the hall. And the man could kiss. A hot mouth that grazed and nipped and melted, urgent sweeps of tongue that sent shock waves of need along her spine and made her lips cling to his. She reveled in the heat and rough texture of his skin, inhaled his scent. Something about him was different, something addictive, and her inability to hold back a measure of herself scared her.

The warm shades of the tan and umber bathroom tiles seemed to wrap around them. He let her slide down the length of his big body until she stood, still wrapped in his arms, still captured by his mouth. If he released her, she wasn't sure her legs would support her.

He caressed her skin from her throat, to her breasts, and across her stomach. The calluses on his hands heightened the sensation, heating her skin every place he touched. His index finger teased back and forth beneath the waistband of her nylon jogging shorts. She closed her eyes, hunger tingling, throbbing, licking through her belly and up her spine.

When he removed his hand, she opened her eyes to see him staring at her with an intensity that stopped her breath. Somehow without her realizing, he'd divested himself of his shorts and sneakers. She'd seen all that hot, smooth skin, the roughness and power, bared for her before, but not glistening like wet marble. The urge sparked and flared to touch every line and angle—the contours of his shoulders, the bulges and sinews of his muscles.

More scars marred his skin, slashing white ones across his torso, knife scars from defending himself in prison. She wanted to kiss each one, soothe him with her mouth. How had he come out of that hellish place as whole as he was?

Her heart gave a solid kick against her sternum before taking off like Serena Williams chasing a corner power serve. She held his hard-hewn face between her hands, studying the raw, primitive need in his eyes. She reached into the double-size, tiled shower stall to flip on the hot water. She yanked off her sneakers and scooped off her shorts and panties. "What I said before still goes. We're all wrong for each other."

He swallowed, seemed to force himself to meet her gaze. "Still warning the ex-con?"

"Ditch the ex-con crap. You say you don't trust others but it's really yourself you don't trust. This is casual, a temporary affair, nothing more." She crossed mental fingers she could keep that promise to herself.

A shadow flickered in his eyes before he shuttered his expression. Most men would do handstands of gratitude for a woman who wanted no strings. Most of the time he was stoic and remote. Wasn't he the one who insisted on casual? She didn't get it. But the pain she'd glimpsed in his eyes was real and raw.

"Sweet," he finally said, his voice rough. "We're clear on that." He grabbed protection from the stash someone had left in the medicine cabinet and reached for her. His dark pewter gaze promised sensual, slow pleasure.

And then they were mouth to mouth, skin to skin, the water sluicing over them, washing away second thoughts, rinsing away *all* thought. She licked his skin, tasted his salty passion. Giving herself up to the deep longing within, she reached for him, felt him jerk in her hand, hot with the same need that stirred her.

His fingers delved into her, driving her higher until she went boneless. "I have to have you *now*."

And then nothing was slow. Not his need, not hers. He lifted her against him so her legs gripped him, and pleasure exploded as he entered her. The three shower nozzles wrapped them together in a curtain of water and steam. He continued to caress her and kiss her, his skillful touch stoking heat, unfurling pleasure, unraveling control. He knew what she wanted, what she needed without her speaking, not that she could utter anything but a strangled cry.

Pressure lapped higher and higher as he moved within her, and her senses reeled. It was too much. He wanted more than she wanted to give of herself. She flung her head back, breathless, gasping, panic sharpening to an unbearable pitch. His possession shot shock waves through her—too intense, too primitive, too powerful. *No, I can't.*

"Mara, let yourself go." His whisper was rough, his breath hot against her skin. "Fly for me. Don't fight it."

Water beat on her head, coursed through her hair as she searched for balance and sanity. She found only him, around her, inside her, body and soul. A hot flash of sensation flooded her legs, her belly, her entire being in a huge, pulsating wave and she clutched at him and cried out, unable to fight him or herself anymore.

And then he surged against her and gasped his release in a guttural roar.

Moments later, rubber-legged and blissed-out, she realized she was again standing—with his support. He soaped them both and turned her to let the water rinse her. Dazed, she barely noticed when he turned off the now tepid water and tossed her a towel.

As he stepped out of the shower stall to dry, he watched her, studied her with those penetrating eyes.

She angled away to hide. As if it wasn't already way too late. Oh God, she'd let go with him and flown. Dangerously high. He'd wrung from her every drop of pleasure and emotion the way she was twisting the water from her dripping hair. And God help her, she wanted him again. With the towel he tossed her, she wrapped the long, tangled mess turban-style. She accepted another towel and dried off, still standing in the shower stall. Away from him.

A glance at him tightened her stomach. He seemed to take up the entire bathroom. Naked, all sexy-eyed and gorgeous. What the hell could she do now to resist him? Necessary, until she got her emotions under control. So casual it was. Wrapping the towel around her for some modesty, she stepped onto the soft bath rug and steadied herself before she met his avid gaze.

He closed the gap between them and pressed her power-button tattoo. His eyes held a wicked gleam and his grin dented the dimple in his cheek. The man didn't play fair.

She batted his hand away. Already his touch was arousing a shivery sensation. "Down, boy. Hey, it must be getting late. We ought to get dressed and go find some dinner."

He cupped her chin, his eyes probing her face, consternation crimping his brow. "Don't act like nothing special happened between us, Mara. We nearly flew over the Golden Gate Bridge."

"No, we did. I mean... I just—"

She didn't know what he saw on her face but suddenly he wrapped his arms around her. "You're afraid. And this time it's not our bad guys. What are you afraid of?"

"Nothing. You're reading too much into the situation."

"You were struggling with something a minute ago. You afraid of me?"

Yes. And of myself and how much I dare give, how much I care. She wriggled away. "Get out. Aren't you the one who said this was casual? Then chill."

"Chill? With you, sweetheart, cooling off isn't

possible. It's still early. Dinner can wait. You've whetted my appetite but not for food."

Before she could object, he scooped her up—again—and marched off to their bedroom. "Hey, what are you doing? Put me down," she sputtered. But an old sci-fi line came back to her: *Resistance is futile.* Especially when down deep she wanted the inevitable.

He dumped her in the middle of the king bed and followed her down, kneeling over her. One side at a time, as if opening the petals of a flower, he peeled back her towel. "I rushed you in the shower. This time's for you."

****

Later they ate dinner at a sidewalk bistro down the block. With color in her cheeks and her lips plumped from his kisses, she looked sexy and well loved. And elegant as always, dressed in black pants and a black silk shirt under the new grass-green jacket she'd bought that afternoon to replace her ruined one. He couldn't wait to get all that off her again.

He ordered steak and she chose pasta.

"Need to replenish all that testosterone with some red meat, big guy?" she teased.

"Read into it whatever you want, sweetheart. I notice you ordered carbs."

She laughed and lifted her wine glass to him. "Touché. Enjoy your steak."

He told her about Kaplan's call. When she heard the agent offered as much support as the trap door beneath a hanged man, she dropped her forkful of seafood linguini. "Suspects? *Us?* He's an idiot!" If Kaplan were there, her irate look would've reduced him to cinders.

"Ex-con here, remember?" Cort said.

Her eyes widened in comprehension. So did his.

Did she forget he'd spent four years in prison? Did she forget he'd committed that robbery along with Leon? The honest bewilderment and affront on her face said she did. He'd never known anybody to think of him without his damn sins on their mind. Then there was that odd thing she'd said about not trusting himself. Made sense in a weird sort of way. Not that he'd let himself get all mushy. Best not to read too much into anything.

She twitched her shoulders in dismissal of his reminder. "You were in for burglary, not cold-blooded murder. Besides, we called 911 to report the attack."

"Happens all the time. I heard cons talk all the time about reporting their own crime to draw suspicion away from themselves that way. Didn't work. They were in prison."

Her look of rebuke and disgust before she returned to her pasta was for the cops or maybe the dumb crooks, not him. He hoped.

When they arrived back at the condo, he expected to pick up where they'd left off. She burned hot and bright in his arms, and he wanted her again. She popped into his mind when he least expected. When he was trying to figure out the puzzle of the ring pieces and their murderous competitors, she wrapped herself around his thoughts and he wanted to know what she thought, felt, wanted. He wanted to bounce ideas off her. And hell, yes, he wanted her in his bed.

But his craving for her was because of the danger. Nothing more. He'd had great sex before. He couldn't remember when exactly but he must've. He could keep their relationship just friends, just business except for the sex. He was fine alone. No problem.

As they reached the top of the stairs, he started to follow her to the master suite.

She turned, placing a hand on his arm. "Casual, remember, Jones?"

"Affair, remember, Marton? That means sex, or it meant sex in our recent past."

"Sex doesn't have to mean always sleeping together." When he gaped at her, she rose on tiptoes to brush a light kiss across his mouth. "Not tonight. Please. First, flying on the red-eye, then... well, I need a good night's sleep before facing Mom tomorrow."

Chapter Eighteen

CORT OPENED HIS eyes and stretched, thinking of the woman who'd kept him awake hoping she'd come to his bed. Or invite him into hers.

To his amazement, Mara'd been the one to quote his demand for casual, no-involvement sex. So why the hell did that bug him? He'd gotten what he wanted. More than once. His body was singing hallelujah. But casual? Not hardly. So he spent the rest of the night in this bed alone, wanting her and wondering why she'd fought her orgasm in the shower. Afterward she hadn't held back. He ought to decide if he really wanted to know what the hell was going on.

He swung out of bed, lowering his feet to the plush dark red carpet. He pulled on jeans and a shirt and hit the bathroom. No sounds throughout the condo, only the distant intrusion of a jet overhead and a car horn below. If Mara was still sleeping, he should wake her. Time to plan strategy.

He padded barefoot down the hall. Rounding the corner to the master suite's door, he skidded to a halt. The door stood ajar. Was it open before? The suite contained its own bath so no need to use the hall one.

"Mara?"

No answer.

He pushed the door inward and entered the room. Bedcovers tossed back on the king-size bed, suitcase open on a luggage rack, bathroom door wide, toiletries lined up on the vanity. He called her name again.

Silence.

No reason to panic. Yeah, she'd backed off after dinner but she hadn't split. Not without her clothing. Without the code, nobody could've gotten in here and carted her off. So where the hell did the woman go? She knew running around out there was dangerous. His gut started a slow freeze.

He dashed to the other bedroom and jammed on his boots before stomping down the stairs. Where he was going to look for her, he wasn't sure, but he couldn't just pace the floor. He opened the door to see—her.

"Thanks," Mara said brightly, a big smile on her face. "I was having trouble managing everything."

He shoved the door, barely caught it before it slammed. Was about to ream her out for scaring the bejesus out of him when he spied what she was carrying—a fiberboard coffee holder containing two humongous coffee cups and a paper bag marked José's Bagels. He closed his mouth with an audible click of teeth.

"The kitchen has no food, nothing except state-of-the-art equipment. DSF's people must order supplies delivered when they plan to be here." She handed him the coffee and bagels before depositing her bag and jacket on a nearby chair.

He gripped the breakfast. Otherwise he'd drag her into his arms to reassure himself she was okay. Judging from the speed at which she'd run away from him after dinner last night, she wouldn't welcome an embrace. If ever again. Smarter for both of them.

"Going out alone here is dangerous," he instructed.

"Those two scumbags know we saw them yesterday. They might think we can identify them. And what if the colonel's men found a way to follow us?"

When she angled her head at his harsh tone, he tried to relax his features. But she merely smiled indulgently, no more frightened by the Murder One scowl than if he'd launched into a lullaby. Although his singing might make her run screaming.

"You were worried about me. I'm sorry," she said gently, as if to a child. "I didn't want to wake you until I could offer coffee. Everything bagels and cream cheese. Toasted. Still warm." Her beaming smile disarmed his ire. She looked good enough to eat, in slim jeans and a low-necked red top and with her ebony hair draped forward over her shoulders.

Immediately he felt the tension drain from his gut. "Don't go off alone again, okay?"

"Only to see my mom." She pried the food containers from his death grip and whipped to the kitchen. "Although I can't imagine how any of those guys would be able to find us at this address. And I went out the rear of the building."

His gut knotted again. Then her thoughtful gesture hit him and he followed her to the kitchen. "Hey, thanks for the breakfast. I need the coffee."

Mara sighed her relief as she set down the containers on the dining table. "Colombian, black, the way you like it." She gathered napkins—no paper ones in this kitchen, only dark-blue cloth—knives, and two square blue plates and arranged them on the table.

She'd managed to keep her cool in spite of wanting to throw herself at him as soon as he opened the door. She flipped the lids off both venti paper cups and inhaled the chocolate steam of her non-fat, no-whip, no-foam mocha before she drank a bracing swallow. Totally sweet he'd been worried about her. She grinned.

His lovemaking had banished the horrors of yesterday and replaced fear with pleasure. He was tender and sexy, forceful and demanding, and she yielded to what her body and soul wanted. Needed. She could fight this tangling of her mind and heart. Sure.

"Mara, you can't play ignorant," he said. "At least some of the bad guys have known our every move so far. Why not now?"

"That same question haunts me. That and the sight of Danita Inglish bleeding on her kitchen floor." She slid his coffee toward him.

He lifted the cup and took a healthy drink. "Idiotic pretentious name. Why venti and not extra large?"

"*Venti* is Italian for *twenty*, as in twenty ounces."

"Pretentious." He glared at the cup. "Like I said."

No argument from her on that. She returned to his other question. "Only that detective knows where we are."

"And Thomas Devlin." Shaking his head, he slathered cream cheese on his bagel.

They needed a distraction. He'd never been to San Francisco before so... "We shouldn't bother Danita's daughter until tomorrow. We have the day until I meet Mom for dinner. How'd you like to see the city?"

****

Seeing the city suited Cort just fine. Spending the day with this beautiful woman walking by his side and putting their quest on hold was strategy of a sort. Mara had phoned to arrange a meeting tomorrow with Inglish's daughter. To their surprise, Ellen Plante didn't slam down the phone. She sounded eager to talk to them.

The day was theirs. If Mara wanted to pretend nothing odd happened between them last night, he'd go with it. For now. But he had questions.

She set a mean pace in green sneakers that amazingly matched her jacket. She carried another of those big-ass bags she favored, this one somehow strapped onto her back as a backpack. About nine o'clock, they'd set out on foot toward public transit. As the morning wore on, the heavy blanket of fog retreated to the bay but a cloud cover kept the day cool.

"We'll hit the highlights if it's okay with you," she said. "I haven't done this since Mom moved here six years ago."

"Sounds good."

The glass window of a Chinese noodle restaurant reflected nobody paying them undue attention. No sign of the Clone Brothers. Or anybody with a military demeanor. As they passed the place where Mara bought their coffees, he checked a man watching the crowd from beneath the small awning. Nondescript, well dressed, not somebody he'd seen before, but Centaur could afford to pay local thugs. When a blonde woman ran up to the man, the two embraced and set off together across the street.

"We clear? No bad guys?" Mara said.

Reading his mind again or had he sighed in relief? He didn't know. Her intuition ought to bother him but for some reason he liked it. "So far."

She laughed.

"I keep thinking about the bad guys, who they are, how many, what they know."

"What do *we* know so far?"

"Spoken like a true research geek," he said, giving her hand a gentle squeeze. He liked the way her mind worked. "We know this shadowy Centaur syndicate wants the jewels. Centaur could have sent dozens of agents for all we know. The Gramornia royal family sent an agent into the country to retrieve them. And the rival prime minister sent security police to stop me from retrieving them."

"We don't know which group killed Danita Inglish or if it's the same people who killed Dante Falco." When he started to comment on her change of heart, she continued, "Yes, I do think he was murdered. Definitely. After yesterday, how could I not?" Her shoulders moved in a shudder of revulsion.

"I'm betting the violence is on Centaur. Devlin said the group is ruthless," Cort said. "Although Colonel Yerik would have no qualms about murder, he has more reason to leave our suspects alone than he does to attack them. The royals might have their spy investigate, even tail us, but murder? I doubt it. But it's all speculation."

"So it boils down to we don't know much at all. Two possible accomplices are dead. We haven't found any ring pieces. Or any proof of my dad's innocence."

He shook his head. No, they had zip. And so did the FBI. But the domino he'd set in action should take down one set of bad guys before too long. If all went according to plan. If not, the downside yanked on that frozen knot in his gut.

They turned left on the wide boulevard of Market Street and continued to the cable-car turntable at the foot of Powell, where one of the tram-like cars was just making its rotation. The brown-uniformed gripman maneuvered a tall handle to walk the wooden turntable around, turning the cable car with it. A crowd of tourists snapped pictures of the operation.

"We taking that?" He nodded toward the red-and-wood-toned vehicle with San Francisco Municipal Railway on the side.

At the small-boy excitement he couldn't keep from his tone, she gave him a knowing smile. "A great way to see the city, nice and slow, up and down the hills. We can get off at the edge of Chinatown, board again later, and ride it the rest of the way."

They paid the three-dollar each fare and climbed aboard. They grabbed places at the end of a wooden bench facing outward. When a family of four wedged onto the seat, Cort scooted close to Mara and curved his arm around her shoulders.

No rumble of an internal-combustion engine, only clatter and click as the cable car rolled along its metal rails. The climb up the steep incline of Powell Street offered a spectacular view of the city.

"An Englishman who made wire cable for mines came up with the idea for the cable cars," she said. "When a horse-drawn streetcar slipped on a wet hillside, he saw the horses killed and wanted to prevent more accidents. The first cable-car line went into service in 1873. At one time there were cable car lines all over the city but the 1906 earthquake destroyed many. Now the city has only two lines. There's a museum farther along the route if you want to see how they work."

"You know I would." Her eagerness to show him exactly what he'd enjoy warmed him more than the rays of sunlight peeking through the cloud cover.

Casual? Hardly. Shit.

****

Rousso buried his nose in his guide book and pulled the baseball cap he had just purchased lower over his face. Pretending to plan his afternoon, he backed deeper into the shade of a restaurant awning from where he could see his targets watching the lazy antics of sea lions.

He could not find their hotel but tracking credit-card purchases led him to the street. Luckily he spotted them this morning. Crowds made it easy to follow at a distance. He did not find Inglish's ring piece in her tawdry apartment, which meant Jones and Marton did not have it either. So what were they doing? Was this sightseeing day a ploy to fool him into thinking they had given up?

His cell phone buzzed. When he saw the caller's number, his blood chilled. His boss, the head of Centaur. The man known only as Z had created the sprawling network in only a few short years, with contacts in many countries. Some said his family used to have money but lost everything in a scandal. Others said he was ex U.S. military. Whatever the truth, Rousso feared the man more than he admired him.

Before the phone could ring again, he punched the button. "Rousso here."

"You've called attention to yourself," the Centaur boss said without preamble. The gruff quality of his voice put Rousso in mind of a knife being sharpened. "I don't like publicity of any sort but witnesses? News broadcasts?"

"I can explain, Mr. Z. No one—"

"Fuck the explanation! Your attack on the

208

ambulance was on television. CNN, Fox, all the networks. No more publicity. Do you fucking understand?"

His Adam's apple bobbed painfully as he swallowed the bile creeping up his throat. He nodded automatically. "Yes, sir. No more fallout. I promise you."

"Where are Jones and the woman now?"

He glanced from his shade to where they had their heads together. "They are standing on the dock at Fisherman's Wharf."

"Fisherman's Wharf? Details."

"I followed them to Chinatown, where Jones bought trinkets, souvenirs, and she bought a bag. My taxi followed their cable car back down the hill to here, where they strolled the shops of Pier 39 and ate Dungeness crab at one of the seaside restaurants. Now they watch sea lions. Sir." He braced himself for Z's reaction.

"*Sightseeing?*" Z's voice boomed, the commanding voice according to rumor he'd perfected during his military career. "What about Inglish's ring piece?"

"They do not seem to be searching. But I do not believe they possess it already," he hastened to add.

Silence. Rousso wiped a palm on his trouser leg. Wished he knew more about Z.

"You have two ring pieces, correct?" Z asked.

"Yes, sir. I obtained the thief Falco's and I have access to another."

"Then quit dicking around and get the one Jones has. He has the Jeweler's or his own. Three should be enough to lead us to the treasure. I need those crown jewels. I have five bidders who are on the phone to me hourly. Are you able to do what I ask?"

Rousso fervently hoped so. His future depended on it. He had not attempted to accost Jones, except when he and Willy needed to escape yesterday. Jones had the hard look of prison, was big and strong. Judging from yesterday, he knew how to fight. "Obtaining Jones's ring piece will mean eliminating him. Maybe the woman."

"She works for Devlin, right?"

Rousso frowned, perplexed by the non sequitur and more so by the smile he heard in Z's voice. "She does."

"Then do her."

Chapter Nineteen

MARA LOOKED UP from the crowded floats and inhaled the sea air redolent with salt and seaweed. In the distance was the Golden Gate Bridge, a ray of afternoon sunlight through the clouds glinting rusty red off its girders.

"Too long since I came to enjoy this view." So far they'd laughed and enjoyed the day without anything more serious than his occasional check for someone tailing them.

Sightseeing and talking about the city's history kept things light, the way she wanted it. Even with her slight slip when he'd fingered a silk scarf in one of the Chinatown shops.

"For someone special back in Maine?" she'd said.

"Office manager at the woodworking school."

"Ah," she said. The gorgeous design featured a dragon in brilliant blues and reds and would look fabulous with her black suit. Not that she'd let on. She had no cause to be possessive, no right to care. "Any woman would like that scarf."

He tossed her the dimpled grin that always weakened her knees. "Jealous?"

His blatant male satisfaction at her obvious attitude further prickled. Her own fault. She'd been too transparent, but she pasted on a sunny smile. "Just curious."

"The woman runs everything, a good woman to keep happy. She's also married and has five kids ages five to sixteen."

Relief doused her ire. Dammit, no cause to feel relief either. "Then by all means, buy her that scarf."

In the end he'd also selected key chains depicting the Chinatown Gate and other city landmarks for the kids while Mara bought a handbag. They spent an hour in the Cable Car Museum before continuing their ride downhill.

She pointed across the water. "Over there is Ghirardelli Square, where the chocolate factory used to be. Now it's mostly shops. Beyond it is Pacific Heights."

"There to our left, Telegraph Hill?" Cort asked. "What's the tower?"

She nodded, pleased he was as interested in the historical surroundings as she was. "Coit Tower, built in the 1930's to honor the fire brigades, as they used to call them. The top is rumored to be shaped like a fire hose nozzle but I don't see the resemblance."

"Guess you'd have to be closer. Or be a fire fighter." He pointed to where one of the smaller sea lions tried to push its way into the crush of animals on a float. The youngster flopped into the water with a big splash. It swam to another float, more crowded than the last. Sea lions piled on top of each other, their massive weight nearly sinking the floats.

"These guys disappeared for a while but came back and are again a nuisance," she said. "Too many of them but killing them is illegal. They climb on boats and private docks as well as here where they're welcome."

"A twist on that old joke about where a gorilla

sleeps." Cort slung his arm around her and kissed her temple.

Tucked close to him, she felt protected and at peace, a moment of calm in their dangerous quest.

"Can't see Chinatown from here," he said.

"No, it's back the other way."

"Your mom must not live in Chinatown or you'd have mentioned it earlier."

"Of course not," she said, arching away to gape up at him. "Mom's Korean."

"Sorry. Dumb mistake." He held up his hands in surrender.

"No, my fault for being overly sensitive." She returned to his embrace. "The ethnic separations are ancient. Chinatown is exclusively Chinese. Not many other Asians live or work there. L.A. has a Koreatown but not San Francisco. The main Korean enclaves are out in the Avenues, near Golden Gate Park. That's where Mom lives with my aunt and uncle."

The breeze blew her hair into her face and she brushed it away. Too long. Since they'd begun their search, she hadn't taken time for a cut or styling.

He released her and turned to lean against the railing. A tress fell across her breast, and he rubbed the strands between his fingers. "Beautiful. Bouncy and alive."

She met his eyes and felt herself falling into their gray depths, like losing herself in an impenetrable fog. He made her feel too much. He bent forward and their mouths touched and fitted together for a greedy moment. She gripped his shoulders and clung to him, diving into his addictive taste.

When he eased away, he caressed her cheek, her

jaw, his fingers trembling. His expression was unreadable in the afternoon shadows that cut deep across his face. "Mara, about last night."

Her stomach squeezed. *Here it comes.* She couldn't head him off with a protest that others were listening. The other sea-lion watchers had moved off toward the street. A lone man stood beneath an awning perusing a guide book but he was too far away to hear their conversation. "What do you mean?"

"You. Me. We have this connection, and I can't ignore it. And neither can you, although you try to." He leaned closer so his intense gaze bored into her. "Sweetheart, having you come for me more than once is a major turn-on, but seeing you fight it isn't exactly an ego booster. Care to tell me what that's about?"

She averted her gaze but couldn't focus on the sea lions. "You're imagining things."

"You said that last night. Didn't wash then. Doesn't now. You have a damn good memory but mine's not bad. I recall you saying something to your sister about not being like your mom. Am I getting warm?"

She bent her head and chewed her lip. This family secret was so personal. But *personal* was what they'd been last night and many nights before. "My parents met in San Francisco when Dad was just starting out with Global Insurance. I don't have all the details. But Mom was the hostess in her brother-in-law's restaurant. She's doing the same job again. They married eight weeks later and moved to Maryland. She was pregnant. Cassie and I did the math a long time ago."

"A whirlwind courtship. Nothing wrong with that. The marriage lasted, didn't it?"

"The marriage lasted but not the relationship. It's like that Johnny Cash song. Something about marrying in a fever and then the fever burns out. She let passion overrule her brain and fell for a totally incompatible man. They never agreed about anything. Not politics. Not household matters. Not us kids. Nothing."

"Big fights, or what?"

"Sometimes. Most of the time, one of them gave in, usually Mom. She'd mutter to herself in Korean and slam a door or something."

She hadn't thought about it in a long time but now saw how the tension had affected her and Cassie in different ways. Cassie became confrontational and defensive but was always looking for love with the wrong man. Just like Mom.

And herself? She wanted love and caring and common interests with the right man. Did that make her the perfectionist Cassie'd always accused her of being? She had no answers. Not today. Not with Cort standing beside her, so strong and sexy and distracting.

He rubbed his nape as he mulled over what she'd said. "I get how you know about the incompatibility. You lived it every day. But you know about the sex thing how?"

"When I was about twelve and Cassie seventeen, she overheard them talking. Arguing was more like it, I guess. She explained it to me. I vowed right then never to let myself fall for a guy strictly because of sex."

"An intelligent decision. Just like you. But you've taken it to an extreme conclusion. So you hold back on good sex and the pleasure two people can give each other on the off chance sex tips the balance with the wrong guy?" The scar-dimple in his cheek winked at her, a sure indication he was having fun with this topic. A whole lot more than she was.

She shook her head, pulled her hair back and up to cool her neck, which was hot for some unaccountable reason. So were her cheeks. Dammit. She avoided his eyes, or he'd see too much. "You make it too simple."

"Sweetheart, nothing about you is simple."

She chanced a look. This time he wasn't grinning. She let her hair down and continued. "Last night was the aftermath of an emotional day. I was exhausted. So were you, after the flight west. The whole thing with Danita Inglish and the two attackers. We'd been through a lot together. I felt... overwhelmed and a bit frightened by my strong reactions to our lovemaking." She stopped there, before she dove into a quagmire.

He kissed her palm. "I'm glad it wasn't me who scared you. But who knows what Cassie really overheard and what you understood from her explanation? You were a kid. You should ask your mom for the truth."

Her mouth dropped open. "Absolutely not. Would you dare to ask your mom about her sex life with your dad?"

"No need. I heard them too many times through the wall. They loved each other. I know because they told me. Love's no guarantee people agree on everything. Or much of anything."

New sea lion watchers joined them on the wharf, likely early diners at the many seafood restaurants and raw bars. Because it was getting late, the two of them left the wharf and headed up Taylor Street toward the cable car turntable. Beyond, sunlight skidded across the rooftops of candy-colored Victorian houses lining the vertical streets.

Cort glanced at her as they walked along. Fear of passion? Maybe. Her parents' fights had stressed her childhood, just like his, for different reasons and in different ways. Her face was so expressive and her eyes revealed everything. Not this time. She was still hiding something, something she deliberately omitted from her revelation. Emotional overload? Crap. What the hell did he know about women's emotions? Not much. Probably smarter of him not to try to find out. Getting in any deeper with her would lead nowhere either of them wanted to go.

But he'd never known sex to be so powerful, so all-encompassing. And he had to wait hours for the night.

They crossed the street, but this time the turntable stood empty. The tracks ribboned up the hill, empty. The ticket attendant said the next cable car was due in about ten minutes. Five other people stood around with tickets in hand. He followed Mara around the barrier and sat on a planter big enough for an oak tree.

She turned to him, her eyes bright with purpose. "Okay, now it's your turn. You've talked a lot about Leon. Is there a reason you've avoided talking about your mom?"

His breath hitched. Yes, there was a reason. Pain. But he'd opened the door. He tucked her arm in the crook of his elbow while he composed himself. He got through the day easier when he avoided remembering how he'd failed his mom. "Fair enough question. I don't talk about her because her death is my fault."

"What? That can't be. You were in prison when she died." Her disbelief almost but not quite mitigated the shame that bubbled up after he spoke the damning words.

"Exactly." He swallowed against the tightness that gathered in his throat. "First I should tell you this isn't my first visit to San Francisco."

"Whoa, really?" She gaped at him with a look of disappointment. "If you've seen Chinatown and Fisherman's Wharf, you should've told me."

"If I've been to either place, I've forgotten. I was eight."

She gawped. "So San Francisco was one of the many places you lived with your parents?"

He hadn't thought about that time in forever. Being here propelled him to relive the year. Painful memories. "Leon moved us here in pursuit of some big score. I have no idea what his target was. I do know I never got to ride on a cable car. Mom pronounced it too expensive. Never mind that Leon always had plenty of dough. She did temp work when she could so she had her own money. She tried not to spend his. I can't recall where we lived—a row house away from the city center. We usually traveled by streetcar and bus. I took a city bus to school."

"How long did you live here?"

"About a year. Just long enough for me to get used to the routine. Then something happened with Leon's big plans—maybe he scored, maybe not—and we split in the middle of the night."

She gave his arm a squeeze. Maybe she'd sensed his bitterness. Hiding his emotions from her wasn't working.

"Tough on a family, a nomad life like that," she said finally.

"Back then I thought of it as a big adventure. Now

I think the stay was more of a fiasco. Might've been when my mother started drinking." A band tightened around his chest. His throat stung as he fought the memories.

She said nothing. Just waited quietly, her hand secure on his arm.

Somehow the pressure inside him eased enough so he could keep going. He spilled all that had festered inside him for the years since the warden told him his mother had died. Accidental, he said, a combination of tranquilizers and vodka. A long downhill slide that might have begun here or earlier. He'd been too young to know.

"First she had daily cocktails. Next she needed a "pick-me-up" at lunch. Then a little here and there all day. At first I wasn't conscious of her descent into an alcohol haze. Too young and stupid, I guess. She kept up a façade of calm stoicism."

"You were just a kid. I can't imagine how alone you must've felt. How helpless." Her understanding gave him the strength to continue more or less calmly. "And Leon?" she asked.

He snorted his scorn. "Too involved in his schemes and redesigning the stolen gems into saleable jewelry that I wonder whether Leon even realized his wife was going under. After the divorce, she got worse. I became her caretaker."

"And took care of yourself, I imagine."

"Some. When the FBI arrested Leon and then me for the Gramornia theft, she had to be hospitalized. A wake-up call for Leon, but too late."

"He must've felt remorse."

Ever the optimist about people, misplaced in

Leon's case, but her words comforted him. "Never knew him to regret a damned thing. When that all went down, I never wanted to see him again. The court kept him locked up but they let me visit my mom in rehab." He didn't add he'd been wearing handcuffs and an ankle monitor.

She'd wept in his arms. *"I warned Leon years ago. I begged him. And look what he's done to you."*

"She got better for a while," Cort said, "but she was alone. I deserted her. I failed her. By giving in to Leon, I betrayed her. If I'd been with her, I could've stopped the slide." His breath hitched and he couldn't continue.

"What was your mother's name?"

"Monica."

"A good strong name. Cort, your mother started down her self-destructive path when you were little. None of it was your fault, not her drinking, not her death. If you want to blame someone, blame Leon. He betrayed you both, first teaching you to pick locks and then dragging you into the robbery. I wish he wasn't dead so I could tell him exactly what I think of him."

She leaned her head against his shoulder, and he felt the tension in his chest ease a bit more. They sat like that until the cable car arrived.

****

Forty-five minutes later Cort held the door to the condo building for Mara. Seeing the city was great but the memory-lane session hit him like three rounds with The Rock. If he could, he'd avoid accompanying Mara tonight. He wanted to hang out in the condo with his feet up.

In the lobby, the security guard hailed them from

his circular metal and glass desk.

"Ms. Marton, a guy came by just a few minutes ago with an envelope for you." The middle-aged guard was thin but with a pot belly that made him look pregnant.

The exhaustion weighing on Cort forgotten like yesterday's weather, he looked sharp at the guard, as did Mara.

"Where is it?" she asked. "The envelope?"

The guard shook his head. "He wanted to take it on up but I told him you weren't in and I'd deliver it when you returned. He wouldn't leave it with me. Said he'd be back."

Mara nodded and thanked the man. She started across the carpet toward the elevator.

"Wait," Cort said. "Did this delivery man know the unit number?"

"Nope, he asked me. But I know better'n to give out that information." He narrowed his eyes. "You think it was some sorta scam?"

"Was he wearing an official uniform, like UPS or Fed Ex?" Mara asked.

He looked upward, thinking. "Blue pants, blue shirt, no insignia."

Cort's gut tightened. "What did he look like? Black, white, brown, old, young?"

"White. Thirty, forty. Average height. Nothing special. Couldn't see his hair 'cause he was wearing a Giants cap. Official, black cap with the orange *S* and *F*."

Mara blinked at the guard's statement and opened her mouth, shut it again.

Cort's fingers curled into his palms. Damn sports

fan, the guard remembered the cap better than the phony delivery man's features. "Did you see his truck?"

"No vehicle. But there was another guy. I noticed him earlier, just standing across the street. Looked at his watch like he was waiting for somebody so I didn't worry. When the delivery guy left, this other guy sorta followed him. Hung back a bit, you know, then slouched along a ways behind him." The guard shrugged in a self-deprecating gesture. "I could be wrong."

"What did this second guy look like?"

"Never got a good look at him. Too far away. But he didn't wear no cap."

The knot in Cort's gut said the Centaur agent named Rousso had found them. Or it could be Colonel Yerik even though Cort had fed him bullshit about having to appear to search to satisfy the FBI.

Chapter Twenty

CORT FLEXED HIS fingers and splayed his hands on the desk, giving the guard a hard stare. "I appreciate the heads-up. You did the right thing. Under no circumstances are you to allow anyone to go up to the unit. You got that?"

The man's eyes widened at the flinty tone. He jerked his head up and down several times in a passable bobble-head-doll imitation.

After an admonishing glare in Cort's direction, Mara beamed her bone-melting smile. She shook the guard's hand. "Thank you for being so alert. We feel safe with you on the job. Will you convey Mr. Jones's instructions to the other security people?"

"Yes, ma'am, I sure will. You got it." His relief at her blandishments was palpable.

Cort hustled her to the elevator before the mutual admiration session got out of hand.

"You didn't have to yell at him," she said in a low voice. "Or use the death stare."

Shit, he might've overdone his warning, but she didn't have to hit on the guy. "Between your good cop and my bad cop, he got the message," he hissed.

Neither of them spoke in the elevator, although they were alone. Earlier he'd noted the security camera and a small mic. Security, crap. Too much like prison.

Once inside the condo, Cort tossed his plastic bag

of souvenirs on a nearby chair. He heaved a sigh. Safety. For now. "What was that about the Giants cap?"

Crinkles fanned the edges of her eyes, testament to her worry. "When we were on the wharf, I saw a man wearing a Giants cap under the restaurant awning. He was studying a guide book."

"Why didn't you mention him earlier?"

She lifted and lowered one shoulder in dismissal. "I didn't think it was important. He was too far away to hear our conversation and didn't seem to be paying us any attention. When we walked back toward the street, he was gone. You're thinking it was maybe the man who killed Danita? Rolf Rousso?"

"It's possible. They didn't get her ring piece so maybe they've decided to go for mine."

"Or they think I have one. The envelope was for me, remember." She shrugged out of her jacket and marched to the kitchen. He followed, noting her trembling hands as she poured a glass of water and began to drink. She collapsed back against the counter, her face pale as paper. "Do you think it was a bomb or something?"

He opened the fridge for one of the green teas he'd bought earlier. What addressing the package to her meant, he could only guess. The likely threat doubled his determination to keep her by his side and protect her. Damn the bastards and damn Leon for putting him in this fix. Fear for her scraped his spine.

He should've been looking for danger this afternoon. He'd been thinking not with his brain but with another part of his anatomy. He nearly exploded with the burst of profanity caroming inside him. Instead, he downed a healthy slug of tea. He should've opened a beer. Better, if he could find any, a shot of whiskey.

A deep breath evened his voice before he trusted himself to speak. "A bomb in an envelope? Maybe. More likely a ploy to get access. Who knows what they're up to? Or if it's Rousso or the colonel. But somebody knows where we're staying. So how the hell did they find out?"

"Someone who knew what he was doing might use my credit card transactions to trace us as far as this street. Other than that, he'd have to ask in every building."

"The guy across the street. Could your boss have sent somebody to watch over us?"

Her exotic eyes widened and she took a step backward. "A bodyguard? But that doesn't make sense. How would that man know the delivery was to me? And if he's protecting me—us—why follow the other man?"

"Good point. But you could call and ask." There was a second call she should make. Now was a good time to find out if the suspicion prodding him was valid.

She blew out a breath and her mouth thinned. "Okay. It doesn't hurt to ask." She retrieved her bag from the chair where she'd deposited it and dug out her phone. "I'm going to freshen up for dinner." She headed toward the stairs and he followed, enjoying the view.

"There's another possibility, but you won't like it," he said.

She turned on the third step. "André."

He smiled as he wound a finger in a strand of hair

dangling by her ear. "I do like how your mind works. Damn convenient this international mogul hooked up with your sister at this particular time. I wonder if he's still in town."

"My mom might have told Cassie we were coming west."

She looked so guilty he kissed her. "And she'd have told André."

She looped her arms around his neck, easier because he stood on the step below her. But the anguish in her eyes said romance wasn't on her mind.

"I should've told Mom to keep it quiet. What if her telling Cassie is what led Centaur to Danita Inglish? Then it's my fault she was killed."

He kissed her again, a mere brush of lips, but his body reacted as always. Save it for later. "Don't even think it. They beat us here. Probably found her the same way you did."

If his words sank in, she didn't show it. She said nothing as she trudged up the stairs.

****

"You didn't need to come with me," Mara said, as Cort left the car behind her aunt and uncle's restaurant. "I'm safe with my relatives. Although considering my aunt, maybe not."

"She a tough cookie?" He pocketed the car keys.

She watched as he checked out the shadowed parts of the small parking area, dimming further as dusk fell. "Let's just say my aunt never lets Mom forget her position. It grates on Mom, being the older sister and having to live with them and work for them. Mom's sister has always been controlling. She finds little errands, demeaning chores for Mom beyond her hostess duties, just to lord it over her. I want Mom out of there and on her own." Her knuckles cramped where she gripped her hobo bag tightly, and she flexed her fingers.

"The big reason she needs your father's pension."

"Yes. This has gone on way too long. I *have* to prove Dad innocent."

"To do that you need to be careful. You'll be okay inside the restaurant. I don't want Thomas Devlin coming after me if you get hurt. Or worse."

His veiled concern warmed her, although the threats around them chilled her bones. Their phone calls had borne mixed fruit. Cort couldn't reach the FBI agent. Devlin had sent no one but ordered her to stick close to Cort. The final blow was her sister's news that André had flown to France to be at his sick father's bedside. Interesting his need to leave happened at the same time as Mara's trip to San Francisco.

Too convenient, too coincidental. She made sympathetic noises to her sister even as guilt cinched a band around her chest. After ending the call to Cassie, she'd texted Sandi to check on André's trip.

As they walked to the front of the white-painted brick building, he slung an arm around her shoulders, making her feel secure. He knew how to watch for danger, how to react, what to do. And yeah, he was hot. He made *her* feel hot—in both senses of the word—and important and feminine, not the ultimate geek. And he made her smile.

Seoul Food was one of a number of Korean and other Asian businesses on Geary Boulevard between the Presidio and Golden Gate Park. A sandwich board in front listed the day's specials. Aromas of spicy seafood stew and kimchi wafted through a vent.

His grin seemed forced, one he'd manufactured to lighten the mood. "You going to ask your mom about her sex life?"

"I'd rather throw myself under a cable car." She glared at him, then wilted. "But I will explain about the ring pieces. If she knows anything, she'll tell me."

"Fine. Then I'll mosey down the street and eat. Be back for you at eight thirty."

"*Mosey*?"

"Hey, we are out west." He kissed her soundly, a thorough enough kiss to curl her toes. "Don't leave the restaurant without me. If these guys are after you, don't give them any openings."

Speechless, she watched him *mosey* down the street, admiring the way he filled out his jeans and the fluid way he moved until he disappeared around the corner.

Inside Seoul Food, the familiar spices and warmth of Korean hospitality relaxed her. No sign of her uncle, who managed the place by hiding from his wife in the kitchen. Her aunt, seating customers, gave her a lofty look, quite a trick for a woman who stuffed her pudgy feet into spike heels to lift her to five foot four. A nod directed Mara toward the back.

Her mother rose from the corner table when she entered the private function room. Shorter than Mara, Su Lin Marton reached up to kiss her daughter's cheek. Mara bent into the jasmine-scented hug, comforted by the familiar. She, not her dad, was now the one who supplied the perfume.

"Thank God nothing bad happened today. I've been worried," Su Lin said in the slight Korean accent that remained after thirty plus years in the United

States.

She scanned Mara as if reassuring herself. At fifty-nine, she maintained her youthful beauty, although with a few wrinkles around her dark eyes. Silver threaded her dark hair, knotted and clasped on the back of her head. She looked chic in tan pants and a pale yellow twinset.

"No need to worry about me, Mom." Mara wished she felt as confident as her words. "I told you about Cort. He's with me, and Devlin will send people if we need assistance."

A young server she didn't know whisked in with a pot of tea and a plate of appetizers, stuffed deep-fried dumplings.

They took seats side by side at the round table, set with white linen instead of the placemats used in the main dining room. Usually when she visited her mother, she shared her small bedroom and ate most meals at the family's row house, but Su Lin always treated her to one meal here. Mara felt a twinge of guilt for what she was about to ask.

"I ordered a variety but nothing stuffed with kimchi," Su Lin said with an indulgent look.

"Thanks, Mom." At her mother's thoughtfulness, she relaxed further. She popped a hot dumpling in her mouth and chewed the savory squid.

The older woman poured tea, and looked up from her fragrant cup. "When I talked to Cassie, her voice sounded hoarse. Is she smoking again?"

Thank God her full mouth afforded her time to consider her reply. "I had dinner with her Friday. She wasn't smoking then. Maybe she has a cold."

"Uh huh." No one put anything over on Su Lin.

But she didn't probe further. "Cassie mentioned something about this detecting with the thief's son."

Mara recognized that oblique statement as a demand for details. If she intended to quiz her mother about a ring piece, she had better comply.

The server brought their entrees. Mara ordered her usual seafood *dolsot*, rice with stir-fried shellfish and vegetables, and her mother the restaurant's newest dish, *japchae*, clear noodles with beef and vegetables, so she could recommend it to customers.

As they ate, Mara told her story beginning with the Jeweler's death and finishing with an explanation of their search for the ring pieces. No hiding Danita's murder but her mom didn't need to know the other hazardous aspects of their search. "Cort wants to prove he's reformed. He wants to return the crown jewels so he can be free of FBI harassment. He's a talented furniture maker."

Su Lin dabbed her mouth with her linen napkin. A smile twitched at her lips. "He is more than that to you. I saw you together through the window. Very masculine and rough-looking, but obviously protective of you. And affectionate." She tilted her head and waited.

Mara felt her cheeks heat. To their right in the kitchen, raised voices battled. In the dining room, silverware clattered. "I think he's sorry he dragged me into this. But he needs my technical help and Devlin Security Force resources. Finding the ring pieces will help prove Dad wasn't involved and you can receive his pension."

"That is your reason for taking part. But there is more to it now. And you want something from me."

"You're right, as usual. Do you have anything of Dad's, boxes of personal items, like jewelry or letters?"

Her mom's shoulders straightened and she set down her chopsticks. "So you think he might have had a ring piece? He might be guilty?"

The vehemence didn't surprise her. Her mom might not have loved her husband but she was loyal. Her throat tight, Mara shook her head. "He was innocent but I have to rule out every possibility. And we don't have much time."

"And Cort needs the ring pieces to find the jewels."

Heat flared, a match struck in her emotional tinder. "It's not about Cort."

"I think it is, at least in part. You are in love with him. I see it in your eyes when you talk about him, when you defend him."

Mara blinked away the tears threatening to burst the dam. She swallowed hard. She couldn't be in love with Cort. So totally the wrong man.

"You and Dad didn't love each other. What do *you* know about love?" She clapped her hands over her mouth. Tears slopped down her cheeks and dripped into her bowl. "Forgive me, Mother, for being so disrespectful."

Su Lin clasped her hand and placed it against her cheek. She murmured soothing words in Korean, words Mara had heard when she'd skinned a knee or lost a tennis match. "Whatever made you think that?"

"You argued all the time. You never agreed." Bringing up Cassie's birth seven months after the wedding didn't seem like a good idea. Nor did what Cassie'd overheard. She blew her nose into the tissue her mother handed her. "Why did you marry him?"

"Look around you, Mara. This is where your father found me. Waiting tables and hostessing. I came from a small town in Korea with no money, no education, and no hope of escaping poverty. Your father was handsome, a rich American who wanted me."

For security, not for passion. "He had to know you were unhappy."

"I was not unhappy. Your father loved me. He was good to me and to you girls. He loved us all. Yes, we disagreed about a lot of things, but we always enjoyed making up." Pink tinged her high cheekbones at this confession.

Mara held up a hand. "Enough, Mom. T.M.I."

The mood lighter, they laughed together.

"He was a good man, an honorable man," her mom continued. "And I had my girls, my house, and my garden." She knitted her fingers together in her lap and looked at them as if her hands were tied. "But now I am back where I started. And my girls live a continent away."

"I think I understand. I'll get you out of here if I can."

"With help from your young man?"

"He's not *my* young man. We're…" She struggled to think. "I don't know what we are. But he's smart and kind and proud."

"And sexy."

Chuckling, Mara picked up her tea and downed it. "He makes me laugh and hurt for him. He listens to me and thinks about what I say. Mom, he built me a desk and he reads all the placards in museums."

Su Lin's knowing laugh rolled out. "You are in love with him but you are afraid."

"Something like that."

"Your situation is nothing like mine. You and I are not alike. If Cort Jones is a good man and you love him, fight for him."

"I don't know. He trusts no one. He doesn't believe in love."

"Self-preservation. He has been hurt by someone he loved, his father. Pride. You said he was proud."

Mara nodded. He'd given her no sign he felt anything but desire. Maybe friendship as well. Not enough. Was she in love with him? Or was it simple lust? Simple? Nothing was simple about the emotions roiling inside her.

"One thing more," Su Lin said, with a catch in her voice. "I have never told anyone because it shames me."

Mara studied the older woman's anguished face. "You don't have to tell me anything."

"You need to understand. I told you I did not love your father when we married. When the doctor warned him about smoking and his weight, I realized I could lose him. That is when I knew I loved him."

Not just loyalty, but love. Tears welled again. She caught her mother's hand and felt the trembling of her emotion in her frail bones. "He knew?"

Su Lin shook her head. "That is my shame. I was afraid to tell Quincy I loved him. Afraid he would not believe me after all those years. He died without knowing."

"I'm so sorry." She rose from her seat and went to embrace her mother.

"Your young man has no family left. Only you. And you are both in danger." When Mara started to protest, her mother cut her off. "No, don't. I see more than you think. Once you know your feelings for him, tell him. Let him know he is not alone."

"That's a big risk to take."

"Some things are worth the risk. I regret every day I did not risk love with your father."

Chapter Twenty-One

MARA HUGGED HER mother goodbye a while later and meandered unseeing through the restaurant's busy tables. Too much to think about. Too much to absorb.

She nearly collided with a server bearing a heavy tray of hot covered dishes. Aromas of spicy chicken and shrimp and the hated kimchi wafted around her as the lids rattled. She apologized to the irate server and scooted away.

Whatever Cassie had overheard got jumbled in the telling to Mara. Or misinterpreted by their juvenile minds. As Cort said. Marriage was about love, but more than love. Her parents made their union work in many ways. They had passion and their marriage lasted. But what Mara had always wanted still held. True love from the beginning. On both sides.

She was about to take a seat on the bench reserved for take-out customers when a sharp voice penetrated her fog.

"Customers need those seats," her aunt snapped. Probably irked because Mara hadn't made time for her. More likely because she had to do Su Lin's job. "Your young man came in. He said to meet him at the car."

"Thanks. I'll visit with you next time, okay?" Mara slipped outside without waiting for a reply. She hustled around back.

Vehicles pinged as their engines cooled in the full lot. Under the halogen safety lighting, she spied their rental car beside the restaurant's panel van. Funny, Cort wasn't in the driver's seat. And hadn't he said to wait inside? Apprehension prickled her nape.

A big hand covered her mouth and an equally hefty arm yanked her backward.

Her heart raced. Her head reeled.

She struggled but the man had her pinned against him.

"Do not make a sound." A man in a tailored suit stepped from behind the van. The accent, the military bearing, the buzz cut—he had to be Colonel Yerik. "I merely want to talk."

His words made no sense over the barrel of his big pistol, aimed at her nose.

****

The aromas inside Seoul Food made Cort's mouth water, although he'd filled up on Cambodian beef in yellow curry peanut sauce. A cup of tea, maybe a dessert, while he waited seemed like a plan. Mara should be ready to go soon.

"Mr. Jones?" A beautiful older woman who looked to be Mara's relative approached him. She wasn't smiling. No surprise. She wouldn't be thrilled about his being with Mara.

"That's me. I don't want to rush Mara. I can wait."

"My daughter left to meet you a few minutes ago."

His dinner congealed into cement in his stomach. He clasped Su Lin Marton's trembling hand. "Mrs. Marton, why did she leave? Where'd she go?"

Her free hand fluttered to her throat. "I don't know. My sister said…" She swallowed hard, cast a beseeching glance toward another woman. "Mae?"

The sister, a stack of menus in her hand, looked distraught, confused. "A man came in. Said he was waiting for Mara. She should meet him at the car."

"What did this man look like?" Cort demanded as he reached for the door handle.

"Like you. Bigger though," Mae said with a shrug. "Tough. Shorter hair. Windbreaker."

Shit. One of the Clones. "Stay here." He blew out the door and booked it around the corner of the building.

Braking to a halt in the parking lot, he scanned the area. "Mara!"

No answer.

Shadows blurred the scene, but their rental sat empty where he'd left it, and more cars filled the small lot.

Every nerve in his body tingling, on alert, he raced between the cars.

Nothing.

A woman's scream split through the traffic's hum. A scuffling noise from the back of the lot sent him barreling that direction.

More scuffling. A male yelp of pain.

"You freak, let me go!"

Mara! He bolted into the narrow passage, adrenaline pushing him like a mighty hand. A dark alley, rank with smells of garbage and worse.

One of the Clone Brothers held Mara pinned against his torso with one arm. His other arm held one of hers stretched in front. The Clone grimaced in pain.

Cort's breath caught and fear threatened to choke him. When Mara's wide gaze met his, he saw anger but no pain or fear. As quickly as his gorge rose, he dialed it down. She needed him to stay cool.

"Let me go, you ape." She struggled in the steely grip, kicked backward with one pointed heel. "Or I'll kick you again."

Give 'em hell, sweetheart. But that could backfire. "Easy, Mara. Don't give him a reason to hurt you."

"Hold it right there, Jones." Colonel Yerik pointed a pistol his way. Not the same one as last time. Even bigger. Long attachment—a silencer.

His relief at seeing Mara whole vanished. "Let her go, Yerik. She was just visiting her mother."

"So you said before about San Francisco. Not credible. I do not believe in coincidence. Sorry to hear about the guard Inglish's demise." He raised his cigarette for a long drag.

"Was that you?"

Yerik snorted. "Not my style. Too high profile and no finesse. And inconvenient."

"And Mara?" Cort clenched his fists as he struggled for patience.

"I warned you, Jones. If you pursue the search for the jewels, she will pay. It seems you—and she—need a demonstration."

"You touch her, Yerik, and I'll blow this thing sky high. Your fucking prime minister will go down so fast, he'll suck you down the drain with him."

"An idle threat. You have no proof of anything."

"I don't need proof, asshole. All I need is an interested TV reporter." At Yerik's raised eyebrow, he took a step forward. Before he could press his advantage, a siren's wail brought up everyone's heads. Mara's mom must've called the cops.

"I do not believe you will go public." Yerik tossed down his cigarette. "Be warned. I can get to Ms. Marton any time I want." He turned to the Clone. "Release her."

The muscleman shoved Mara toward Cort.

As she stumbled away, he caught her in his arms. Could only watch as the men disappeared down the alley. He kissed her forehead, her cheeks, her lips, thanking the powers that be he'd reached her in time and cursing himself for giving Yerik that window. He should've stayed at Seoul Food for dinner, kept her within reach.

"Are you all right? They didn't hurt you?"

"The damn freak burned me." Movements rife with fury, she pushed up her sleeve to display an angry, round wound.

Son of a bitch's cigarette. Cort clutched her shoulders, then held her closer. He'd encase her with his whole body if he could. Over her head he stared down the alley where the men had disappeared. If he had laser vision, he'd cut through buildings and incinerate Yerik and his goon.

"How bad is it?"

When a clatter on the pavement announced arrivals, he released her.

Casting a glance around him, she pulled the sleeve down. "Stings like hell, but don't tell Mom. Here she comes with the police."

****

"Kind of late for you, Kaplan. Out on the town?" As if Cort could picture the rumpled FBI agent doing anything but working. He propped his cell phone under his chin as he wrestled with a corkscrew.

"If you call still being at my desk out on the town." Pencil tapping echoed through the connection.

"You have news for me or your usual threats and warnings?"

"Funny guy. No threats but I can deliver the other two. Your detective friend informs me the car involved in Danita Inglish's death has been found in long-term parking at San Francisco International Airport."

"Anything like clues inside? The killer's gun's too much to hope for."

"Bingo," Kaplan said. "Wiped clean of course. And sitting beside it was a dead man. Big dude wearing a dark windbreaker."

"Sounds like the guy I saw running from Inglish's building."

He flipped the lever and the wine cork popped loose. They'd purchased a bottle of local wine, a pinot noir. Mara preferred red wine to white, like he did. He'd urged her to let him open it now. She could use a little mellowing after being terrorized.

"Looks like it's him," Kaplan said. "Local rent-a-thug who won't be missed, according to the detective. Took a slug to the temple."

"He was probably Inglish's killer."

"And a clear warning. No witnesses. If you want to turn the ring piece over to me and let the FBI handle the case like you wanted before, I won't object."

Cort nearly dropped the phone. Stop? Let the FBI run with the ball? Tempting, considering Mara's safety. But with Colonel Yerik in the mix, he had to keep going. "Kaplan, your concern warms the cold corners of my heart. But like you told me before, people will talk to me or Mara easier than to the Feds. I'll stick with it.

For now."

"Don't say I never gave you an out, Jones. You and the lady watch your backs." With that the agent disconnected.

Too many disparate details and no more ring pieces. Cort stowed his cell and carried the open bottle and two goblets into the living room.

Mara glided down the stairs, brightening the room. Barefoot and wearing a red silk caftan, she moved with such sensual grace, his breath caught. As he settled on the couch, anticipation rippled through him. He poured them some wine and handed her a goblet.

"You're brooding. Bad news?" She curled up on the other end of the sofa—not beside him—and tucked her feet beneath her. She sipped her wine, staring into it as if seeking answers.

No answers for him there, but maybe a duller edge to his returning headache. He sipped the wine and savored before downing a healthy slug. He didn't know wine but he knew what he liked. Fruity, nice and dry. "You're the quiet one but *I'm* brooding? Not bad news. Hell, except for a thug in long-term parking." He recounted his conversation with the FBI agent.

"Don't even consider trying to convince me to stop, if that's what has your forehead all knotted up." She sank into the cushions and closed her eyes.

"Too late. You'd still be in danger." What was she wearing under that slithery garment? Maybe nothing? He slid closer and soaked in her just-showered scent.

They'd bought burn cream and bandages on the way back to the condo. She'd winced but hadn't complained as he tended the ugly wound. Every dab with cream stabbed him in the gut. Hurt him more than it pained her.

"How's the arm?"

"Okay. Ibuprofen helped. I'll heal." She settled back and sipped more wine.

Except for her abnormal quiet, she seemed back to herself after her ordeal. She'd held up like a trouper while the cops questioned them and even afterward. Su Lin had glared but said nothing when he and Mara swore the attack was a mugger after her purse. She recited a generic description—average height, average weight, ski mask. Both the patrolman and her mother shook their heads. He bet Mrs. Marton gave her sister hell for falling for the thug's line. Ice still gripped his gut when he thought about how Yerik had terrorized Mara.

He pulled himself back to present worries. "Too many questions and too many seemingly insignificant details. Every new clue, every new event tumbles through my head and causes a shift like the pieces in a kaleidoscope. Until I see no pattern at all. We're as far away as ever from finding the location of the crown jewels."

She rallied, sat up straight, brisk and back into the puzzle. "One of them will make it all click. Maybe Danita's daughter has her mother's ring piece or knows where she hid it. Like in a safe deposit box. My apartment building has locked storage areas in the basement. Maybe hers does too and she stashed it there." She poured more wine.

He raised an eyebrow. She never drank more than one glass of wine. "Rough dinner with Mom? Or are you still shaken up?"

"Both. A little. Mom's worried about me, doing

this search with you."

"Hanging out with the Jeweler's ex-con son."

"Actually no. More about the danger. Even before today's *mugging*. She seemed quite impressed with you. She thinks you're sexy."

He grinned, satisfaction and sensual energy flaring. "What does her daughter think?"

She drank some wine and set down the glass. "She agreed to look through her stuff in storage to see what she has of Dad's."

Cort saw the ambivalence on her expressive face. Both mother and daughter hoped she'd find nothing incriminating, but if there was a ring, at least they'd have an answer. High price for success. "And the other question?"

She affected a puzzled look but the flush on her cheeks gave her away.

"Come on. Give. Mom revealed all."

"You wish. You were right that whatever Cassie overheard, we misinterpreted. Dad fell in love with Mom but she married him for security."

"To get out of the restaurant job she's been forced to come back to many years later. That's it? That's all?"

"What? You thought she gave me an X-rated version?" She swung her feet to the floor and pushed to her feet. "You can stay here drinking wine. It's been a long day. I need Z's."

WTF. He reached for her hand. "Hey, sweetheart, you're wearing that slinky red thing and sharing my wine and you're going to bed? Alone? Remember last night? You're not still afraid of letting go? Or are you playing games?"

"No games. I don't mean... sorry." Her dark eyes

held no guile, only pensiveness. "Just I have some thinking to do. About the rest of what Mom said. That's all. Okay?"

He didn't understand. But he nodded.

Halfway up the stairs, she turned back. "I forgot to tell you. While I was at Seoul Food, I got a text message from my airline source. More enigma to confuse matters."

After her odd rebuff, he couldn't work up much enthusiasm for whatever she'd dug up. "Yeah?"

"Get this. During the two days after André told Cassie he had to go to France, they have no record of anyone named André Rozmer or any permutations of the two names boarding any flight commercial or private out of D.C. or Baltimore."

****

After Cort heard Mara close the door to her room, he pulled out his cell phone for the call he dreaded.

"Don't you know the difference between the time zones, Jones? Middle of the night here."

"Sorry, but you don't sound like I woke you." A good thing. He needed Thomas Devlin alert.

"I don't sleep much. You wouldn't have called if it wasn't important. What's up?"

"I fucked up. Yerik got to Mara." A sharp intake of breath on the other end. "She's all right. A warning. But, Devlin, *he fucking burned her!* My fault." *Shit.* He'd meant to hold it together. He closed his eyes and breathed.

"I'll take it out of your hide later. Tell me."

As calmly as possible, Cort related Yerik's assault and warning.

"This wasn't your fault," Devlin said when he

finished. "You told Mara to stay put until she saw you. She didn't. She went into that parking lot unprotected. Trust yourself. You saved her, didn't you?"

"Same thing she said." They'd argued about who screwed up. He was supposed to be protecting her, but no use flogging the same dead horse with the man whose help he needed. "I can't let her go down with me. Can't you speed things up? Get Yerik and his thugs out of the picture?"

"I almost have an arrangement. What's underway takes time. Hang in there a little longer."

"The coronation is less than a week from now. Time's running out and I'm not even close to knowing where Leon hid the crown jewels. My life isn't worth shit but Mara—" He hauled in a ragged breath. "She could die."

Chapter Twenty-Two

THE NEXT MORNING, Ellen Plante welcomed Mara and Cort to her modest row house. Mara hated the reason they'd come, but all too necessary. Someone was cutting down possible accomplices like trees in the woods where Cort lived.

And how André Rozmer fit into this puzzle was anyone's guess. She hated continuing to sneak research behind Cort's back but she could do only so much on her smart phone. She should've brought her tablet but had packed fast and forgot it. Not like her. Her chest felt clogged, as if her lungs had seized up.

"Thank you for seeing us, Ms. Plante," she said to the woman seated opposite her on a comfortable looking green tweed armchair that matched the sofa where she and Cort sat. "I know this is a difficult time for you and your family."

"Least I can do," Ellen replied. Clad in a modest navy-blue dress, she was a slimmer, younger version of her mother. She clutched a wadded tissue. "You tried to save my mother's life. She might've made it, too, except—" Her voice wavered and she wobbled her hand to indicate the attack on the ambulance. Words too painful to utter.

Mara knew exactly how she felt, tears never far away, the ache in her chest as if by a tight strap. She'd experienced the same raw anguish when her dad died.

For Ellen to lose her mother to senseless murder, the grief must be compounded with outrage and helplessness.

She caught a glimpse of Cort beside her. Stoic as usual, except for the tourniquet grip on his knees. She didn't sleep well last night and suspected neither did he. She would rather have spent the night in his arms but needed to sort out her jumbled feelings.

She ought to be able to come to a rational decision. But no. Her conclusions flipped like pancakes with every toss and turn in her lonely bed. When he cut his gaze toward her, she looked away, afraid he would see her turmoil.

Family photographs papered one wall. A dollhouse and a toy box stood in one corner along with a pink tricycle, its handles decorated with pink and purple streamers. The broken cake on the floor beside Danita must've been for Ellen's daughter Shayla. Her fifth birthday. Tears burned Mara's eyes.

"What is it you want to know?" Ellen straightened her shoulders and tucked away her tissue. "Something about the Gramornia crown jewel robbery? That's the reason those men killed her, isn't it?"

Relieved the connection to the robbery was out in the open, Mara nodded. She explained, beginning with how Leon's death renewed the search for the crown jewels by several parties and ending with Cort's and her reasons for the search. "Your mother was one of the museum guards suspected of complicity in the robbery eleven years ago."

"If my mama knew where those crown jewels were hidden, you can bet she'd have turned them over to the cops years ago."

Mara blinked. *Did Ellen just admit her mother's guilt?* She and Cort exchanged a glance.

Ellen sighed. "Yes, Mama was part of that robbery. She gave the thieves the security information and looked the other way. Biggest regret of her life, she always said."

"Did she ever say why she did it?" Mara asked gently.

"Me." Ellen sniffled. "To my everlasting sorrow. She was a single mom with only a high-school education. She made a decent salary but wanted college for me. The Jeweler, your father—" she gave Cort an apologetic look "—offered her more money than she could've made in twenty years walking those marble floors. He got her to give him copies of the security set-up. Lured her in with promises of an easy life and a future for me. Never happened, of course."

The success Ellen achieved since Danita lost her museum job proved the two women's drive. She sensed Cort's impatience so she dug for courage. "At the time, my father questioned all the suspects. Did your mother ever say anything about those conversations?"

Ellen's broad forehead crimped in thought. "Only that she kept telling him she didn't know anything. Same thing she told the FBI."

"Did she ever talk about a ring?" Cort cut in with what was Mara's next question. "Something the Jeweler might've given her?" Tension edged his voice.

"That jagged thing? Too big to wear? Lord, yes. What about it?"

Finally! Mara could barely sit still.

Just inside a rounded archway that led to a dining area and kitchen, she caught the slight movement of a pink sneaker and a black braid. *Shayla.* A small oval face peered out. Grief shadowed big brown eyes, and something else. Guilt? Surely she didn't feel guilty for her grandmother's death.

"The ring is what the killers were looking for. What *we're* looking for," Cort said, pulling her attention away from the child. "It might help lead us to the hidden jewels. We don't think they found her ring." He scooted to the edge of the sofa. "What did she do with it?"

Ellen plucked another tissue from a box beside her and blew her nose. "She dragged that ring with her wherever we lived. Said the Jeweler told her it was a key to the treasure. More than once she got ready to give the damn thing to the cops and confess, but she couldn't face the idea of prison. Couldn't bring herself to throw it away neither. Like that old story poem about the sailor and the albatross. You know the one?"

"Yes, ma'am. But the ring?"

"Gone. Seemed like a good omen to me the day that thing disappeared."

"Gone?" Cort's voice broke on the word.

"Lost is more like it. When she moved into that apartment. We were unpacking stuff and it just never showed up."

"Did your mother have a storage locker or safe deposit box?"

"No bank box, and we went through every crate and suitcase in the basement locker. Good riddance, I thought then. But not now, I reckon. I'm sorry."

Cort slumped against the cushions. "Not half as sorry as I am."

Now was Mara's chance. "Did she ever say my

father asked her about the ring?"

Ellen shook her head. "Nobody ever asked her about a ring. Not until now."

No proof for Global Insurance, but good enough for Mara. Dad didn't know about the puzzle ring. He was innocent. She'd known it all along. Her shoulders relaxed. She closed her eyes, and slowly, silently, the dread and tension flowed away on an exhaled breath.

When she opened her eyes, in the doorway was Shayla's small fretful face. The child chewed her lower lip and looked like she might burst into tears. Mara's heartbeat quickened.

"When I was a little girl, about four," she began, raising her voice a little, "I admired the cameo my dad gave Mom. The brooch was his grandmother's and very precious to him. This cameo contained a small diamond chip. That bit of shine and the beautiful woman's silhouette drew me like a magnet. Little girls always seem to like shiny jewelry."

Cort's brows shot together so tightly in a WTF expression he could've held a pencil between them. Mara shook her head slightly and he said nothing.

Ellen's eyes widened. She seemed not at all thrown by Mara's off-the-wall family story. "I know what you mean. Mama used to have a gold necklace. It belonged to her mama but she had to hock it years ago. You know, after…"

"A shame to lose precious pieces with memories like that," Mara said. She slanted a quick glance at Shayla. The child riveted her dark eyes on her. "When Mom was busy, I took to sneaking into my parents' room and playing with her jewelry. One day I took out the brooch and put it on to wear to my best friend's house. To show off, you know?"

Ellen nodded, apparently caught up in the story.

Cort sat back, his posture tense and his expression intent.

"Sometime that afternoon, the cameo fell on the floor. I stepped on it and broke the clasp. I felt terrible. Guilty and scared to death. What would I tell my mother?"

"What did you do?"

"The worst possible thing. I hid the cameo in my secret treasure box and hoped Mom wouldn't know the piece was missing."

Ellen smiled. "That so never works."

"Too true. When she discovered the loss a few days later, she thought she left it on a jacket and it fell off. She didn't blame me or even ask me or my sister about it."

Cort followed her slight nod toward Shayla. When his brow smoothed, she knew he understood her subterfuge. "And you kept this guilty secret?" he asked.

"For two years." Actually only five days. Her parents had argued about the loss. Her mom cried and shut herself in their room. Mara'd felt sick to her stomach. Even then she knew her father's mantra by heart. *Once a crook, always a crook.* "Finally one day I confessed and handed the cameo back to my mother."

"Let me guess," Ellen said. "She didn't punish you half as much as you feared because she was so glad to see the cameo."

Mara smiled. "The punishment wasn't the spanking or even the grounding I expected. I had to work off the cost of the clasp repair with chores like putting away toys and setting the table. The worst part was my older sister's teasing." Not really. The worst part was how disappointed her dad was. *Once a crook...*

She glanced toward the dining room but Shayla had disappeared. Mara's heart sank.

"I appreciate your story, but—" Ellen dabbed at a tear-dampened spot on her dress. "I'm sorry I couldn't help you."

"We have other people to see. Thank you for your time." Cort got to his feet and held a hand out to Mara. "Especially now. I know it's rough."

"If you ever run across the ring," Mara said, extending her card, "please call me."

"If it shows up. Maybe when I pack up Mama's things." Tears welled and she snatched up another tissue.

Mara trudged to the door, her heart as heavy as her hands were empty. She'd had such hope. She took a deep breath. "Would it be all right if I spoke to your daughter?"

Ellen's face pinched with doubt. "I reckon so. Just a—"

"Mama."

All three turned toward the childish voice.

Shayla trudged into the middle of the living room. Tears swam down her face. She pressed her small hands against her stomach, cupping them tightly around something.

Mara's breath stalled. She ached to go to the girl, but if Shayla had come this far, she had to do the rest on her own. Mara gripped Cort's hand. He squeezed back.

Shayla's mother went to kneel in front of her. "You can tell me, baby. It's all right."

The child opened her hands. In her palms lay a

large gold ring with a jagged edge.

****

Cort sat in the leather armchair he'd pulled in front of the living-room windows. Instead of the view of the Golden Gate's lighted silhouette, he stared at the two separate ring pieces in his hand.

"Dammit, how many of these are there?"

Like the first, the new section had a raised design, this one a small *X*. One edge was finished and smooth, the right-hand outside rim with the endings of each of the four lines. The left-hand jagged edge did *not* fit the right side of Leon's. Another piece would go between them. And another on the left.

The new piece yielded more words and more mystery.

"... THE ... HOLD
... AND ... GOLD
... FOUNT ... YOUTH.
... OUR ... TRUTH."

The words were a poem, a simple rhyme. But too clever and too cryptic.

Thanks a hell of a lot, Leon.

Gold for damn sure meant the gold scepter and crown. Something in the new word *hold* tickled at the back of his mind. The place *hold*ing the jewels? Or *hold* onto? Fountain of youth maybe? Did Leon hide it in Florida? Mara'd done a search for the words on her phone, looking for similar poems or something, but found nothing. Not enough words, she said. Still, some knowledge hovered just out of his reach like a wind-blown dollar bill. Like whatever seemed out of kilter at Falco's trashed house.

His brain fucking hurt.

He'd seen the light in Mara's eyes when Ellen said Quincy Marton interrogated her mother and that was all. Finding a way to clear her father had been a carrot he'd held out, not realizing how important it was to her and her mother. He was a total jerk.

Hell, he was no detective and no puzzle solver. Give him ten board feet of cherry and he could cut it and put together a fine chair or an elegant box. Figuring out this riddle went ass backwards from the way he thought. He swore softly.

"So you couldn't sleep either," a soft voice said behind him.

She padded around the chair in bare feet, her hair tied back in a sleek tail. She looked damned cute in the sleep tee that just reached her knees, as sexy as in the red silk robe. Too bad it wasn't a tad shorter. If he wasn't so torqued, the saying across her breasts—"Geeks know all the right MOVs"—would've made him smile.

"Happens when I'm pissed at myself for being dumb as a drill bit."

"How were you to know the ring had more than three parts?" Her exotic eyes heavy lidded, she smiled as she perched on the upholstered chair arm. The wide seat left enough room for her to prop her feet, giving him a fine view of her bare legs. Her scent invaded his senses, coiling tension inside him.

Shayla had handed over the ring piece without a qualm. "Gramma said she hated that ring," she bawled. Apparently she'd rationalized taking the ring was helping her grandmother. Once she realized Danita wanted it back, she was afraid to say anything.

Until she heard Mara's story.

As soon as Cort had tried to fit the ring piece with his, his heart dropped like a carpenter's plum bob. The gap between them and the two jagged edges meant at least two more pieces were out there. At least four, maybe five. Or more.

"I shouldn't have assumed Leon's ring was the same as the one he made me years ago."

"This entire thing is frustrating but what can we do but keep going? We have more suspects back east, don't we?"

"Little Miss Sunshine," he groused at her cheery tone. "Good thing you're useful."

"And fun to have around." She propped her elbow on the chair back. "Dealing with frustration is par for the course in my work. Computers are the devil's invention, and don't get me started on dead ends in research."

The thin cotton stretching across her breasts diverted his attention from the ring. He twisted in the chair for a better view. "Your brain's good for more than research. Good call drawing out little Shayla with your story."

"Thank you, sir. You couldn't see her face where you sat, but the anxiety in those big eyes reminded me of myself."

"So your story was true?" At her nod, he said, "*That* was the extent of your—what did you call it?— 'youthful mistakes'?"

"I wish. You might as well know. I too was a thief once."

He choked back a laugh and clutched at his heart. "Tell me it isn't so."

Mara swatted him on the arm. "This geek wanted

to belong to a gang of popular girls. Joining meant taking a dare. I shoplifted a bottle of nail polish from the local drugstore."

"How'd you get caught?"

"I think guilt was tattooed on my forehead when I got home." She grimaced. "Cassie gave me a hard time and I burst into tears. Dad wrung the truth from me."

"Punishment?"

"Big time. I had to return the polish and apologize. Dad made me work off the amount of a fine he made up. But worse—"

"Was disappointing him." One of the reasons she tried so hard to be perfect. Hard to imagine any two different fathers than hers and Leon. The FBI must've had their heads up their asses to think Marton had anything to do with the robbery.

"I wasn't worthy of his trust. It seemed forever before I saw approval in his eyes."

"Was the dare worth the punishment?"

"Not even close. And the next day I told the gang I didn't want to be like them or part of them. But enough about me." She waggled her shoulders as if shaking off the memory. "Back to recovering the ring piece. Good on you, having us leave in a funk."

"The bad guys could've been watching. Or not. But we need the odds in our favor. If they think we didn't come up with Danita's ring piece, we're one up on all factions."

And they could fly home. The Oakland detective had phoned with the all-clear.

They sat quietly together for a few minutes, Mara watching the lighted bridge, Cort watching her. His mind blurred as he pictured her without the shirt.

"My feet are cold," she said. "Do you mind?" She tucked her toes beneath his thigh.

The contact shot heat into him. Breath backed up in his lungs. His jeans were too tight. Was she teasing or seducing? She knew how she affected him. "Mara."

She cleared her throat. "I've thought some more about stuff Mom said yesterday."

"Yeah?" He circled her slim ankles with his fingers. Her calves lured his touch but he quashed the urge in favor of seeing where she was going.

"Mom respected Dad. She was loyal. She's still loyal. You should've seen her bristle when she thought I might doubt him. Looking at a relationship from the outside isn't the best way to understand. Everyone fails sometimes."

Her stare made his stomach twitch. She meant him.

"Sometimes it's a parent failing a child," she continued. "Danita thought she was securing her daughter's future by taking Leon's deal. Instead, she failed Ellen and herself miserably. All relationships involve risk and work."

Risk? No shit. He could fail Mara like he'd failed his mom. Like Leon failed her. She learned her parents' relationship wasn't what she'd thought. He wasn't wrong about his parents'. What it meant for him, he'd examine later. Time to throttle back from the brink before she started talking relationship with him. "But you didn't quiz her about—"

"Their sex life." Her cheeks probably blazed but the dim light showed him only the way her hands fluttered to them. "No, but I got what I need to know. She said making up after their arguments was one of the good parts of their marriage."

257

He couldn't resist any longer. His fingers slid up her calves—smooth, soft, warm—to rest on her bare knees. "And what did you learn from this revelation, grasshopper?"

She wrinkled her nose. "A Kung Fu master you're not." Her arms twined around his neck. The smile she sent him was quicksilver and flirtatious. "I learned I don't have to be afraid of passion leading me into the wrong relationship."

"Now you're talking." Passion rammed though him with the force of a runaway cable car. "You're the sexiest woman I know, tempting as hell in that skimpy shirt. Don't play games. Tell me what you want."

"I want you, Cort. Make love with me." From a small pocket in her shirt, she drew out a foil packet.

Chapter Twenty-Three

"YOU DON'T HAVE to ask twice, sweetheart." He tugged her onto his lap for better access to the good stuff.

Sensual energy flared like a whirlwind, wild and hot. As his hand moved up her legs, the cotton shirt bunched until she slipped it off. "Damn, you're beautiful." He growled when he saw she wore no panties. She tugged at the ribbon binding her hair and shook it loose over her bare shoulders, then twisted around to straddle him, pressing herself against him.

As he feasted on her breasts and his fingers found her center, she made little urgent sounds of delight and need. She stripped off his T-shirt and tossed it behind the chair. When she undid his belt, he slid his jeans and boxers to the floor. She skimmed her soft hands down his chest, his belly, until she closed a fist around him. He groaned with pleasure and lifted her onto him. She sighed and began to move with him.

His whole body tightened at the play of fingers, the strokes of tongues, the sweet and hot surging of their bodies as he thrust away the frustrations, the fears, the lies. When he felt her climax, he let himself go in a hot burst of release and cried out in wonder.

Afterward they left their clothing where it had landed. He carried her up to bed and they made love again. Sated, he tucked her in the curve of his body.

Mine, he thought, acknowledging a connection with her beyond the physical.

New. Surprising. Shocking. Too tired to wrestle with the notion, he cuddled against her backside and drifted toward sleep.

"Cort," Mara said sleepily, "you were a kid, trapped in the war between the two of them. Your mother's death wasn't your fault. If it was anyone's fault but hers, it was Leon's. You couldn't have stopped her. Trust yourself."

****

Rousso poured himself a glass of wine from the hotel mini-bar. Too oaky for his taste, like many American wines. But he needed the fortification before his call connected.

"About time. Your attempt at invading their condo was a fucking bust. You'd better have accomplished something this time." Z was long on demands, short on patience, as usual. He remembered only failures.

Rousso set down his wine and gripped the cell phone with a sweaty hand. "Yes, sir. Covered my tracks in California. Hired help will not talk to the cops or anyone ever again."

"As expected. And Jones?"

Rousso's surveillance had paid off. Jones and the woman frowned as they left Inglish's daughter, but arrived at the condo building looking much too pleased with themselves. "I do not know how they accomplished this, but he and the Marton woman returned east with ring of Danita Inglish. They have two."

There was silence as Z analyzed his announcement. Rousso knew better than to expect praise. "Don't waste more time. Get their two rings. Then the jewels."

"I will take care of situation right away." Nerves were eating away at his English fluency. He had to concentrate.

"Don't fucking screw this up," Z ordered, threat dripping blood from fresh kill, "The cops and Feebs are tripping over each other to solve those murders, my sources tell me. If they sniff out your trail, you're done. Don't call me until you have success to report."

With a trembling hand, Rousso closed the phone. Even if he obtained the crown jewels, Z would continue to perceive his difficulties as failures. His chances of moving up in Centaur were nil. If he failed again, Z would have him gutted like a pig.

Time to cut his losses. With enough money, he could disappear and create a new life.

****

"So how was your trip to California with lover boy?" Sandi plunked her butt onto the guest chair beside Mara's desk.

Mara continued to scroll down the report she was reading on screen. "Productive. Eventful. Saw my mom. Fisherman's Wharf."

"Huh-uh, hon. You're not getting away with the abbreviated version." Her friend sipped from the water bottle she always carried. "I already know the bullet points. I want the details. You did the nasty with him, didn't you?"

Mara blew out a breath and sucked in another. She slid away the mouse and swiveled to face Sandi. She needed a sounding board that wasn't her mom.

"Several times. And nasty? Not even close. Amazing, mind-blowing might be a start. He's so

261

intense, but tender, too, you know? When he looks at me, he really focuses on me and it's like the world goes away." She didn't have the words to describe how sex with Cort made her feel. How *being* with Cort made her feel. What she felt for him was so sharp and intense, it hurt. She dropped her hand as she realized she was rubbing her chest in the area of her heart. "I don't want to fall for him. That road leads to heartbreak."

"Get out. Seems like the road's leading to a relationship. In the meantime, you have to put up with the enormous suckatude of a gorgeous hunk who appreciates you and has the hots for you. I should be so lucky. And the problem here is?"

"He doesn't love me. He doesn't want love. His parents loved each other but made each other miserable. For me, it'd be like my parents all over again, in reverse. Except this party will end once our search ends. Then he's gone, back to the woods." Where he didn't have to worry about who to trust and who would trust him. Where he'd be alone again as he'd been for years. The image made her head ache. She pressed fingertips to her eyes.

"For sure, as long as you're drowning in a pity pool."

"No, I've got to reboot and just enjoy the time I have with him."

"He's still here, then? He didn't go back to Maine?"

She shook her head. "I left him setting up meets with our remaining suspects." After the former museum director, a curator, and another guard, they had nowhere to turn.

"Then use that time. If he's as intense as you say,

the man's in serious lust. To stick with the road metaphor, for men, great sex is the road that leads to love. I have three brothers. Trust me. You have to show him this route won't lead to crash and burn."

"Sure. That's all." Cort Jones didn't trust himself, living under his father's shadow, fearing his bad seed. How much did *she* trust *him*? Could she? What if the temptation of the crown jewels was too much to pass up? No, no, he wasn't his father. She wanted to trust him, or maybe it was passion driving her after all. *Frak!*

"Excuse me, *chicas*. Here's a package for Mara." A grinning Max Rivera deposited a box bigger than her briefcase on her desk.

She thanked him, standing to peer at the package. "But since when do field operatives do mailroom duties?"

"Practicing for an undercover role," he said with a wink. "Shh. Don't give me away."

"Hel-lo, anyone who believes that flunks a gullibility test. Unless it's *under-the-covers* work with your fiancée." Sandi shook her empty bottle at him. "More likely you need that report you've been bugging me about."

"Busted." He hunched his shoulders in a show of contrition. "Since I was on my way here, I offered to deliver. The mail kid's cart was piled up. Sent in overnight mail."

"I appreciate it, Max. Thanks again." For convenience she usually had packages delivered to work rather than home. But overnight? What could be urgent?

"The report is ready. I was getting ready to send it to you. Follow me and you can even have a hard copy."

Sandi headed for the door, and Max followed. "See you later, Mara," she said. "Think about what I said, okay?"

Mara nodded, waving her off as she recognized the return address on the package. Her mother. Could Mom have gone through the stored stuff already? They'd seen each other only yesterday. Mara and Cort arrived in D.C. today at noon, and she immediately came to work to get caught up.

Her fingers shook as she ripped at the tape with a box cutter. Inside the bubble wrap, she found a white envelope with her name in her mother's writing. With trembling fingers, she opened the letter, handwritten on plain white paper.

I found these things among my stored belongings. I had forgotten about them. The pictures were ones from your father's Global office, and the big brown envelope was delivered when I was packing up the house. I was such a mess then that I stowed them without looking. I hope what you need is here. I understand you must hurry.

There is one more thing to tell you about your father. Don't blame Cort Jones or his father. Your father didn't want you girls to know, but his heart condition was very serious. The doctors prescribed pills but he wouldn't take them unless he felt bad because they affected the one area we always agreed on. If he had taken his pills, he might still be alive.

Mara couldn't finish. She set the letter on her desk. Tears clawed her eyes and clogged her throat. Why did her dad have to be so macho? So the drugs made him impotent. He'd still be alive, wouldn't he? Maybe he could've cleared his name. Maybe her mother would have found the courage to tell him she loved him. Maybe—

She pressed her fist to her mouth to stop a sob. Maybes and whys were futile. All she could do now was try to prove him innocent to Global Insurance.

She'd look at the photos later. The bulky padded envelope came out next. An official return address, a law firm in the District. Bickham, Dixon, and Kress. Not one she recognized. Her knees watery, she sank onto her chair.

****

Another piece of the puzzle but what the hell did it mean? The FBI didn't seem to know any more than Cort did.

He closed his cell phone and hit the remote for sports. A classic match-up. Colts stomping all over the Bears. Perfect after his day playing phone tag with the former museum director. Nobody wanted to talk to him. There was a shocker.

He'd just stretched out on the sofa when Mara opened the apartment door.

He set down his just-opened bottle of ale and vaulted up. "Hey, what's this?" He relieved her of the cardboard box with the shipping label and placed it on the cocktail table.

"Stuff from my mom." She kicked off her heels and set down her big bag—the one from Chinatown, covered with a red Asian dragon.

He was about to ask but decided to wait when he took a closer look. Her sunny yellow dress was at odds with the wild and puffy aspect of her eyes. Crying?

"I hope you had a better day than I did," she said, waving her arms like she was signaling with semaphore flags. "We thought finally we'd tracked down the authentic Han horse. You know, the one stolen from the Tate Museum? But it was another copy. Centaur again, damn them. Fingers in every art-crime pie. Is there any wine?"

He trailed in her wake as she whisked to the refrigerator. "A bottle of pinot. Don't know if you're supposed to chill it, but it's in the fridge. The wine merchant said it was excellent." Cort figured that meant at least decent.

"Whatever." She bent over to search inside. "What's this? Shrimp? Chopped veggies?"

He dragged his gaze from the view of her shapely backside. "Um, on my run, I found these shrimp on sale. Thought I'd make shrimp creole."

The manic look in her eyes softer, she dragged out the wine bottle. She brushed a kiss across his lips. "Cort, that's so sweet. If I have some of this wine now, will it spoil the dinner?" She slammed open the drawer where she kept the corkscrew.

"No problem." When she fumbled with the tool, he took the bottle and corkscrew from her. In her state of mind, whatever its source, she'd probably stab herself. What the hell was in the package? He poured a healthy amount into a glass and handed it over. "You gonna tell me what this is all about? Not just the Han horse."

"Give me a minute." When he nodded, she took a long pull on the wine, then sighed. "Thanks. I saw a salad in the fridge too."

He felt his face heat. "Baby greens and grape tomatoes. Bottled balsamic vinaigrette though. A guy can create only so much in a day." He'd begun taking his turn at kitchen duty. Tonight he'd wanted to impress her with more than his usual basic chicken or spaghetti with bottled sauce. But that goal dropped in priority. Now he was worried about her.

Bottle and glass in hand, she marched back to the living room and paced as she downed the wine. She straightened CDs on a shelf. Arranged the throw pillows on the sofa.

"Did you talk to your sister?" Maybe that was what put her in such turmoil.

"Ah, yes, about dear André. Cassie's floating on clouds. He offered to take her to France next trip. As if. She bragged about him flying by private jet. But I can find no record of that. I'll search the databases next for other flights. No record of Rozmer, Senior in hospital either." She drained her goblet. "Any luck with new suspects?"

He returned to his former spot on the sofa, eyeing her as she poured more wine.

"The former director hasn't returned my calls," he said. "The guard hung up on me."

"We're quite the pair. Drink up," she said, nodding toward his beer. She hoisted her glass again and took a modest sip before setting it down. "Okay, I'd better get to this before I'm too sloshed to know up from sideways. Jet lag is probably working on me too."

"The box?" he prompted.

She lowered her head in an almost prayerful pose. "From Mom. She found some things of Dad's in storage. Pictures from his office." She unfolded the top flaps and lifted out a lumpy brown envelope. "And this from a law firm in the city. I don't know them. Addressed to Dad."

"There's no postage," he pointed out. "So no date

stamp."

"Delivered by messenger, I suppose. The letter inside is dated a week before the Smithsonian robbery." She drew in a shaky breath, closed her eyes a moment then reached inside the envelope. "And this." She deposited a bubble-wrapped object in his open palm.

Anticipation revved his pulse, but his heart stalled out when he realized the implication for Mara. No wonder she'd been crying. Everything she'd always believed about her father crumbled to dust. He peeled apart the wrap. Inside was a gold ring.

Fat tears puddled in Mara's beautiful eyes. Her shoulders shook with silent sobs.

Seeing her grief as her world fell apart wedged pain between his ribs like a pounded spike. He started to take her in his arms. "Mara."

She held up her hands and shook her head, swallowed hard, backed away. "No, I'm all right. I'm dealing. Dad did conspire with the Jeweler. And not just after the robbery. He knew before. He got Global to give him the case so he could manage the evidence. He lied to everyone."

Cort racked his brain for some explanation for Leon sending Quincy Marton a ring piece that didn't involve larceny. He had to try to comfort her. "Maybe your dad let Leon think he wanted in. Maybe he was going to use the ring piece to talk Leon into—"

"No." The look in her eyes almost burned a hole through his chest. Picking up her wine, she trailed to the breakfast bar where she straightened the sections of the *Post* he'd left there. "Don't try to make up excuses for him. Or me. I'm the child of a crook."

Just like me. He'd tell her that didn't make her one,

but coming from him, the advice would be damned hollow.

As she continued her manic pacing and fussing, he examined the new ring piece. Like the others, it contained words on the inside and a raised shape on the outside, this one a small acute angle. What could the symbols mean? He needed Sherlock Holmes. The new one locked between the other two with a slight twist that aligned the text. He added the new words to the old in the chart he'd drawn on his legal tablet.

"What does the new ring piece add?" she asked, stopping to peer at the paper.

"... THE WOODEN HOLD
... AND ROYAL GOLD
... FOUNTAIN OF MY YOUTH.
... OUR HONOR, TRUTH."

When Mara finished reading the four lines aloud, she blinked. "Not much help, is it?"

"Not yet," he said, working on the new wording. "Something. Not sure what, but maybe it'll come to me." He lifted the wrap packing the ring. "Was this opened?"

"No. The envelope was still sealed. Why?"

"Your dad didn't open anything. Maybe Leon was offering him a bribe but he didn't even know what was inside so he couldn't have taken it."

A pained groan tore from her throat. "He knew what it was. He didn't have to open it. You're grasping at straws."

"And you're jumping to conclusions. But now we have three rings. We have to see this thing through. Get the whole story." He hovered, ready for when her coiled spring ran down.

"I have the whole story. Right here." She withdrew a sheet of business size stationery from the envelope. "I'm guessing this is the Jeweler's handwriting."

He accepted the paper. "I recognize it. Yeah."

In his typical meticulous script, Leon had written, *"I'm sending this to you, Q, because I know you'll do what I expect with it."* He signed it with his initials.

Cort saw crowding Mara's eyes the emotions that had blasted through him after the crime. Impotence. Grief. Anger, building to rage. Rage alleviated the pain but left a bitter taste that never abated. His arms ached to hold her but the timing was wrong. Soon. She'd need it and so would he. "I'm sorry."

"I know. Keep reading."

Chapter Twenty-Four

BELOW THE MESSAGE was a list.
D. FALCO
G. HAUPTMAN
D. INGLISH
L. JONES
Q. MARTON

"I think it means there are five puzzle ring pieces," she said, her voice ragged.

"So along with Danita Inglish, Dante Falco and the guard George Hauptman did receive rings. But probably not this letter. Leon wouldn't have let them know the other conspirators." His gut clenched at the suspicion the Centaur agent had Falco's ring piece.

"So why did my dad get this list?"

"And why didn't the FBI jump on it? Maybe it came after your dad died and they'd already collected his files."

"Why would Leon have it sent then? No, the FBI just missed it. Somehow." Her frown said she questioned that supposition. "Dad was in on the crime. Either before or after."

"Still doesn't make sense to me. No more than a dozen other mysteries in this mess."

"The widow Hauptman lied to us." She jabbed her index finger at the list.

"Maybe not the first time but definitely when you phoned her. My friendly FBI agent called just before you came home. The cops have no record of her so-called break-in."

"You think she found George's ring?"

"Bet on it. And she didn't want us to know. She meant her threat to sic the cops on us to keep us away. If she thinks she can find the crown jewels with one ring piece, good luck." Even with three, he wondered if they had enough of the clue.

Mara did a good imitation of his Murder One stare. She folded her arms. "We should pay the widow another visit."

"Definitely. Unannounced. One more thing from Kaplan. The cops do have a file on her brother. Seems Hugo Evans has been in trouble since he was a teenager. A couple of assault charges, one conviction. Not the sharpest chisel in the kit. Poor impulse control. He worked part time for a landscaping contractor until he whacked the boss across the back with a shovel over a salary dispute. Did a few months in jail for assault."

She huffed her exasperation. "What does it mean?"

"Hard to say. Now. We need to make a list of what facts we have and go from there."

"I should've done a background check on him. I've been too naïve. Say it. I know you're thinking it." She wove her fingers together as if to still their agitated fluttering.

Her bleak gaze and pale face punched him in the chest. He captured her hands. Cold, clammy. "Thinking what?"

"That it's better not to trust because it doesn't hurt as much when people fail you."

"I've thought that, yeah. But I'm beginning to wonder what that philosophy has caused me to miss." He tugged until her arms wrapped around his waist and her scent lowered his tension a notch. For the first time since she'd come through the door, he felt warmth spread through him. And the odd feeling of coming home.

She sighed against his chest, tears dampening his shirt. "You already know. Pain."

"But what else? You could've kept that envelope with its damning letter and ring piece secret. You didn't have to share it. You found your answer, even though it's not what you wanted. But you trusted me enough to share it with me. Thank you."

When she'd cried herself out, she excused herself and went to soak in a hot tub. Bubble bath, he guessed, with a scented candle burning nearby. Aromatherapy she'd called it the last time. Pampering, he'd countered. Which she needed at the moment.

Later he made sure she ate some shrimp creole,

which turned out not bad. Mara laughed for the first time when he told her he'd copied the recipe from TV.

Later she fell asleep on the sofa and he carried her to bed. As frustrating as it was for him to hold her without making love with her, sleep was what she needed. So he tucked her against him and watched her beautiful features as she relaxed into sleep.

He'd never been this involved this long with any woman. She was smart and brave, and she made him smile more than in years. Sex with her made him feel like he was coming with his whole body. She made him feel alive again. And he wanted to make her happy.

His search for the ring pieces had dragged her through hell. She never complained about the threats they faced, never folded even when she was scared to death, and she was as determined as he was. She'd shown him the ring and the letter when every instinct must've screamed to hide them. She was amazing.

He didn't know what to do with his warring feelings. A dangerous need to connect with her in every way, a heady joy when he was with her, and hungry impatience when he couldn't see her, hear her voice, touch her.

They were racing against ruthless enemies, one greedy for power, another for wealth. And a third unknown adversary, probably the Gramornia spy. Sooner than she knew, their quest would end and *they* would end. That notion gnawed at him.

In his half-asleep state, key words from the verse popped out at him in 3-D. He jolted with the realization and forced himself to settle again, afraid he would wake Mara. The memory he'd been struggling with clicked into place.

Not efficient, but effective and elegant. *Damn you, Leon, you son of a bitch. Why there?*

The prince's crowning was three days from today. Thousands of miles away. Cort would climb out of bed and into his truck right now except he needed to throw their competitors off the trail. And keep Mara safe.

Then recover the jewels to send them to Gramornia in time. A long shot.

****

"I'm sorry about your father," Thomas Devlin said. "But I agree with Cort there must be some other explanation. A man who stood for honesty his entire life wouldn't jump off the rails like that."

"Thank you, sir." Mara had searched her brain for a plausible reason for the Jeweler to have sent her dad the letter and ring piece, a reason that didn't involve larceny. She found no answer but the obvious one. "The truth is tough to accept but I'm handling it."

Maybe if she said that often enough, she'd believe it. But dammit, he was Dad. How could he be a crook? She said a silent prayer Cort and Devlin were right and proof would present itself. Somehow.

"In case you're wondering, this information makes no difference to me. You're one of my best employees, Mara. I trust you completely. That hasn't changed and won't."

She swallowed against the tight knot in her throat. If Devlin didn't see her as tainted by her dad's transgression, maybe there was hope for her.

"Thank you, sir. I won't let you down."

"And I won't ask you where Cort thinks the jewels are hidden. You can have a few days to do what you need to, but I'm concerned about your safety. I don't need to remind you people have died."

She suppressed a shudder. "I need to see this through. At least returning the jewels will give me and my family some peace of mind." Cort didn't want her to accompany him, but she'd insisted she'd be safer with him than alone where the bad guys could snatch her and try to use her as leverage. "We hope we can get away tonight without a tail. The Centaur agent or whoever is always either one step ahead of us or right behind."

"You're checking for bugs in the apartment?"

She nodded. She'd swept the place daily. "The scrambler chips and GPS blockers in our cell phones are still working."

"We need to set you up with one more security device on your cell. And there's another possibility I should've thought of sooner," Devlin said, picking up his interoffice phone. "Go to the parking garage. A surveillance tech will meet you there."

****

Cort hooked the three ring pieces together again. Studied the raised symbols on each. An arc like a backward *C*. An *X*. And an acute angle or an *L*. He'd tried to get some shuteye before their overnight drive, but his brain wouldn't shut down, jetlag or no. So he'd spent time on Mara's computer searching for codes, symbol meanings, hieroglyphs, anything that might yield a damn clue to their significance. And the rest of the day at the table with his printouts trying to figure things out. Found zip.

What he knew for sure was the symbols did have significance. They hadn't been fused on later but had been molded as part of the ring pieces. No accident the symbols were designed to line up in a row. Everything Leon did was deliberate.

He lowered his head and rubbed his aching eyes. Leon was a dark cloud swirling over him, a malevolent presence casting a shadow on his life until he could find the crown jewels and turn them over to the FBI.

"What the hell, Leon?"

Enough. Rolling the kinks from his shoulders, he left the table and changed into sweats. A long run would clear his head. As soon as he hit the pavement, he felt the heavy humidity that presaged a thunderstorm. The midday traffic spewed exhaust in his face. Fucking perfect. He couldn't get to the clean air of Maine soon enough.

The bad guys had dogged his every move. He couldn't let them follow him to Leon's stash. If Centaur and not the FBI got the crown jewels, he would deserve being hounded. How to manage blowing town in secret was a problem to ponder while he ran.

An hour later, soaked from sweat and drenched from a short but soaking downpour, he dragged up the steps and into the apartment. No Mara. She should be home by now. He picked up his cell phone from the counter. A message, but from Thomas Devlin. His pulse had started to calm but anxiety kicked it up again.

"Come to my office immediately. Don't drive the truck. If the colonel's men are there, don't let them see you leave."

****

Forty excruciating minutes later Cort strode into Devlin's office—this time on his own, no guard escort. No sign of the two dickwads who'd strong-armed him that first time.

"Where is she? What happened?" he barked, as the admin closed the door behind him.

"I'm right here." Mara jumped up from the conference table. She held out her arms as if to say, "I'm fine."

Without thinking, he catapulted across the office and dragged her into his arms. He drank in the feel and smell of her, reassuring himself she was whole and safe.

"So that's how things are." Thomas Devlin, on his face the kind of indulgent smile usually reserved for puppies, rose from his desk chair and ambled toward them. "Sorry to be so cryptic. Hazards of my work. As you can see Mara has not been abducted by aliens of any stripe."

Cort's heart thudded a few more times before it settled to a quieter beat that allowed him to hear the ticking of the antique clock and the hum of computers. Maybe he'd overreacted but after Yerik's attack in San Francisco, he was taking no chances. So screw it if Devlin thought his behavior entertaining.

"He called because we thought you needed to see this," Mara said, gesturing toward the conference table. "Turns out the bad guys' crystal balls won't give away our secrets anymore."

On the table were two rectangular cases the size of his cell phone, one gray, one black. "Electronic trackers? I've checked under both vehicles every day. What the hell?"

"Right. A surveillance tech found this GPS transponder tucked up high in the right rear wheel well."

He dropped onto one of the side chairs, a fireball

burning his gut. "They used a decoy for us to find and a duplicate. Want to bet my truck has one exactly like this?"

"Two actually," Devlin put in.

Cort looked up blankly.

"There were two," the other man continued. "The other was in the left rear wheel well. An unlikely scenario, I grant you. I've never run into this before. The black one's sold in this country as well as Europe, and the gray one's a design used by various military in Europe. Gramornia uses them to monitor their own vehicles' locations. We can turn these against your adversaries."

He nodded but didn't comment. Devlin had something up his sleeve. He got that. But the rest... "Dammit, Mara. I'm an idiot. I should've—"

"Cram it with the guilt, Cort." She planted her hands on her hips. Temper glowed like hot coals in her dark eyes. "If anyone failed here, it's me. I'm supposed to be the technical whiz. But, as Mr. Devlin pointed out, neither one of us is a trained security specialist. And he didn't think of it until today. So stifle yourself, mister."

She looked so adorable railing at him, he nearly smiled. Instead he let her justification calm his tension. "Yes, ma'am. No guilt here. So how do these gadgets work?"

"The transponder sends out a signal to the receiver, which can read it as far as a mile away," she explained, taking the chair beside him. "The receiver can be plugged into a computer's USB port, so the user can see the location on screen. Using GPS mapping, the transponder tells the receiver exactly where it is at all times." She held up the black case. "The tech told me this model has a battery life of up to four months. The gray one longer."

"Before I go rip the suckers off my truck, any idea why *two* trackers?"

"Not the FBI," Devlin said, swinging into his executive chair at the head of the table. "They probably couldn't get a warrant to bug you."

Cort smacked a fist into his palm. "That leaves Rolf Rousso and Colonel Yerik. A damn wonder they didn't trip over each other."

"Discovering these now is good news, given you need to get out of town without them knowing you've gone."

Cort thought about it, then rose and wandered the room. Moving fueled his brain with a spark of an idea. "The black tracker has to be Rousso. The military one Yerik. I hope. We need a plan."

Devlin placed his elbows on the table and steepled his fingers. "Things are coming together in your favor. The Gramornian royal guard arrested the prime minister an hour ago along with several of his deputies."

"You're involved in that somehow, sir," Mara said, her brow furrowed with speculation.

Before Devlin could reply, Cort held up a hand. "I'm the one who kept her out of it. Let me take the heat."

He turned to her. "Once Yerik added to the threat, I asked Mr. Devlin to help. He acted as go-between to eliminate the threat from the colonel. I kept it quiet because I didn't know if what he planned would work. Yerik hurt you and I want to see him taken down." More than taken down. He'd have risked arrest to pound the asswipe into the dirt.

"I'll make a note in my smart phone you kept this from me. Payback comes later."

"Duly noted." If Devlin hadn't been there, he'd have kissed her within an inch of her life. And she could pay him back any way she wanted. "I look forward to it."

Color suffused her cheeks.

"I've been scared to death since he burned me. I felt like I had knives in my chest. Even yoga didn't calm me." She closed her eyes, breathing deeply. "How did all this work? Go-between with whom?"

"A contact at the Gramornian embassy," Devlin said. "My contact kept it under wraps while proof was found that Prime Minister Turkof was plotting against the royal family. They also have proof of Yerik's involvement, but they don't know where he is. They don't know he's in the country. He probably used false papers."

"We don't know his location either, although he's been monitoring us. Until now." Cort nodded toward the transponders.

A diabolical smile curved Devlin's lips. "I think my Gramornia contact can arrange something that will make everyone happy. Everyone but Colonel Yerik."

Chapter Twenty-Five

"GET IN THE back, you idiot. Let me drive." With jerky movements, Yerik maneuvered behind the sedan's wheel. Why couldn't he have a comfortable automobile like this in Gramornia? Once Turkof took over, perhaps he would.

His men had phoned him, panicked over their target's erratic behavior. They did something to the computer, he was certain. But when he checked the program, all appeared in order. Now he would see for himself what was going on.

After Gregor settled into the backseat, Yerik steered into traffic. "You say Marton left work at seven o'clock and has been driving around the city for an hour?"

"Yes, sir. Aimlessly as far as we can tell." Egor, beside him, nodded over the laptop screen. The man's nervous sweat made Yerik wrinkle his nose. "She's not very far away. If you'll take the next left. Sir."

After the earlier downpour, the sky cleared of all but a few wispy white clouds. Within five minutes, Yerik pulled to within four vehicles behind Marton. Raindrops on the pavement and on vehicles reflected the ambient light and made it hard to see. He couldn't spot the red coupe but it had to be there, blocked from his view by larger, taller American vehicles.

"She seems headed home now," Egor said.

The transponder guided him past Dupont Circle, where Marton should've turned. Her flat was only blocks from the crowded hub. Where the hell was she going?

He turned to Egor, but his man merely looked as puzzled as he felt.

When she led him west on Massachusetts Avenue toward Embassy Row, Yerik started to sweat. No matter what she was up to, he wasn't going to take the chance of driving too close to his country's embassy.

"She has stopped up ahead," Egor reported.

"In front of the Westin?"

"Yes sir. Perhaps she has been waiting to meet someone."

"Killing time. A possibility." He should berate Gregor for offering an opinion without being asked, but given the circumstances, he would let it go. He steered to the curb and killed the engine. A yellow sign indicated a no-parking zone, but what did he care? "We shall wait to see what she does."

"I do not see it," Gregor said. "No red car ahead. Only a black limousine."

A limousine. The skin on Yerik's nape prickled. Perspiration broke out on his hairline. He reached for the ignition. "Can you see any sort of insignia?"

Tires squealed and brakes screeched. Vehicles converged from ahead and behind, blocking any exit. People in flak vests leaped out, guns drawn. They surrounded his car.

"Colonel!" Gregor squeaked from the back.

Egor slammed shut the laptop lid. A look of panic froze his broad face.

Yerik reached inside his jacket for his 9mm. He

flicked off the safety and fired. A bullet smashed through the computer on Egor's lap. He screamed, a shrill and unearthly cry above the echoing blast. The next shot shattered the man's skull. Blood and gore sprayed the passenger window. The lifeless body slumped to the side.

Before Yerik could turn to silence Gregor, the driver's door flew open and a pistol jabbed his temple. A gloved hand snatched the pistol from his hand. Two brawny arms yanked him from the seat like a rag doll. A man and a woman slammed him against the hood. A thud on the rear bumper meant Gregor received similar treatment.

"Embassy of the Principality of Gramornia Security," the woman said. Hearing her speak in his native tongue fizzled the last molecules of bravado. "You're under arrest for crimes against the crown. And for stalking one of our diplomats."

What? Who? He tried to twist around but was pushed back against the car as the male guard bound his wrists behind him with a zip tie.

When the guards dragged him upright, he saw the limo's doors open. The uniformed driver helped out a blonde woman in a pink suit.

The daughter of the ambassador.

Before his brain could tackle the conundrum of how an embassy limo came to have his transponder attached to it, Mara Marton joined the blonde outside the limo. The driver doffed his cap. Cortez Jones.

Yerik had been taken for a ride, to use the American expression literally. His gut felt knotted with razor wire, and a cold sweat beaded his torso, but he straightened his shoulders. He was a soldier after all, albeit on the losing side.

If his hands weren't bound, he'd salute his adversaries. Instead he dipped his head in a sharp nod.

****

When Cort saw Yerik nod in their direction, he planted his feet to stop from going over there and beating the asshole to a pulp. Mara started walking toward the man, but he caught her elbow.

"What are you doing?" he asked over the noise of cop voices in two languages and the rumble of high-power engines. The smells of exhaust and pavement still hot from the day's sun mingled with another, grisly smell.

"I have to face him down. Rid myself of this fear."

Recognition slapped him between the eyes. He'd faced his father, saw the man he'd hated and feared no longer powerful, but withered and weak. The meeting didn't eradicate his hate but instantly dissipated the fear.

Mara had begun their journey nearly paralyzed by fear of the violence threatening the two of them. He saw her grow into decisive purpose and courage. "I'm going with you."

"I shall remain here," the Gramornian ambassador's daughter said, no less regal for her petite stature. "It has been my honor to assist in capturing this traitor to my country. And my pleasure to meet the people responsible for uncovering the plot. Thank you."

"My pleasure entirely," Cort said as the three exchanged handshakes.

"Thank you so much for allowing us to ride with you," Mara added.

"My father did not want me to participate, but I'd

not have missed this for the world." The other woman returned to the limo. As if by magic, her real driver appeared to open the rear door.

Gramornian guards stood on either side of Colonel Yerik, ready to pounce even though his hands were bound behind him. U.S. Diplomatic Service and D.C. police milled around, as if unsure of jurisdiction.

"It appears you have won," the disgraced colonel said as Mara and Cort walked around puddles and approached him. He held his head high.

Cort held her elbow. No way was he letting her get closer than three feet. No matter how under control the guards had the colonel.

"You have a lot to answer for." Indignation fired her words. Her shoulders trembled and she fisted her hands. "Treason, assault on Cort and me, and now murder. Your prime minister has been arrested. You're done."

"Treason?" His voice was aloof but strained. "Perhaps. All in the perception. I prefer to think of my efforts as loyal opposition."

Her shaky laugh held no mirth. "Whatever. I hope you rot in prison."

"A short sentence, Ms. Marton." The skin tightened across his face, sharpening his features and thinning his mouth. "In Gramornia I face a short trial and a firing squad."

She stared a long minute. "I'd sentence you to fifty years, enough time for you to consider the distinction between opposition and treason."

Cort waited until Yerik's bleak gaze swerved to him. "She's way too nice. Personally, I'd like to be there to see those bullets rip you to bloody fucking shreds."

Blown away with admiration at Mara's bravery and boldness, he released her. They walked away together to Devlin's waiting car.

The car drove them back to Crystal City, where they retrieved Mara's coupe, complete with the remaining transponder. If their plan worked, Rousso would think she'd worked late and was just heading home after nine o'clock.

As soon as they entered the apartment, Cort took her bag and deposited it on a chair. He pulled her into his arms and kissed her with all the pent-up emotion and heat building since learning their vehicles were plugged in to the bad guys. She looped her arms around his neck and opened to him with matching ardor. Their tongues caressed and danced. He ached to take her to bed and make love to her all night. On a sigh of reluctance, he ended the kiss, too damned aware of what else he had to accomplish before they could blow this town. He buried his nose in her fragrant hair and inhaled the woman.

"You were amazing back there." He had to tell her just how amazing. "When we started this high-wire act, you had no idea of the dangers involved. Truthfully, neither did I, but prison taught me to watch my back."

"No kidding. I fell apart like a broken marionette and panicked all over you." She caressed his cheek, probably too rough with stubble against her soft palm. The same passion burning in him glowed in her eyes along with the awareness their time was short.

"Understandable. But in San Francisco and tonight, you were a super hero. Fighting back, standing up to the slime. I've never seen more courage."

"He was in handcuffs," she reminded him with a smile.

"I wouldn't put anything past someone like Yerik."

"You were pretty good too, letting two females backseat drive all over the District."

"I suffered, but I'll live." After another kiss, he released her.

She gestured toward the kitchen with a sigh of apparent regret. "The pizza we had in Mr. Devlin's office was okay but I'd planned a celebration dinner before we left."

He rooted around for the beer he'd hoped for after his run, but opted for a tea. They had a long night ahead. The sadness in her eyes tugged at his chest. "A bittersweet celebration. I'm sorry as hell learning Leon's hiding place comes at such a price."

Something was off about Leon sending Marton a ring piece. He'd get it sooner or later.

"I know." She ambled to the kitchen and poured a glass of water.

"And we have a couple more tricks before our high-wire routine is over."

She snapped her fingers, as she remembered something. "I didn't get to tell you earlier what I came up with about André Rozmer. More digging yielded some interesting information. He *is* negotiating wine distribution contracts while he's in the Baltimore area."

"I hear a *but* in there."

She smiled ruefully. "I found a plane flight. He took a private jet from La Guardia to San Fran the same day we did. No info on where he went out there."

"Maybe he was the man who followed the fake delivery guy. But why? How does he figure in all this?"

He had an idea but they had no time. Save it for later. "We can leave as soon as it's safe. I want to get the crown jewels and turn them over to the FBI before Rousso knows we've left D.C."

One day to go before the new prince's crowning.

Mara measured out water for the coffee maker. When she retrieved the coffee beans from the freezer, she hummed with surprise. A metallic clink on the countertop told him what she had.

Smiling, he leaned his butt against the breakfast bar as he opened his tea. On the counter were the linked ring pieces he'd stashed in the freezer when he went out to run. "Speaking of hiding places, I see you found mine."

"Not what I expected to see in my freezer." She shot him a sly look, mischief in her eyes. The rich aroma of freshly ground coffee filled the kitchen as the beans whirred. "Another attempt to find meaning in the raised symbols?"

He hooted a laugh. When he realized she was trying to cheer him up, warmth curled in his chest. She'd been dealt a body blow about her father but she was thinking of him. "Thought I'd see if freezing gold morphed the runes into the answer to the Sphinx's riddle."

"Maybe the Sphinx's but I'm guessing not Leon's."

"No answers, ancient or new. I left the rings chilling while I ran. Seemed safer than carrying them in my pocket on the streets. Figured the freezer was another layer of protection along with the security system."

"Linked like that, they look like copper pipes,"

Mara said. "You know, for plumbing."

Cort stared at her, then at the rings. His brain flashed back to a workbench littered with Dante Falco's bump key, a keybit, and other tools...

The hairs rose on the back of his neck as his gaze and his mind raced. He set down his tea so hard that liquid splashed out the top. "Son of a bitch."

"What?" She ambled over and picked up the joined rings.

"In Falco's basement, the burglar dumped drawers of tools and junk onto the surface of his workbench. When the rock and then the Molotov cocktail went through the window, I forgot everything else. For days I've tried to figure out what was bothering me about the incongruity of what I saw on the bench."

"And?" she prompted.

"Along with his burglary tools, copper pipe. All shiny bright and unused. He had many talents, but fishing toy boats from the nameless muck in toilet drains to give him entry into people's houses? Not the fastidious Dante Falco I knew. Not likely. And I saw no plumbing tools. So why have short lengths of copper pipe?" He picked up the linked rings. "After that drawer, no more were dumped out. The rest of the basement was untouched."

Her luscious mouth formed an *O* as she saw what he was getting at. "What better place to hide his ring piece than mixed in with similar rings?"

"Clever. Except his ruse didn't work." He ran a finger across the remaining jagged edge, where either another ring would join these. "The Centaur guy has his ring piece."

"We can pay another visit to Twyla Hauptman.

289

Persuade her to give us her husband's."

He shook his head, pulled her into his arms. Nothing better to soothe his niggling doubts. "No time to spare. Forget the Widow Hauptman. Forget Centaur. Their rings will do them no damn good. Even if they had the rest of the rhyme, they wouldn't know where to go."

"What about the symbols, the runes, you called them?"

"Maybe we'll find the key to that once we get to the hiding place." He shrugged off the plague of a puzzle. Now he had some plaguing of his own to do. He kissed her and poured a mug of coffee. "One for the road. How about you pack while I carry out the next part of our plan?"

"Fine. But how long do you think it'll take?"

"Forty-five minutes tops. I'll go out the alley in case Rousso's watching."

At the door, she reached for his free hand. "Be careful. He has a gun and doesn't hesitate to kill."

No one had worried about him for a long, long time. The caring and concern in her eyes thawed something dormant in his wary heart, something that rumbled to life and hummed. He didn't need the confusion of such soft emotions. He needed to be sharp and focused.

"No sweat, sweetheart. I'm not doing anything dangerous," he said, his mouth set in a grim line. "Just devious."

Chapter Twenty-Six

WOULD CORT BE safe? Would Rousso or whoever else was out there get to him? Mara's stomach churned as she headed to the bedroom with her mug of coffee. She dragged an overnight bag from beneath the bed.

Just as well they had no time. She hardly felt like celebrating. And not because of her father's guilt. She wasn't okay with that, but her boss's validation of her as a person helped. Her anguish had to do with Cort. As soon as they found the crown jewels and turned them over to the authorities, she'd never see him again. Her heart bumped so hard she dropped onto the bed. Cort desired her, wanted her, cared about her, but he wasn't interested in her love. He'd spent so many years repressing emotion, he could feel nothing but the darkness of his father's ghost and the weight of his crime.

When tears threatened, she jumped to her feet. "Dammit, no. Stop it."

After throwing some clothes and toiletries in her bag, she hit the shower. The hot spray massaged her tense shoulders as she soaped up. For a few more days, she would be with him. Until then she had to ditch her silly girlish dreams.

Focus on the goal. Determination, not desire or dreams.

A few minutes later, clean, dry, and marginally more relaxed, she stepped out of the tub, a small towel wound around her damp hair and a thick white one wrapped around her body.

Her stomach took a swoop when she spied Cort in the doorway, all muscle and masculinity, one brawny shoulder propped against the doorjamb. "Don't scare me like that. I didn't hear you come in."

"Sorry. Guess we're both on edge."

She sagged against the tile with relief he was safe and apparently successful. She had an idea what he'd done but decided to let him tell it. "What did you do with the transponders?"

"Yerik's is on the table." His grin punched in his dimple and sped up her heart. "And the other, you know that Starbucks around the block?"

She frowned, confused. "Yeah, but what..."

He stepped closer and unwound the big towel, let it drop to the floor. His hot gaze perused her body with such intimate slowness, heat pulsed inside her with an insistent beat.

"Always a couple cabs parked outside while the cabbies load up on caffeine for their shift. I took a Yellow Cab over to the Renaissance off Connecticut."

"A hotel?" When his hand skimmed along her hip, she could scarcely breathe, let alone ask a sensible question.

"Hotel seemed like a good place to catch a return trip. The first cab now has an electronic hitchhiker tucked under the backseat. It'll ride around the city all night sending its signal. Rousso will be chasing his tail. Not us."

Even if the cabby changed shifts, the car would

keep going. She puffed out a breathy laugh, allowed him to tug her against his hard torso.

He lifted the small towel from her hair and slid his fingers through the damp tresses, gently massaging her scalp and working out the tangles. "Mmm, even beneath the soap, I can smell the scent of your skin. Unique, an aphrodisiac."

His words and the sensual caress made her head spin. He smelled damned good too, salty and male. Her legs nearly gave way. "What about the FBI? Don't you want them to know where we're going?"

"Not yet. I don't trust Leon. The raised runes bug me. I have to know this ring puzzle is for real and the crown jewels are still there before I call Kaplan."

"I understand." Cort feared what the FBI would do if this turned out to be another of Leon's merry chases. They would make Cort's life harder than ever. For his sake, she prayed his father had played it straight this last time.

"And, Mara, tell your sister nothing. *Nothing.* We still don't know André's game." His eyes searched hers. For agreement? Or deception?

That he still didn't trust her sent a chill through her. "I know. I won't. I haven't told her we're leaving town." *You can trust me.* But if he didn't after all this time, telling him so would make no difference. "I still have frequent-flier miles. We could get to Maine faster than driving."

He shook his head. "I checked the schedules. Flying to a small-market airport like Portland gives meaning to the Maine saying, 'You can't get theah from heah.' Now we're not bugged, we can make better time driving and stay under the radar."

He planted his big hands on her bottom and pulled her harder against his erection. "We still have time before we need to leave."

Dreams versus determination? Well, maybe one more diversion wouldn't hurt. She intended to make it one for the memory banks. "Let's make good use of it then."

"Hoped you'd say that." He picked her up and carried her to the bedroom.

As soon as he deposited her on the bed, she bounced up and worked at his belt buckle. "You stripped me. Now it's my turn."

"Sweetheart, if you want control, be my guest."

She kissed his eyes, his mouth, his scars, his tattoos. Holding his gaze, she yanked his shirt off over his head and threaded her fingers through the dusting of chest hairs. *I want to memorize every line and angle, the taste and feel and heat of you so I never forget these weeks together.*

When she'd rid him of every stitch of clothing, they tumbled onto the bed together.

The very male scent of him, the heavy contours of his muscles, and the languid heat in his eyes enthralled her. She caressed his chest, toying with the whorls of crisp hair, teasing the flat coins of his nipples with her tongue, and he sank into the bed, head thrown back as if his body were too heavy to move. She slid down him, pleasure rippling through her, thrilling at the dark leap of passion in his half-closed eyes. She heard soft moans and realized they came from her as she rubbed herself over his engorged length.

When she closed her mouth around him, he lifted off the bed. His hands reached for her but she slithered out of reach.

"Not yet," she murmured.

"You're killing me, woman." Both his fists gripped the bed covers.

She hummed as she licked and suckled and tasted, driving them both higher. When she heard her name moaned, she slid upward and straddled him. His hand covered her abdomen and dipped between her legs, building sensation, making her senses reel. With no other man had she ever found such complete immersion, such fever, such freedom. With him she could hold back nothing, no longer wanted to. Need roared in her ears, and she covered him with protection and lowered herself onto him. The edgy thrill, the sparking of circuits, the thudding of her heart—this was where she belonged. Locked together, bodies, hands, and gazes, they stilled, the moment spinning out on a thread as bright and hot as sunshine. He moved, slowly, languidly, thrusting with her, prolonging her torture, as if he too wanted to stretch out the time. Pleasure pulsed through her veins, slicking her body, carrying her to the beckoning peak.

When liquid sparks pulsed in her body, she let go, soaring with white hot pleasure, her whole body rippling above him, around him with explosive spasms. She felt him seize up and join her, the liquid fire fusing them into one.

****

At the highway rest stop, Mara held the restroom door for a woman with a baby in a stroller. The woman smiled widely and thanked her in Spanish.

"*De nada*." The limit of Mara's Spanish language fluency.

She spied a coffee kiosk in the food court and hustled over. She'd napped some of the five hours since they'd left D.C., but she needed coffee before taking over the wheel from Cort. Rather than her usual mocha, she ordered a French roast. Caffeine, smoothed out with a little milk, a little sweetener.

She headed for the door. Cort must've finished filling the truck with gas and would be anxious about getting back on the road.

When her jeans pocket vibrated, she opened her cell phone and looked at the screen.

Cassie. At this time of night?

The scrambler and GPS blockers were still intact so it would be safe to talk to her. "Hey, sis, you're up late."

"You didn't answer before. It went right to voice mail." Cassie's whiny plaint was nasal, as if she'd been crying.

"Sorry. Guess I turned it off by accident." She'd doused it so she could sleep uninterrupted and just turned it back on in the restroom. "What's up?"

"André. He's gone."

"Gone? You broke up?"

"I don't know what else you'd call it." Cassie hiccupped her way through a stream of consciousness recital of their evening. Romantic picnic on the boat in the Inner Harbor, wine, chocolate. Then André received a phone call and said he was leaving the country and wouldn't return. He turned around and left her at her door. Boom. "Mara, he was The One. I know it. And he's never coming back."

"Never?"

The honk of Cassie blowing her nose came through

the phone loud enough to stress the scrambler. "Never. His French accent made dumping me sound so smooth and sexy, but it's still the same result as in English. 'It's been great, baby, but it's over. I'm outta here.'"

Mara murmured soothing words, forcing herself not to say I told you so. "If he can drop you so coldly, he's not the man you thought he was."

Cassie sniffled. "I thought tonight was special, that he'd… oh, I don't know anymore. Livvie's not here. She's sleeping over at her best friend's. Can you come? We can cry over a chick flick, like old times."

Mara closed her eyes, the pain in Cassie's voice tightening her chest. She hadn't told either her or Mom about finding Dad's ring piece. She couldn't. Not yet. She hadn't been able to find the words. The truth would come out once this quest ended. The press would be all over the return of the Gramornia crown jewels and the puzzle ring. She would let her family down easy.

But not now.

André was gone. For good, in both senses of the word. Mara'd pegged him for a sleaze from the start. She had to tell Cassie something but she'd promised Cort. Maybe generalities. Just in case. "I wish I could but I'm halfway… across the country."

"But— With Cort? Why?"

"I'll tell you all about it when I return. Love you. Hold on, Cass. It'll be all right." She saw Cort motioning to her through the glass doors. "I can't talk anymore now. See you soon."

Mara understood for the first time how Cassie felt—a hole in her chest, scraped out by a serrated blade—the same way *she* felt knowing her affair with Cort would end soon. When they parted, the hole would be a crater. She loved him, this intense, protective, fearless man. Maybe passion wasn't to blame, but she'd allowed herself to fall for the wrong man anyway, wrong because he couldn't love her back, couldn't trust himself not to fail her.

On a sigh she pushed through the doorway and crossed the pavement to the truck.

Cort helped her adjust the driver's seat. "Phone call?"

"Cassie," she said. "André has left. Again. This time it seems for good."

"Maybe it is good. I didn't trust that guy."

Better to keep the rest of the conversation to herself. She hadn't told Cassie anything important. He was so focused on secrecy and retrieving the jewels she didn't want to worry him.

Rationalizing? Maybe. Her pulse rattled, and her gut felt hard as a rock.

****

Cort watched Mara handle the big pickup in and out of the swarming lanes of traffic. He hated the Jersey Turnpike. Old and dangerous. Jersey drivers were worse than the hell-drivers in Boston. Cars and trucks whizzed by approaching warp speed. Normally he hated turning over the truck to someone else. No one knew her eccentricities like he did.

But Mara insisted he sleep. She was doing all right, plugged in and bopping to her iPod. She'd pulled back her hair into a single braid, showcasing her beautiful bone structure.

"I'm comfortable driving this monster now," she said with a wink.

Reading his mind again or just the scowl on his

face? He smoothed his features. "I'm surprised you're not frying with curiosity at where we're going."

"Approaching cinder status but I conceal it well. Are you going to tell me now? If so, let me tune my iPod to "Pomp and Circumstance.'"

"Tune away." Good. She wasn't too ticked at him for holding back on her. "Maine. We'll stop at my cabin first. If Leon isn't screwing the world with this puzzle ring, the crown jewels are hidden at an old fishing camp not far away."

"The fountain in the poem is a pond?"

"The camp's on Fogg Lake but he meant the spring in the woods just beyond the shack. I own the place but haven't been there in years."

She reached out and squeezed his knee. "Your dad took you there?"

"When I was a kid, we fished sometimes when he needed to chill after a heist. Part of his plan to program me included the camp, along with rock climbing and wilderness survival."

"I'm surprised you returned to Maine at all."

"But for the Birch Lake Woodcraft Center hiring me I probably wouldn't have." Or did he come back because of Leon rather than in spite of him? He couldn't blame his father for his own stupidity. The closer he got to solving the puzzle, the less hatred burned in his chest.

The Newark exit signs meant the Parkway was next. Rosie would guide her if he fell asleep.

"So your dad bought a fishing camp in Maine as a getaway?" she prompted.

"Not exactly. It used to belong to his father."

"And he passed it down to you. That's really

sweet."

He snorted. "Vasco Mallory was a jewel thief like Leon. The Royal Canadian Mounties threw a party when the old reprobate died. He's buried in Montreal. He taught Leon everything he knew, except Leon took the family profession a step further by becoming a jeweler to eliminate tracing his stolen goods. Leon changed his name from Mallory so American cops wouldn't make the connection."

She was grinning like a kid with a new toy. "Wait a minute. Vasco. Leon—"

"And Cortez, yup." He'd been waiting for her to make the connection. "My French-Canadian great-grandfather—name plain old Jean—had a thing for explorers. Thought about changing my name but never got around to it. Probably won't now. The FBI would think I was plotting something."

"I've kinda grown used to Cortez," she said. "I can't wait to see this fishing spot."

"*FOUNTAIN OF MY YOUTH* is a play on words. My grandfather used to joke the spring beside the camp was the fountain of youth—"

"So he named his son for Ponce de Leon," she finished.

"Leon was grateful he chose Leon and not Ponce." He slewed over a little in his seat so he could gauge her reaction. "The fishing camp's only about an hour away from my place. I can be there and back no problem. And you'll be safer staying at the cabin."

"No frakking way." Her eyebrows clashed in fury over her nose. "I've come this far with you. I deserve to see where the jewels are hidden. And *if* they're hidden. You don't trust me. That's it. You *still* don't trust me."

He heaved a sigh. That wasn't it. At least he didn't think so. Or was it that she didn't trust him? She had every right not to. "Not true. If Rousso has discovered somehow where the jewels are or he's followed us, it's too dangerous."

"I suppose going there alone isn't too dangerous for you." She shot each word like a dart.

No point in denying the danger for either of them. "Maybe I could use a lookout," he conceded. "No promises."

Chapter Twenty-Seven

MARA DROVE ON as Cort slept beside her. At first he seemed to wrestle demons in fitful dreams. The Centaur guy? Or his father? When he talked about Leon now, his tone wasn't so harsh, his words so angry. Maybe he was coming to terms with the man's nature.

Finally when they reached the northern Connecticut state line, he fell into a deeper rest in spite of a hard rain that gave the wipers a workout. Stopping for a quick breakfast in Portsmouth, New Hampshire, woke him up, and he took over the wheel for the last leg of their marathon.

As they entered Maine, the rain gave way to drizzle and fog. "We've outrun the rain," he told her, "but it'll catch up. Storm's heading down east as usual."

After Portland they turned away from the interstate onto two-lane country roads that wound past lakes, over rolling hills, and through farmland and villages with white steeples and antique shops. She caught glimpses of mountains in the distance, their tops still snow-capped. Trees had just unfurled their leaves in new mint green, and irises were blooming. The whole experience felt like going back in time.

"There's the school," Cort said, his mouth a taut line.

A white wooden sign announced the Birch Lake Woodcraft Center.

"I didn't expect a whole campus," she said, gawking at the six Shaker-style wooden buildings painted barn red. Paths wound among the workshops. "Impressive."

He didn't comment, but sat up straighter. His work here had contributed to the school's growth.

"Do you want to stop? You can deliver your friend's souvenirs."

"Finding the crown jewels comes first. I'll stop by her house sometime."

His face was again drawn into hard lines. This man who'd confronted hardened criminals and survived prison shrank from the disapproval, the rejection of people he worked with. People who already knew his prison record. She could cry.

Or hug him, but now wasn't the time for either.

Cort gunned the engine to propel the truck past the school as fast as was prudent on the narrow highway.

"Maybe you could give me a tour someday," she said, offering hope.

"Doubt it. I'm probably never going back there."

She dug her nails into her palms. "Your boss let you go only when the board pushed him into a corner. He'll welcome you back when this is over."

When Cort made no comment other than an inarticulate grunt, the equivalent of a shrug, she was grateful. If she were less selfish, she wouldn't feel this gnawing ache at her own words— *"when this is over."*

****

"Here's my cabin," Cort said, stuffing down mixed emotions as he eased into his parking area. "I was lucky to find a furnished rental with a barn not too far from the school."

"It's cute," Mara said, settling her hood on her hair as she exited the truck.

Cute? Only a woman would call an old log cabin with a hand-planked door and a roof with two different colors of shingles *cute*.

She gestured at the barn, to the left of the house. "This is so isolated. All your tools and wood are valuable. Do you have a security system?"

"Spoken like a city girl who works with security. Oh, I forgot. You had to be burgled before you got a system."

"Guilty. But answer the question, mister."

"My security system consists of my friend's son. Whenever I'm gone, he stops in every day to check on things." A couple different tire treads dented the rain-dappled ground. The kid probably drove his dad's truck. One set of tracks looked fresh. He was here earlier today.

"I'm sure that keeps everything safe." She peered at the single lock as he inserted the key. "Not even a dead bolt."

"This is Maine, sweetheart, not Washington, D.C. Unless I'm going out of town, I don't even bother to lock the doors." He ushered her inside.

A fine layer of dust coated everything. Maybe he should've had somebody come in and clean. But that would do little to brighten up the shabby and colorless space, so different from Mara's bright and cheery apartment. Worn rag rugs, threadbare gray sofa, brown chair, all part of the rental.

Dark. Depressing. Lonely.

He deposited their bags beside the door and switched on the ceiling fan light. Good thing the bedroom door was closed. He probably didn't make the bed before he left.

She made a beeline to the one piece of furniture not part of the rental. A cherry trestle table with some contemporary touches in the base. "Yours." She ran a palm over the glass-smooth surface. But dusty. "Gorgeous. Feels like fine china."

He couldn't help grinning like a fool. "A prototype for a new design. Turned out okay. I liked it so I kept it."

He watched her admire the table for a moment before he broke the spell. "We can clean up and rest for a while before I go to the lake. Maybe the rain'll stop by then."

"Before *you* go to the lake?" She stood in the middle of the small living room, her arms planted on her slim hips.

"I'm still thinking about that." And agonizing over whether he'd foiled Rousso.

"The bad guys know all about you, including this cabin, but you said yourself no one but you and Leon would know about the lake. I'll be safer with you." She pulled her jacket more tightly around her.

He'd been wrestling with that very problem for days. "The cabin's cold. I'll fetch some wood for the wood stove and then we'll discuss it while we eat the sandwiches we bought."

"Way to duck the issue."

He winced on his way out the door. He stalked around the barn to the woodshed. After gathering a couple logs, he stared into the woods. What she'd said was true, but he needed to think. A moment without her warmth and sweet smile derailing his brain, without her apparent faith in his too flawed character, without her challenging him to rethink… everything.

Like returning to the Birch Lake Woodcraft Center. Maybe they would rehire him. But did he want to return to this hermit existence, as she liked to describe his life?

Without her.

He hadn't wanted to feel anything for her but lust. Not admiration for her courage and determination. Not respect for seeing this through with him when she no longer needed to. Not this burning drive to be with her, to argue with her, to comfort her, to bask in the warmth of her glorious smiles. But he felt all of that, and more. Deep emotions he never thought to experience.

And yes, he trusted her. She'd given him no reason not to. Not once. It was himself he didn't trust. She'd said that often enough he had to acknowledge it as truth.

And yes, she'd be safer with him at the lake. Having her with him just felt right. Adding one last log to the pile in his arms, he headed back to the cabin. A load seemed to have been lifted. He didn't even feel the weight of the firewood.

When he opened the cabin door, he nearly dropped the logs. Adrenaline gushed through his body.

Mara stood, ashen-faced, by the faded sofa. The man in the dark rain slicker behind her kept his left arm clamped around her waist. His right hand held a pistol, the muzzle pressed against her temple.

"Close the door," the man said. "Do not try anything. I would hate to scar this beautiful face." He pressed the pistol's muzzle into Mara's throat hard enough to pierce the tender skin.

"Mara," he gritted out, "are you hurt? Has he—"

"I'm okay. He… he came out of the bedroom. I—" She grimaced. Fear was stark in her eyes.

He nodded, focused on sending Mara strength, forcing an appearance of calm, as if his heart wasn't hammering against his sternum hard enough to explode out of his chest. As if fear for her wasn't cutting him like glass. As if fire wasn't roaring through his body.

When he'd willed his rioting emotions to simmer, he kicked the door shut. The new tracks. His mind raced with possibilities. The man seemed to be alone. Was André not part of this plot?

A closer look—big nose, thinning hair. "Rolf Rousso in the flesh."

Respect and surprise flashed across the Centaur man's narrow face. "I would like to know how you discovered that. No matter. Rousso is as good a name as any."

"You followed me in the Metro. Was the delivery man in San Francisco also you?"

"You are an observant man, Jones. Pity it will do you no good."

The response was oblique but Cort sensed he'd hit the mark. "These logs are heavy."

He flicked his gaze to Mara's pale face. He had to get them out of this fucking mess alive. Somehow.

"You may put the wood down, but keep your hands where I can see them," Rousso said. Never removing his pistol from Mara, he turned to watch Cort walk to the wood stove. "Do not bother with a fire. We will not be here long."

"How did you find me?"

The creep laughed. "Very clever placing my

transponder in a taxi. But I had other means of knowing your movements. A short visit as the cable repairman a few weeks ago and my electronics allowed me to listen to everything said. Ms. Marton could not resist telling her sister." Mara sucked in an audible breath. Rousso's gaze flicked between them. "Once I knew you were headed to this cabin, it was a matter of chartering a private jet."

Reality pelted Cort like the cold rain outside. His gaze lasered to Mara. "Is this true? You told your sister?"

Tears glistened in her dark eyes. She started to raise a hand but Rousso clamped down on her.

"God, no, I didn't. Cassie wanted me to go to her. I thought if André was gone, it'd be safe to tell her why I couldn't. But I swear I didn't tell her where we were headed, only cross country."

She closed her eyes on a shudder. Fat tears fell as she shook her head slowly. She seemed to close in on herself.

And then he knew.

She hadn't told Cassie. Rousso saw his doubt and played them both. The slime had researched him and used what he heard in Cassie's house. A logical leap they would come to the cabin.

A tangle of emotions like frayed rope knotted up Cort's insides. He'd yielded to one moment of doubt and lost Mara's trust.

He'd lost *her*.

"Ah, André the romantic boyfriend," Rousso said. "A tragic turn of affairs."

"Not your source then?" Cort said, forcing himself to focus on what must be done and not on Mara's anguish. Or his. Damn, he was a fool. And damn Rousso for manipulating them both.

He edged toward the wrought-iron poker in the rack beside the stove. His only possible weapon. If Rousso removed the gun from against Mara's cheek, maybe—

The Centaur agent shook his head. "Not my source, but helpful nonetheless. He encouraged Cassie to talk about whatever Ms. Marton knew about you."

That explained why they knew everything so fast. But André had to be something more than a wine importer. Too convenient, his hooking up with Cassie. Too many damn coincidences.

Another step closer to the poker.

Rousso's mouth curved in a predatory smile. "Move away from the stove. Place the ring pieces on the sofa where I can reach them."

Cort wasn't giving up, not when Mara's life was at stake. He could take Rousso if the man let down his guard. If his shadow of a life had taught him anything, it was patience. Seeing no recourse, he dug the ring pieces from his jacket pocket and placed the connected length on the sofa arm. When Rousso bent to retrieve them, maybe…

"You have *three*?" Surprise hiked Rousso's voice half an octave. "Whose is the third? No matter. Bravo." He directed Mara to hand him the rings.

Cort choked back a curse. Another chance missed.

Rousso had probably planned to kill them once he possessed the ring pieces. But the man didn't count on the clue poem not giving the specific location. The Jeweler was cagey to the end.

No one could obtain the jewels, not without Leon.

Or his son.

Rousso peered inside the rings. He dragged Mara to the kitchen table. She sank onto a straight-backed chair, her limbs rigid. He shoved a piece of paper and pencil at her. "Add the new words to the lines written here."

Hand shaking, she picked up the pencil. She looked shell shocked as she copied the words. Rousso never wavered with the gun. Cort fought the urge to charge the fucker.

He stared at the lines already written and the realization hit him. "You have Falco's ring piece." Which meant he'd killed the old second-story man. Or had him killed. "Hauptman's too? Obtained in that break-in?"

Rousso sneered, a beast of prey gloating over his kill. "So the police questioned you?"

"Police? No. Twyla Hauptman never reported the burglary."

Rousso's eyebrows shot up in denial. "But— Forget it." He snatched the paper and read.

STEEL WITHIN THE WOODEN HOLD
PROTECTS THE JEWELS AND ROYAL GOLD
BESIDE THE FOUNTAIN OF MY YOUTH.
THUS WE KEEP OUR HONOR, TRUTH.

"What is this? A trick?" he roared. "It does not have location."

"Yes, a trick. Nobody better at deception than Leon. Only he knew where he'd hidden the crown jewels. He kept the location secret."

Rousso spat out a string of words in a language Cort didn't recognize. The blistering outburst could be nothing but curses upon Leon. When the bastard wound down, he yanked Mara to her feet. She gasped when he again dug the pistol's muzzle against her throat.

He turned to Cort. "But *you* know where the jewels are hidden. Why else would you have driven to Maine under cover of darkness?"

"Cort, don't tell hi—"

Rousso clipped her on the cheekbone with the pistol butt.

She yelped, cringing to the side and gripping the table, but he held her fast.

Cort started forward. "You asshole!"

"Stop," Rousso ordered, pointing the pistol at her.

Cort stepped back, hands fisted at his sides. "Mara?"

Blood welled from a small cut where purple already stained the skin. She managed a nod. A tear trickled down her swelling cheek but she looked more furious than afraid.

Hang in there, sweetheart.

"Take me to the hiding place and I will not harm her. I will let you both live." Rousso pocketed the ring pieces. "Once I have the jewels in my possession, you will be free to go."

Cort ground his teeth until his jaw ached. No choice. But the camp was *his* territory. If he could surprise Rousso, he could get the gun. They could escape into the woods. "You have me cornered. I'll show you where Leon hid the crown jewels."

"Much better." Rousso gestured toward the door with his pistol. "Outside."

When Cort opened the door and walked into the drizzle, he saw another vehicle parked beside his. He hadn't heard the big black SUV pull up.

Chapter Twenty-Eight

"MY... COLLEAGUES," ROUSSO said. His arch tone made them seem more like minions than equals.

Two people exited the SUV. The widow Hauptman in a hooded rain jacket. The other was a human monolith who had to be her brother Hugo, likely the man who'd mugged Mara. Six foot seventy and wide as a UPS truck. He held a pistol, smaller than Rousso's but equally lethal.

Three of them. Hell fucking damn. They were knee deep in goat shit now.

And puddles. Droplets of misty drizzle chilled him and slid off the bridge of his nose, and plopped into the icy water around his boots. Good. If he was cold, so were they.

He watched the interaction among the three of them while Rousso brought his cohorts up to date. Twyla's eyes narrowed into furious little black beads as Rousso finished his narrative. Hugo, tight by his sister's side, looked blankly at everyone. Easily manipulated, Cort observed, but loyal to his sister.

No love lost between Twyla and Rousso. Wouldn't hurt to kick up dust between them.

"Twyla, I'm wondering why you never reported your so-called break-in to the cops," he said, stretching his stiff lips into a smug grin.

"Jones is not only curious one," Rousso said icily.

Flags of color stood out beneath the artificial pink on her cheekbones. She sputtered like a dying lawnmower. "Didn't see no need of cops. Jones was the only one needed to believe I had a real robbery. After you and Hugo trashed my house, you scared the life out of me when I got home from work. Cops'd only add to the mess."

Cort wasn't surprised the woman who sealed her furniture in clear plastic didn't want a mess. If he'd had more time, her vanity might have brought the cops to her house for a different reason, one that could've wrapped up the search. And Mara wouldn't be shaking in her sneakers with a gun against her soft skin.

He bit down hard on the memories, the emotions that threatened to spring free. He wouldn't think about that, about her. They were done, once this was over. He'd known it all along. Now he'd seen that truth in her eyes.

Twyla aimed a hate-filled glare at him. "And *he* ain't my boss. We work *together*."

Hugo's broad forehead crimped. "Yeah, work together."

"In a manner of speak," Rousso said, his accent thicker, his English less fluent, but his tone no less sinister. "Remember who is in charge, Mrs. Hauptman. Your ring piece would be useless trinket if not for my enterprise. Do not let this man cause trouble between us."

"Worth a shot." Cort figured his mouth was his only weapon. So far.

Fear shone too bright in Mara's eyes, but underlain with something else as she studied him. Steel. Encouragement.

And trust.

Jesus. Her fear nearly tore him apart, but it was the trust, trust in him to get them out of this hell, that scorched his insides like battery acid. After he'd doubted her, she still trusted him?

****

Mara slid from the SUV into the fog. Trees and underbrush surrounded the small party. Mist blotted out the sky. Despair lancing her heart, she shivered against the chill. *How will anyone ever find us in this wilderness?*

"Move," Rousso ordered, gesturing to her with his wicked black pistol. "This will be right place, or you will pay for your man's deceit."

Her man. No longer. But Cort wouldn't risk her life, even now that he despised her.

Twyla Hauptman had driven the rented SUV, with Rousso and her in the back. The bumpy ride on the rutted track stretched her nerves as taut as a tennis racquet. Swollen and puffy, her bloodied cheek throbbed. Rousso offered her a tissue. She refused. She would take nothing from the bastard.

Cort hopped down from his pickup, in front of the SUV, with Hugo holding a gun on him. She'd known as soon as she heard Hugo speak he was the behemoth who'd accosted her in her foyer. She would recognize that raspy voice anywhere, anytime.

Cort's grim features were granite, his eyes set in cool, piercing bullet-gray. A mask of vigilance. He led the way down a narrow path to what appeared to be a log shed with a rotting wooden shingle roof. Beside the camp, the lake shimmered through the rain's blurry curtain. No "fountain" in sight. The spring lay in the

314

woods.

His clever attempt at dividing the enemy buoyed her. Some. Enough to layer her terror with determination. So far only in the form of poison-filled glares Rousso's way. Not that she got any reaction. But at least her heart rate slowed from four Ghz to one. Well, maybe two.

She'd failed Cort when he began to trust her, betrayed his precious trust. Rousso must've known about the Maine cabin from some earlier conversation he'd overheard. Even her general *halfway across the country* must've clued him in. Why did she tell Cassie anything? She'd ruined everything.

Love for Cort welled up inside her, an ache that gripped her heart for what she'd lost. She was her father's daughter after all. He'd betrayed everything he believed in for a chance at fortune. She'd betrayed Cort's trust, and for nothing. Her chest ached as if she inhaled broken glass.

Worse for him, she'd proven him right. *Trust no one.* Not even himself. He would retreat into these woods. He would exist, not *live*, his days behind a wall of loneliness.

That is, if they lived through this day. The thought nearly brought her to her knees.

Suck it up, Mara Lin.

She swallowed a hot, hard lump and straightened her shoulders. Since that first night she met him, she'd learned to be stronger in the face of danger. To survive this day, she had to be strong. She had to be brave. She had to be smart.

Any chance with Cort was blown to hell. But maybe she could help give them both a chance to escape. She could scream at the idea the Centaur gang could end up with the crown jewels. Any chance of redemption for Cort would be lost.

She'd seen in Cort's eyes he was primed to take advantage of an opening. She would do anything to create that opening.

Anything.

When they reached the small fishing shack, Rousso shoved her toward Twyla. Mara stumbled on the rough ground. As she dropped onto all fours, pebbles stabbed pain into her palms. She bit her lower lip against an automatic outcry.

"Son of a bitch!" Cort spat. "You didn't have to hurt her again."

"Just reminder. This will be truth," the Centaur thug sneered, his accent even thicker with the tension rife around them. "Or Hugo *will* hurt Mara. Sometimes my large friend does not know his strength."

His mouth a grim slash, Cort pointed to a sheet of weathered plywood weighted to the ground with a football-size rock. Dead leaves and evergreen needles littered the surface. "That's the hiding place."

Mara pushed to her feet. Blood droplets bubbled from abrasions on her palms. She opened her hands to the drizzle. *Use the pain to focus.*

Twyla tugged Mara's braid to pull her closer. She now held Hugo's pistol. Maybe they didn't trust King Kong with a gun for more than a few minutes. Mara, Hugo, and Twyla stood no more than five feet from the lake's edge, a good twenty feet beyond where Cort and Rousso jockeyed for position beside the plywood.

Mara sent the widow her version of Cort's death stare, then averted her gaze. She didn't dare look at

Hugo, whose beefy hands could crush her. Instead, she focused on Cort.

His gaze flickered toward her and away with no hint of emotion. "No deception, Rousso. This is an old root cellar, wood lined with stones, used to store potatoes and other winter vegetables back when this was a year-round farmstead."

Rousso's eyes widened. "In the ground? But the dampness, the weather?"

"Gold and jewels would be fine in any case. But remember the verse—*STEEL WITHIN THE WOODEN HOLD.* Leon must've reinforced the original."

Mara's chest tightened so she could barely breathe. Handing over the jewels was a death sentence. The longer to open the *wooden hold* and pull them out, the longer they lived to stop this travesty. She scrambled for an idea.

"Rousso, why does Centaur want these crown jewels so much?" she asked. "There must be others much easier to steal."

"Not your concern," he barked. "Is just important."

"I bet your boss has private collectors lined up to buy either pieces or the whole collection," she went on. "You'll be in big trouble if that hiding place is empty."

"He's in trouble with his boss already," Cort said, studying his enemy. "All those deaths, the cops, the fuck-ups. I hear Centaur doesn't allow mistakes." He made a slashing motion across his throat. "What about it, Rousso?"

The flush on the Centaur agent's face and the fever in his eyes screamed of desperation. "Perceptive, Jones. But you will not trick me to reveal more. Open it."

Cort knelt on the damp grass. He brushed away the

winter's detritus with his hands, then picked up the rock.

"Do not." Rousso raised his pistol.

Mara recognized the longer nose on the weapon's muzzle as a silencer. Who would hear them in these woods anyway? The inanity of it nearly provoked a giggle. She started to shake off the delirium but a spasm in her cheek made her gasp.

"Wouldn't think of it," Cort said mildly, not even looking up. He tossed the rock aside. The plywood lifted easily and flipped over and out of the way.

Mara was too far away to see into the hole no matter how she craned her neck.

Twyla took a step forward. So did her brother.

"Stay there," Rousso ordered the widow. "Keep gun on her."

Glowering at the man, Twyla returned to Mara's side. The brother took another step, and another, then hovered midway between the two groups. Curious but afraid to cross Rousso.

Everyone's attention focused on the hiding place of the Gramornia crown jewels.

And not on Mara.

She tore her gaze from the dark hole to study the older woman. With the hood covering her perfectly teased and sprayed helmet, Twyla's peripheral vision was impaired. Sure, she had the gun. At the moment aimed only generally toward Mara. Twyla didn't look any more comfortable with that pistol than Mara would be. And the rain was making the grip slippery, less than secure. Could she use the gun if she managed to wrest it away? She would have to.

God help me.

If she screwed up, she would die. Cort next. Hell, they were both going to die anyway. No way would Rousso let them live. She drew in a deep breath to steady her fried nerves.

Cort, what do I do?

But his focus was on the hole. If she made a move, could he react in time?

"What the hell's in there?" Twyla's grating whine yanked Rousso's head toward them and yanked the chance from Mara.

Rousso stepped closer to the hole and peered inside. "A steel safe. Water and fireproof kind. Good. For last time, open it."

Cort drilled both hands through his hair and shook off the rainwater. On his belly, he reached inside. A metallic clank resounded through the small clearing. Again. And again.

"What?" Rousso scowled, exasperated.

Cort sat back on his heels and erupted in a belly laugh. More of an animal howl than mirth. Not quite what Mara expected.

"I can't open it without the ring. *The whole ring,*" Cort said, as he subsided into a chuckle. He shook his head, amazement on his face. Respect too, if she read him right. "My old man created an unbeatable puzzle. No one involved in the burglary, himself included, could retrieve the jewels without the others. I thought the raised symbols were a key to something. Shit, the symbols *are* the key."

He slanted a glance toward her. Checking on her wellbeing? Sending a message?

A key. Of course. Damn, she wished she could see. But this might be their chance. She was ready—on the balls of her feet, arms loose. God, did she dare? She would have only one chance.

"What do you mean, *the key*?" Rousso demanded.

"The safe is locked. Did you think he'd leave it here unlocked for years? To open it, you need a key. Each of the five raised symbols has to fit its matching slot. Only then can it be turned and the tumblers will fall into place. I need the complete puzzle ring."

"Move back." When Cort obeyed, Rousso withdrew a penlight from his windbreaker pocket. He aimed it inside the hole and studied what he saw for a moment.

"Yes, this is right. Clever." He backed up and gestured to Cort to resume his position beside the in-ground safe.

He returned the flashlight to his pocket and instead withdrew the three pieces Cort had yielded earlier, plus a fourth. Falco's, Mara assumed. He tossed them to the ground beside Cort.

"That's only four," Cort pointed out as he tried to fit the last piece with the others. "This is an outside piece. Where's the missing one?"

Everyone turned to Twyla Hauptman.

Mara had assumed Rousso possessed it along with the others. Twyla had kept herself and Hugo in the game by maintaining possession of her one asset, even though she shared the inside wording with Rousso. It probably suited him to use her and her brother for his schemes to obtain the others.

"No, absolutely not," Twyla snapped. "I ain't givin' up my George's ring piece."

"You foolish bitch," Rousso spat. "Yours must fit with others to open safe and retrieve jewels." He waved his pistol toward her.

Mara forced herself to breathe evenly. *In. Out. Easy now.* She watched Twyla. And Twyla's pistol. Not Rousso. One gun was all she allowed herself to think about.

Hugo turned toward the one who'd been ordering him around. "Don't you swear at my sister," the big man ordered. "She's been helpin' you."

"Sorry, Hugo," Rousso said, in an oily tone that boded no good.

Would he shoot his two allies? As well as Cort and her? Her pulse pounded and her stomach roiled.

"You shouldn't yell," Hugo said. "I don't like yelling."

"I did not mean to yell. We want to see crown jewels, all of us, do we not?"

Hugo nodded deliberately, in almost comical slow motion. Twyla scowled, still reluctant to give up her only insurance.

"Twyla, the ring, if you please."

"Fuckin'-A," she whined. "Reckon I got no choice. But you better not try nothin'. I got a share of that treasure coming to me."

"Of course. Your share."

She reached across her body with her left hand to her right-hand jacket pocket. The unnatural twisting motion compromised her right hand's steadiness. The gun dipped. As she withdrew the ring piece, the gun wobbled. Slipped in her wet hand.

Chapter Twenty-Nine

MARA TOOK A deep breath and swung up her left arm against Twyla's right. Knocked the gun loose. A loud crack split the silence. The weapon fell to the ground.

Hugo bellowed.

Mara blinked away the aftershock and fumes. With her right hand, she snatched the ring. Emitting a Serena roar, she executed a perfect serve.

The ring drilled into the lake with a sharp splash.

Mara's ears rang from the gun's report, but she heard Twyla screech like a wounded owl. *"My ring, my ring!"*

Mara risked a glance across the clearing. Cort wrestled Rousso for his gun.

Yes!

The smaller man seemed to have some martial-arts moves, but Cort was bigger, stronger. Prison had taught him how to fight dirty, to fight for his life.

She dived for the dropped pistol. Had to get it before the behemoth came to his sister's aid. She scrabbled around on the ground in the ferns and new grasses. Came up with the weapon, fumbled the wet metal but held on.

The screaming banshee recovered and charged her.

Panting, her heart racing like a greyhound, Mara pushed to her feet. Across the clearing, the cracks and thumps of hand-to-hand combat lured her to search out Cort, but she kept her eyes on her opponent.

"Stop right there!" She held the pistol in both hands. She willed her grip to be steady and firm, as if she knew what she was doing.

Twyla halted, her face a twisted mask of hatred, clown garish with rain-streaked makeup. "You slope-eyed bitch! You wade in and get that ring or I'll kill you."

Mara ignored the threat and prayed the widow had the good sense to stay put. The few Devlin employee self-protection classes she'd taken covered defending herself against muggers grabbing her from behind or coming at her with a weapon. Not against this spitting cat who would attack with tooth and claw. Twyla and her brother probably aided Rousso in murdering Falco. As repellent as taking a life was, she would shoot if she had to.

"Hugo! Help me!" Twyla yelled.

"I... can't."

Hugo was no longer vertical. He lay on his back, a beached whale. Crimson stained the light blue fabric of his windbreaker.

Twyla spun toward his weak croak. She ignored Mara and raced to her brother. "Hugo! Baby brother, speak to me!"

When the pistol fired, the bullet had struck Hugo.

Twyla shot her own brother.

Weeping and wailing in near hysteria, urging him to hang in there, she tore off her jacket and wadded it against the bullet wound. Hugo lay still, apparently unconscious. Or dead.

No reason Mara could think of to keep the woman

from tending him. She kept the gun aimed at the pair while she circled to where she could also keep an eye on Cort's battle.

Rousso stood spread-legged behind him. Cort kept Rousso's arm trapped against his body. He gripped the man's hand with both of his. Tried to shake loose the pistol.

Oh God, please let him be all right. She wanted to help but allowed herself only brief glances his way. She couldn't take her eyes off the other two. Twyla or Hugo might have another weapon.

Rousso kicked, sweeping Cort's legs from beneath him. The men fell to the ground in a welter of limbs and guttural sounds. Cort maintained his grip on Rousso's wrist. The pistol clattered onto the door of the safe, an arm's length or more down in the hole.

Thank God! Mara bit her lip. If she cried out, she might distract Cort.

Rousso yelled and swung a fist.

Cort blocked the blow and with his other hand landed a solid punch on Rousso's chin with a thunk of bone on bone. His head snapped back.

Cort pounded him again. Rousso lay still. Cort pulled back his arm for another blow. His chest heaved. He let his arm drop.

He sat back on his heels and looked at her. "Mara?"

Before she could answer, the clearing filled with a dozen men and women in black flak jackets. They carried enough weapons to supply an army.

"FBI. Stand down."

An agent in a rumpled suit marched over to Cort and helped him up. Kaplan, she guessed. Another FBI agent relieved her of Twyla's pistol.

"Thanks," she said to the woman. "I don't think I could've held that another second."

A medical crew rushed in behind the initial invasion. And behind them, Thomas Devlin.

Her boss crossed to her as an EMT draped a blanket around her chilled shoulders. He clasped both her hands in his big warm ones. "Mara Marton holding a gun on anyone is a sight I never in my wildest dreams thought I'd live to see. How're you doing?"

"I'm okay." And to her surprise, she was. She wouldn't let herself think about Cort. She couldn't even look at him. Or the ache in her chest would become unbearable.

****

As if the weather gods knew the danger was past, the skies began to clear. The drizzle stopped and patches of blue appeared above the trees.

Things happened quickly after that. Cort stood to one side as agents cuffed and led away Rousso and a weeping Twyla Hauptman. The EMTs took Hugo away on a gurney. One told an agent the bullet had punctured one of the man's lungs, but he'd probably live.

Live to stand trial, Cort thought with satisfaction. Hugo might be limited upstairs but he knew the things he'd done were crimes. Both Hugo and his sister would go to prison for a long time, nearly as long as Rousso.

He glanced at Mara talking quietly with her boss. She looked wet and dirty, and more beautiful than ever because she was okay. He'd known fear in prison, fear for his own life, how fear tasted and how it prickled his scalp and roiled in his belly. But that was nothing compared to the paralysis, the dry-mouthed cold sweats he felt seeing her held at gunpoint. The blanket the EMT gave him warmed his shoulders but the ice in his gut would take a long time to dissipate.

How the hell did she manage those fancy moves to save the day? He wanted to ask but she was better off if he left her alone. She'd said more than once he should trust himself. How could he trust himself when nobody else should trust him? Devlin had a clear field if he wanted her. Frozen barbed wire twisted in Cort's gut but he forced himself to look away from them.

The FBI diver splashed out of the lake. He held up the ring piece in the sunlight peeking through the thinning clouds. This part of the lake had a sandy bottom, not mud. The gold would've disappeared in mud. They'd have had to cut open the safe.

Kaplan handed him the ring. "You do the honors, Jones," he said. "You been through hell to get this far. That million-dollar reward from Gramornia should go a mile or two toward making it up to you and Ms. Marton."

Cort hadn't known about a reward. That didn't concern him at the moment. "How'd you find us? How did you know to come?"

"Thank Thomas Devlin for that one. And whoever put up a cell phone tower in these godforsaken woods. Ms. Marton pushed a link on her phone that sent Devlin a direct SOS with GPS coordinates."

Cort shook his head, speechless. She must've sent that signal when Rousso first grabbed her. Fear hadn't stopped her from acting, from using the same tactic that called him to her rescue more than a month ago.

A conflicting stew of emotions swirled inside him, made his eyes sting. He swallowed hard. He began this quest because he wanted freedom and a full life, but without her, his future looked empty. He would laugh at the irony if he didn't hurt so much.

"Jones?" Kaplan asked. "You okay?"

"Fine, just fine. Let's get this safe open. I want this over with." The sooner he handed over the crown jewels, the sooner all these damn people would leave him alone.

He connected the new ring piece with the others, creating a six-inch tube of gold. *The key to the treasure.* If for once in his life Leon played it straight. Unless the crown jewels weren't there. What happened then? He hoped the prince could be crowned with them.

But for himself, it didn't matter as much. The FBI knew he'd been honest with them.

Now it was up to Leon.

He tossed off the blanket. As he lay on the tarp that spread beside the hole, he sensed the crowd gathering closer. Mara's sneakers appeared at the edge of the hole. He didn't look up.

The raised runes fit perfectly in the circular lock on the safe. He twisted it to the right, praying he didn't hit another roadblock, like a combination. But the lock turned. The tumblers clicked. With his jaw clenched tight enough to crack a tooth, he grasped the handle and pulled.

"The safe opened," Kaplan murmured above him.

Inside the deep metal box lay a black duffel bag, the waterproof kind boaters used. With the FBI agent's help, he hoisted it out and placed it on the tarp. When he began to work the zipper, Kaplan stopped him.

"Not yet," the FBI agent said. "I promised the Gramornian ambassador I'd wait until the prince's emissary could be here to witness the contents. He's on his way."

****

Mara huddled by the woodstove in Cort's cabin trying to thaw her icy hands. The scent of wood smoke drifted in the air, and the snap of flames warmed her skin.

A technician had swabbed and bandaged her palms, which barely stung, and her cheek, which throbbed almost as much as her heart. Another EMT treated Cort's knuckles but said no bones seemed broken. He'd have more scars. So would she, inside.

The duffel lay on the faded sofa, a homing beacon to everyone's gaze. The wait for this damn emissary was taking too long. If she'd ever had a chance at a future with Cort, she'd lost it. She wanted to leave before she broke down.

Most of the FBI people had driven away, leaving only Kaplan, two other agents, and Devlin as buffers to the tension between Cort and her. The two of them gave a preliminary statement to the special agents while they waited.

Kaplan clicked off the digital recorder and folded his arms. "Ms. Marton, how did you manage to disarm Hauptman and toss the ring? Some self-defense moves?"

Mara felt her face heat. "Not exactly. I play a lot of tennis. I was hoping for a swing at the pistol but when she took out the ring, I came up with a better tactic. I threw up my arm like tossing up the ball—" she demonstrated "—and knocked the pistol loose. Then I grabbed the ring and served it into the lake. That's all."

"That's all?" The agent scratched his balding pate.

"You have my congratulations."

"Thanks. I have no field operative ambitions, but now I think I'll take more of the self-defense classes DSF offers."

The laughter around the table—Cort even smiled—diffused her tension.

When it was clear no one had any more to add, the agent said, "Twyla Hauptman lost her bartending job a week ago. Boss wanted a younger, prettier face behind the bar. She could've fought the firing." He continued tapping his pen on the table. "But that may have been the reason she became even more desperate for the money Rousso promised her."

"He wouldn't have paid either one of them a dime," Cort said. "After killing us, he'd have shot them. No loose ends and more bottom line for Centaur."

Mara shuddered, agreeing. "He deserves life in prison. Maybe he didn't push Dante Falco off that balcony, but he ordered his death. And he killed Danita Inglish and that hired thug in San Francisco."

"Rousso's a stone killer, no question." Kaplan barked a humorless laugh. "Rolf Radulescu—his real name—is a native Romanian. Grew up rough in the slums of Bucharest. Clawed his way out and up with various criminal enterprises. Seems he had ambitions in the Centaur hierarchy. As it is, he'll be lucky to survive. Centaur doesn't tolerate failure. Or betrayal. Word is he made a private deal with a West-Coast Russian Mafia boss for the crown jewels."

"So I wasn't far off ragging him about his Centaur boss being unhappy with his screw-ups." Cort's thin smile resembled Rousso's noxious one.

The crunch of tires on gravel brought everyone's

head around. One of the FBI agents crossed to the door to admit the newcomer.

The man who walked inside was tall and movie-star handsome, dressed in a black turtleneck, pressed jeans, and a short black trench coat. The last man Mara expected to see.

André Rozmer.

So the French son of a bitch was the agent of the Gramornia prince, not that of Centaur. Bile rose in her throat as she rose to her feet. She wrapped her arms around her waist to keep inside the anger bubbling to a boil.

Like her, Cort remained at the table, his hands clenched into fists, his scowl shooting death rays at André.

André spoke quietly to the agents. He handed them a set of credentials. Then he held up a finger, asking for a moment. He approached her.

"I must apologize, Mara, for so deceiving you and your sister." That too charming French accent now struck her as smarmy. "I attended Oxford with the new crown prince of Gramornia. From time to time, the royal family asks me to carry out little favors for them, you see. I had to know how close you were to finding the crown jewels and if you would really return them. I had no choice." He dipped his head in a very small, very Gallic bow.

The little rush of adrenaline spurting through her had a calming effect. "You had a choice all right. You could have *chosen* to declare yourself to Cort or me. Instead you *chose* to seduce my sister. To make a fool of her before you tossed her aside like an empty wine bottle."

She turned aside and stalked across the room to where Thomas Devlin stood by the sofa with the others. To her relief, her boss didn't touch her. She couldn't have tolerated another person's contact at that moment. With one exception. But she didn't trust herself to look at Cort.

The duffel lay in a pond of light beneath the skylight. Everyone gathered around to watch as André unzipped the bag.

He lifted out an object wrapped in soft cloth. As the fabric fell away, a sunbeam flashed on the brilliance revealed. The scepter's shaft of old gold gleamed and the gemstones in its round headpiece reflected the rays, scattering light around the room.

"Leon didn't lie," Cort murmured, emotion roughening his voice. "This time, the old man didn't lie."

Next was the crown, with fleurs-de-lis around the base and four arches on top. Mara knew from studying the robbery that the jewels winking along its edges were pearls, emeralds, rubies, sapphires, and diamonds.

In quick succession, André and Kaplan lifted out the other pieces of the royal regalia, equally magnificent and encrusted with gems—a smaller crown called a diadem, two swords, three ornate diamond-and-emerald rings, and a slim dagger in a gold hilt.

"All of it seems to be here," André declared. "And just in time to be polished up for the coronation tomorrow. The royal family has arranged for a security detail and a private jet. They await my call." He began wrapping up the pieces.

"There's a little formality," Kaplan interjected softly. Like the others, he could barely drag his gaze from the treasure on the brown sofa. "An inventory and photographs. An official statement and receipt. But we'll have you ready to go by later this afternoon."

André opened his mouth as if to object, but closed it again. He honored the agent with that same little bow.

"If you will all excuse me," Thomas Devlin said, "now that I know my employee is safe, I'll be returning to D.C."

Mara's mouth felt like she'd been sucking on bitter herbs but she forced herself to speak. "If you're going to the airport, I'd appreciate a lift. Time I got back to work."

Her boss looked at Cort, who stared stoically into space, then back at her. "Sure. Get your things. Glad to have your company. Plenty of room in the chartered jet." He'd told them earlier he'd been on the tarmac, ready when he got her signal.

The FBI agents were busy with André and the crown jewels. Hard as it would be, she couldn't leave without facing Cort one last time.

He was loading more wood into the stove. She stood there a moment before he looked at her. His face a mask of steely resolve and simmering emotion, he seemed to be grinding granite with his molars. The pulse throbbed in his throat. His familiar scent made her want to lean into his warmth and hard body.

She blinked back the tears that stung. She could barely suck in enough air to speak. *God, how could this be any harder?*

"I know I totally screwed up everything. I'm sorrier than you can imagine. I committed the one crime you can't forgive. But I swear the only destination I gave my sister was general. I never said Maine. And I might as well confess the rest. You asked me not to tell anyone at work what we were doing. I couldn't do that. I needed help from a friend, another researcher in my office while we were in San Francisco. I should've told you.

"And I want you to know I'm in love with you. I understand it's over between us. If your parents loving each other didn't guarantee happiness, neither did my parents' loveless marriage. There are no guarantees. A relationship needs tending—shaping, smoothing, and polishing, like your furniture—and I failed what relationship we had. I wish you a good life. Maybe someday you'll be able to move beyond the past and come to trust yourself."

Lines bracketed his taut mouth. He nodded but didn't speak.

She turned and walked away. She collected her bags.

"You ready?" Devlin held the door open for her. He took her overnight bag from her.

She tilted her head, thinking. "Not quite." She stalked to where the others hovered over the crown jewels. "André."

When he turned around, she reared back and punched him in the face. The arrogant Frenchman stumbled, then slammed down on his Gallic butt. The pure pleasure she felt from striking the blow eclipsed the pain exploding in her knuckles.

André stared up at her in shock. Blood trickled from one nostril.

"That's from my sister." She whirled around, catching a glimpse of the others.

The two agents gaped.

Thomas Devlin grinned.

Cort looked as if his eyes might fall out and roll across the floor.

She marched out the door. Tears shimmered and fell, blinding her. Her boss caught her as she crumpled.

Chapter Thirty

End of June

THE SIGHT OF Mara's red coupe pulling into the sunlit driveway sent Cort's pulse soaring into the stratosphere. He dropped the instructions for setting up the professional-grade Delta cabinet saw and headed to the shadowed barn doorway.

He'd wavered all day between certainty she would be too curious to ignore his invitation and gut-wrenching fear she'd trash the email and shine him on.

But she came!

Everything else had been wound up. The new Gramornian prince was crowned with all the regal paraphernalia. Rousso implicated Hugo in Falco's murder.

In spite of strict security, Rousso was killed in jail, probably contracted by Centaur. A fight in the corridor drew away the guards. When the dust cleared, he lay bleeding out from a stab wound. No weapon and nobody saw a thing. Good riddance. Saved prosecuting complicated cases—crimes in D.C. and three states.

The FBI said Rousso was about to cut a deal for intel about Centaur. He'd already divulged enough to tease—the leader was an ex-military American called only Z.

Cort mustered the courage to phone Dante Falco's daughter. At least he had good news, that the killers were caught and one was dead.

The Gramornian royal family had been so ecstatic about his part in ending their difficulties with the prime minister, they doubled the reward. Cort had enough money to set up his own workshop and even advertise his furniture.

Now he had to fix the most important part of his new life.

He strode into the sunshine and crossed the lawn to meet her.

She stood staring at the house. He'd felt the same amazement when he first drove down the narrow gravel lane to this house. Tall hedges beside the lane rescued the residents of the McMansions on both sides from viewing the blight of this residue of rural history. He saw the place as more of a time capsule, an oasis in plastic suburbia.

When she heard his steps on the gravel, she turned. The sight of her expanded a bright balloon in his chest, beginning to fill the void growing there since she'd walked out his cabin door. She wore a short yellow skirt that showed off her killer legs and a lime-green V-neck top that almost gave a glimpse of her power button.

She wasn't smiling. He needed that smile to make his world right.

He swallowed, unable to speak. *Thanks for coming* and *welcome* were inadequate. He was so damn happy to see her all he could do was grin. He stuffed his hands in his pockets.

Her wary expression warned him he'd better find some words or she might climb back in that little car and drive back to D.C. He'd sure had enough time to think of what to say. A month of staring at his cabin's drab four walls. A month of stagnation at the workbench. A month of pondering what he was losing and facing what she'd told him all along.

"What *is* this place?" Her gaze swept the plank-sided barn and the whitewashed farmhouse with its metal roof and wide, low porch.

"My new digs."

"You left the woods of Maine for an old farmhouse in suburban Virginia?"

Closer now, he saw the small v-shaped red scar on her cheek where Rousso had struck her with the pistol. He wanted to deck the man again.

He took her arm and led her up the porch. Not protesting, she trailed along as if expecting to wake up from this fantastical dream.

"Kick in the head, I know. Found I missed... certain things. Hundred-year-old farmhouses don't drop out of the sky every day, except maybe in Kansas." She stared at him like he was Oz himself, or maybe the Wicked Witch. "Farmer sold the land except for this three-acre lot. You drove past one of the developments to get here. When he died, his heirs couldn't agree on what to do with the place, so it sat empty for most of ten years."

"Until now."

"You got it." He was renting for the time being, with an option to buy. But that depended on her. *"I'm in love with you."* Her words had kept him going. She might've meant them then but by now she probably hated him and Devlin had made his move.

Grow some brass ones, Jones.

The front door led through a foyer into a living

room-dining combo. "Hardwood floors, working chimney. Needs a lot of work. I'm sort of camping out until I can buy furniture. And build some." He tried to pretty up the potential, but in reality, what he was showing her wasn't much. Paint peeling on the walls and mantel. Worn and stained floorboards. Packing boxes, still loaded, as seats around his trestle table, the one she liked.

"It's fine. The floors look in good shape."

"Maple. A little work should bring them back. One of the heirs has bought furniture from me. A desk, dining room set. He did some renovations—the kitchen, wiring, plumbing. He's the one renting it to me."

"Ah," she said as if she understood.

If only she did. If only she could read his mind and they could jump ahead without him walking on nails barefoot.

"Cort, you got me out here to see some sort of proof my dad is innocent. What's the deal? Did you make that up?"

"Never. I do have proof. But give me a minute. You want a drink or something?"

She gave the stainless appliances and the granite countertops a survey, her big green handbag clamped against her hip. "Water would be nice."

He handed her a glass, took a green tea for himself. As she drank, he watched the line of her throat, the way her hair draped her shoulders. Longed to put his lips on both.

"The little urn on the counter," she said, nodding in that direction. "Your father?"

He huffed out a breath. "Thought I'd scatter the ashes in the backyard. Put Leon in the sunshine for a change. Now his crime's paid in full and the jewels restored, it's fitting."

"You've forgiven him?"

"I won't go that far. Maybe in time. Let's say I've come to terms with who and what Leon was."

When she set down the glass, he suggested they go outside. The brick patio spread beyond French doors and looked onto an expanse of weedy lawn and more blocking hedges, over the tops of which he could see green hills, not the cookie-cutter houses on either side. All in the eye of the beholder, who was blocking what view.

She moved up beside him and he inhaled her spring-rain scent. Damn. If he didn't have something to do with his hands, he'd be reaching for her. Good way to get punched out like old André.

"Why are you smiling?"

He wrapped his hands around his bottle. "Thinking about the way you decked the Frenchman. Nice right cross."

"Thanks." She frowned. "André tried to see Cassie again. To apologize, I guess. She slammed the door in his face."

"Good for her. How's she doing?"

"She bounced back as usual. New neighbor has a lot to do with it. Single dad about her age with a daughter in Livvie's class. My mom's there now too. My share of the reward money came in handy. I brought her back East. She's living at the house with Cassie and Livvie while she looks for a condo."

"That's great. Really great." How lame could he be? If she didn't hate him, he'd bore her to death with small talk.

She set her bag on a big empty ceramic planter. He pictured her tending flowers and sitting with him at a table out here—real wood, teak, not cold iron like Falco's.

From the don't-mess-with-me look in her midnight eyes, she wasn't giving him anymore time to soften her up. As if. "My dad. Some nebulous proof. What's going on?"

"I'll get to that. Bear with me." He set down his bottle and reached for her. He held her hands so she couldn't run from him. Damn but her skin was soft. He'd missed the feel of her so much. "But I have to... I have something else first. Please hear me out."

Her eyes gleamed, two dark pits of suspicion. Shit, but he'd earned her mistrust.

"Seeing Rousso and Hauptman hold a gun on you slammed me in the gut with fear I've never felt in my life. I was too numb afterward to think coherently. When you walked out my door, I felt empty, cold, like the sun had been stolen from the sky.

"You trusted me to keep you safe, even when I didn't trust you. Or anybody. You kept telling me it was myself I didn't trust. That I wasn't responsible for my mom's death. You were right. It took stewing in my own juices for a month to accept it as truth. As reality. And to move past it, like you said. I should've been there for Mom, but I'm finally out from under Leon's shadow. I'm no more my father than you are yours. Except yours really was innocent."

"Cort, you don't have to—"

"Yes. I do. Let me finish or I might not be able to get it all out." He kissed her knuckles but held on. She didn't try to pull away. He still had a chance.

"Okay."

"I screwed things up between us. I was so paranoid about trust I couldn't see what was reasonable. Like you consulting somebody in your office. And comforting Cassie. I should've known Rousso would research me and know about the cabin. I was out of line and I'm sorry. You don't know how sorry. I wanted to end the Gramornia thing to get on with my life."

He swallowed to lubricate his tight throat. "But without you, I have no life."

"Cort, I—" Her beautiful eyes shimmered with tears.

"God, Mara, I love you. I've never said that to anybody. Never felt this way before. You reach the places inside me I've never let anybody else touch. It's like before you my life was gray as my T-shirt and now it's in Technicolor. With you I feel like my whole body is smiling. I miss going to sleep at night with you in my arms and waking up beside you. I miss watching you sleep. I miss arguing with you and laughing with you. Don't take the color and life away, Mara. Don't hate me. I want a future with you. I want—"

But he couldn't finish because she was in his arms and kissing him. Her fierce embrace blanked out all coherent thought. All he could do was drink in her sweetness and let the scent and the warmth of her wash through him.

She ended the kiss and blinked at him through tears. Of joy, he thought. He hoped. "Of course I don't hate you. I told you I love you and I still do. You're an honorable man, but you had to learn that about yourself the hard way. I love your gentleness, your strength, your passion for your work." She smiled wickedly.

341

"And your passion for me."

"And Thomas Devlin?"

"My boss? What does he have to do with us?"

Her obvious bewilderment was all he needed to know. "Nothing at all." He leaned his forehead against hers. His heart still raced like a hamster in a wheel. "Thank God. Can we go inside now? I need to sit down."

Laughing, she led the way.

They took adjoining kitchen stools, the only real furniture in the house other than his table. Except for upstairs. He opened teas for them both. His had spilled onto the bricks when she jumped him. He kissed her gently on the small scar. "Does it hurt?"

She shook her head. "The doctor said it'd fade in time."

"Your badge of courage."

"Funny. I think of it that way too." Her gaze dropped to his arms. She traced a finger over the snaking lines. "Your tattoos. They've faded."

"Laser removal takes time. A few more treatments and I'm finished." Then he could put that outward sign of his painful past behind for good. Because of Mara, most of the inner pain was gone too. "You probably want to know about your dad now."

"Cort, I came to terms about my father's guilt. But it's okay if you want to try—"

He kissed her to shut her up. "Not try, sweetheart. Only do, according to a famous philosopher. I kept thinking about the cryptic letter that came with your dad's ring piece. Why would Leon list the conspirators for him? None of the others knew any names. So I gave Leon's old attorney a call. Hogan Fox retired after

Dad's trial, so his name's not on the law firm now."

"He phoned me after Leon died. To get me to agree to talk to you. So?"

"His old law firm is Beckham, Dixon, and Kress. Ring a bell?"

Her bottle halted mid-air. "They sent Mom the package with the ring."

"After Quincy died. Right?"

She nodded. "Mom said it came when she was packing up his things. What does that have to do with it?"

"Everything, according to Fox. Leon didn't trust anybody. Yeah, yeah, I know," he added when she grinned. "The packet with the letter and ring piece was self-protection. It was to be sent to your dad if Leon was to die suddenly or under suspicious circumstances. Otherwise I'm guessing he was going to reclaim it before he and the others went to get the jewels. Or maybe he had another identical one stashed away somewhere. Who knows?"

"I don't understand. The ring piece was mailed years ago."

"And never opened until it reached you. Fox turned over all his files to others in his firm. He said he explained what to do with Leon's package but the assistant got the instructions wrong. Instead of mailing it if *Leon* died, she mailed it when *your dad* died."

Her face lit up like Christmas morning.

"*'I'm sending this to you, Q, because I know you'll do what I expect with it,'*" Cort quoted.

"Because he knew Dad would do the *right* thing. He would investigate. He would inform the police of the identities of Leon's accomplices in case one of them killed him. My dad was the honest man I always knew he was."

"Exactly."

She frowned. "But finding the rings wouldn't have led either the FBI or Dad to the crown jewels."

"Right again. Either he just wanted revenge or he figured they'd come to me with the verse once they had the rings."

"And you would find the jewels. Which you did." She beamed through happy tears.

"Fox is calling Global Insurance about your dad's pension going to your mom. He said he'd see she got back payments. The whole law firm will be on it. They're worried you'll sue them. The wheels are turning." He lifted his green tea for a toast.

But again Mara jumped him. The liquid spilled across the countertop.

He didn't care. Her kisses were the only sustenance he needed. He locked her in place with his legs, reveled in the hot sweep of her tongue, the shift of her body against him, the silken feel of her hair brushing his fingers. Blood whooshed in his ears and the heavy pull of desire hardened his body. But he had one more bit of good news to impart. Maybe two.

He set her away from him with a last taste of her delectable lower lip. "Hold that thought, sweetheart."

"There's more?" She looked so sexy with her lips shining from his kisses and her eyes twin pools of black that he nearly forgot what he still had to say.

"About that, no. About us, definitely. This farmhouse doesn't look like much, I know."

"It has more potential than that cabin you lived in." Her smile morphed into concern. "But leave Maine?

What about the woodworking school?"

"Seems the boss didn't tell people he fired me. He said I took a leave of absence."

"I'm biting my tongue not to say I told you so. And?"

"He asked me to come back. Offered a raise and a co-teaching position in the nine-month class. But I'm done with living in the woods. Light and open spaces are for me. And a certain woman who brightens everything."

"And this house?"

"It's solid so the repairs are mostly cosmetic. The heirs have released it for sale, at a reasonable price. Four bedrooms, room for a family. Someday, I mean, if you want. If you don't like the house, if you'd rather stay in D.C., we can look for something el—"

"Cort, stop. Shut up." When he stopped babbling, she smiled. "I love you. I love the house. I've had enough of living in a cramped city apartment. I've always wanted a big old house I could fix up. We can work on it together for when that family comes along."

"I love you so much. Damn, now that I've let those words out, I'm going to drive you nuts saying them all the time."

She laughed, music he wanted to hear for the rest of his life. "I'll hold you to it."

His heart thudded so hard his chest hurt. His body flamed with summer heat. He wanted her so much he could barely focus. "I, um, did buy one piece of furniture. It's upstairs in the master suite. Would you like to try it out?"

Her smile bloomed, slow and sultry. "Show me."

So he did.

A word about the author...

Occasional bouts of insomnia led to Susan Vaughan's writing career. When she couldn't sleep, she made up stories to fill the long, dark nights. Her stories throw the hero and heroine together under extraordinary circumstances and pit them against a clever villain. Besides curling up with a good mystery or romance, Susan enjoys walking her dog, boating, traveling, and volunteering. A former teacher, she is a West Virginia native, but she and her husband have lived in Maine for many years. Susan is the author of 16 novels and one children's book. Find her at www.susanvaughan.com, where you can sign up for her newsletter or contact her, or at https://www.facebook.com/susanvaughanbooks.